Jonathan Kellerman is the Number One *New York Times* bestselling author of more than forty crime novels, including the Alex Delaware series, *The Butcher's Theater*, *Billy Straight*, *The Conspiracy Club*, *Twisted*, *True Detectives*, and *The Murderer's Daughter*.

With his wife, bestselling novelist Faye Kellerman, he co-authored *Double Homicide* and *Capital Crimes*. With his son, bestselling novelist Jesse Kellerman, he co-authored *Lost Souls*, *A Measure of Darkness*, *Crime Scene*, *The Golem of Hollywood*, and *The Golem of Paris*.

He is also the author of two children's books and numerous nonfiction works, including *Savage Spawn: Reflections on Violent Children* and *With Strings Attached: The Art and Beauty of Vintage Guitars*. He has won the Goldwyn, Edgar, and Anthony awards and the Lifetime Achievement Award from the American Psychological Association, and has been nominated for a Shamus Award.

Jonathan and Faye Kellerman live in California and New York.

Praise for Jonathan Kellerman

'Kellerman's psychology skills and dark imagination are a potent literary mix' *Los Angeles Times*

'Exceptionally exciting' *New York Times*

'Ingenious and horrifying' *Sunday Times*

Also available by Jonathan Kellerman

FICTION

ALEX DELAWARE NOVELS

When the Bough Breaks
Blood Test
Over the Edge
Silent Partner
Time Bomb
Private Eyes
Devil's Waltz
Bad Love
Self-Defense
The Web
The Clinic
Survival of the Fittest
Monster
Dr Death
Flesh and Blood
The Murder Book
A Cold Heart
Therapy
Rage
Gone
Compulsion
Bones
Evidence
Mystery
Victims
Guilt
Killer
Motive
Breakdown
Heartbreak Hotel
Night Moves
The Wedding Guest

OTHER NOVELS

The Butcher's Theater
Billy Straight
The Conspiracy Club
Twisted
True Detectives
The Murderer's Daughter

WITH FAYE KELLERMAN

Double Homicide
Capital Crimes

WITH JESSE KELLERMAN

The Golem of Hollywood
The Golem of Paris
Crime Scene
A Measure of Darkness
Lost Souls

GRAPHIC NOVELS

Silent Partner
The Web
Monster

NON-FICTION

With Strings Attached: The Art and Beauty of Vintage Guitars
Savage Spawn: Reflections on Violent Children
Helping the Fearful Child
Psychological Aspects of Childhood Cancer

FOR CHILDREN, WRITTEN AND ILLUSTRATED

Jonathan Kellerman's ABC of Weird Creatures
Daddy, Daddy, Can You Touch the Sky?

Jonathan Kellerman

THE MUSEUM OF DESIRE

arrow books

1 3 5 7 9 10 8 6 4 2

Arrow Books
20 Vauxhall Bridge Road
London SW1V 2SA

Arrow Books is part of the Penguin Random House group of companies whose addresses can be found at global.penguinrandomhouse.com.

First published in Great Britain by Century in 2020
(First published in the United States by Ballantine in 2020)
First published in paperback by Arrow Books in 2020

www.penguin.co.uk

A CIP catalogue record for this book is available from the British Library.

ISBN 9781787461208

Printed and bound in Great Britain by Clays Ltd, Elcograf S.p.A.

To Adeline

THE MUSEUM OF DESIRE

CHAPTER 1

Eno trudged up the road. Big fancy property like this, maybe a chance to hit a lick.

His last stretch at County had ended eighty-two days ago, then he was back on the street looking for bank. Trying a few things that didn't work out so having to do *this.*

Bright Dawn Cleaning and Maintenance.

He'd filled out a half-page questionnaire: *Have you ever been convicted of a felony?*

Hell, yeah.

He'd checked *No.* Later he found out from dudes at the Cyril you weren't even allowed to ask anymore. He'da lied anyway, it was good to stay in practice.

Looking for shit to steal was Eno's thing when he was at rich-people houses doing landscaping or roofing. His specialty was small stuff no one would notice till he was long gone. Street sale or pawn at one of the places that didn't ask questions.

He thought of himself as careful but *not* careful was not noticing an old Mexican maid at a house in Hancock Park after he spotted a little gold box on a table from outside a sliding glass door. The door unlocked, shiny thing just sitting shouting *Come and Get Me!!*

Maid's looking from around a corner. Being sneaky, whose fault was that?

That had earned Eno three months at County while waiting for trial. All charges dismissed because the maid went back to Mexico. Plus they never found the box because Eno had ditched it in some bushes before the cops showed up.

Lack of evidence, his PD announced. Proud of herself, like she did something.

Maybe he should go back and look for the box in the bushes. Nah, be careful.

So now he was pushing a big plastic wheelie can up a long private road early on a Sunday morning. The can full of gloves and bleach and soaps and rags and Windex, a broom and a shovel attached to the side.

Another party house to clean up. Worst job he'd ever had, getting up at five a.m. to start at six, being driven all over the city in a service van, Laquitha at the wheel, glaring at him and the other cleaners like *they* were the garbage.

Like they were special-needs kids on a special-needs school bus; Eno knew about *that.*

He'd worked two houses this month, not a single lick. No surprise, he guessed; the places were mostly empty except for rented furniture.

The disgusting shit people left behind, even with the gloves it grossed Eno out.

He'd do it just until something better came along. If nothing fell into place soon, maybe he'd take the next step: mask and hoodie up, get weaponated, do the *gimme-your-money-motherfucker!!!*

Targeting drunk downtown club yuppie scum weaving around like worms. Lots of clubs walking distance from his room at the Cyril. What a shitbox *that* was, not much better than a cell.

At least Section 8 was paying for it.

As he pushed the wheelie, he tried to concentrate, always a challenge.

Yeah, easy enough to take the next step and just go for the gold. Unless you got blowback from a drunken yuppie. Eno had never been a fighter and at forty-three he had no muscles left.

Motherfucker fought back, Eno would have no choice.

Bang.

Maybe *too* big a step.

Meanwhile he'd do this. Pushing uphill, his mind wandering. Nothing at the top except other people's shit.

He stopped for breath, arms and chest and legs aching. A few more steps and the drive curved around and he finally saw the house.

Whoa! Biggest one so far. More like one of them castles, with two of those things that stick out on castles on either end, whatever they called 'em. The whole thing *looked* like it was made of gray castle-stones. Then Eno saw it was just regular stucco with lines in it. Fake-out, but still, like a castle.

As he got closer, the house got even huger. Like it was put there to make him feel small. All that was missing was one of them water thingies they put around castles, alligators and dragons swimming around snapping their jaws. One of them . . . mokes.

That would be something, big moke full of monsters, just waiting to grab you by the business. Chain-saw teeth, before you knew it, you were a street taco.

Eno shuddered, imagining, stopped for more breath, resumed wheeling. Man this was steep.

Not only didn't this castle have no moke, there was nothing out front period, not even a lawn, just dirt.

Why couldn't the company drive him up from Benedict Canyon? He'd asked Laquitha.

No answer, bitch just sped off.

Leaving him with a fucking *hike.* Eno hated hiking, reminded him of when he was doing state park service as part of his first arrest at fifteen in San Bernardino.

He finally almost got to the top. Place was a joke lick-wise; halfway up, he'd seen an alarm sign from a company he knew had went out of business five years ago. A *Protected By Video Surveillance* sign but no cameras.

On top of that, the gate on Benedict was left wide-open since like three a.m. Saturday when the party ended. The crap that was gonna be left behind, sitting there, all clotted and sticky, a pain to scrub.

Another pause to breathe then he made it to flat ground. The place was *huuuge,* would take every minute of the seven hours Bright Dawn gave him. Twelve bucks an hour plus the shit lunch they packed for the workers. Huge place but a one-man assignment.

The rules were always the same: Start with the outside, then do the inside, there'd be a back door left unlocked.

Eno looked up at those two tall things, what did they call them . . . tur . . . bines? No, turbits. Coupla turbits sticking into the sky. Darker gray than the sky. Everything gray.

June Gloom his aunt Audrey used to call it. But this was May.

Eno called it L.A. shit-air.

Maybe there'd be *something* here, not just red cups, empties, used condoms and needles. He looked for access to the backyard. Nothing on the left, there was a stone wall blocking him. But walking to the right side of the castle showed him another iron gate, wide open.

Nice iron, all fancy with squiggly things and flowers and twisted bars. The metal by itself some serious bank but he had no way to transport it. Years ago, he'd gotten into copper wire, did real good selling to places on San Fernando. Then, at a plumbing supply yard on Alameda, he got nailed by a junkyard dog that came outta nowhere and busted by a rent-a-cop with a Glock.

That had earned him five months at County, grand theft pled down to petty, the first forty-five days in the infirmary healing his leg. The rest of his sentence they had to put him in protective because all the regular cells were taken up by gangsters.

Maybe scrap metal wasn't his thing.

He pushed the wheelie through the gate opening. What shoulda been a driveway but was dry dirt. Like someone built the castle then hated it and decided not to finish.

It took a while to get past a long wall of fake-stone but finally he reached the backyard.

More nothing-green, just a wall of trees all the way at the back, like someone was trying to take out a forest. Facing the back of the castle was one of those covered things rich people used for sitting in, a round dome roof covered by dead brown vines that reminded Eno of coiling snakes.

Over to the right was an empty blue hole where a big pool woulda been if the hole had water. At least one lucky break, he wouldn't have to fish out used condoms. But around the fake-stone pool deck he spotted some, along with red cups and broken bottles.

Eno wasn't paying attention to any of that. His eyes were to the left of the pool. Something different.

A super-stretch Town Car, white, one of those prom specials.

Eno had ridden in one when he was nineteen. Invited by his friends when they graduated high school even though he'd dropped out in tenth.

First, he'd said, *Nah.*

They'd said, *Hey, E-man, fuck graduation, you can still party!*

So he went. And had a pretty good time, until the girl he was fingering gave him a funny smile then barfed all over him. Everyone, including the girl, laughing. Eno knew right then and there that he wasn't fitting in, would never. So he left and walked four miles home. Aunt Audrey was up, watching Discovery ID. Wrinkling her nose and saying, "Whoo, someone stinks like a pig with the runs."

Laughing but also pissed off at Eno. Not letting him use the bathroom to clean up, he had to go outside and shiver naked while he hosed himself off.

So *fuck* proms and stretch white Town Cars. Fuck this *job,* he was *definitely* gonna mask-and-hoodie and take the next step.

But meanwhile, maybe something shiny in the limo.

Then he thought: What was a car doing here? Someone still inside? A stoned-out loser sleeping it off? Bunch of losers? After an orgy?

Maybe he'd get to roust some naked chicks, get looks at their tits as they panicked to get dressed.

Smiling, he left the wheelie in place and strutted toward the limo. Tried to peer through the windows. Tinted too dark.

"Hey," he said, not as loud as he'd meant to be.

No answer.

"Hey."

Nothing.

"Dude. Party's *over,* you need to *leave."*

Still no answer.

Stoned out? Or just shining him on.

Like he wasn't there.

That made Eno's face feel hot, same feeling as before his assault beef, some loser in a Bakersfield bar saying he was a fag and getting razored across the face down to the bone.

"Hey!" Shouting, now.

Feeling his body tighten in a way he hadn't felt in a long time but liked, Eno flung open the driver's door.

Saw what he saw and felt his stomach go nuts. Like *he* was going to barf.

He trembled, mouth-breathed, felt his heart racing. Turned to look at the back of the limo but a sliding black glass panel blocked his view.

He backed away. Frozen.

Then—he couldn't explain it but he just did it. Opened the rear door and looked inside.

Oh, shit, *bad* idea. Now his stomach felt like it was shooting totally out of his mouth like *all* his insides were coming loose.

Oh, shit, this was different this was bad-different.

He slammed both doors shut, felt what was left of his breakfast burrito shoot up and out and miss the limo's spotless white paint and land on the dirt.

What to do now? He'd seen lots of things but he'd never seen anything *like* this, what to *do*?

Reaching into his jean pocket, he pulled out the phone he'd just bought from a homeless guy on Grand Street. Piece of shit, ten bucks, thirty-three minutes left.

Use the time to call the company? Nah, no one was in the office this early.

What would they say, anyway?

So 911 here we come.

Eno's day to be a solid citizen.

CHAPTER 2

When it comes to murder, nighttime's the right time. So when Milo calls me, I often find myself driving to crime scenes on dark L.A. streets.

This time, the phone rang just after nine a.m. Lovely Sunday in May. Robin and I and Blanche, our little French bulldog, had taken a leisurely two-mile walk followed by a pancake breakfast.

Robin was washing, I was drying, Blanche's sausage body was prone on the kitchen floor as she snored and let out periodic dream squeaks. My phone, on vibrate, bounced on the kitchen counter. Milo's number on the screen.

I said, "What's up, Big Guy?"

Detective II Moses Reed said, "Actually it's me, Doc. He asked me to phone you."

"Busy, huh?"

"We're all busy. This is utterly horrible."

Reed's a terse young man; it takes a lot to get him using adverbs.

I sat down and listened as he explained, images tumbling into my brain. Robin turned from the sink, pretty eyebrows arching. I shook my head and mouthed *Sorry,* and said, "Where, Moe?"

"Private road called Ascot Lane, off Benedict Canyon. Easy to miss, kind of like your street, but this one's more like a big driveway, only goes to one house."

He sighed. "Half mile north of the Beverly Hills border."

But for a couple thousand feet, someone else's problem.

I said, "Give me half an hour."

"Whenever you get here, Doc. No one's leaving for a while."

In the movies when detectives encounter terrible things they frequently banter and tell tasteless jokes. That may be because screenwriters or the people who pay them are emotionally shallow. Or the scribes haven't taken the time to hang out with real detectives.

I've found that the men and women who work homicide tend to be thoughtful, analytic, and sensitive. Despite a certain gruffness, that certainly applies to Milo.

My best friend has closed over three hundred fifty murders and he's never lost his empathy or his sense of outrage. Notifying families still rips at him. He eats too much, sleeps poorly, and often neglects himself while working two, three days in a row.

Once you stop caring, you're useless.

Milo leads by example so the same approach is taken by the three younger D's who work with him when he can pry them away from other assignments.

When he can't, it's just him. And sometimes me. Rules are often bent. Milo was a gay soldier when gay soldiers didn't exist, a gay cop when LAPD was still raiding gay bars. Things have changed but he continues to disdain stupid regulations and often overlooks social niceties in a paramilitary organization that prizes conformity.

Murder solve rates have dropped but his rate remains the highest in the department so the brass looks the other way.

This morning the sense of anxious gloom I've seen so many times at murders—stiff posture, tight faces, sharp but defeated eyes—extended to the two halfback-sized uniformed officers blocking the entrance to Ascot Lane from Benedict Canyon.

They'd been given my personal info and the Seville's tags but checked my I.D. anyway, before the bigger one said, "Go on in, Doctor," in a defeated voice.

To get to them, I'd nosed past half a dozen journalists stationed on Benedict as they tried to rush the Seville before being shooed by another pair of cops.

Different emotional climate for members of the press: a heightened energy bordering on ebullience. Misfortune is the mother's milk of journalism but with the exception of war correspondents, those who suckle the teats of tragedy are rarely forced to confront evil directly.

I'd kept the Seville's windows open and as I climbed the road, a bee-swarm of words followed me.

*"Who's **he**?"*

*"Vintage **Caddy**?"*

*"Are you the **owner**?"*

*"Sir! Sir! Do you rent out your house for **parties**? How much do you **get**? In view of this, was it **worth** it? He the owner, Officers? Yes? No? Aw, c'mon, the public has a right to know—if he's not the owner, how come **he** gets in?"*

If I'd said anything it would've been, "I get in because it's bad and strange."

I drove through a wrought-iron gate propped open by two bricks and began to climb. Halfway up, another cop waved me on. The road ended at a flat acre or so of brown dirt crowded with vehicles. Four white coroner's vans, a scarlet fire department ambulance, half a dozen patrol cars, two blue-and-white Scientific Division vans, a bronze Chevy Impala I knew to be Milo's unmarked, two black Ford LTDs, and a gray Mustang. I wondered who'd scored the sports car.

Like a lot attendant at a county fair, a fourth uniform waved me to the far-right end of the dirt. When I got out, she said, "Walk around there, Dr. Delaware," and tried to smile but failed.

I said, "Tough scene."

"You have no idea."

The path she'd designated took me along the right side of the massive house that fronted the expanse of soil. A semicircular drive of cracked brick girded the house. What you'd expect to see at a grand English manor, which was what this pile of faux-stone was striving to be.

Strange-looking place, thirty-plus feet high, graceless and blocky with a double-width entry fronted by curvaceous gold-painted iron over glass.

But for the lack of gardens and a pair of strange turret-like projections erupting from either end of the pretend-slate roof, one of those country homes featured on genteel PBS dramas. The kind of place where plummy-voiced tweedy people gather to natter, get soused on *mah-tinis,* and labor to make their way through all seven deadly sins.

Long walk to the back. At the end of my trek, I reached crime scene tape stretched across the drive. No one guarding the tape. I ducked under.

Given the dimensions of the frontage and the house, the rear of the property was surprisingly skimpy, much of it taken up by an empty Olympic-sized pool and a massive domed pavilion set up with cheap-looking outdoor furniture. At the far end, a wall of pines constricted the space further.

Another uniformed duo saw me and approached. Recheck of my I.D.

"Past the pool, Doctor."

Needless direction; on the far-left side of the property was a crime scene tent big enough for a circus.

I headed for the main event.

◆

The tent's floodlit interior smelled of people. Lots of them, suited and gloved and masked, worked silently but for the rasp and clop of equipment cases being opened and shut and the snick-snick of cameras.

Everyone knowing their role, like a colony of ants swarming a giant larva.

The object of all the attention was as white and fat as a larva. A stretch Lincoln Town Car, its blunt snout pointed toward the house. Oversized red-wall tires, chrome reversed hubcaps, a strip of LED lighting running just under the roofline.

Party wagon.

The doors I could see were wide open but the interior was blocked by squatting techs.

Four heads rose above the roof on the other side of the car.

To the far right was Moe Reed, ruddy, baby-faced, blond, unreasonably muscled. Next to him stood a taller, freckled young man with a red spiky do: Sean Binchy. Leftmost was a handsome, ponytailed woman of forty with knife-edged features and piercing dark eyes aimed at the forensics symphony. Alicia Bogomil had tinted the ends of her hair platinum blond. Feeling secure in her new position as Detective I.

To the left of the three was the tallest man.

Bulky, slope-shouldered, full-faced and jowly, with pallid skin ravaged by youthful acne, a high-bridged nose, and a curiously sensitive mouth that tended to purse. His hair was coal black except where white had seeped from temple to sideburn. What Lieutenant Milo Bernard Sturgis calls his skunk stripes.

He saw me and walked around the limo. Brown suit, brown shirt, limp black tie, gray desert boots. The only splash of color, conspicuously green eyes brighter than the morning.

We go way back but this wasn't the time and place for a handshake.

I said, "Hey."

He said, "Big production, huh? First responders got here at six twenty-seven, fourteen minutes after the 911 call. Place is vacant, used as a party house, most recent party was a rave-type deal that started eleven p.m. Friday night and stretched to Saturday around three. The cleaning service didn't send a guy until this morning and that's who found it. He says he phoned it in right away. After throwing up. He's in the FD van, getting looked at. Said his chest and tummy hurt. Addict with a long sheet, so who knows what's going on."

"He interests you?"

"Not as the main offender but I wanna have a chat with him once he's cleared by the EMTs."

I said, "Criminals clean up rich people's houses."

"Apparently. This prince calls himself Eno, full name's Enos Verdell Walters. For the most part, his pedigree's not violent. Weed, meth, crack, and all the crap that finances weed, meth, and crack: shoplifting, theft, forgery, fraud. But there was a knife ADW a while back, he cut some guy up pretty viciously."

"You researched him right away."

"Nothing else to do while the science majors do their thing."

I pointed to a camel-colored splotch a few feet from the limo's right passenger door. "That Walters's breakfast?"

"Breakfast burrito." He grimaced. "I think I'll be off Mexican for a while. Maybe food, period—hey, here's the miracle diet I've been hoping for."

Patting the convexity of his gut.

I thought: *I'm sure you'll recover.*

I said: "When can I take a look?"

"Right now if you're up for it."

"Why not?"

"Don't," he said, "make me answer that."

He pulled out a set of rubber gloves and handed it over like a sacramental wafer.

CHAPTER 3

The tech working the front of the limo was broad and male, the one at the rear smaller, probably female. Milo tapped the man's shoulder softly.

The big tech looked over his shoulder and exhaled. A mask-muffled voice said, "Lieutenant."

Milo said, "Sorry for sneaking up on you, George. This is Dr. Delaware. Can he take a brief look?"

George's mask tented. Lips forming something that might've been a smile or a frown. "What you'd like is what we do, Lieutenant." Sharp tugs at the edges of the mask. Definitely a smile. "Unless one of the pathologists comes by and contradicts you."

"You expecting a doc?"

George stood and pulled his mask down on a face suited for a sitcom dad role: a bit soft at the corners, crinkly world-weary eyes. "I requested one but probably not. It's psychotic at the crypt, big de-comp, stinks like you know what. Truth is, I was happy to get out of there."

He frowned. "Even with this."

The smaller tech stood and faced me. Female, young, bespectacled. "Knees hurt, I'm ready for a break."

They both left the tent.

I inhaled through my nose, exhaled through my mouth, and stepped forward. Gloved but still careful not to touch anything, I began taking fast-action mental snapshots.

My brain works like that, registering images and saving them. Forever.

Snap one: in the driver's seat an elderly black man.

Leaning slightly to the right.

Both hands resting in his lap.

Black chauffeur's suit. White shirt. Black tie. White hair. Bushy white mustache.

Black hole in the left temple to his left cheek. Brown crust rimming the wound but no other blood until you got to the knees. Then, lots of it, slick as an oil slick as it glazed the lower part of both legs and descended to dove-gray leather seating and plush black carpeting.

No blood on the impeccable gray mohair roof of the limo. A partition sectioning driver from passengers was black glass but for a gold-plated audio speaker in the center.

No spatter there. Not a speckle anywhere.

The chauffeur's chocolate skin had turned chalky in splotches. Slightly parted lips revealed perfectly aligned white teeth.

Dental perfection courtesy a skilled dentist. A bridge had come loose and dangled awkwardly.

I peered closer. No stippling around the wound that I could see but dusky skin tone made it hard to be sure.

Rigor hadn't set in. Or it had come and gone. The dried blood said probably the latter.

Eight to twelve hours with no obvious decomposition. Cool May weather? But it's rarely that simple.

I stepped back and walked to the rear of the car.

Three dead people occupied the rear seat, pressed close to one another, knees touching.

Closest to the door was a white male in his thirties wearing a black sport coat, a black T-shirt and slacks, black loafers, no socks. Thick, dark hair. Lean, good-looking.

Like the chauffeur, coated with blood from the knees down, a similar pool sludging the carpet.

Unlike the chauffer, no bullet wound that I could see.

I said so to Milo.

He said, "There is none, don't know what got him, yet."

I turned back to the car. The good-looking man's fly was unzipped. His limp penis rested in the upturned left palm of his nearest seat-mate.

Older woman. Sixties, maybe even seventies, full-faced with a squashed, veiny nose. Eyes shut behind steel-framed glasses. Puffy cheeks had been rouged clumsily, creating clown-like cerise circles. Heavy arms swelled the long sleeves of a black wool dress, and stout legs encased in fishnet stockings were stuffed into square-toed black pumps, instep flesh humping above the strap. Gray hair curled from beneath a black felt tam. No jewelry, no adornment.

Like the chauffeur and the man whose member she fondled, bloodied from the knees down.

Again, no bullet wounds I could see.

I circled to the opposite side of the limo. The young D's were still there. They greeted me but didn't move.

The final victim was a brown-skinned man, Hispanic or Middle Eastern. Thin, bony-faced, with meager, elfin features. Sparse dark hair cropped short was flecked with silver. A filmy thatch of chin hairs struggled to be a beard.

Tough to estimate his age. My mental Nikon settled on thirty-five to forty-five.

Like the three other victims, dressed in black. Baggy suit, blousy white shirt, clip-on black tie, black canvas slip-ons.

I thought of a funeral procession waylaid and slaughtered.

Male Number Two's cause of death, obvious: bullet hole in the center of his forehead.

Washed in blood from the knees down. Nothing to do with a small-caliber wound.

I returned my attention to the woman in the center. Stern, matronly. An appearance bizarrely at odds with the organ in her hand.

I said, "Nothing makes sense."

Milo said, "And here I was hoping for immediate wisdom." But he didn't sound surprised.

"Any I.D.s?"

"Let's catch some fresh air, I'll fill you in."

CHAPTER 4

I followed him out of the tent, across a strip of cement and a wider belt of dirt, up the steps to the domed pavilion. The structure was impressive at a distance but tatty up close, brick floor cracked and buckling, cement columns crudely molded. The roof was rusting iron covered with dead vines that fought one another for space.

Vipers in a feeding frenzy.

Milo said, "Okay to sit, this area's been gone over." He plopped down on a flimsy-looking plastic chair and made it groan. "Lotta crap cleared away, most probably garbage from the party. Lovely stuff—condoms, cups, little baggies with remnants of granular stuff."

The other chairs looked grubby. I stayed on my feet.

He said, "Any impression at all? I'll take improv."

I said, "To my eye, they've been dead for a while. I'd guess no more than twelve hours but maybe I'm missing something and they were partygoers from Friday night?"

"You're not missing anything. The company that books venues swears the place was cleared out three a.m. Saturday. That wouldn't mean much but every C.I. and tech says the condition of the bodies doesn't match that long of a time period, even with cool weather, there'd have to be more decomp."

"The car was moved here after three. How'd it gain access to the property?"

"Same way you and Mr. Walters did, open gate. Cleaning company asks for that, closes up when the job's over. Nothing inside, anyway, just cheap rental furniture."

He pulled a panatela from an inside jacket pocket. Rolled it between thick fingers but didn't unwrap it.

I said, "Didn't see any maggots on the bodies."

"There weren't any, just a few blowflies buzzing around the driver's door when we arrived. Walters opened two doors then shut them. After he threw up. Looks like the closed car formed a sealed environment."

"Any cameras on the property?"

"Not a one."

"Who owns the place?"

"Don't know yet, cleaning company punted to a rental agent and she hasn't answered my call."

He held up the cigar and squinted, as if close inspection would reveal secrets. "What'd you think about all that blood at the bottom?"

"Doesn't fit the wounds," I said. "As if it got poured on them postmortem."

"*Everything's* wrong about this picture, Alex. Holes only in the driver and the little guy? Joe Stud groped by a woman old enough to be his mother, looks like a church lady? What the hell *is* that, Alex? Something creepy-Oedipal? Or whatever you guys are calling it nowadays."

I shook my head.

He said, "Yeah, yeah, yeah, too early to expect wisdom."

He looked over at the tent. "When the call came in, four bodies in a stretch, I was thinking, just what I need, a gang thing with a hip-hop angle. Or worse, some kids partying got wiped out by who-knows-who. Then I get here and it's even crazier."

He returned the panatela to his pocket. "Everyone's weirded out,

Alex. Even George Arredondo—the big tech—before he went scientific, he was on the job, patrol in the toughest part of Lancaster. Ten years of violent domestics, meth monsters, child murders. Nothing bothers him. *This* does."

He got up, paced the pavilion, sat back down, rubbed his eyes. "Don't hold back, I'll settle for wild theory."

I said, "Four victims, variation of method. So maybe they were killed separately, at different locations. At some point, they're collected, cleaned up and costumed postmortem, placed in the car and driven up here. Then they're splashed with blood and left to be discovered. It feels like some sort of a production. With all those steps, moving the bodies, probably more than one person. Or one bad guy who had plenty of time, a safe place to work, and the ability to escape on foot. Or he'd stashed one of those mini-bikes in the trunk."

"A physically fit psycho," he said. "Or a gang of zombie fiends. Wonderful. What else, keep ideating."

The cigar made a second appearance. As I thought, he smoked. When I began talking, he stopped.

"We're talking a killer or killers who knew the gate would be left open with no one around. That could mean a past partygoer. Or someone with a link to either the rental company or the house itself. What about the victim I.D.'s?"

He pulled out his notepad, flipped a page. "The men all had their wallets in their pant pockets, nothing on the women. The driver's Solomon Roget, seventy-eight. I googled him. Legit livery driver, home address near Pico-Robertson, the limo's registered to him along with a 2001 Cadillac sedan. The poor guy with his fly open is Richard Peter Gurnsey, thirty-six, Santa Monica, the little guy is Benson Mauricio Alvarez, forty-four, lives near downtown."

"Victims from all over the city," I said. "Any purse on the woman?"

"Empty. Got the Gucci clasp but Alicia informs me it's a cheap-shit copy. No blood on it, so it was placed after the red bath."

I said, "A prop."

He frowned and turned pages. "Gurnsey—he goes by Rick on his social media pages—has a law degree and works in business affairs at Sony Studios in Culver City. He put himself all over Instagram. Mountain biking, scuba diving, hang gliding, fooling in the gym. He also liked showing off his matte-black BMW and he likes women. All young and cute, no apparent fetish for grannies. Roget has no internet presence and neither does Alvarez, who's mentally challenged. I reverse-directoried his address. Group home for people with developmental issues able to 'mainstream and live semi-independently.' "

I said, "A mentally slow forty-four-year-old, a narcissistic hotshot, a woman who looks like everyone's straitlaced aunt, and their chauffeur. It's like they're characters in a play. Roget doesn't advertise?"

"Haven't found anything yet. He doesn't appear to work for a company and the limo is registered to him personally so I'm thinking freelance."

"I wonder how he got business."

"Maybe word of mouth? Don't know much about anything, Alex. Let's go back."

Reed, Binchy, and Bogomil were waiting for us just inside the tent. Off in a corner, near the limo's rear tire, stood a coroner's investigator working her phone. Gloria Mendez pulled down her mask and waved. No trace of her usual smile.

I waved back. Her thumbs stayed busy.

Milo said, "Hey, kids."

The trio said, "Sir," in unison, but looked at me. Expecting wisdom.

I repeated what I'd told Milo about multiple offenders and the theatrical quality of the body dump.

Moe Reed said, "Makes sense."

Sean Binchy said, "Total sense."

Alicia Bogomil said, "The posing, Doctor. The way Gurnsey was . . ." She blushed. "Do you see this as a sexual thing?"

"Could be," I said. "Or it could all be about power."

"So are sex crimes."

Reed said, "Sex crimes are about sex *and* power." To me: "Right?"

Milo said, "What Dr. D. would like to tell you but won't because he's kind and empathic is we're starting with a lot of weird and nothing else."

Alicia said, "So what do we need to do, L.T.?"

"Same as any other case, kiddo: learn about the victims."

"Speaking of which," she said, "I just took a closer look at the woman. Like I told you, the purse is cheap-phony. She's also wearing a lot of makeup but it was put on sloppily and where her skin shows through, here"—touching the space between her cheekbone and her ear—"it looks raw. Wind-whipped. And there are blood vessels all over her nose."

Reed said, "Street person?"

"That's what I'm thinking."

Milo chewed his cheek. "Alvarez's assisted living place is near downtown, lots of shelters and SROs and encampments. There could be a link between the two of them."

I said, "Alvarez has some sort of mental disability. Maybe she does, too."

Binchy looked troubled.

Milo said, "What, Sean?"

"Someone taking advantage of the weak." His freckled face registered sadness. A detective who still believed in inherent goodness.

Bogomil said, "Gurnsey doesn't fit with that. Unless he did charity work downtown or something like that."

Milo said, "I like all this thinking—see, I told you Dr. D. would inspire us. Okay, you all know what you need to start with."

Binchy said, "Canvass the neighborhood."

"Every house up and down Benedict."

"Then four death knocks," said Reed. "How're we dividing it?"

Milo said, "We're not. I'll take all of them."

The three detectives said nothing.

"It's called benevolent leadership," he said. "Let's get moving."

Three *yessirs* and they were gone.

I said, "Taking on your favorite job. Feeling emotionally resilient?"

"What the hell, they're young and tender, and I've already got a mood disorder."

"What's that?"

"Personal variant of bipolar. Half the time I'm pissed off, the other I'm merely irritated."

He strode to the limo where George Arredondo was still working, had a brief conversation with the tech, repeated it with the bespectacled woman. Then over to Mendez for the same.

Shaking his head as he returned. "Gloria says they've got copious samples of everything, we'll see what the lab says but with the big decomp case don't expect anything quick."

We exited the tent again and took a quick walk through the house. Empty, gray, echoing, nothing but more lawn furniture, tatty beanbags, and detritus from the party.

Outside, Milo stretched, fooled with the knot of his tie, and looked up at a bluing L.A. sky. "So much evil, so little time. You don't have to come death-knocking with me, Alex. On the other hand . . ."

"Good way to learn about the victims."

"I thought you'd see it my way. Leave the Seville here, I'm in the mood to drive. More than that, I'm feeling all *official*."

As we headed for the front parking area, I texted Robin and told her I'd be gone all day.

Bad?

Complicated.

Ooh. Worse than bad. Okay, love you.

Love you, too.

◆

A skinny, stick-legged man was exiting the FD ambulance, elbows gripped by two EMTs.

Medium height, caved-in thorax, long gray hair, ragged beard. He wore a brown T-shirt several sizes too large, droopy jeans, and sneakers. The hair flapped as his head shook from side to side in protest.

"Our reporting person," said Milo. "Care to meet him?"

"Wouldn't miss it."

As we walked toward Enos Walters, Milo said, "The posing. You said stage production. It reminded me of one of those museum dioramas."

I said, "What would you title it?"

"Un-civilization."

When Walters saw us he tried to break free of the EMTs' grip, couldn't, and shouted, "Fuck this! I'm no suspect!"

Milo said, "Let him go, guys. Mr. Walters, Lieutenant Sturgis, we spoke briefly before."

"What, you think I can't remember?"

"You were a little shaky—"

"Wouldn't you be, seeing something like that?" Walters shook himself off like a gun dog shedding water.

The taller medic said, "His blood pressure's been all over the place and his atrial beats are premature. We recommend hospitalization for observation."

"Fuck that," said Walters. "I'll outlive you, asshole."

Milo said, "Up to him."

"Fucking-A."

"Your decision, sir." The EMTs returned to their ambulance and drove off.

Enos Walters said, "Shitheads strap me down, wanna take me to some hospital where they wanna fuck me up."

Raspy voice accustomed to anger, speech slightly fuzzed as it emanated from between sunken lips. No teeth on top, a few on the bottom, cracked and brown.

Milo said, "Sorry for the inconvenience—can I call you Enos?"

"Ee-*no,*" said Walters. "Ee-nos sounds too much like . . . I had enough of that—okay? Got it? Ee-*no.* Can I call myself what I want?"

One scrawny hand balled, the other scratched a deflated cheek. Crude blue-black tattoos climbed up a stringy neck: lopsided crucifix, tiny devil, incongruously pretty pink rose in full bloom. Under the beard, a haggard hatchet face was dotted by eruptions of nasty-looking pimples. Meth rash.

Walters's eyes bounced and roamed. "Believe this shit? Build a castle and let assholes party in it?"

"Crazy," said Milo.

Walters tensed and stepped back, nearly tripping but waving off Milo's helping hand. "*I* ain't crazy. My heart's okay, too, I'm not celling up in some fucking ward."

"No offense intended, Mr. Walters. I meant the situation."

"Yeah. Whatever." Eyelids twitched. "I need to get out of here."

Milo produced another panatela. "Smoke?"

"Don't do that shit, used to do Viceroys," said Walters. "Quit last year. Being healthy. Been here since six thirty, gotta get the fuck out."

"Sorry for your inconvenience. Could you please tell us what happened when you got here at six thirty?"

"More like six twenty." Walters looked at the cigar, snatched it, and slipped it into a jean pocket. "Why not, you tried to stick me in that death wagon so yeah, you owe me."

His eyes bounced around. "I'm being a citizen and you hold me. You guys are something."

Milo said, "When you got here at six twenty—"

"Yeah, yeah yeah," said Walters. "Listen carefully, I ain't repeating."

Rocking on his feet and fighting for concentration, he told the story, the pace picking up with each sentence until he was racing, spewing out words, barely intelligible.

Brain alleyways detoured permanently by speed. When the verbal flash flood stopped, Walters was mouth-breathing hard.

Lots of words, no revelations.

Milo said, "Thanks. Could I please have your address and phone number?"

"Why?"

"For the record."

"I don't do the record," said Walters. "And I don't got no phone."

"You called 911—"

"On this." Fishing a burner out of his jeans. "Runs out in a few minutes, you won't reach me so don't waste my time."

"How about your address?"

"The Cyril."

"On Main?"

"Yeah."

"Room number?"

"It changes," said Walters. "Now let me outta—"

"The company you work for, Bright Dawn—"

"Bright Dawn Assholes Corporated. I'm finished with that shit."

"'Cause of this?" said Milo.

"'Cause of everything. Start early, end late, fuck-all pay."

"You ever clean this property before?"

"First time. Last time."

"Who's the owner of the company?"

"How should I know?" said Walters.

"Who pays you?"

"Irma."

"Last name?"

"How should I know? Why's it matter?"

"Filling in details, sir."

"I was a sir, you wouldn't detain me like a fucking prisoner. For doing the right thing."

"Appreciate your help, Mr. Walters. Irma—"

"In the office. Ask for the bitch with the fat ass."

Milo smiled.

Walters said, "You think I'm kidding? Like this." Stretching his arms.

"The people in the limo, recognize any of them?"

"Why would I?"

"Okay, thanks, Mr. Walters. You can go now."

Walters's gnarled hands slapped his hips. He stood there.

"Something the matter?" said Milo.

"How the hell'm I gonna do that? I got dropped off."

"The company won't pick you up?"

"I'm over with them. Don't want nothin' from them." Walters jutted his negligible mandible and stretched out a palm. Tattoo on his inside wrist. Ridiculously buxom naked woman smoking a cigarette. Below that: *Viceroys. Taste That's Right.*

Below that what could have been an old razor scar.

Milo pulled out his wallet and handed over two twenties.

Walters inspected the money. His eyebrows rose. "Huh." He teetered away.

Milo said, "He'll probably walk all the way downtown and use my money for crank."

I said, "Oh, you enabler."

"Does that mean I have to attend meetings? Anyway, he didn't add a thing."

"He's emotionally unstable so I don't see him helping you in court."

"Court? Talk about jumping guns, you just vaulted an arsenal. Yeah, so much for ol' Eno. You know why I asked about knowing the vics."

"The Cyril's downtown."

He nodded. "SRO, a dump among dumps. But Walters didn't throw off any tells and he's not exactly a criminal mastermind."

He hitched his trousers. "Time to deliver some really bad news. Whose day do we ruin first?"

"Gurnsey lived the closest."

"There you go," he said. "Thinking efficiently."

CHAPTER 5

We got in Milo's Impala and he rolled it slowly down the drive. Nowadays journalism's a short-attention-span business; at least half the reporters had left. When those that remained saw us, they tried to compensate with arm waves and revved-up volume.

Milo said, "You hear something, Alex? I don't." Nosing past the throng, he turned right on Benedict. Eno Walters was down the road a thousand feet, walking unsteadily and smoking the cigar.

Milo pulled up alongside him. "The press get hold of you?"

"I told 'em to fuck off."

"Good man." Another twenty exchanged hands.

Walters looked at it suspiciously, then jammed it in a jean pocket.

"Want a lift to Sunset?"

"Why? So you can lock me up again?" Hunching and working his lips, he turned his back on us.

"Love the job," said Milo, putting on speed. "Makes me feel like one of the popular kids."

◆

Richard Gurnsey had lived in a forgettable three-story building the color of Swiss cheese left too long in the fridge. Vintage seventies, when boxes were nailed up all over L.A., style be damned.

Beach city but at a mile from the beach, no salt-aroma or view of water.

No security, either. A weathered front door opened to a linoleum foyer sour with mold that T-boned a few feet later at a brown-carpeted stairway.

Milo sniffed. "Not what you'd expect from a hotshot studio lawyer."

I said, "Maybe he was just a gofer who padded his online résumé. Or he's frugal and spent his dough on all that recreation."

"Wine, women, and song, the rest foolishly." He inspected a bank of bronze mailboxes oxidized black at the corners. Four units per floor, R. Gurnsey and J. Briggs in 3B.

Milo said, "Maybe a live-in girlfriend if we're lucky. If we're lottery-lucky, she's in."

We climbed the stairs. Now the carpeting was blue, an uninterrupted hallway ending at a blank wall.

Music from behind the door to 3B. A pro-tooled female voice exhaling over an acoustic guitar loop of C major and G major. What qualified, nowadays, as folk.

Milo gave the V-sign. "We're buying tickets, at least scratch-offs."

He knocked on the door.

A male voice said, "Hold on."

The music lowered but persisted. "Who is it?"

"Police."

The music died.

"About what?"

"Richard Gurnsey."

"Ricky?" The door creaked and opened on a tall, shirtless, blue-eyed man in his thirties. Denim shorts rode low on his hips. Slightly taller than Milo, so at least six-four. He had bushy too-yellow hair and eyebrows to match, patchy, three-day gray-blond stubble, a burgeoning double chin. But for the neck flesh, lean, with a long-limbed beach-volleyball build. A deep tan said a mile to the sand was no obstacle.

Milo said, "Morning, sir. Lieutenant Sturgis, this is Alex Delaware." Talking as he flashed his badge.

Sometimes he chooses shiny metal because it's a better choice initially than the business card that specifies *Homicide*.

The man said, "What's up with Ricky?"

"You're his . . ."

"Roommate. Jay Briggs. What's going on?"

"Unfortunately, Mr. Gurnsey's deceased."

Briggs's eyes bugged. "What?"

"We're really sorry to—"

"What?" A massive fist hammered Briggs's right thigh, leading my gaze to knees clumped with surfer knots. "What the—*what*? This is totally *fucked.*"

"Could we come inside, Mr. Briggs?"

"You're telling me Rick is—oh, shit, what happened?" Jay Briggs ran his hand through his hair.

Before Milo could answer, he said, "Whatever," and stepped away from the door. It began to swing shut. I caught it and we stepped inside.

Small living room, more of the moldy sourness from the lobby. Décor was a brown corduroy couch worn bare in spots, a chipped black steamer trunk used as a coffee table, and three pine-and-burlap chairs—red, yellow, blue. The same blue carpeting as out in the hallway. On the table, crushed beer cans, empty beer bottles, a jar half filled with salsa, bags of corn chips. A paper Trader Joe's bag crammed with more empties tilted precariously near the open entrance to a plywood kitchenette. Two surfboards stood propped in a corner. To the left, a hallway led to three open doorways.

Jay Briggs padded to the fridge, fished out a can of Heineken, popped the top, took a long deep swig, and sat cross-legged on the floor.

"What, some drunk hit him?"

Time to show him the card.

Briggs's mouth dropped open. "Homicide? I don't get it. Who? Where?"

"When's the last time you saw Ricky?"

"I dunno," said Briggs. "I guess Friday, but not for long, he was going out."

"With who?"

"Some chick."

"Who?"

"He didn't say. He never said, it wasn't like there was anyone regular."

"Casual dating," said Milo.

"You could call it that," said Briggs. "More like going fishing. Ricky was always ready to fish. A lot of times he caught something."

"Any details on his Friday night catch?"

"I don't even know if he had anyone in mind, just that he was going out." Briggs threw up his hands. "That was Ricky. It was like his . . . hobby."

"Women."

"He lived for 'em." Briggs's mouth sagged. "You're saying he got into trouble 'cause of that?"

"We don't know enough to say anything, yet. Was Ricky discriminating in his choices?"

"Was he a racist?" said Briggs. "No way, equal opportunity, he liked 'em all."

I said, "Not picky."

"About what? Looks? That depended on his HL." Small smile. "Horniness level. Murdered? Jesus. Where did it happen?"

"Up near Benedict Canyon. You guys ever go up there?"

"We?" said Briggs. "We didn't go places together anymore, we just roomed."

"Anymore?"

"We knew each other in high school. I b-balled and ran the mile and Ricky covered sports for the paper."

"Which high school?"

"Fontana High. We weren't like tight bros but then we met up a couple years ago, bar at the beach—The Hungry Croc, now it's called something else—had a few beers and started to conversate. I had just moved back from Tucson, had been looking for a place. Ricky said he had a two-bedroom near the beach, would never let go of it 'cause of the rent control but he didn't need the second bedroom, I could have it cheap."

Briggs sighed. "It's been working out fine, he works days, I work nights. That's what I mean by not talking much."

He flexed big hands. "Oh, shit. I can't handle the rent myself."

"What do you do nights, Jay?"

"Take care of an old guy. Professor Van Ness, he's like a hundred, can't move but his brain's still okay. I take care of him at night, mostly he sleeps so I can, too. Sometimes I have to change a diaper but it's cool. I like helping people, used to assistant-coach middle school b-ball in Tucson, then the school, it was a private school, Christian school, had money problems so I decided to come back."

"Ricky was a lawyer at Sony."

"Um, not exactly," said Briggs. "He went to some law school but didn't pass the bar. To be honest, he was more of a paralegal."

"Ah," said Milo.

"He was pretty smart," said Briggs, sounding uncertain. "Said he didn't want the hassle of being a lawyer, the main thing was to make enough bank and have free time to party."

Our eyes swept over the mess on the coffee table.

Briggs said, "That's on me, Ricky was kind of a neat freak."

I said, "When were you expecting him back?"

"When he didn't come up Friday, I figured Saturday. When he didn't come up Saturday, I figured maybe tonight. But there was no way to tell."

Milo said, "Did Ricky know a guy named Benson Alvarez?"

"Uh-uh, who's he? Some Mexican gangster?"

"Did Ricky do any charity work?"

"Like what?" said Briggs, as if the concept was absurd.

"Volunteering his time, helping the homeless, people with disabilities, stuff like that?"

Slow head shake. "Only thing I know is he gave twenty bucks to United Way at the office. Asked me if I wanted to also. I said when I have more, I will, dude. Ricky was cool with that. Ricky was always cool."

"So not much into volunteering."

"Not that he told me," said Briggs. "To be honest, Ricky had time, he'd spend it on one thing." Shaping an hourglass in the air.

I said, "Did he ever have a long-term relationship—girlfriend, ex-wife?"

Briggs said, "Not since I knew him."

"He never mentioned a bad situation?"

"Never. But Ricky wasn't much to bitch. Didn't talk about his love life, period, just sometimes he'd come home looking happy and I'd say, 'A hot one, huh?' And he'd smile and give the thumbs-up."

"Friendly guy."

"He liked everyone," said Briggs. "Sometimes I wondered if that would get him into trouble."

"In what way?"

"I mean, it's okay to be okay with people, right? But not all people are good people, right? I mean sometimes it pays to be a little . . . not paranoid, just a little suspicious. Watch your back, right? I had an ex-wife, right after high school. She lied and told me she was pregnant then she cheated on me, then she got to keep my truck."

He frowned, remembering.

I said, "You're careful but Ricky wasn't."

"Ricky liked everyone," Briggs repeated. "Now look what happened."

Milo said, "You're thinking he got friendly with the wrong person."

"It's possible, no?" Briggs recrossed his legs. "I guess what I'm saying is the guy had no walls around him and sometimes you need walls."

His hands clasped on his knees and he rocked a couple of times. "He was my friend, I don't want talk smack about him."

"Of course not," said Milo. "But if you know something that helps find his killer, you need to tell us."

"Yeah . . . it's just, all this me-too shit going around. You know?"

"Ricky didn't always treat women right."

"He'd say he did. Because they had fun, too."

We waited.

Look," said Briggs, "I'm not saying he ever roofied anyone. Did a Harvey or a Cosby, that kind of thing."

Long arms folded across his bare chest.

I said, "But . . ."

"But he . . . oh, man, don't take this the wrong way. Okay?"

"Okay."

"Okay," said Briggs. "He didn't need to be a perv, chicks liked him."

As if that mattered. Milo and I waited.

Briggs said, "I'm just saying his way wouldn't be mine." His cheeks ballooned. He let the air out slowly. "He liked to get them a little . . . relaxed. Then, once they were in the mood . . . already doing it . . . he liked to stand them up. Sometimes in . . . both ways, you know?"

I said, "Anal sex by surprise."

"That makes it sound twisted, he never really forced anyone, they were already in the groove." Briggs unlaced his hands and waved them. "It was more like . . . he called it shifting gears."

"How'd his dates react?"

"He never said they had problems with it."

"Not your thing," said Milo.

"I mean . . . I like to know where I'm going so I assume a chick does, too." Small smile. "Not that I been doing much. Between the job and hitting the waves. Also I try to do some volleyball."

I said, "Ricky's sport was women."

Emphatic nod. "In school, he was never a jock, so I guess for him . . ."

Milo said, "What did he use to relax his dates?"

"Nothing weird," said Briggs. "Sweet drinks, he said chicks always went for the sugar, liked to pretend they were doing 7UP or something."

"He mixed them sweet cocktails."

"No, he'd buy them. Getting them to try stuff during dinner. Or at the bar."

I said, "Stuff with parasols."

"He said little paper things."

"He didn't party here?"

"He brought a few home but I can't tell you who. I'd only know the next day, I'd come home he'd be washing sheets, giving me the V-sign. Like I said, I work nights. Even on the weekend."

Milo said, "Seven-day job."

"Professor Van Ness needs me. Also, I need the money, got loans." Briggs's head dropped. "I didn't want to talk smack about Ricky like he's some sort of freak. He was just a friendly dude who liked to have fun."

"Sure," said Milo. "Okay, tell us what else you know, Jay."

"Nothing," said Briggs. "A couple of times, he bragged. Like the few times when we were both home. I'd be in my room, Ricky would have the door closed. I'd be getting ready to leave and he opens it, does this."

Hushing himself with a finger on his lips.

"Someone's sleeping."

"Exactly. But not him. He'd open his robe and peel off his rubber and give this big smile."

"Mission accomplished," said Milo.

"What can I say, it made him happy," said Briggs. "Nothing wrong with happy, right?"

"Ever see who he was with?"

"Never."

"Deep sleepers."

"I guess."

"Think they were unconscious?"

"I don't know. I hope not. I don't want you to think of Ricky as a bad person. 'Specially now that he's—this is freaking me out. This is the last thing I expected to hear."

Milo said, "You okay with us seeing Ricky's room?"

"Sure." Briggs pushed himself upright. "You need my permission?"

"You're the sole occupant now."

"Yeah. *That* sucks."

First door up the hall.

Moderate bedroom, small en-suite bathroom with a tub-shower combo. The walls of Rick Gurnsey's sleeping quarters were painted maroon, the ceiling, white, the floors faded oak laminate partially covered by an imitation Persian rug. Bare-topped wicker nightstand, king bed with a white spread tucked tight, both facing a sixty-inch streaming-compatible flat-screen.

In the skimpy closet two navy suits with a Saks Fifth Avenue Men's Store label shared space with a charcoal suit from Neiman Marcus, a black leather jacket with no label, three pairs of black, Diesel slim-cut jeans, same number of dress slacks: black, navy, cream linen. Dress shirts in blue, pink, and white. On the floor, two pairs of Nike runners, black and brown calfskin loafers, intentionally scuffed brown suede boots, red rubber beach sandals. The top shelf held a Dodgers cap, a gray knit stocking cap, and a cheap-looking panama.

The top drawer of a wicker dresser under the TV was filled with Calvin Klein briefs and socks rolled inside out. In the middle drawer, polo shirts, tees, a black silk Nat Nast bowling shirt with golden saxophones embroidered on the front.

In the bottom drawer, twelve packages of Ultra-Sleek XL ribbed and lubed condoms ("For her pleasure and yours"). One package opened, three rubbers missing.

"The simple life," said Milo. "Long as it's ultra-sleek and lubed."

He checked the bathroom. White tile and towels. The toilet seat lid was shut.

Milo said, "Endearing himself to his visitors," and opened the medicine cabinet. A couple of Speed Sticks, OTC analgesics and cold remedies, a boar-bristle shaving brush, cream from Truefitt in London, a walnut-handled razor and a week's worth of blades. Off to the right, given its own space, sat a small blue glass canister. Milo squinted at the label, handed it to me.

Cannabis blended with "a host of other botanicals." Inside, a waxy, fragrant paste the color of beer.

The entire top shelf was more condoms. Another ten packages.

Milo said, "His date comes in here, sees that, what's she gonna think?"

I said, "Sounds like Ricky arranged things so they wouldn't be thinking much."

"Then he shifts gears."

"A woman's caught off guard, thinks about it later, doesn't like the memory. Could be a motive."

"So what about the other three victims?"

I shrugged.

He laughed. "I was hoping you wouldn't say that."

Jay Briggs was across the hall, in his own quarters, smoking. Two-thirds the size of Gurnsey's room, set up with a plastic carton for a nightstand and a mattress on the floor that dipped under Briggs's weight. He'd put on a crushed-looking gray T-shirt. Piles of equally tortured-looking clothing littered the floor randomly.

Briggs stood. "Anything?"

Milo said, "Just doing our thing, Jay. I know I can trust you to stay out of Ricky's room until our forensics crew gets here."

"They're coming here? When?"

"Probably sometime today, they'll call first so give me your number, please."

Briggs recited, Milo copied. "Thanks. They'll also take your fingerprints."

"Mine? What for?"

"To eliminate you from any prints we find in Ricky's room."

"I never went in there."

"Then your prints won't come up."

"I have to do that?"

"Any reason you wouldn't want to?" said Milo.

Briggs's lips twisted. His eyes raced to the right, then back.

"They use a little computerized gizmo, Jay, you won't even get your fingers dirty."

Briggs chewed his cheek. "Here's the thing. I've been busted. A long time ago. DUI. Twice."

"Couldn't care less, Jay."

"But here's the thing. Sir. I lied about it when I applied for the job with Professor Van Ness. I *need* the job."

"No background check, huh?"

"They said they did," said Briggs. "I was figuring, *Oh, shit, I'm screwed.* But then they hired me so I figured it didn't come up."

"How long ago were your busts?"

"Like . . . fifteen years ago."

"Sometimes minor stuff doesn't make it to the files, Jay. Sometimes they're wiped off the record."

"Really? Cool."

"Whatever the situation, same answer: Couldn't care less, this is about homicide."

"Okay, sure, I'll do it. Sure, thanks, anything to help."

"There you go," said Milo. "Now give us contact information for Ricky's parents."

"They both died," said Briggs. "He talked about it once, some kind of accident. Then he said don't bring it up again, just wanted you to know. 'Cause I'd asked. Right after I'd moved in. Shooting the bull, you know? I'm telling him about my family, trying to be polite, ask about his. That's when he told me."

"Any sibs?"

"I have four, he had none. He liked that, said he got all the attention. I told him brothers were cool, sisters could be also. I hope you analyze pretty soon. There's bad energy floating around since you told me. Like I'm out in the water waiting for a wave, see this red tide floating toward me."

I said, "You and Ricky both surf?"

"Nah, just me. His only sport was chicks."

Milo said, "Where's Ricky's BMW?"

"We've got two spaces and his has been empty since Friday. Like I said I figured he'd hooked up with a hot one."

Briggs knuckled an eye and sucked in breath. "Guess he didn't. Once you guys leave, I'm getting out of here, too. Take a run. A walk, something."

Milo said, "The girls Ricky brought home. Remember *any* names?"

"Can't remember what I never knew, sir."

I said, "Did he have a type?"

"What do you mean?"

"Tall, short, blond, brunette."

"All I know was what Ricky said. White, black, Mexican, Chinese. Whichever fish were biting."

CHAPTER 6

When we returned to the car, noon had passed. "Next closest is Mr. Roget. I'll try his number."

No answer, no voicemail. Milo started up the engine. "Damn. If he lives alone, I'll need a victim's warrant."

He drove east on Arizona.

I said, "If there's no one to talk to, maybe Leon Creech can help."

"Why him?"

"They're both older guys who drove livery independently."

We'd met Creech last year, the driver of a hundred-year-old victim as well as her murderers. Informative, courtly, professional.

"Leon, there's a gent for you," said Milo.

"It's worth a try."

"Sure, why not, but first let's see if Solomon Roget lives with someone I can traumatize."

He didn't.

No answer at Roget's first-floor flat in a well-kept Spanish duplex on Hi-Point north of Olympic. A single vehicle sat far up a driveway that had been swept clean recently, under a gray canvas cover. Generous vacant space behind it. Enough for Roget's limo.

Milo lifted a canvas corner. Black Cadillac.

"Wait here for a second." He walked around the left side of the building, disappeared for a few seconds, returned. "No one in the backyard, no answer at the service door. I'll push paper once we're through spreading gloom."

As he turned to leave, the door to the second-floor unit opened. A young, sweat-suited blond woman with a left-arm sleeve tattoo stepped out to the landing. In her arms was a swaddled baby. Long, stringy hair, droopy fatigued eyes.

"Hi," said Milo.

"What's going on?"

"Police."

"For him?" said the woman. "Oh, shit, don't tell me he's a bad guy or something. We just moved in."

"You're talking about Mr. Roget."

"Don't know his name, just that he gets to keep two cars in the driveway 'cause the landlord likes him so we have to pay for a night permit." She pointed to a dusty red minivan across the street.

"Tough deal," said Milo. "Mr. Roget live with anyone?"

The woman's eyes rounded. "He *is* a bad guy?"

"Not at all," said Milo. "Does he live alone?"

"Why?"

"Something bad happened to him."

"Oh." Unimpressed.

"Anybody live with him?"

She shrugged. The baby bounced. "Never saw anyone."

"How long have you been living here?"

"A month," she said. "It's not *fair.* The *parking* thing."

"Big problem for you," said Milo.

"I mean, is that legal?"

"Don't see why not."

The woman's mouth dropped open. Milo headed for the car, muttering: "Milk of human kindness."

When she thought we weren't looking, she flipped us off. Or maybe she didn't care.

No answer at Leon Creech's house, either.

Milo pulled out his cell. "Happen to remember the street?"

I said, "Wooster."

He stared at me. "I was kidding. You remember everything that goes into that brain of yours?"

"I try to filter."

"Not even gonna ask. Let's cruise by."

Creech's mint-grin stucco traditional was one of the few single dwellings on a block of duplexes and apartment buildings. He owned the property, a traditionalist holding out.

We spotted him from a hundred yards away, dusting off his navy-blue Town Car. Tall, stooped, a human crane, filmy white hair flying away as he worked. Dressed for something important in an olive-green cardigan over a pink golf shirt, immaculate seersucker pants, white New Balance running shoes.

Concentrating on the car, stepping back to check his reflection in the paint.

We parked and crossed the street. Milo said, "Mr. Creech."

"Lieutenant! Long time."

"How's everything been going?"

"Passed my driving test with flying colors." Creech gave a thumbs-up. "When I see you it reminds me I served, too. Brings back my MP days in Seoul."

Same thing he'd mentioned the first time we interviewed him.

"And, Doctor, how are you?"

"Fine."

"That's good. So what's up? Another idjit doing something criminal? Not at that dump, the Aventura, they closed it down, got cranes digging up everything."

"Nope, somewhere else, sir. Do you know a livery driver named Solomon Roget?"

"Solly? What's up—" Creech's lips quivered. His long face lost definition. "Oh, no."

"Afraid so, Mr. Creech."

"Solly?" said Creech. He touched his chest. "Oh, my my. Solly and I go way back, he was driving when I was still working for the school district. Solly Roget? Really? Haitian, salt of the earth, couldn't find a nicer guy. When? Where?"

"Yesterday, a house in Bel Air."

"Bel Air? Like a Manson thing? Where in Bel Air? I used to drive there. Mrs. Meldock, Mrs. Davis, Mrs. Robertson, I was the guy for the ladies who lunched."

Milo said, "Off Benedict Canyon."

"Not that big one, looks like an office building, you have to take off your shoes even in the motor court—the agent . . . Mort Medvedev?"

"No, sir."

"Where, then?"

"Sorry, can't give out details just yet, Mr. Creech. When's the last time you saw Mr. Roget?"

"The last time." Creech tapped his lower lip. "The last time would have to be . . . couple of years ago? Yeah, two summers ago, some violinist. At the Bowl. We were both doing a drive-and-wait, got put in parking spots right next to each other."

"In your Town Cars."

"What else?"

"Yesterday, Mr. Roget was driving a white stretch—"

"That monstrosity? Oh, boy." Creech's palm slapped his own cheek lightly. "Piece of garbage, you can't get axle stability in something that big. Unless you build it like a semi and then it's too stiff for livery. No resale value, Solly picked it up cheap a long time ago. I told him don't go there, my friend, the kind of people want to ride something like that you don't want to know. Guess I was right. Who were the customers? They the ones who did it?"

Milo said, "Doesn't look like they were."

"What then, a robbery?"

"It's complicated, sir. We're just starting out and trying to get to know Mr. Roget."

"Been two years but I don't see Solly changing from the way he was when I knew him. A sweeter guy you'd never meet. You ask me, that was part of his problem. Too nice. Got taken advantage of."

"By who?"

"Customers passing bad checks—him taking checks, period, was naive. Not getting everything up front."

"You know all this because—"

"He told me. At the Bowl. We had plenty of time to talk. I brought snacks, he also did. We snacked and talked. So were they lowlifes, the passengers?"

"We're still gathering information, Mr. Creech."

"You want, Lieutenant, you can give me names, I'll see if they ring a bell."

"You and Solly shared clients?"

"No, but people who use drivers use drivers."

"Okay," said Milo, "but please keep the names to yourself."

"Promise. Shoot."

"Richard Gurnsey."

"Nope."

"Benson Alvarez."

"Nope. We talking gay guys?"

"Don't seem to be."

"Just two guys in the back of a super-stretch," said Creech. "Doing what?"

"There was a woman, too, we don't know who she is."

"A hooker?" said Creech. "An orgy?"

"No, sir. Like I said we're just starting out, Mr.—"

"Sorry, sorry, Lieutenant, I'm just upset." Creech patted his chest again. The precise spot that roofed his heart. He winced.

"You okay, sir?"

"Me? I'm fine. I'm just . . . this is hard to hear, guy like Solly. Easygoing—what the kids call laid-back. Nothing bothered him. His snacks were Haitian. He made them himself, didn't have a woman to cook for him. Cornbread, *that* I liked. Some kind of meatball, frankly, too spicy. I gave him potato chips and apple slices. We had a pleasant time and could hear the music in the parking lot."

I said, "Do you know anything about his family?"

"I know he had one," said Creech. "Couple of kids, living in Florida. One's some kind of doctor, the other's . . . I think also. Son and daughter, he was proud of them. Whole family came from Haiti on boats, worked their way up, Solly's wife cleaned rooms. Then she died."

Creech's voice caught. "He had it rough. But you'd never know it, always smiling."

"How did he get clients?"

"What do you mean?"

"We haven't found a website."

"I have one," said Creech, with sudden pride. "Did it last year, move into the new age. But it's a half-half deal. You get more clients but not always high-quality and then they rate you. The kids, they don't even know how to tip, to them it's Uber." Uttering the last word as if it were a disease. "Nowadays you sell a cookie at a counter, you get a tip. You drive idjits all night, you don't. That make sense?"

I shook my head. "So if Solly had no website—"

"I asked him that, he told me he did the tear-offs. Those things on bulletin boards, little fringies with flaps? You tear them off, they've got a phone number."

Milo said, "That's it?"

"When we were at the Bowl, that's what he had."

"Where did he hang his tear-offs?"

"Beats me," said Creech. "My opinion was, not smart. I told him at the time. Anyone can rip off a free piece of paper, you don't know who you're dealing with. Am I right? You're here, so obviously I am."

"Obviously, you are, sir."

"Yeah," said Creech. "But here's the thing, I don't want to be."

CHAPTER 7

Doctors in Florida, uncommon surname, easy trace.

Hillaire B. Roget, M.D., FAAOS, headed the Ocala Bone Institute. Specialties: geriatric orthopedics and diabetic wound management.

Milo took a deep breath, switched to speaker, and called.

The chain of communication was receptionist to nursing assistant to nurse practitioner to physician. Sped up by Milo's rank and explanation: "It's about Dr. Roget's father."

Within moments a soft voice said, "This is Hillaire Roget. What happened to my father?"

"There's no easy way to tell you—"

"Oh, no."

"I'm so sorry, Doctor. Unfortunately, your father's deceased."

"No," said Hillaire Roget. "God *no* . . . the police? So not natural causes?"

"I'm afraid not, sir." Milo braced himself with one hand on the steering wheel. "Your father was the victim of a homicide."

"My *father*? How? What happened?"

"We're still trying to work that out, Dr. Roget."

"At his house? A home invasion?"

"No, sir, he was found in his car."

"Oh, no." Muffled weeping. A long moment passed. The soft voice had weakened. "Sorry . . . I *told* him to stop driving. A man of his age by himself with strangers? I always worried something would happen. What, a robbery?"

Milo said, "Had he had bad experiences driving?"

"I'd assume," said Hillaire Roget. "But he wouldn't have told me . . . excuse me."

Another break.

"Oh, my, this has knocked me over, Lieutenant. Father was a kind man. A kind father. My sister and I have always adored him. After our mother died, he raised us by himself. He never hit us. Never raised his voice to us. He always said he believed in honey, not vinegar, and believe me, we could be imps. His patience . . . but such a stubborn man! I *wanted* him to move here with us, begged him, but he wanted his independence. Why couldn't he listen?"

Milo said, "So you're not aware of any specific incidents?"

"He'd *never* have told me," said Hillaire Roget. "He still thought of me as a ten-year-old—my age when Mother died. When I became an adult, I tried to protect him, but he never relinquished his role. *He* was the protector. Period. Was he taken advantage of by people he drove? Probably, because he's—oh, this is hard—he was such a generous man. Far too trusting. And that's after going through hell growing up—Haiti, the Duvalier times, I don't know if you're familiar but it was horrendous back then. The secret police would visit, people would disappear. Father never lost his good cheer. Never."

"That's what his friend told us."

A beat. "A woman?"

"No, sir," said Milo. "Did he have a woman friend?"

"He did fifteen years ago, that's why he stayed in L.A. when we moved back to Florida."

"Name, please."

"Lillian Adams, but she's deceased, Lieutenant. Cancer, just a few years after my sister and I moved—that would make it twelve years ago. That's why we thought he'd finally join us here in Florida. But he wanted to be independent. Now look where it got him—which friend told you about him? I wasn't aware he had any friends. Not that he was a loner, he liked people. But when he wasn't working his pleasures were solitary."

"Another driver his age named Leon Creech. What activities did your father enjoy, Doctor?"

"Mostly reading. English and French. He also played the violin." Strangled chuckle. "Tried to play. When he practiced, my sister and I would smile and get as far away as possible. He was no musician but he was a highly intelligent man, Lieutenant. Wanted to be a doctor but in Haiti unless you were a planter's son or a politician's son, forget it."

"So he became a driver."

"No, that was later," said Hillaire Roget. "When we first came to Florida on the boat, he worked as a maintenance man and went to night school. Accounting. Then Mother died and he picked us up and moved to L.A. and got a job working for the gas company. Bookkeeping. Then the gas company retired him, cost cutting, he got a pension but he was bored. So he began driving. For limo companies, then himself. This Creech, is he a good person?"

"Sterling," said Milo. "He spoke highly of your father. He also told us your father refused to advertise online and got customers by posting ads on bulletin boards."

"Those *tear*-off things," said Hillaire Roget. "Primitive. My sister and I teased him but like I said, stubborn. Did someone he drove do this?"

Milo said, "It's very early, Doctor. We're working out the details."

"Do you have a suspect?"

"No, sir."

"Any clues—what do you call them—leads?"

"Not yet, sir."

"So nothing," said Roget. "Good God, this is unreal . . . will there be an autopsy?"

"Yes, sir."

"Can you at least tell me *how* he died?" said Hillaire Roget. "Do I want to know?"

"Single gunshot wound. He wouldn't have suffered."

"Father hated guns. Never touched a firearm after he was discharged from the Haitian army. I want to come out as soon as possible to bring him back. When may I do that?"

"I'd give it at least a week or so, Doctor. I'll call you. And you call me anytime you have a question. Here's my number."

"Hold on, I'll get a pen." Scratchy noises. Exhalation. "Okay."

Milo recited the numbers slowly. Hillaire Roget recited them back.

"That's it, Doctor. Are you and your sister the only close relatives?"

"Just us," said Roget. "My sister and I work together. Madeleine's a podiatrist."

"No family here in L.A.?"

"None. God, how are Madeleine and I going to tell our kids? They last saw Father two Christmases ago. We flew him out, first-class. He kept making fun of that, snooty-hooty this, snooty-hooty that. Teasing us about why we picked him up at the airport instead of letting him drive. The kids love him. He loved them . . . this is . . . a horror."

"Again, Doctor, so sorry. Do I have your permission to enter and search your father's residence?"

"Why would you need my permission?"

"Without it I'll need to apply for what's called a victim's warrant. I'll certainly get one but your permission would speed things up."

"Of course, whatever helps," said Hillaire Roget.

"Would it help to talk to your sister?"

"I doubt she can add anything and I'd rather inform her myself—*that's* going to be wonderful. This is the most horrid day of my life. This and when Mother passed."

◆

Milo clicked off. "That was fun."

He looked at his Timex. "You up for Alvarez? Take us a while to get downtown."

"Sure." I texted Robin. *Not sure when I'll be back.*

No prob, I'm in the studio.

Making a left turn on Olympic was tricky but Milo seemed to enjoy the challenge. Setting off a chorus of car-horns, he muscled into an eastbound lane.

I said, "Gurnsey and Roget had no local family ties."

"Easier victims."

"Alvarez lives in a care facility and if the woman's homeless, she'd be the most vulnerable."

"Predator," he said. "But what the hell's the payoff?"

CHAPTER 8

Skaggs Avenue sits west of Chinatown, in a tight little circle of obscure streets shadowed by the pasta-bowl entwining of the 101 and 110 freeways.

The areas in and around downtown L.A. have been flirting with renewal for decades, with uneven results. A smidge of optimism had made it to Skaggs in the form of crisp, three-story apartments with security parking. Multiple *For Sale* signs said only a smidge for awhile.

The older properties ranged from fifties dingbats to wood-framed Victorians and Craftsman bungalows nailed up a century ago before earthquakes were taken seriously. A surprising quantity of improbable construction has survived, social Darwinism meets real estate.

Casa Clara Adult Residential Care was on the 800 block of Skaggs and one of the survivors: a two-story Craftsman painted cantaloupe orange, with a wraparound front porch complete with two rocking chairs. The paint looked fresh.

No signage; from the street, just an eccentrically colored house.

A front area behind a low wire fence and gate was cement. Triangle cutouts in the gray surface sported drought-loving succulents. That and the paint said someone was paying attention.

The gate opened on a walk-right-in pathway. From the street, no apparent security. Then the details asserted themselves.

The rocking chairs were bolted to the wide-plank porch floor. Iron bars grilled every window and the four-pane mini-window in a vintage carved mahogany door. Sticker from an alarm company and two serious dead bolts on the door. Maybe to counteract all that, a yellow happy-face decal beamed just below the top bolt.

Milo rang the bell and evoked a wasp-buzz.

Nothing for several seconds, then a female voice sang out, "Wuh-*uhn* second!"

Footsteps. The same voice, louder, trilled, "Who *is* it?"

"Police."

The upper half of a face filled the four panes, pale skin and blue eyes waffled by the iron grid. "Um, I.D., please?"

Milo obliged with the badge. The door opened on a tall, slim woman in her twenties wearing a crimson Harvard sweatshirt, ripped gray jeans, and black flats in need of polish. Square face with a strong chin, upturned nose, narrow mouth, pert chin. Oversized glasses in tortoiseshell frames hazed the eyes, which verged on turquoise. Long caramel-colored hair was gathered in a free-for-all high pony. Long pale fingers moved restlessly, as did her shoulders and the eyebrows.

She smiled at us, what appeared to be a sincere attempt at warmth. The fidgeting reduced the impact, but still, good intentions.

"Someone finally got going on Benson? Please tell me he's okay."

She squinted past us at the street. "Is he in your car? Can I go out and get him?"

Milo said, "Benson Alvarez."

Enthusiastic nod. "We call him Benny. So he's safe. Good. We've all been so worried since he didn't come home Friday. I immediately reached out to his DPSS worker but she never got back to me so I phoned you guys. The guy I spoke to started in with an adult has to be missing twenty-four hours before you can file a report. I told him Benny wasn't your typical adult and he said okay, he'd look into it. I wasn't sure he meant it, so good, he did."

She shifted to the right, blue eyes shooting past Milo. "Um, I don't see him in your car. *Is* he being held somewhere? I can't leave myself but maybe Andrea can authorize an Uber to pick him up or something."

Milo said, "You're his caretaker?"

"I oversee the facility. We're Level One, the most able residents, they don't have individual caretakers. It's by accident that I'm dealing with this, usually I do the night shift because I'm going to school for my master's during the day. But Marcella—the day person—asked if she could trade to take some vacation time with her boyfriend."

She stopped, caught her breath. "That was oversharing, sorry. So where and when can Benny be picked up?"

Milo rubbed his face. "Could we come in, Ms. . . ."

"Justine Merck. Why, what's happened?"

"It would be better if we discussed this inside—"

"Something *happened* to Benny?"

This time, Milo used the card.

Justine Merck read and swayed and clutched the doorjamb for support. "Homicide . . . Benny? Oh, God, no!" One of her feet gave way and began skidding out from under her.

I caught her by the arm, Milo gripped the other, and we guided her inside.

Like the interior of most genuine Craftsman structures, the ground floor was dimmed by dark wood walls and matching ceiling coffers. A cheap plastic fixture dangled overhead, casting merciless light.

Off to the side was a living room furnished with couches that looked as if they'd been rescued curbside. But the space looked well tended and smelled of lemon-scented cleanser.

Big room, uninhabited. No sights or sounds of human habitation from anywhere in the house.

I said, "Is anyone else home?"

Justine Merck, now crying and gulping air, shook her head violently.

We sat her in a decrepit armchair facing a sofa and waited as she took several breaths.

"The other residents are at the zoo with our student volunteers. We go there a lot because it's open and relaxed. Benny loved it. The flamingos, he loved their color. Even though they smelled bad. He'd joke about that, hold his nose and make a funny face—oh, here I go again, you don't care about any of that!"

Milo said, "Actually we care about anything you can tell us about Benny." He produced the wad of death-knock tissues he keeps in his jacket pocket and gave her one. She dabbed and sniffled.

Milo said, "Justine, when it comes to a homicide investigation, there's no such thing as oversharing."

She hung her head, tapped her knees. Placed both hands on her temples and pressed until the nails blanched. "In a couple of hours, they'll be coming home and I'll have to tell them. I should also call Andrea, she'll know what to do. Or maybe she won't. This never happened before."

"Who's Andrea?"

"Andrea Bauer, she owns Casa Clara and other havens. She lives in Santa Barbara but she comes here regularly. I told her about Benny not coming home, she said follow up with the police. This morning she called me back and said you guys were looking for him. That's why when you showed up . . ."

Tears.

"Could we have Andrea's number?"

"Sure." Slow recitation, hurried jotting.

I said, "Justine, tell us about Benny."

"Like what?"

"The kind of person he was."

"Sweet," she said. "Sweet, nice boy—I mean he was a middle-aged man, I'm not intending to juvenilize him. But that's what you think of when you think of Benny. Innocent, like a young boy. Just the gentlest little guy."

"How mentally challenged was he?"

"He was officially classified as DD—developmentally disabled—but it wasn't severe. I think he tested out in the midseventies—his IQ. He could read a little, although usually he faked it."

"Pretended to be higher functioning than he was."

"I mean everyone needs to feel good about themselves, right? It's not like he lied or bragged or did stupid stuff. What I'm talking about is like the time he got hold of one of my textbooks and ran this little plastic magnifying glass over it and started humming and nodding, like he understood it. I said, 'So what have you learned about educational curriculum, Benny?' He looked up at me with the sweetest expression and said, 'I learned you're smart, Justine.' That was Benny, always a nice word for everyone. Everyone loved him. Who'd hurt him? I don't *understand*!"

Milo said, "So he went missing on Friday."

"He was supposed to be back by three. I arrived at four, usually it's seven but Marcella had to get ready for her trip so I helped her out. Marcella was super concerned, she said she'd drive around looking for him but couldn't do it for very long because she had to get ready for her trip. I told her not to worry, I'd take care of it. Which is when I began making calls. When I didn't hear anything Friday or Saturday and then today, I was really scared. But hopeful, you know? Benny's Level One, maybe he could take care of himself for a bit."

She looked at us, doubtful. "I always try to be hopeful even though it's stupid!"

Her hands began to shake and her eyes glazed.

I said, "You go to school during the day and work all night? Tough schedule."

"It's actually not that bad. When I'm here I mostly get to sleep unless a resident has an issue and when they do it's almost always short-term—bad dreams, someone wants water or a snack. Also, I only have classes twice a week—graduate seminars, both in the afternoon, so I can catch up on the other days."

"How did the other residents react to Benny not coming home?"

"A couple asked, I told them Benny had an appointment, he'd be back. No one argued. They're like that. Docile—does that sound patronizing? They're *cooperative,* very gentle people. And Saturday was a field trip, Descanso Gardens, they came home exhausted. It'll be like that today 'cause of the zoo. We try to keep them occupied."

"Where did Benny go on Friday?"

"To his job. An art gallery, sweeping up," said Justine Merck. "Obviously I phoned them first, they said he'd been there until two, two thirty, as usual, seemed fine when he left. It's not a strict schedule, they basically let him hang around."

I said, "He likes the zoo but chose not to go."

"He liked having a job. It made him feel . . . meaningful—this is a nightmare!"

The first tissue was soaked and compressed. Milo gave her another and she blew her nose noisily.

"I even looked for him right here. In his room, every other room, the backyard. Even though I knew that was irrational. Wanting to do *something,* you know?"

I said, "Of course. How many doors are there?"

"The front where you came in and in back, from the laundry area to the backyard."

"So if no one was at the rear of the house, someone could come and go without being noticed."

"I guess so." Justine Merck wrung her hands. "We don't lock them up, it's not a jail, the whole point is fostering independence. Benny loved his job. Loved art, loved to draw."

Milo said, "Was he talented?"

She slumped. "He drew me stick figures. I told him they were fantastic."

"What's the name of the gallery where he worked?"

"Verlang Contemporary, it's on Hart Street, not far."

"Benny walked."

"It's less than a mile, and he always went during daylight. When he started, a student volunteer accompanied him. After a week, he insisted on doing it himself. That's consistent with our approach."

"How long had he been working there?"

"Months," she said.

Milo said, "What's Marcella's full name and number?"

"Marcella McGann. Hold on." Justine Merck stood, took a moment to steady herself, hurried out and returned scrolling a cellphone. She read off the number. "But like I said, she's on vacation."

"Where?"

"Mexico—Cabo, I think. With her boyfriend, they'd been planning it for a while."

I said, "You get up at night when the residents have issues. Did that ever include Benny?"

"Not often. And he'd never make a fuss, just come down and tell me he couldn't sleep. We'd chat for a while and I'd walk him back up. He wasn't malfunctioning or anything, if that's what you're getting at. I just got the feeling he sometimes had ideas in his head and didn't know what to do with them. At night and when he was awake."

"What kind of ideas?"

"I don't know, maybe I'm totally wrong," she said. "But people like him think a lot. They're just like anyone else. Sometimes he'd get a look"—she tapped her head—"and I'd be like, 'What's going on up here, Benny?' Sometimes he wouldn't answer, sometimes he'd look up at me with this puppy smile and say, 'You're so smart, Justy.' "

Tears welled. She wiped them away.

I said, "A gentle guy."

"The gentlest. Why would anyone hurt him? Unless it had something to do with the neighborhood. Something he ran into while walking back."

"You've had problems in the neighborhood?"

"Fewer than you'd expect, but sure, it's like any other urban thing. I mean I'm not judging and disparaging an entire region because it's low-income, but my first year of grad school I had a placement at one of the downtown shelters and it was scary. Not most of the homeless, just a few. You'd get some who were totally irrational with major anger issues."

She touched her left forearm. "I got my arm sprained once. Ladling out food and a guy, a total schizophrenic, thought I wasn't moving fast enough and grabbed me and twisted."

"Scary," I said.

"Petrifying. So when Benny still didn't show up, I thought, What if he ran into someone like that? He'd be defenseless. But you can't imprison them. There are always risks to be weighed. Right?"

We nodded.

She threw up her hands. "Working with the disabled, nothing they teach you in school prepares you. Like that shelter, how could I be ready for that?"

Milo said, "Any problems between Benny and the other residents?"

"Of course not. Andrea selects for gentleness, she doesn't want to waste time on discipline and control."

"Okay. What about Benny's family?"

"He didn't have any family."

"No one at all?"

"Isn't that *sad*? That's how he ended up here. He was an only child, lived with his mother, she had him late, died two years ago when she was in her late eighties. You see that with Down syndrome. Older parents, three of our residents are Down. But Benny wasn't Down, he was just UDD—undifferentiated developmental delay."

I said, "He was living with his mother until she died?"

"He was the one who found her, he got all terrified and ran out of their apartment and sat on the curb crying. A neighbor saw him, found out what happened, and called 911. Benny was put in adult foster placement until he got in here."

Milo said, "No cousins, aunts, that kind of thing?"

"No one," said Justine Merck. "That's true of most of our residents. They're kind of like foundlings. It's society's responsibility to take care of them."

"How about a look at Benny's room?"

"Sure. You'll see his art. How much he loved it."

She took us up a mahogany staircase softened by brown shag. The house's second floor was the same mahogany. Nature prints taken from commercial calendars hung askew at irregular intervals. Five open doors on each side of the hall. Some were set up with a bunk bed, others with a single.

Benny Alvarez had roomed alone in a beige eight-by-eight space at the rear of the house, probably built as servants' quarters. A single, narrow window, the view partly obstructed by the broad, rust-edged leaves of a towering sycamore. The *Sesame Street* quilt on the bed was neatly tucked, a matching pillow fluffed.

I said, "Did Benny make his own bed?"

Justine Merck said, "Oh, yes, he took pride in it. He was always neat and clean. Loved to wash his hands and was the first to line up for shower time. He was picky about his clothes, too. Buttoned his shirts up to the neck even in hot weather."

I thought: *Military dad? Convict dad?*

I said, "What do you know about his father? His upbringing, period."

"Nothing, just what I was told about his mom. With some of them you get abuse histories but not Benny. He was well taken care of by his mom and his foster parents."

"Speaking of which, what's their name?"

"The Baxters but they moved back to Utah two years ago. That's why Benny came here."

Milo and I took in the tiny room. Other than the bed, only one piece of furniture: a white three-drawer dresser. Resting on top, several sheets of paper covered with stick figures.

Milo rifled through the drawers, then checked a small closet. Meager wardrobe, a pair of sneakers on the floor, nothing on the shelf. I thought of Rick Gurnsey's condom stash. Two men, so different, slaughtered and abased together.

We turned to leave.

Justine Merck said, "Darn. I was hoping you'd find something. Like I said, I'm stupid, so I never stop hoping."

She watched us from the door until we drove away. Two blocks later, Milo pulled over, entering the shadow of the freeway. "Another one with no local family."

We each pulled out our phones.

His research began with the basics on Andrea Bauer and Marcella McGann. McGann's Facebook page portrayed a heavyset, brown-haired woman in her thirties. Favorite music and movies, nothing unconventional. Three photos with an equally chubby boyfriend named Steve.

Dr. Andrea Bauer lived in Montecito and donated to worthy causes. Ph.D. in sociology from Yale, inherited wealth from a deceased developer husband. Buddhist, pacifist, vegan, self-labeled as an "activist," mother of two, grandmother of one. Lots of images on the Web for her, all at fundraisers. Angular, pretty woman in her sixties with short iron-colored hair brushed straight back from a clear, tan brow.

Nothing remotely nasty in either woman's background. Perfect driving record for McGann's five-year-old Nissan Sentra, Bauer had gotten a few speeding tickets in her Porsche Panamera GTS. The 101 north. Heading home in a hurry.

As Milo continued clicking, I looked up art galleries on Hart Street and found Verlang Contemporary. An image search revealed a narrow storefront on the ground floor of an ornate, gargoyle-encrusted twenties building. Gray limestone, somber and impressive; maybe built as a bank.

The elegance diminished by a discarded shopping cart up the block, chips and stains on the stone.

I ran a map search. As Justine Merck had said, not far—.61 mile from the cantaloupe-colored house.

Twenty minutes if you ambled, add a bit more time for the possible distractedness of a mentally challenged man with a creative mind.

Milo clicked off. "Hate when everyone's law abiding."

I said, "Short walk home so he was likely abducted sometime Friday afternoon, kept somewhere until he was murdered on Saturday. Skid Row isn't that far so what Justine told us about the soup kitchen might be relevant. All kinds of people on the street."

He frowned. "Damn men's jail isn't that far, either. Scrotes walking out to freedom, who knows what they'd do."

He placed a call to Dr. Andrea Bauer, got voicemail. The same for Marcella McGann.

"Okay, let's have a look at that gallery."

The brief ride took us past residential and commercial buildings of varying ages and conditions and a fetid homeless encampment occupied by six vagrants, none of whom recognized Benny Alvarez or the woman in the black hat. The outdoor inhabitants seemed strangely serene when questioned, an attitude buttressed by Milo's distribution of singles and cheap cigars. As we left, a man called out, "God bless you, General!"

The limestone building housing Verlang Contemporary was another holdover, flanked on the north by an eighties motel called The Flower Drum festooned with English, Japanese, and Korean signage and on the left by a two-story block cube housing New World Elegant

Jewelers. (*WE BUY GOLD!!!*) Off in the distance, the pagoda roofs of Chinatown pierced the smog, strangely quaint against the brutalist towers of municipal government.

Verlang's windows were dark but for a *Closed* sign. Same for two neighboring art emporia: AB-Original Gallery and The Hoard Collection. The building had two additional stories, no lights from within.

Milo said, "Entire place looks dead. Maybe not enough talent to go around."

He drove to Hill Street, headed south to Sixth, then west. Traffic had congealed, tempers were fraying, horns farting. He switched on the police band and used it for background. The inflectionless, nonstop dialogue between dispatchers and patrol officers often lulls me drowsy. When I woke up, we were passing the county art museum on Wilshire just east of Fairfax.

He said, "Rise and shine. Let's get some coffee."

"Drop me at home and I'll make a pot."

"Not decaf, dude."

"No prob."

"Kenyan?"

"I think we've got that."

"Think? I was hoping for a guarantee."

"Life's rough," I said. "On the other hand, we definitely have biscotti. Robin baked some with candied citron."

"Robin bakes?"

"Robin does anything she puts her mind to. One of the good things she got from her mother was a book of home recipes."

"Biscotti," he said. "Lovely language, Italian. Okay, fine, doesn't have to be Kenyan. See? I'm doing what you tell me, being psychologically flexible."

Sitting at my kitchen table, he downed three large mugs of Jamaican coffee and half a dozen biscotti before yawning.

Robin had come in two minutes ago and sat down with us. She smiled. "Want to take a nap, Big Guy?"

"Appreciate the offer but I'm calling it a day." Leaning over, he pecked her cheek then bent and ruffled the folds of Blanche's neck before pushing himself up.

I walked him out of the house and down to the Impala. "What's next, Big Guy?"

"I do grunt work and you enjoy life. Something comes up, I'll let you know."

He walked to the driver's side. Stopped, backtracked, squeezed my hand with both of his. Like being swaddled by oven mitts. "Yeah. Thanks."

CHAPTER 9

Monday at two p.m., he called and said, "Three able detectives canvassing thoroughly, zero information."

Tuesday at four p.m., he texted: *Don't know if it's too short notice but Andrea Bauer's coming by in an hour.*

I'd just completed two custody reports and Robin would be working late, finishing a "dire emergency" repair on the neck of a celebrity rocker's red-sparkle Telecaster. Koko Moe didn't play a note and used the instrument the way a drum majorette employs a baton. But she needed to look "hot and hyper and hot," and a limp, decapitated instrument wouldn't cut it.

I went to Robin's studio, kissed her, and looked at her workbench. "Artistic fulfillment."

"We take it where we find it, darling."

At two forty-seven, I arrived at Milo's windowless, closet-sized office on the second floor of the West L.A. station. Other detectives work in a big room downstairs, saturated with human noise and clanging locker doors.

Years ago, my friend had been shoehorned into the apparently unworkable cell by a corrupt, soon-to-retire police chief who promoted Milo to lieutenant in return for silence about "errors of judgment" that would've jeopardized a huge city pension.

The chief felt smug, certain he'd gotten the better end of the deal. Unaware he'd earmarked the perfect den for this particular grizzly.

Lieutenants typically operate desks but Milo had leveraged the ability to keep working cases. When administrative tasks came up, he ignored them. Ditto memos, meetings, and paperwork outside the pages of blue-bound murder books.

Two subsequent chiefs had bristled, as organization men always do when iron rules rust. But their initial resolve to change things had fizzled: The department needed every bit of good P.R. it could cadge, and Milo's success was too blatant to mess with.

The cramped space barely accommodates his desk and chair plus one additional hard-backed seat. The visitor's throne might as well have my name engraved on a brass escutcheon as I'm the only person who occupies it. Witnesses and persons of interests are taken to interview rooms and when the young D.'s show up, they stand in the hall and report.

For the meeting with Dr. Andrea Bauer, Milo had selected the nearest of the rooms. But as we approached the *Reserved* sign dangling from the doorknob, he kept going.

I said, "Change your mind?"

"She's from Montecito," he said. "We're offering valet service."

We headed down the stairs, left the station, and stood near the curb. Butler Avenue was a steady stream of unmarkeds and official vehicles entering and exiting the staff lot across the street.

I said, "Why's she coming here?"

"She called and offered. I don't argue with someone with the net worth of a midsized Caribbean country."

"You researched her finances."

"After she called, I took a superficial look at the numbers. She's coming down for a board meeting at The Music Center, figured it would be efficient to stop by. Still haven't been able to reach her employee, McGann. I'm hoping Bauer can direct me."

He glanced at his Timex.

I said, "Nothing from the crypt?"

"The decomp case still rules, all four of my bodies are in the fridge closet, can't even get a commitment for autopsy schedules. Adding to the joy, I got into Solomon Roget's apartment yesterday and turned up nothing but a pile of those tear-off ads he posted who-knows-where. An appointment book woulda been nice, guy had to have some way to organize his schedule."

"Whoever killed him took it."

"That would be my guess. Along with his cellphone. He uses some small-time carrier, I subpoenaed his account, heard nothing, will keep on it. I also drove around near his apartment checking out supermarkets and convenience stores. If Roget posted at any of them, his ads have been taken down."

"What about cameras?"

"The places I found, none are directed at the boards, the concern is pilferage, not free advertising. I also talked to the agency that rented the house for parties. Place has been vacant for a year, some sort of nasty divorce. Still unlocked by the way, I just got back, rechecked every one of twenty-plus rooms. Nothing bloody. The murders didn't go down there."

I said, "Nasty divorces kick up all sorts of passions so maybe the dump spot wasn't chosen randomly. Who are the feuding parties?"

"Ansar versus Ansar. Mom split with the kids, is hiding out somewhere in the Middle East."

"Maybe I can get you specifics. There are judges I can call."

"Oh, yeah, that's your other job, isn't it? Great, thanks, terrific—okay, here's our philanthropist."

A maroon Porsche Panamera had turned onto Butler from Santa Monica and continued to glide toward us. Milo waved, the car stopped, he pointed to the staff lot, hustled across the street, and used his key card to raise the barrier. I waited and a few minutes later he emerged from the lot with a woman wearing a black hoodie, black tights, and red ballet shoes.

Same face and coif as her pictures but Andrea Bauer had let her hair go white. Artful white, shiny as chrome, every strand in place. She moved quickly but with the slightly off-kilter gait you see in women who've sacrificed stability for extreme thinness.

Milo doing all the talking, Bauer staring straight ahead. By the time the two of them reached me, her hand was out. She allowed me a brief shake of her fingers. Stiff and cool, nails cut short and buffed. Her nose and chin were sharp enough to cut paper, her eyes nearly black.

"Nice to meet you, Doctor. Good to hear the police value behavioral science." Deep, slightly abrasive voice; Lauren Bacall with a cold.

I smiled. "Dr. Bauer."

"Andy." She looked at the station door. "Never been in a police station before. Time for everything, I guess."

We stepped inside and Milo offered her the elevator.

She said, "The stairs, use it or lose it," and climbed ahead of us. Medium-sized woman but able to take two steps at a time. At the second floor, Milo outpaced her and held the door to the tagged interview room. He'd set it up friendly: table in the center, three chairs on three sides, bottled water, plastic cups.

Andrea Bauer took the center chair without instruction. "Interesting. I imagine the environment alone intimidates suspects."

Milo said, "All kinds of people come in here."

"Such as?"

"People helping us out."

He sat across from her. I took the side chair.

"What do you call them, sources? Informants?"

Milo smiled. "People helping us. So what would you like to tell us about Benny Alvarez?"

Andrea Bauer's thin lips turned down. "This has been incredibly difficult, I've never dealt with anything like it. Benny was a sweet, innocent human being, Lieutenant. I was pleased to be able to take him in. Was he probably abducted on the way from work?"

"We don't know yet."

"Can you tell me if he suffered greatly?"

"I don't believe he did."

"It's utterly mad," said Andrea Bauer. "I can't imagine anyone deliberately wanting to hurt him. But I suppose I'm being naive. There's all sorts of evil out there, isn't there?"

"Unfortunately, ma'am. How did you come to take him in?"

Andrea Bauer crossed stick-legs and looked up at the ceiling. "It was a couple of years ago. I was full-up at the Skaggs facility but a caseworker called and just about begged. There was a vacancy at my place in San Diego, it's the largest—twenty residents—but the worker felt the move would be difficult for Benny, his experiences had been rather limited."

I said, "Emotionally or geographically?"

"Both. From what I gathered, he'd lived with mother in Echo Park then with his fosters only half a mile from there. The worker described him as having the mind of a child though I learned later she was selling Benny short."

I said, "He functioned higher than she thought."

"Most people don't understand but I'm sure you do, Dr. Delaware. The concept of mental age is given more credit than it deserves—mind of a six-year-old, mind of a ten-year-old. But it doesn't work that way, does it?"

I shook my head. "A slow adult is qualitatively different than a normal child."

She turned to Milo. "What your psychologist means, Lieutenant, is that an adult with cognitive impairment can function low on one measure and high on another. Benny was a prime example. His reading skills were just about nil but his vocabulary was pretty darn good—

you'd meet him and think he was okay. On top of that, he could function socially and had no physical stigmata—small stature but he looked normal . . . no pain? You're sure?"

Milo said, "He died by a single gunshot that would've been rapidly fatal."

Andrea Bauer sank an inch. "Oh, God, how grotesque. And you have *no* idea who could've done this?"

Milo said, "Not yet. Could we go back to his history, for a sec? You had no vacancies but you found a way."

"I had to do some shuffling, make sure no one else was put at a disadvantage. I'd just accepted a resident at Skaggs but she hadn't moved in yet. Williams syndrome, slightly lower-functioning than Benny but one part of that diagnosis is extreme sociability. On top of that, she'd moved around a bit so I thought she might be okay in San Diego. So off she went and Benny got the slot at Skaggs."

She recrossed her legs. "Small victories, gentlemen. That's how you need to look at it."

I said, "You take a personal interest in the residents."

"There's no reason to work with people unless you're interested in them."

She edged closer to the table, grazed a water bottle with her fingernails. Clipped utilitarian nails but nothing ascetic about her: The hoodie was cashmere, a four-carat diamond stud glinted from each ear, and a platinum ring set with a round yellow diamond at least twice that weight banded her left ring finger.

"That probably sounds glib but I mean it," she said. "I never set out to run facilities, fell into it after my husband died. He owned all kinds of things—office buildings, apartments, shopping centers, reinsurance companies, and just before his stroke, he picked up four dozen old age homes and drug rehab centers as part of some sort of trade. I was ready to sell everything, wanted no part of warehousing human beings. But then I thought, *Hey, it's been years since I've worked with human beings, why not give it a try?* So I held on to a few locations. The goal was to create spaces for unaddicted people born with cognitive problems. Nothing grand. Bill—my husband, was all *about* grand, I'd had enough of grand."

"Something manageable," I said.

"I'm not going to sit here and tell you I'm Saint Andrea. The state and county pay me handsomely for each resident but every penny is plowed back, I make no profit. Don't need to, Bill set me up." Fleeting smile. "Grandly."

"Are all your places Level One?"

"The one in San Diego—that was my first, it used to be an old age home—is larger so we have a few Level Twos. But I stay away from anything below that. The point is to offer maximal quality of life in a relaxed manner. You visited Skaggs. Did it seem anything other than comfy and nurturing?"

Milo said, "It seemed nice, ma'am."

"When Bill ran it, it housed addicts and was painted a horrid pea green."

She rolled the edge of a cashmere sleeve, looked down at a diamond-studded Lady Rolex. "Got to get over to Disney Hall. Tedious meeting, but one commits."

Milo said, "Is there anything else we should know about Benny?"

Head shake. No movement of hair. "On the drive down I tried to pick my brain but came up with nothing. What seems likely to me is this was a robbery—a mugging that went wrong or just one of those crazy random things."

"Did Benny carry money around?"

"When they leave the facility, we give them ten singles and a limited-use cellphone. Two numbers programmed: 911 or the facility. But maybe someone wanted the phone, didn't know it was useless. Kids kill each other over shoes, why not a phone?"

I said, "We were told Benny had a job at an art gallery."

"Marcella arranged that," said Andrea Bauer. "And for the first week she or a student volunteer walked him to and fro. He learned quickly, had an excellent sense of focus."

Milo said, "Meaning?"

"He could divine a route, set a goal, and reach it, Lieutenant. That's what Dr. Delaware and I meant about mental age. In some ways, Benny was like a fully operational adult. If we felt he was in danger, we'd never have allowed it."

Her thin face shimmered as a tremor ran from chin to eyebrow. She twisted the massive ring. "Will it be necessary to publicize Benny's living arrangement? I'd love to avoid media coverage. For my residents' sake."

Milo said, "Far as we're concerned the less press the better."

"I concur." She stood. "Sorry I couldn't be more helpful."

Milo said, "Thanks for taking the time."

Andrea Bauer's smile was cool and knowing. "To be perfectly frank, I wanted to meet you face-to-face to make sure Benny was getting optimal attention. There are people I know, Lieutenant. And now I'm reassured that I won't need to contact them."

CHAPTER 10

The trip down the stairs was the Andrea Bauer–led race in reverse. Once outside, she shot Milo something vaguely smile-like, crossed Butler Avenue, and jogged into the staff lot.

Milo said, "She *knows* people. Nothing like a threat to brighten my day."

I said, "Her main reason for coming here was self-protection."

"Alvarez disappears Friday, it's already Tuesday and I'm supposed to shield her from bad P.R.? The brass has stifled to the max because the mayor's official line is The Westside Is Safe but a story breaks tomorrow in the *Times.*"

"Could work in your favor," I said.

"Tips? With all the loonies, a double-edged sword but let's see. Meanwhile the kids are still canvassing, I extended it two miles in both directions."

Andrea Bauer's Panamera exited the lot and sped off.

He said, "It could work in my favor—lemons to lemonade, huh? You ever sink into a sump of bitter, soul-leeching pessimism?"

Not since I made my way from Missouri to L.A. at sixteen and could stop hiding from a drunken, raging father.

I said, "I try to avoid it."

We returned to his office.

I said, "Lulling the victim's the key to predation so Benny Alvarez's sense of focus might've worked against him. Overly fixed on his goal and not paying enough attention to his surroundings. The same might apply to the woman, if she was a heavy drinker and chronically impaired. Gurnsey, too, for that matter. Too intent on sex to evaluate risk."

"Caught up in a honey trap."

"Who better than a hungry bear?"

He rolled a pencil between his fingers. "What about Roget?"

"My bet would be collateral damage," I said. "Wrong limo, wrong time. Or maybe the car was a factor: Someone wanted a flashy stage. But he could also be seen as taking undue risks: older man driving strangers, keeping no record of his fares."

"Use him for his wheels, then do him and display him with the others," he said. "Because why waste a corpse? We're talking Hitler-level cruelty, Alex."

"Cruelty and power lust. Literally manipulating human beings."

His fingers drummed a paradiddle on his desktop. "All that said, let's dot some i's and see what the computer says about Dr. Andy's business practices."

Several interviews with Andrea Bauer in glossy throwaway magazines repeated the gist of what she'd just told us. Precisely the goal of interviews in glossy throwaways.

She owned nine facilities: three in California, four in Arizona, two in Idaho. No serious complaints had been lodged against any of them. No mechanics' liens for unpaid bills, bankruptcy filings, or other evidence of financial weakness.

The extent of Bauer's involvement in the legal system was three civil suits in just as many years, two in San Diego County and one in Tempe. What appeared to be routine slip-and-falls, everything settled by her insurers. Online ratings skewed toward positive but that was meaningless; praise can be purchased and, in general, the internet's a compulsive liar's dream. But the lack of criticism was noteworthy and it made Milo's shoulders droop.

"Sued three times," he said. "Considering how many lawyers are lurking around that's just about saintly. Too bad."

He swiveled away from the screen. "Time to move on. Agreed?"

I nodded.

"Now tell me—scratch that, therapeutically *suggest* to me where exactly we relocate."

As I thought about that, he checked his email and deleted anything administrative.

I said, "The killer knew the property would be accessible. How about a closer look at the party hosts?"

"Rental agency finally coughed up the names," he said. "Coupla rich kids, seniors at Beverly Hills High. Meaning the partyers were probably kids, too. You see a teenager setting something like this up?"

"There was a sixteen-year-old in Florida, murdered his parents before throwing a house party."

He pulled up the Beverly Hills High School website. "The academic day ends just before four. Let's try to catch them as they wheel their little roadsters off campus. Anything else, meanwhile?"

"You get the cause of death for Gurnsey and the woman?"

"Crypt's been giving me radio silence, not even a text from Basia, which isn't like her. I'd take the time to drive over but with the big decomp case I'm not gonna be a welcome presence. Not to mention my nasal passages being ruined for a month."

"Why's the decomp high-priority?"

"That's what *I'm* trying to figure out, it's not even a murder," he said. "Three floaters bob up in Wilmington Harbor a week after a fancy fishing boat goes down five miles out. Big Coast Guard search, nothing until what's left of two anglers and a hired captain make an appearance. Lots of shark and crab damage but from what I've heard so far, not even a hint of human transgression. What the hell, I'll try Basia again."

He punched a preset on his cell. Sat up straighter when Dr. Basia Lopatinski, formerly of Warsaw, Poland, said, "I was just about to call you."

Basia had offered crucial info on his last case, a murder at a wedding, and was his new favorite at the crypt. Petite, blond, graced with a mile-wide smile and natural ebullience, she sounded weary.

Milo said, "Tell me you're assigned to the limo case and my faith will be restored. Tell me you've already got scientific factoids and I might even go to midnight Mass."

She laughed. "Another lapsed Catholic? You are so kind. I have been assigned one of your victims, the woman. It's rather frantic here so we're splitting up the splitting up."

"What's the big deal with the boat, Basia?"

A beat. "Keep this to yourself, okay? The owner of the charter is a friend of the governor and there could be serious liability issues."

"Sealed lips, kid. How much longer before things settle down?"

"I hope a few days—we're talking extreme putrescence, Milo. Shreds and globs. We know who these people are but actual scientific identification is necessary for insurance purposes and it's a nightmare. We've stopped answering the phone because attorneys are calling so frequently. On top of that, even with a gas mask the smell is unbelievable. Okay, on to more pleasant things: I completed the autopsy on your female victim but put that aside for now, something very interesting came up before I began cutting. The copious blood ranging from her knees to the floor of the car isn't human. It's canine. And turns out the same applies to all four victims."

"Dog blood?"

"Theoretically, at this point, it could be any type of canid—coyote, wolf, hybrid of either. But domestic dog would obviously be the most probable."

"Jesus," he said. "Any human blood mixed in with it?"

"That I'm not able to answer yet. I requested that the crime lab keep the limousine in their auto bay and exhaustively sample seats and carpeting. We'll be doing the same for clothing. That's a lot of analysis, a definitive answer will take days."

"How'd you discover it?"

"No precipitin had been done at the scene, which isn't breach of procedure, with a multiple the obvious assumption is going to be human blood, why wouldn't it be? But the pattern was off. Too much contrast between the relatively sparse amounts of low-caliber gunshot blood near Mr. Alvarez's and Mr. Roget's wounds and the volume below. Making it even odder, the woman had no obvious wounds at all but was still drenched in blood at the lower extremities and the same went for Mr. Gurnsey. I ran an ABO to see if we had admixtures among the victims and it came back no ABO, just DEA—that's a canine grouping. I was shocked so I repeated and got the same result. Followed up with a precipitin, again not human. I then took a look under the microscope and sure enough, there were a few scattered nucleated erythrocytes. That can happen in canids but not humans, our red blood cells never have nuclei. I went to my colleagues and they tested their victims. Same results. Everyone's astonished."

"Someone murdered four people then threw pooch blood on them."

"I wouldn't describe it as a lusty throw, Milo. That would have created more spatter. This appears to be more of a careful pouring. By the amount of blood, perhaps from a sizable receptacle."

"Bucket of blood."

"The phrase did come to mind," she said. "As to what it means, perhaps you've got something psychopathological that Alex could help you with."

"Alex is right here."

Basia said, "Oh. Hello. Anything come to mind?"

I said, "First for me, too, Basia."

"This *is* a strange one, guys. Including variety in cause of death. The driver and Mr. Alvarez were shot by the same .22 but turns out Mr. Gurnsey was stabbed three times in the upper torso with a thin, double-edged bladed instrument. It wasn't spotted until we disrobed him because there were no defects in his clothing. So he was cut either while wearing something else or while naked. Either way, he was re-dressed postmortem."

I said, "Costumed."

"Hmm . . . interesting thought, yes, there is a theatrical quality to it, the ostentatious car, the sexual posing."

Milo said, "What killed the woman?"

"That remains undetermined though I'm leaning toward asphyxiation. I'll be doing more tissue dissection and microscope work but so far all I've found are a few ocular hemorrhages. That's suggestive but not definitive, a small quantity of burst blood vessels can be caused by all sorts of things, including lifestyle issues. And this body gives up plenty of evidence of that: congested lungs, boggy hypertrophied heart. Both are present with asphyxia but also in chronic drug use and alcoholism. She certainly presents as a likely longtime abuser: that outdoor skin you see on the homeless, liver almost completely cirrhotic, gallbladder dangerously enlarged, both kidneys are disasters. There are also changes that could be compounded by age and/or substance abuse: vascular deterioration of the brain, her thyroid gland isn't much to speak of, and her esophagus displays several highly erosive splotches, probably cancerous."

Milo said, "Not a paragon of health."

"An orthodox conclusion would be she didn't have long to live," said Basia. "But who knows? I've seen people with brains like Swiss cheese and hearts enlarged to the size of a bull's who survive far beyond expectation."

I said, "Would her brain damage affect her consciousness and make her easy prey?"

"Her being intoxicated obviously would and I suppose if she had chronic brain damage that wouldn't help. If nothing shows up on the tox, Dr. Krishnamurti agrees asphyxia will be the ruling by process of elimination. One more thing: We haven't been able to identify her because her fingerprint ridges are abraded and shallow. You see that with various skin diseases but some people just don't have good ridges, especially as they age. On top of that several of her fingertips are scarred—old wounds, most likely burns. The computerized system failed so I inked her by hand and that produced a bit more definition. But not enough for AFIS. I'll try moisturizing and if that doesn't bring up the ridges, we can slice off the skin, plump it up with saline, make a glove, and see if that works."

"Thanks for everything, Basia. Any idea how long the bodies sat in the car?"

"I was told no blowflies were spotted outside because the car was a closed environment. Still, if the car had been sitting in sunlight for a prolonged period, even with temperate spring weather, I'd expect more tissue deterioration. So probably no sooner than Saturday night."

Milo said, "Makes sense, it's a conspicuous vehicle, why risk being seen during the day? What about time of death?"

"That's a bit trickier," she said. "Rigor had come and gone and I didn't find any evidence of freezing or refrigeration. But again, the lack of decomp suggests the victims were killed and stored in a well-insulated space before being transferred to the limousine. A naturally cool environment—a cellar, say—or strong air-conditioning could've been enough. Also, moving bodies can disrupt rigor. The most I can tell you is twelve to thirty-six hours prior to discovery. But if we're assuming the bodies sat there for around twelve hours and we factor in time to clean them up, dress them, put them in the car, we need to tack on additional time. The big problem is drive-time. We have no idea where they came from."

"No freezing. So not long-term storage."

"Most probably not."

I said, "Basia, could we go back to the causes of death for a sec? Like you said, four victims and three separate methods is unusual for a mass murder. So maybe we should be thinking about this as individual killings grouped together, methods tailored to each victim."

"Tailored how?"

"Smothering someone's harder than shooting them. The woman's compromised health might've made her more suitable than the men."

"Hmm. It's a thought, Alex. She was carrying plenty of weight—one hundred eighty-one pounds on five foot four. But the muscles of all four limbs were extremely atrophied, meaning a good deal of her bulk was nonfunctional fat. So, yes, she could have been overpowered fairly easily. What about knife rather than gun for the fittest victim, Gurnsey?"

I said, "A more personal death. The way he was posed fits that."

"I'll say. Personal *and* demeaning. But the woman was demeaned as well."

I said, "She could've been a player in his scene."

"Hmm . . . you could be right. They certainly don't present as a likely couple."

Milo said, "Any defensive wounds on Gurnsey?"

"As I said, I'm not doing him but I don't believe there were."

"A sneaky knife attack also fits up close and personal, Basia. One thing we've learned about Gurnsey is he lived for sex. Guy like that, gets in a compromising position, lowers his guard, the killer slips in the blade."

"Cuddle turns to cutting," said Basia. "Okay, gentlemen, time to sift through more marine sludge but I promise not to forget you. When I finally get home tonight, I will drink Tokaji and search the literature for cases where animal blood was used as a supplement to a human homicide. There's a ritualistic feel to it, no?"

Milo said, "Satanic ghouls prowling the Westside? God forbid, Basia."

"My, you *are* getting religious."

"Parochial school memories never die."

"How true," she said. "Sometimes I still dream of nuns. And I won't tell you the content of those dreams. Good luck, gentlemen."

Milo said, "One more thing, Basia. Can we get quick DNA on the dog blood, at least find out the breed? I get hold of a suspect, he's got a black Lab, whatever, it's another brick in the wall."

"We're not talking a live animal, Milo. The amount of blood, survival would be out of the question. But sure, once I have multiple samples I'll send them out. Now back to my gas mask."

Milo said, "Too bad the governor wants to be president."

"Doesn't everybody?"

"Not the people I want to hang out with."

She laughed. "Yes, that would be a grim soiree."

He put the phone down and faced me. "Like you always say, kiddie psychopaths practice on animals. Maybe this one never stopped."

I said, "This feels different from a practice run. All performance, no rehearsal."

He shook his head and rubbed his eyes. "Doing that to a pooch. Why does that make me even madder?"

CHAPTER 11

Beverly Hills High is a twenties-era French Normandy concoction sprawling across twenty prime acres that had once served as a racetrack. By three twenty Milo and I were parked near the main motor exit watching for either Shirin Amadpour's one-year-old white Porsche Boxster or Todd Leventhal's two-year-old black Dodge Challenger to emerge.

The Dodge was the first to show, snorting and bucking as it waited behind a silver BMW halted by a crossing guard.

Young male at the wheel, young female next to him. We followed as the car made its way north to Wilshire, turned left on Beverly Drive, and continued into the core of the Beverly Hills business district. Keeping two car lengths behind and being treated to a symphony of tailgating, jerky unsignaled lane changes, and braking so sudden it juddered the Challenger's frame.

Milo said, "Stupid kid lives on the 600 block of Alpine but he's driving for fun. Hopefully he won't be pulled over by BHPD before he gets there."

His hopes were fulfilled as the Challenger was allowed to continue its clueless journey past Santa Monica Boulevard and east on Carmelita Avenue.

I said, "Warren Zevon got the name for his song from this street."

"Huh." He liked Zevon's music but wasn't in the mood to fake interest.

The black car hooked a quick left at Alpine Drive and continued half a block before careening over the curb and landing in a driveway of a homely, square house faced with gray shingles. In Beverly Hills, seven million bucks.

The driver, smallish, ferret-faced, and sporting a blond fade hairdo, got out swinging a black backpack. Slamming his door he stood next to the car and thumbed his phone. The girl unfolded herself from the passenger side. Pretty and slim, taller than her companion, clutching an identical backpack. Both of them had on charcoal-colored T-shirts and jeans and matching polychrome sneakers. A sheet of black hair tickled an area two inches below the girl's waist.

Out came her phone. Down went her eyes. Two sets of adolescent fingers worked manically.

Milo said, "Modern romance," and bounded out of the Impala.

Neither kid noticed our approach. That level of space-out, as vulnerable as Benny Alvarez.

Did the future portend a planet teeming with easy victims?

Finally, when we were a foot away, the girl looked up. Huge brown eyes sparked with alarm.

Milo's smiling "Hi, guys" made matters worse. Her mouth dropped open and she grabbed the boy's arm. He kept scrolling. "Whuh?"

"Todd—look."

Milo said, "Todd Leventhal? Shirin Amadpour? Glad we caught you. Lieutenant Sturgis, Homicide."

The girl gasped and squeezed Leventhal's skinny biceps.

He kept texting.

"*Taw*-odd!"

Harder squeeze. Leventhal's gray eyes rose slowly, favoring us with a neutral stare. The cropped part of his hair was etched with rising thunderbolts. The top of the do was three inches of off-white straw. "Yeah, you called. What happened afterward at the party. No idea."

"I'll give you an idea," said Milo. "Someone was killed at the house you rented."

"Don't know about it."

"Yes, we don't," said Shirin Amadpour. "That sounds terrible but we just throw parties."

Milo said, "It's a regular thing for you guys?"

Leventhal shrugged.

Amadpour said, "Basically."

"How often?"

"Three, four times a year."

"Kind of a hobby?"

The question perplexed Amadpour. "I guess."

Leventhal's eyes slitted. "No way. We're in it for the money."

Milo said, "Capitalism at work."

Amadpour said, "No, socialism—Instagram, Snapchat, Twitter."

"What I'm telling you is we make *money,*" said Leventhal. "It's business, okay? Forty bucks guys, twenty girls." A glance at Amadpour. The smile a carnivore gets picking out a steak.

I said, "Girls pay less."

"Ye-ah." The unspoken word: *stuuupid.* "'Cause girls are worth more. They're like a . . . guys come because a girls."

Amadpour took that as praise and beamed.

Milo said, "The feminine mystique."

"Huh?"

"So how many people showed up last Friday?"

Another shrug from Leventhal.

Amadpour said, "We didn't count."

"How about an estimate?"

Leventhal said, "Three hundred. Give or leave."

Amadpour said, "Yeah."

Milo said, "How much do you guys pay to rent the house?"

Leventhal said, "Why? You want to do competition?" Giggling at the thought.

"Just trying to get an overall picture, Todd."

"We don't know jack about what happened after."

"I know but just for the report."

"The report," said Leventhal. He smirked. "They wanted seven I got 'em down to five."

"Thousand or hundred?"

Both kids cracked up. Leventhal said, "You get a place for hundreds, let me know."

Milo said, "See what you mean about bank."

Amadpour said, "But we really basically do it for fun. And basically for practice."

"Practice for what?"

"The future. I'm going to be an event planner and Todd's going into finance."

Leventhal shot her a peeved look. "You don't know for sure what I'm doing because I don't know for sure, I might be a sports agent." His eyes dropped to his phone. An index finger tapped the side lovingly before touching the screen and lighting it up.

Milo said, "How about holding off for a sec."

"Why?"

"We're having a conversation."

"That what this is?"

"*Taw*-odd! Be nice to them!"

Leventhal said, "What? They're not being nice to us. They think we know something about what happened."

Amadpour said, "No, they don't." To Milo: "You don't think that, right? All we did was throw a party."

Leventhal huffed.

I said, "Any problems at the party?"

Shirin Amadpour cocked a hip. Black hair swooshed. "Nope, it was totally perfect."

Leventhal said, "We don't have problems. We get the right people."

"As staff or guests?"

"Both."

Milo said, "How do you build your invitation list?"

"List?" The boy snickered. "Yeah, we make a stone list. Like the Babylonians with their hydroglyphics."

Amadpour said, "We use the Sosh-Net. Like two days before."

Leventhal said, "Everyone who comes, we want. We don't, we use football players from the U. to tell them bye-bye."

"We're careful," said Amadpour. Pouting. "We try really hard."

Leventhal shot her a peeved look. "We don't try, we succeed. The money keeps out you-know-who."

Milo said, "Who?"

"Ha."

I said, "Forty for guys, twenty for girls."

"We might go forty-five next time. Even fifty."

Amadpour said, "But probably keep the girls at twenty."

Leventhal said, "Maybe twenty-five."

I said, "So nothing unusual happened Friday?"

"Nah, Friday was easy-peasy," said Leventhal. "Agency said no cars, there's too much dirt on the property, which was cool, made it easier, the football players could filter at the street."

"Anyone argue with them?"

"Nope."

Amadpour said, "Where did the . . . you know happen?"

"Behind the house," said Milo. "In a car."

"Proves it," said Leventhal, doing a little jig. "We didn't *have* cars so we're *not* responsible for what happened later."

I said, "When was the party officially over?"

"Officially and unofficially is the same, dude. Two. Then me and her looked around and we were outta there by two thirty."

"What were you looking for?"

"Anything," said Leventhal. "There was nothing."

Amadpour frowned. "It *was* kind of creepy. Being there, dark, the house was like a . . . it's big."

"The football dudes were also there," said Leventhal.

"But then we were there by ourselves, Todd."

"Whatever. There was nothing freaky." His hand rose and grazed thunderbolts.

Amadpour said, "I thought it was creepy. That house, big and ugly and cold-like."

"Whatever." Leventhal hefted his backpack and looked at Milo. "We've got no responsibility except overall safety and security at an event we initiate and manage competently."

Milo said, "That sounds pretty legalistic, Todd."

Orthodontic grin. "My dad's a lawyer and so is hers and they told us. Even though they still give us shit."

"About what?"

"Making our own bank." He nudged Amadpour. "They're scared we'll make so much we won't need their asses."

She said, "I'll always need my parents."

He said, "You never know. We could be kings of the world."

"I'd be a queen."

"It's a metaphor." Another grin. "From a movie."

"Which one?"

"Forget."

Milo said, "So what'd you guys do after you left?"

"We ate," said Leventhal.

"Denny's," said Amadpour. "In Westwood."

"Waffles and links," said Leventhal.

"Tuna salad," said Amadpour.

"Okay?" said Leventhal. "Can we go live our life?" His hand brushed Amadpour's cheek. She colored at the jawline. Lifting his backpack, he began walking toward the gray house.

Milo said, "None of this seems to bother you, Todd."

The boy stopped. Turned. "Why should it bother me?"

"The fact that a murder happened where you'd just thrown a party?"

Todd Leventhal looked as if he'd been spoken to in Albanian. "I don't know who it *happened* to."

Milo loped toward him and handed him a card. Leventhal held it to his skinny flank.

Amadpour took the time to read her card. Her lips moved. *Homicide.* She said, "I'm so sorry for whoever it was."

The two of them entered the house.

Milo said, "The Todd-ster's a pretty cold dude, no?"

"Not the most charming lad."

"Didn't pick up any tells. You?"

"Nope."

"Can't think of any motive he'd have other than he's cold."

I said, "Despite his business skills, he probably isn't smart enough to coordinate the level of the production we're looking at. And why would he call attention to himself?"

"Production. That's really stuck with you."

"Hard to think of it as anything else."

"This one, hard to think of anything, period."

We drove back to the station. He said, "Story breaks tomorrow, meanwhile it's time for you-know-what."

"I don't know what."

"No progress? Take a meeting. I called it for nine a.m. tomorrow, me and the kids. Any chance you can make it?"

I checked my phone. "I was going to do something more amusing but sure."

"What?"

"Stick hot pokers in my eyes."

He laughed for a long time. Good to hear.

CHAPTER

12

Wednesday morning, news of the killings broke. The story was pushed to the rear by political viciousness, not much by way of detail, not strictly accurate. ("A multiple shooting in Beverly Hills during the early-morning hours . . .")

The sketchiness meant the department had continued to suppress details but nowadays details don't matter, it's all about emotional contagion. I knew the internet would be ping-ponging the story, leading to freelance guesswork and tips ranging from psychotic to encouraging. Milo's name was listed as primary investigator but his office number wasn't. Someone calling with information would have to make an effort.

At ten to nine I arrived at the same room where Andrea Bauer's interview had taken place. Reed, Binchy, and Bogomil walked in together four minutes later. All three in casual plainclothes, what could be taken as an internet start-up business group.

Milo had been in the room long enough to fill a whiteboard with the death shots of four victims, the forensic details available, and the time line Basia had given.

At the bottom, a snapshot of Lassie that raised the detectives' eyebrows as they settled.

Four chairs were arranged in a semicircle facing the board. On the table, coffee pitcher, cups, and a big box of pastries from a West Hollywood French bakery. The boss picking up patisserie for the troops.

Milo snatched a cruller, demolished half, brushed crumbs from his shirt, and pointed to the board. "Nourish yourselves, scan this, then group therapy begins."

Binchy took a chocolate croissant, Bogomil broke a bear claw in half, Reed sat down.

"Not healthy enough for you, Moses?"

"I'm watching my sugar intake."

"I watch mine, too. As it rises." Finishing the rest of the cruller. "Okay. Like I told you all yesterday, no info of value from the kids who threw the party. They don't keep written records and Alex doesn't see them as able to pull off a complex multi. I agree. I'm assuming still nothing from the canvass."

Reed said, "We covered every house from Sunset to Mulholland. Hard to find anyone home but those that were didn't see the limo enter or anything else out of the ordinary."

"Coroner's TOD estimate fits with the car being brought there in the wee hours, when it was still dark. So they could be telling the truth."

Reed nodded. "We did get a few complaints but not just for that house, for parties in general. Parking, noise, trash."

Bogomil said, "Like we're supposed to drop a homicide investigation and take care of rich cranks."

Binchy said, "It does mean lots of people knew it was a venue. Maybe also that it was left unattended after parties."

Milo said, "Good point, Sean." He smiled. "And depressing because it expands the suspect pool. I double-checked with Bright Dawn and they only cleaned the place one other time this year, back in January. A benefit—breast cancer, different crowd, older folk. I asked for a guest list, they said whoever throws the event keeps the records. The group's called Daylighters, small, limited to big donors. I've got a call in to their office. Alicia, did you have time to look for other agencies?"

Bogomil said, "So far I've found four. None uses that property."

Reed said, "What about another angle, L.T.? Nasty divorce can breed all sorts of ugly."

I said, "I found out which judge is handling the case and left a message."

Silence from the three of them. The kind of sludgy inertia that sets in when there's nowhere else to go.

Milo said, "Next: phone accounts. Alvarez didn't have one and if the woman is homeless, probably the same for her. I've subpoenaed Roget and Gurnsey's cells and Roget's landline. At the very least we'll know who they talked to last. With the canvass over, let's take a look at where Roget posted his ads. Now the forensics, such as they are."

He summed up, including Basia's asphyxiation theory for the woman and her lack of fingerprints. The latter brought frowns to three faces.

Bogomil mouthed, *Wonderful.*

Milo said, "Basia's gonna try to scare up something." He turned to me. "How about some psychological insight?"

I said, "This is more guesswork than insight. If we view the slaughter as a true multiple, it's likely all four victims meant something to the killer. But these four are as varied as they come. So far the only commonality is the lack of local family ties but, again, why such a mixed group? Another way to look at it is one victim was the primary target and the others were added later as supporting players. To my mind, the most likely primary is Rick Gurnsey."

I described Gurnsey's sexual behavior.

Alicia frowned. "Bad boy who tried to sneak in the back door? Yeah, that could annoy someone."

"If he got aggressive, he was more than an annoyance," I said. "At the very least his behavior was high-risk. The murderer had a firearm but chose to stab him, and the lack of defense wounds says Gurnsey was caught off guard."

"Up close and personal," said Reed. "Cut during an intimate situation."

"That's how it feels to me, Moe."

"An angry woman?" said Bogomil. "Then why the others?"

"Don't know," I said. "We could also be talking about an angry husband slash boyfriend. Or most likely, two people working in concert because this slaughter involved a lot of subduing and transferring."

"Vengeful couple," said Reed.

"Supporting players," said Binchy. "Like casting a movie."

I said, "Right from the beginning the crime scene's felt theatrical to me. Given Gurnsey's behavior, the way he was posed, his having a wider social net than the others, I'd concentrate on him. Past relationships, people he worked with."

Bogomil said, "The woman was just as posed as Gurnsey. And choking her out was pretty up close and personal."

I said, "It's possible both of them were primary targets. On the other hand, her age, her looks, her possible homelessness, could be thought of as factors chosen to humiliate Gurnsey."

"You jumped me with your alleged manhood so I'm showing it to the world, soft and small? I guess that makes sense." She smiled. "As the girl in the room, I can say that."

Milo said, "Hopefully we can I.D. her. We find out she's an heiress with a big life insurance policy, we'll shift our perspective."

Alicia played with the pale ends of her hair. "The men were wearing normal clothes but to my eye, she was in what looked like vintage. Like someone went into the costume room and played dress-up. So yeah, there is that production feel to it."

Binchy said, "A chauffeur's uniform could also be seen as a costume. Choosing a chauffeur—and a car like that—is also pretty theatrical."

Milo said, "This is good. Keep thinking and don't be afraid to guess. Anything else?"

Silence.

"Okay, good point about the clothes, Alicia. I'll have the lab check for labels. Onward."

He tapped the photo of Lassie, told them about the dog blood.

They sat there.

Finally, Bogomil said, "Bastard."

Meeting over, the young D's dispersed, everyone begging off Milo's offer to take the pastries with them.

He said, "Maybe it was the dog, ruined their appetites." He brought the box back to his office, placed it in the scant space to the left of his computer, and shot it a longing glance. Phoning the crime lab at Cal State L.A., he spoke to the director, Noreen Sharp, about the clothing.

She said, "We talking fiber analysis?"

"A list of the labels will do just fine, Noreen."

"Easy enough. This is some complication you got yourself, Milo. We had to use the truck bay for the limo, pulled up a fair amount of prints. The crypt hasn't sent over your victims' bio-data yet so I can't tell you if they mean anything."

"I'll get that done for you. What do you think about the dog blood?"

"I think," said Sharp, "that it's bizarre and monstrous and totally over-the-top. We've dealt with canine transfers over the years, mostly hairs we could trace to bad guys. Dumping blood? Who'd *do* that? We're still scraping away the carpet gook, it's like cleaning grease from a barbecue. There's a lot of surface area so we used a new computer program from Israel to tell us how many samples we need to cover enough ground. Multiple drench-spots makes it tough, the program's not set up for that, so it probably overestimated when it came up with a hundred seventy-eight and mapped where they should come from. We'll go with that so obviously it's going to take time."

"Appreciate it, Noreen."

"It's what we do. Does Dr. Delaware have anything to say about this? I mean, let's face it, it smells psycho."

"He thinks it smells theatrical."

"Hmm," she said. "Maybe they're not that different. Okay, let me get you those labels."

Milo's next call was to Basia's office at the crypt. He got her assistant, requested the bio-data be sent to Sharp. Was putting his phone down when a text pinged. He read and shook his head.

"Labels on all the clothing were removed—tech could see the stitch-marks."

I said, "Her clothing could've been altered or she got it from a donation bin with the labels removed."

His computer dinged a text. "Gurnsey's phone records. Here we *go.*"

Six months of calls. "This is gonna take time."

His arm dipped into the pastry box. Random selection produced a chocolate cinnamon roll.

He said, "Go home, enjoy the benefits of hearth and home. I'll content myself with calories."

CHAPTER 13

Custody evaluations pay most of my bills but I prefer trauma and injury suits because kids who've been injured deserve compensation and no one gets hateful.

Thursday morning, I was finishing the final report on a case I'd worked a couple of weeks ago. A three-year-old had swallowed bug bait left out by the manager of the apartment where he lived with his mother. Full recovery after a stomach pump, now the litigation. My job was evaluating the child for emotional repercussions.

I'd told the attorney the boy seemed fine, that I wouldn't be offering any radical predictions.

He said, "No prob, I just need the basics with your stamp of approval."

I rechecked what I'd written, auto-signed and emailed, went into the kitchen for coffee. When I got back my cell was bouncing on the desktop.

Milo said, "Got through Gurnsey's calls, separated business from personal. I'm having the troops backward-directory each number to see who actually answers. The media coverage brought in eighty-eight tips so far and one might even be interesting. A woman phoned an hour ago, said she'd been at a party at the same house. Which is interesting because the address hasn't been released. I asked when, she said January, a benefit, she preferred to talk about it in person. Which is different, no? Most people'll do anything to avoid a face-to-face. She lives in Little Holmby, you could walk there. Can you make it in an hour?"

"Sure."

"Her name's Candace Kierstead. Here's the address."

I was in running clothes but hadn't run. Showering, shaving, and shifting to work duds, I left the house, fast-walked down the Glen, sharp-eyed, facing traffic, crossed Sunset at the light, and continued south and west to Conrock Avenue.

Little Holmby is a tranquil pocket of traditional architecture sandwiched between the imperial estates of Holmby Hills and the town-sized campus of the U. Conrock was a predictably pretty street lined with immaculate houses just large enough to forestall teardown fever.

Milo's Impala was parked on the east side of the street, midway up the block. When he saw me, he got out.

"You actually walked?"

"I thought it was an executive order."

"More like I enabled your addiction to fitness—say nothing. Body-shaming folk such as myself is malignant." He slapped my back. "Thanks for coming on short notice. We're going to that one."

He pointed to a vanilla-covered Mediterranean fronted by a precise emerald lawn. No car in the driveway. Maybe stashed behind a black-iron gate.

His knock was moderate—a friend dropping in. The woman who opened the door was thirty-five to forty, medium height and slender, with true-blue eyes and long brown hair that crowned a pleasant, unremarkable face. Oversized tortoiseshell eyeglasses rested atop a small, thin nose. No makeup or jewelry. White top, white jeggings and flats.

"Ms. Kierstead? Lieutenant Sturgis. This is Alex Delaware."

A tentative, whispery voice said, "Candace. Please come in."

She led us through a black-granite foyer into a living room furnished with art deco pieces that looked real. Pointing to a pair of silver velvet club chairs, she kicked off her shoes and folded onto a facing gray sofa. Bare walls. Behind the couch, a long narrow table held a framed photo of Candace Kierstead and a silver-haired man significantly her senior. Somewhere with a cathedral in the background.

Between the couch and the chairs a round bronze and mirror-top table was set up with a white porcelain coffee set and a plate of graham crackers.

Milo said, "Thanks for seeing us, Ms. Kierstead."

"I felt I had to call. Do you want to ask questions or should I just tell you what I know?"

"Whatever makes you more comfortable."

"This is the first time I've ever called the police, I'm not sure anything makes me comfortable. Except for once, a few years ago, when my husband thought he heard a prowler. Turned out to be an opossum on the roof with little babies. Can you believe that? We love animals, of course we let them be."

I said, "This close to the mountains we do get critters."

"I've seen coyotes," she said. "In the morning when I run. The look in their eyes . . . rather menacing."

Placing her palms together, she dropped them to her lap. "I'll try to make this brief. Last night, I heard from a friend of mine about that hideous house on Benedict. She lives nearby, said there'd been police and reporters milling around Sunday morning and then a detective came to her house but wouldn't tell her much."

Milo said, "Unfortunately, we can't give out details at the beginning stages."

"She understood that, but still, it's good to know what's happening in your neighborhood, right? Anyway, she called me because she knew I'd once been there. Last January, a benefit for Daylighters, it's a cancer advocacy group. I didn't think much of it. Then I read the paper and it mentioned a mass shooting on Benedict Canyon and I said wow. Then

I remembered something and figured I should tell you. But it's probably not relevant."

"Thanks for taking the time, ma'am."

"Would you like some coffee? A biscuit?"

"Coffee would be great, thanks."

"Black, cream, sugar, sweetener—stevia's what I've got."

"Black's fine."

"Certainly." She poured and handed us cups. Grim but with steady hands. Nothing for herself. As we sipped, she took hold of her hair, drew it forward over her right shoulder and onto her chest. A dangling hand twisted the ends.

"So," said Milo, "what happened when you were at the house?"

"Before we get into anything, I'd like to know something. If what I tell you does turn out to be relevant—and I don't think it will—will I have to go to court or anything?"

Milo put down his cup and smiled. "We're a long way from that, Ms. Kierstead."

"You're saying you don't know who the—what do you call them—the perp is."

"We're just starting out, so anything you can tell us will be highly appreciated."

"But still," she said. "Going to court? I wouldn't like that."

"It's unlikely that would be necessary. But honestly, we do need to hear what you have to say before that's clear."

"Okay. Makes sense . . . another thing. Sig—my husband—doesn't know I'm doing this, so I'd appreciate if he doesn't find out. At least for now."

"No problem."

She tapped her teeth. "All right, here goes. Daylighters is a small group. We require a minimum donation but we're not snobby. I'm actually one of the youngest members. Mostly it's Sig's peers. His first wife passed from breast cancer."

She licked her lips. "I guess I'm a bit nervous."

"Take your time," said Milo.

"Okay . . . what I'm trying to get across is we're a well-behaved group, not some crazy party animals. Maybe what happened wouldn't stand out in another setting but . . . back when I danced with the San Francisco Ballet, I saw all kinds of things . . . sorry, back to January. We call it The Newer Than New Year's Fling. Two hundred or so good people, a grand buffet, champagne, full orchestra, dancing. To be honest, too classy for that house. It's rather vulgar, isn't it? And gloomy, all that gray stone."

I said, "It is different."

"Exactly. So. Everything was rolling along according to plan. I was on the steering committee, had to stay on top of things. So I circulated, checking. I can't tell you how many times but several and on one of them it happened—I think I will have some coffee."

She poured, sweetened, sipped, and placed the cup back in its saucer. "The property, we brought in lighting but not enough so it was dark in some of the distant spots. Mostly behind a gazebo, along the rear of the property. I wanted to make sure no one would go back there, trip and fall. Some of our people are on the elderly side."

A well-shaped silver fingernail tapped the cup. She reached for a graham cracker, snapped it in two, studied both halves, and placed them next to the cup. "I heard it before I saw it. Heavy breathing, my first thought was, *Uh-oh, someone did fall.* So I hurried over."

Deep inhalation. "I'm no prude but I was thrown pretty hard." Eyelids lowered and rose. She gnawed her bottom lip. "Heavy breathing? You know what I'm getting at."

Milo said, "Two people having sex?"

"Against the rear hedge. Standing *up*. The woman's back was to me, her dress was up to her waist, and the man was . . . I'm sure I don't need to draw you a picture."

"No, ma'am."

Candace Kierstead said, "I stopped in my tracks but he turned and saw me. And that's when I got scared because he looked really angry. As if I was the intruder."

Deep sigh. "I'd helped compile the invite list and this guy was *not* on it."

"What about the woman?"

"I never saw her face but from the back she looked too . . . I'll be perfectly frank, she looked too young. Young legs, at least. That's not the Daylighters' crowd. I'm a good ten years younger than every other woman in the group. These were definitely crashers. And *he's* getting irate? I thought, *How dare you!* So I managed to collect my courage and came right out and said, 'You need to stop this now and leave.' Something to that effect. You'd think he'd be embarrassed and get moving. Just the opposite. He just gritted his teeth and kept going. Faster! So I ran off to get Sig but by the time I located him and got him back there, they *were* gone. And when I asked the security people, they had no clue. Sig said I shouldn't make a fuss, it would poop the party. But now that something's happened at the same place, I just thought I should tell you."

Milo said, "You thought right. What did the man look like?"

"Thirties, dark hair." Quick intake of breath. "To be frank, somewhat good looking. In a certain way."

"What way?"

"Not substantive good looks. The kind of guy you see all over L.A., spends too much time in front of the mirror."

Milo took out his phone, scrolled to Richard Gurnsey's DMV photo, and showed it to Candace Kierstead.

Her hand flew to her mouth. "Oh, my God, that's him! He's a mass murderer? I got that close to a serial killer?"

A tremor began at her shoulders and coursed down her torso.

Milo said, "You were never in danger, Candace."

"But—"

"He's not a murderer."

"What then?"

"He's a victim."

"Oh," she said. "So telling you this *is* important. Wow." She played with her hair. "Who is he?"

"As I said, can't get into details."

"Oh, of course, sorry—so he actually came back there? Was it also a benefit? Was exploiting a good cause his *thing*?"

Milo said, "May I show you some other faces to see if you recognize them?" and scrolled to Benny Alvarez's social service I.D. photo.

"No," she said. "Never seen him."

Same response to Solomon Roget and the unidentified woman. "Who are all these people?"

Milo smiled. "I wish I could be more specific—"

"Sorry, sorry . . . I have to say, Lieutenant, they're a diverse group, aren't they? If they're also victims, it's as if someone's trying to kill a variety of people. To murder the world."

She got up to use "the little girls' room," returned moments later.

Milo said, "Can you tell us anything more about the woman having sex?"

"I really can't, Lieutenant. Never saw her face."

"Height?"

"Hmm. Average? Not super short or tall."

"Build?"

"She had a good figure, like I said, nice legs."

"Hair?"

"Hmm. Probably brunette but I can't swear to that because the lighting was extremely weak. There was just enough to see what he—what they were doing." She tapped her cheek. "I don't want to go out on a limb but I think her dress was dark. At least it wasn't shiny bright—not lamé or satin or anything along those lines. As I said, most of it was bunched up—you know, now that I think about it I didn't see any underwear on the ground. So obviously she came prepared for . . .

whatever—she did have a rear, that was certainly in full view. Not that hipless boy thing they like on models nowadays, how does anyone live up to that?"

Surveying her own svelte body.

Nothing Milo and I could say that wouldn't come out wrong.

We thanked her and stood.

She said, "Take the biscuits with you. That way Sig won't be tempted, he's a big snacker and he needs to watch."

Milo cruised a couple of blocks before pulling over and parking on a street indistinguishable from Conrock. "Helpful citizen, God bless her."

He found the shot of Gurnsey he'd shown Candace Kierstead and studied it. "Richard, Richard, what sins did you pay for? Maybe she's right about his returning to the same place, some kind of memory thrill. Though how would he know about a teen party?"

I said, "If the first time was a big thrill, he could've googled the address from time to time."

"Five months between parties," he said. "Patient guy."

"Sexual fantasy's a great motivator and sounds like he was into risk-taking. He'd stand out in a bunch of teenagers but age difference didn't stop him at the Daylighters' bash."

He turned to me. "Ricky and a fellow risk-taker. But she's not dumped in the limo."

I said, "No reason for her to be there. Gurnsey was promiscuous, he probably moved on."

"Or he didn't, Alex, and wanted to relive the same scene with the same girl and she agreed? A boyfriend or a husband finds out, ounce of prevention and all that. Gurnsey gets stalked before the party, overpowered, stabbed, stashed somewhere, and finally dumped."

"Him and three others? Simple jealousy doesn't explain that. To my mind the production thing fits better."

"So what's the story line?"

"No idea."

We sat for a while. He started the car. Grumbled and shot forward.

A block later: "None of this is remotely sane."

I said, "At least we know focusing on Gurnsey is the right approach. Look at his calls on the days prior to both parties. The same number shows up twice you'll be legally allowed to smile."

He flashed a fierce grin and yanked so hard at his cell that it snagged in his pocket. Freeing it, he speed-dialed. "Moses, you still working Gurnsey's calls . . . forget all that for the time being, just concentrate on these dates . . . yup—a week prior to both. There's a number in common don't try it, just find out who owns it. I should be back in ten."

CHAPTER 14

Reed stood outside Milo's office door. Troubled look on his baby-face. Detective colic.

He said, "Got a number Gurnsey called three times in January and once last Wednesday but it's—"

"A non-traceable beater."

Colossal shoulders dropped. Maybe the Richter scale at Cal Tech could feel it.

Reed said, "Sorry, L.T. By-the-hour cheapie. A 410 area code, which is Baltimore but geography doesn't matter, these things are bought and sold in bulk."

I said, "Still, maybe someone's got a Baltimore link."

Neither detective was impressed by the suggestion.

Milo said, "Who answers?"

"You said not to call them."

"So I did. Okay, let's give it a go."

Reed handed him the phone list. "The one underlined in red."

Milo lurched into his office and jabbed at his desk phone. Slammed down the receiver.

"Out of service. Guess it's no surprise someone who slaughters four people is gonna be careful."

His eyes returned to the list. "The numbers you marked in yellow are what?"

Reed said, "I made a list of anything that comes back to a personal number, not business. Eleven numbers but one is the roommate, Briggs. I marked his *R.*"

He took a step into the office and pointed. "Briggs and Gurnsey don't talk that much, last time was four days prior to the murder, which matches what he told you about Gurnsey going away for the weekend. I haven't finished backward-booking all ten but the six I have done are females. I've listed them on the back."

Milo flipped and read. "Admirably organized, kid. Finish with the last four, meanwhile I'll start contacting."

"Um, one more thing, L.T. I know you wanted Alicia to keep checking the stores for those tear-off ads but I already asked her to do something else and couldn't reach her to call her off until just before you got here."

"What'd you ask?"

"Run background on the six females. Maybe she should finish the last four?"

Milo smiled. "I defer to your initiative and judgment, Moses. Send her up when she's got everything."

Bogomil showed up twenty minutes later with a sheaf of papers. Milo and I were both in the office; no room for anyone else larger than a toddler.

I stepped out. She said, "Thanks, Doc," and handed Milo her work product.

Milo said, "That was quick."

"Thank God for the backward book, DMV, and the social network. No one's invisible anymore." She flinched. "Except our suspect, but we'll get him, too." Smacking a palm with a fist. "We *will.*"

Milo tapped the papers. "Anything interesting?"

"Ten females between the ages of twenty-eight and forty-four, residences range from Santa Monica to Pasadena. Two with DUIs, one four years ago, one six years ago, no jail time for either. Three have jobs at the studio where Gurnsey worked: couple of office managers and a human resources clerk. The others are two lawyers, an accountant, three nurses, one doctor."

"Impressive memory, Alicia."

Bogomil blushed. "No big deal, it's a technique I do, drawing up categories and making a mental list."

"Who were the DUIs?"

"The HR person and the doctor."

"Please don't tell me the doctor's a neurosurgeon."

"Didn't check specialties, L.T. If you want I can do that."

"No, it's fine. Back to Roget's ads, please."

Bogomil saluted and left.

Milo said, "It's so nice when the kids turn out right."

He studied the list. "All over the city, days of driving. Think I could start with phone screens?"

I said, "If you turn the calls into psych tests."

"What am I looking for?"

"Anything that surprises you. Start with how they react to being called by a detective. Then tell them you're Homicide and see what that elicits. Step three is informing them it's about Gurnsey, after which you probe their relationship with him. Nothing too personal: how long they dated, most recent contact, you're trying to get a feel for what kind of guy he was. Someone who weeps too much or can't hide her callousness would interest me immediately. But there's no guarantee there'll be no acting going on so you'll want face-to-face."

"Got it," he said, rising and squeezing past me to the doorway. "When I'm finished, I'll let you know. Sooner if big question marks pop up."

Nice way to say *Adios, let me do my job.* Sometimes, he can be subtle.

CHAPTER 15

By Friday, ten a.m., I'd taken a four-mile run followed by a brief stroll for Blanche as a cool-down. Robin was busy in the studio, so breakfast for the other woman in my life, coffee for me as I checked my service.

Even professional screeners have trouble filtering noise and it was mostly that. Except for a call from Judge Martin Bevilacqua.

Marty was a smart, organized jurist who tried to be fair when cynicism didn't get in the way. The custody cases I'd worked in his court had turned out as well as could be expected.

I reached him in his chambers.

"Alex."

"Thanks for getting back to me."

"I was intrigued. Ansar's not your case but you're asking about it."

"Police work."

"That aspect of your life, huh? Can't let go of the excitement?"

"Keeps life interesting. I called because some murder victims were found at the Ansar property."

"Victims, plural?" he said.

"Benedict Canyon."

"Oh. Didn't put it together because the news said Beverly Hills and I've been working Ansar long enough to know it's L.A."

"Minor inaccuracy."

"Okay for the media but no such thing in my field. People hate each other they pounce on every misplaced letter. Murder, huh? Maybe it's not a surprise. These two *despise* each other." A beat. "You're not telling me one of them was a victim?"

"No," I said.

"Who, then?"

"It's a strange one, Marty."

"That aspect of your life, aren't they all? Strange, how?"

"This needs to stay between us. Four victims with no apparent relationship to each other."

"A gang thing?"

"Are the Ansars gang-connected?"

"Not to my knowledge," he said. "What their cousins do over in Afghanistan, who knows? What do you want to know about them?"

"The basics of the divorce."

"It's public record, you can get a transcript, Alex. But you generally don't bullshit me so I won't sentence you to reading thousands of pages of yakkety-yak. The gist is Matin and Ramineh Ansar have been here fifteen years, both are U.S. citizens. He's rich from banking and real estate, she says also from graft. She's rich from inheritance, he says also from graft. Bottom line, there's enough money on both sides to feed the sharks so the damn thing drags on. The custody aspect's what you'd expect. Two kids, boy, girl, they gave them American names . . . Dylan and Courtney. Cute little kids, four and six, mutual accusations that amount to crap because of the crap expert witnesses the sharks have hired. World War Three, obviously, is the money."

I said, "She claims she financed the bulk of his ventures, he says she's a lazy princess who did nothing but spend."

"Ah, great oracle of Beverly Glen. What makes it especially stupid,

Alex, is they're wasting time, money, and stomach acid on a relatively small amount. Twelve million, basically the house and some art—yeah, yeah, I know, for the average person it's a big deal. But trust me, either of them probably has overseas dough, they could afford to split the U.S. estate down the middle. You'd think they'd respond to my sage advice to do just that. You'd be wrong."

"Who are the sharks?"

"Trapp and Trapp versus Charteroff."

"See what you mean."

"Even they're getting worn out, but the principals won't budge. Surprisingly, the kids were doing okay, per the therapist—Alfree London. You were busy so I'm using her. One suggestion they did take was separating her from the expert witness shrinks."

He tossed out two names. "You feel otherwise?"

I said, "No, they're whores and Alfree's a good therapist."

"Unfortunately, she hasn't been able to therapize because Mrs. Ansar took the kids out of the country. Not much I could do other than write an order to return because she blindsided Mister, neither had asked for travel restrictions. He was certain she went over to Europe, hired private eyes who traced her to Paris then Monte Carlo then Belgium before the trail got cold. Can't see her heading back to Kabul but you know how it is when people don't think straight."

"Why's she so angry?"

"What do you think, Alex? Matin watches too much porn and fools with other women. He claims she's been sexually unresponsive for years and hints she's gay. What the truth is, who knows? Or cares. Hopefully the kids aren't in some Taliban kindergarten. Anything else?"

"Not that I can think of. Thanks, Marty."

"As long as we're talking, a new one landed on my desk yesterday. Likely to be equally vitriolic but the parties are only semi-big rich, so at some point it'll end. You up for it?"

"Happy to take a look."

"Good man," he said. "After mass murder, you're going to glide through it."

I was on my third cup of coffee when Milo rang my private line. I summarized what I'd just learned from Bevilacqua.

He said, "Can't see how it relates. Talked to most of the ten women on Gurnsey's call list, got a coupla question marks. I can come to you to go over it."

He drove up six minutes later, meaning he'd phoned from the road, assuming a drop-by would fit my schedule. Despite all the Old Sod gloom, a closet optimist.

He strode in, one hand clutching his olive-green vinyl attaché case. Blanche trotted up and nuzzled his cuffs.

"Hey, pooch." He stooped to pet her and slipped her a Greenie treat from a jacket pocket. He smiled as she gobbled, then his lips turned down. "Speaking of dogs, just got DNA on the"—looking down at Blanche—"the you-know-what."

Another glance at Blanche.

I said, "She's smart but no need for code."

He bent for another head rub. Sighed. "Two donors for all the blood, pit bull mixes, one male, one female. The vet Basia spoke to said the poor things were probably totally drained."

I said, "Lots of pit mixes in shelters."

"That's what I figured. Evil *assholes*—that coffee I smell? Let's use the kitchen so I can spread out."

He placed the case on the floor next to the kitchen table, began scrounging in the fridge.

I said, "Anything I can fix you?"

"No, I'll self-serve . . . just a snack—this turkey?"

"Left over from last night and all yours."

"Music to my ears." He cut the meat thick, added tomatoes and lettuce, and made himself a deli-sized sandwich on dark rye.

I brought two mugs of coffee to the table. He said, "Mind reader," took a swallow, then three bites, unlatched the case, and placed two sheets of yellow legal paper next to his plate.

His forward-slanting cursive. Names and details, numbered 1 to 10.

"The first three are the women from Gurnsey's work. They all claimed to be just friends and that matches their sosh pages—they have boyfriends and don't seem to have actually dated Gurnsey. They describe Gurnsey almost identically: easygoing, fun company, never hit on them though he could get 'flirty.' Their contact with him was lunch at work, sometimes dinner afterward in a group. All three were either star actresses or genuinely horrified to hear what had happened. No problem with a face-to-face but they doubted they had anything to offer and I'm inclined to agree."

He took another bite of sandwich. "Now the non-work crowd. Three met Gurnsey on dating sites but Gurnsey hasn't been on for three months, seems to have reverted to old-school, as in cocktail lounge pickups. Mostly places not far from his apartment: Shutters, Loew's, an upscale bar in the hip part of Venice. I've got Moses and Alicia checking out the locales, see if anyone remembers Gurnsey. One woman—the doctor—met him at a fundraiser. Young Professionals Saving the Bay, back to her later. One of the nurses came right out and said she and Gurnsey dated but not for long and that matches her only exchanging three calls with him months ago. She also sounded genuinely shocked about his death but not in a personal way, more like hearing about anyone getting killed. I asked her to describe him and at first she went quiet."

He opened the case again, produced pages of notes. "I say, 'Something the matter, Leslie?' She says, 'Look, I don't want to dis the dead but frankly, Ricky was a total horndog. Nice guy but out for one thing only.' I probed about Gurnsey getting overly aggressive, she insisted no, he never forced anything, just got verbally persistent and that got boring."

"No anger on her part."

"Not that I picked up, she really did sound bored, Alex. I got similar descriptions from Five and Six—one of the lawyers and the accountant. The accountant used the same phrase—total horndog—and the lawyer called Gurnsey a 'low-rent lothario.' Both of them put up with him for a few dates because he was 'basically nice,' 'cheerful,' 'well-groomed,' and 'generous, always picked up the tab.' The accountant also acknowledged he was good looking and knew how to behave in public. The lawyer said he enjoyed good food and wine, even though . . . hold on . . . 'Ricky wasn't really sophisticated or knowledgeable about culture. He was a nice guy but I was looking for more.' "

I said, "His public persona was fine, private not so much."

"Exactly. Get alone with him, sooner or later he's making a move and being pushy about it. Maybe a pain in the ass. Literally, based on what Briggs and Candace Kierstead told us, but so far no one's complained. Onward . . . Number Seven, another nurse, said it wasn't that Gurnsey dispensed with the niceties like a lot of guys, on the contrary he could be a total gentleman. But eventually he'd show his entitlement by . . . 'Ricky could be holding the door open for you and kissing your fingertips one minute, then he'd want to put you up against a wall and jam it in and assume you wanted it as much as he did. But he did take no for an answer.' Again, no animosity. More like a game she didn't want to play. She's the oldest, forty-four, told me she'd been married twice, didn't want to have to 'deal with another guy's issues.' "

He turned to the second page. "Nurse Number Three. The least recent, four dates with Gurnsey five months ago. Gurnsey was 'cute and okay but a little pushy when it came to sex. We didn't mesh.' She works at Cedars so I asked Rick and he knows her. Straight shooter, lovely, no way she could be involved in anything like this."

He tapped the list. "Now the two I want to meet soon. Nine is the other lawyer, a woman named Joan Blunt. Works at a B.H. firm. Haven't been able to talk to her yet, got blocked by her secretary, no call-back after three tries and that twangs the antenna. She's the second oldest, forty-one, and if her Instagram page is accurate, she looks like a movie star. She's also *ahem* married to another legal eagle, one kid, nice house in Encino. Which gives me a motive. Like you said, a jealous hubby. But also like you said, why kill three other people? She and Gurnsey exchanged a dozen calls, always at night, with some of the conversations lasting ten, fifteen minutes. Combine it with the stonewall—you'd think people, especially a lawyer, would figure out that's gonna backfire—and I definitely want to talk to her."

His finger traveled to the bottom of the list. "Last and certainly not least: Ellen Cerillos, M.D., she of woke ocean consciousness. *Her* front desk I couldn't even get to. Group practice in Sherman Oaks. Twelve-step voicemail then I got cut off."

"One of the DUIs," I said.

"And look at this."

He pulled out another sheet from the case. Printout of an online map, his handwritten red marker line connecting the Benedict Canyon house and the clinic's location on Moorpark Street.

Six miles due south, a fifteen-minute drive taking it slow.

"Doesn't mean much by itself," he said. "But."

He drank coffee. "Kierstead said the woman she saw was youngish and Blunt's older than she is. But like I said she's a looker. And fit, runs marathons. Kierstead's got kind of a prim, matronly air, no? I can see her thinking Blunt was younger."

He chomped the sandwich, continued eating as he got to his feet. "Ready to consult a lawyer?"

CHAPTER 16

Kagan, Kiprianidos, Blunt, and Shapiro occupied one of a dozen suites on the third floor of a determinedly undistinguished steel and gray-glass building on Wilshire just west of Robertson. Cheap black carpeting, cheap white doors, Thai food aromas wafting from somewhere.

I'd looked up the firm as Milo drove. Aviation and air-transport law. No associates, just the four partners. Joan Blunt had solid qualifications: B.A. from Penn, J.D. from Berkeley.

Her website photo was the Instagram shot Milo had commented on. Accurately. Milky oval face graced by full lips, enormous blue eyes, firm, dimpled chin. All of that under luxuriant black hair.

Broad, square shoulders suggested vitality. So did her extracurricular interests: marathons and piloting jet planes with instrument certification.

Her waiting room was three stiff-backed chairs on either side of a brown-marble floor. No one waiting. Magazines filled a plastic wall rack. Chagall prints not even pretending to be real hung on three beige walls: cows, fiddlers, bemused brides floating midair.

A young ponytailed blonde in jeans and a black T-shirt looked up from a no-nonsense reception desk and smiled automatically. Behind her, more beige. The kind of wallpaper you see in hospitals because it's easy to clean.

Milo introduced himself. The receptionist's smile flickered and fizzled.

"Um, you called before."

"We did."

"I'm sorry, she's super busy. If you want to make an appointment—"

"Not necessary, we can wait."

"Um . . . it's not necessary."

"It is for us."

"Um . . . hold on—please have a seat. Okay?"

We remained on our feet but moved back a few inches to give her the illusion of privacy. She punched an extension. Nervous eyes scanned us as she spoke softly into the receiver. Frowned.

"In a moment."

A "moment" was twenty-two minutes. For the last fifteen, we'd relented and sat, thumbing through *Air & Space, Elite Traveler, Soar,* and *Flying.*

I'd taken in a whole lot of data I'd never need—maintenance costs on a ten-year-old Gulfstream III—by the time a throaty voice said, "I have ten minutes. Come."

Joan Blunt stood to the right of the reception desk. Perfect posture and shorter than I'd expected from the strong shoulders in her photo. Five-three, tops, a lot of it trim but no shortage of curvy torso.

Even more gorgeous than the photo. Like her receptionist, she wore jeans under a simple top—a maroon crewneck. Brown flats, no makeup, the abundant dark hair drawn back on both sides by tortoiseshell barrettes.

That level of beauty could've taught her to coquette her way through life. Instead, she'd worked hard and done well at good schools and learned to fly planes at five hundred miles an hour. Her posture, the authority in her voice, the functional work space, said *Take me or leave me.*

She turned to the right and began walking without waiting for us to follow.

Milo said, "Thanks for seeing us, Ms. Blunt."

Without stopping, she said, "Joan. And you are?"

Milo always uses his rank. This time, he said, "Milo Sturgis. This is Alex."

"Milo. Alex. Fine, let's get this show on the road."

No style upgrade in Joan Blunt's private office. A desk larger but no less utilitarian than the receptionist's, a pair of the same stiff chairs. One window provided an eyeful of the office building across Wilshire. The desktop was clear but for two framed photos facing away from visitors. Diplomas on the wall behind the desk—her B.A. in history magna cum laude—shared space with a certificate from the U.S. Air Force.

Before our butts hit the chairs, she said, "So someone murdered Rick Gurnsey. Wouldn't have thought it."

Milo said, "He didn't seem the type to get murdered?"

"Too easygoing. Does that sound ridiculous to you?"

"Of course not—"

"It probably does. I understand that anyone can get killed, I was in Iraq. What I meant was Rick always seemed utterly inoffensive. Can't see him generating that level of hostility."

Joan Blunt smiled. Her eyes didn't. "You're talking to everyone he knew?"

"Something like that."

"Or maybe just everyone he dated?"

"That, too."

Joan Blunt said, "So it wasn't a street robbery or something like that, it was personal."

We said nothing.

"Got to keep it close to the vest, huh? Now's when you're going to ask how I met him and the nature of our relationship?"

"That would be helpful."

"It won't be," she said. "There's no *there* there. But fine, here's the whole sordid tale: My husband cheated on me so I filed for divorce and began the process of taking as much from him as I could and bucking myself up with mindless sex."

"Rick was—"

"A vehicle. One of several. How'd you connect him to me? His phone?"

"Yes."

"So you know we spoke a total of—what—ten times? Making dates, breaking them, a bit of flirting, why not? The breaking was always me. Something coming up here at the office or I needed suddenly to travel. Rick was a nine-to-fiver."

Milo said, "Where did the two of you meet?"

Joan Blunt said, "I thought I answered that. I was on the prowl, he was an easy catch."

"That's how. We'd like to know where."

"Why?"

"It might help us understand Rick. His social habits."

"You think they got him killed?"

"At this point, we've got more questions than answers, Ms.—Joan."

Blunt's smile spread slowly. A woman used to calling the shots. "Can you tell me when he was murdered?"

"Sometime Saturday morning."

"Six days ago," said Blunt. "And you still don't know his habits?"

"It's a tough case, Joan."

"Guess so but Ricky never impressed me as a mystery man. Where did we meet? He picked me up at Coast, the lounge at Shutters. When I left my husband I moved from our house in the Valley to an apartment in Pacific Palisades. But you probably know that."

"Actually, we don't."

"Oh," said Blunt. "Of course, I haven't changed my DMV, better do that soon so my churl of an ex doesn't get hold of my registration and throw it out. Anyway, I'm in a tiny little place with no charm but at least it's close to the beach so Shutters seemed like a practical choice for meeting men. I didn't want to do the online thing, too many unknowns. I trust my own intuition and ability to read people. Not that it was easy, I'd been out of circulation for a while. But at some point, you just dive in."

Brief, furious glower. "Unlike the churl, who circulated the whole time—sorry, I'm doing what I despise, bleeding in public. My dad was a colonel in the air force. He'd be giving me the death-stare."

Milo said, "You and Rick both happened to be at Coast?"

"Yup. He was already at the bar when I arrived. Cute, nicely dressed, well built. Nice hands with clean well-shaped nails, I always look at the nails. And he was *obviously* interested."

Another smile, this one broader, flashing luminous teeth. "The moment I sat down he was sneaking looks at me. Then I allowed him to catch my eye and he smiled. The second time, I smiled back. The third time, he bought me a drink. Then he came over. Pretty boilerplate, but I was primed and ready."

I said, "You were both interested—"

"For him sex was probably a state of being. For me, it was a mission and I *was* horny as hell. And lonely. The churl had taken our daughter to visit his parents. That night, I was *going* to meet someone and Rick was the cutest guy in the lounge. I talked to him long enough to decide he was safe and brought him to my apartment. Before the door closed we were up against the living room wall."

Blue eyes turned to gas flames. Daring us to judge.

"I'd seen it in the movies but never did it that way. Not the most comfortable position but I figured time to be open-minded. In the end I was okay with it but had to eventually lie down. Rick *loved* it. And afterward he was *so* well behaved. Soft-spoken, solicitous, not one of those where-are-the-frozen-waffles troglodytes. We hooked up maybe . . . six, seven times, essentially the same deal: drinks, sometimes a light dinner, and . . . I don't need to spell it out. The seventh time he tried to explore me anatomically in a way I didn't welcome and that was it."

"Did he get pushy about it?"

Joan Blunt smiled. "Literally or figuratively? No, he started poking around, I said uh-uh, he pouted a little so I . . . gave him compensation. But that was enough for me, he'd become boring. Not a genius. I told him it had been fun but now it was over. It's the kind of thing guys do to women all the time. That's not a political statement, merely fact."

I said, "Time to chart another course."

Joan Blunt cocked her head to the side and touched a fingertip to her lips. "That's rather insightful or you're faking it well. Are you single?"

"Sorry, no."

She laughed. "At least you're apologizing."

Milo said, "How did Rick take to being dumped?"

"He sent me a couple of weepy-face emojis, called a couple of times, are you sure, Joanie, we can just do it the regular way. I told him it had nothing to do with that and he gave up. As much as I'd like to think of myself as irresistible, I knew he'd just find another green pasture."

"Why?"

"Handsome, inoffensive, reliable erection, good stamina. He was made for dalliance."

I said, "Did he ever talk about having conflict with anyone?"

"Never. He didn't talk much period, thank God. I wasn't interested in learning about his psyche or his family or his aches and pains. This was all about reassuring myself."

She grinned. "And, of course, having fun."

Milo showed her the photos of the other three victims.

Blank look. "Who are they?"

"People Ricky knew. Please don't be offended but I need to ask. Where were you Friday night through Sunday morning?"

Joan Blunt said, "Really? Like in the movies? I spent the entire weekend from Friday afternoon through Sunday night with Brooklyn, my daughter. Friday we were in my apartment streaming movies, Saturday we saw a matinee of *The Little Mermaid* at the Pantages, Saturday evening we had dinner at Ivy at the Shore, Saturday night we watched TV in bed—bingeing on *Chopped,* this month she wants to be a chef. Sunday, we went horseback riding in Griffith Park. Sunday night, I drove her back to you-know-who. If you must have them, I can get my CPA to dig up the credit card slips."

"At your leisure," said Milo.

"You're serious."

"If it's not a problem."

"I fucked Ricky so I'm a suspect," said Joan Blunt. "May I ask why the mixed message? 'At your leisure.' If it's so relevant, why dawdle?"

Milo smiled. "I'd order you to do it A-sap but if you flew combat, you outrank me militarily."

"I flew Apaches. How high did you get and what did you do?"

"Sergeant, military police and some medic."

A crescent of pearly teeth. "Then I expect you to salute me when you clear out of here." She checked an orange-banded Apple Watch. "Which is now. I told you ten, you got sixteen."

We stood. Milo took the time to get a closer look at her military certificate. I managed a peek at the two framed photos on her desk.

She said, "Historical document, Milo. I'll get you those slips," and left her office. By the time we caught up she was talking to the receptionist.

"Chrissy, call Hal Moskowitz and have him contact my platinum Amex account . . ."

No notice of our presence. We slipped out the waiting room door.

◆

In the lobby, he said, "What do you think?"

"Tough woman but no tells that I noticed."

"Same here but she could probably shoot someone without too much hesitation."

"What was the commendation for?"

"Valor under fire. Captain Joan Sybil Blunt."

I said, "All the more reason not to suspect her."

"You're invoking the patriotism defense?"

"She's gifted at focusing. If Gurnsey was her target she'd have found a way to take him down clean, not mix her methods and add three other people to the mix. And two dogs. She owns three, two doodle types and a collie, obviously adores them."

"How do you know that?"

"Picture on her desk. Mother, daughter, pooches in a love fest. Daughter's a blond version of her."

We left the building and headed for the unmarked.

"One lawyer down, time for a doctor," he said. "Give Gurnsey credit for one thing: He was comfortable with women smarter than him."

"No reason not to be," I said. "Brains weren't the organs that interested him."

CHAPTER 17

Dr. Ellen Cerillos's name was listed at the bottom of a ten-physician roster. Valley Oaks Women's Wellness Center took up the ground floor of a wheat-colored building on Moorpark just east of Van Nuys Boulevard. On the second, a six-dentist group specializing in oral surgery and cosmetic reconstruction.

Joan Blunt's waiting room had been small and silent. This space was the size of a double garage and crowded with women, several of whom held babies in their arms. A notable number of the babies squalled. That noise reduced a piped-in new-age music soundtrack to bleeps, burps, and fragments of synthesized tones.

Interesting mix of fragrances: infant-poop, zwieback, perfume, antiseptic wipes.

Heads turned as Milo and I stepped in. Stares followed us as we took our place behind an exhausted-looking woman at the reception window who appeared precariously ready to deliver. An earnest conversation continued between her and a gray-haired receptionist. Scheduled C-section, still working out insurance details. Two other women worked in the front office, both busy clicking keyboards. The only people not paying us any mind.

One of the waiting patients nudged the woman next to her and pointed at us. Murmurs circulated; vocal relay race fueled by curiosity.

The weary woman stepped away and found a seat. The gray-haired woman said, "Yes?"

Milo leaned close, showed his card, covering *Homicide* with his thumb. His voice was soft, conspiratorial. "Is Dr. Cerillos in?"

"She's with a patient."

"Could you please tell her it's about Richard Gurnsey."

"Who's that?"

"A friend."

The receptionist cocked an eyebrow. "She's booked until seven, why don't you try later?"

"We may have to," said Milo. "But if you could tell her."

"The police, huh?" Loud enough for everyone to hear.

"Yes, ma'am. We'd appreciate if—"

"The *police,*" she repeated, cranking up the volume. As if sharing a joke with an audience. "*Hoe-wold* on."

She got up slowly, walked to the right, and disappeared. Half a minute later, the door to the inner office opened. "Must be a good friend. Fifth door to the right."

Returning to her desk, she shuffled forms and held up a finger. "Ms. Langer? Step back up for a sec."

The fifth door was open. To the left, the names of three M.D.'s and a trio of racks for charts.

Inside, room for one practitioner at a time. The white-coated woman behind the desk was in her thirties, narrowly built and buttermilk-pale but for the merest sprinkle of freckles across broad, flat cheeks and a nub nose. Cute in an elfin way. A high-backed desk chair made her look small.

She said, "Please close the door," and avoided looking at us.

The tint of her eyebrows said her hair had probably begun as strawberry blond. She'd dyed it flame orange and styled it ragged and boy-short. Three thin gold hoops glinted in her left ear, four decorated her right.

Once we'd sat down, she aimed rusty-brown eyes at us. One hand drummed a memo pad atop the desk; the other clutched the tubes of a stethoscope. More framed paper than free space on the wall. I found hers on the far right. M.D., Stanford. Internship, residency, and fellowship in high-risk pregnancy, UC San Francisco.

Milo said, "Thanks for seeing us, Doctor."

"I'm really pretty busy."

"Then special thanks."

"The police about Rick? Has he done something?" Ellen Cerillos plucked at a white lapel.

"Doctor, I'm sorry to have to tell you this but Mr. Gurnsey's deceased."

Cerillos's mouth dropped open. Smallish, misaligned teeth. The lack of childhood dental privilege said maybe a poor girl who'd worked her way up. "I don't understand—deceased? How?"

"I'm afraid he was the victim of a homicide."

"Oh, my God." Cerillos sank back in the enormous chair.

Milo said, "You asked if he'd done something. What came to mind?"

"Nothing. It's just . . . if the police were here . . . I mean I didn't assume anything had happened *to* him." Both hands took hold of the stethoscope.

"How well did you know Rick?"

A rosy flush climbed up Cerillos's neck, shooting from the hollow above the center of her collarbone to a small chin. "We dated. A couple of times. How'd you connect me—oh, his phone?"

Same deduction Joan Blunt had made. The cellular age.

Milo said, "Yes, Doctor."

"This is unbelievable. I've never known anyone before who was—

Are you here because you think I can help you in some way? I'm sure I can't."

"You and Rick dated a couple of times. Literally, as in two?"

"Maybe three," said Ellen Cerillos. "Four. That's it. Four." The same number of calls between her and Gurnsey.

"Did you stop because of problems?"

The flush took off again, commandeering Cerillos's entire face. "I didn't stop, he did. As in see you soon then not calling anymore. I was surprised, there didn't seem to be problems. At least as far as I could tell." She tugged at a sprig of red hair. "Talking about my social life with anyone is embarrassing, let alone the police."

"We're at the beginning of the investigation, Doctor. If you could just bear with us." Cerillos glanced at a desk clock backed by a pharmaceutical company's label. "A few more minutes, I've got a waiting room full of patients."

"We'll do our best. So four dates, then he stopped calling. Kinda rude."

"I thought it was. I decided I wasn't going to call him. Then I relented. For closure, you know? You wonder. I reached him at work, he didn't sound surprised that I was asking."

I said, "As if he was used to it."

"Exactly. As if that was his pattern. So I said to myself, *Okay, Ellie, you've been played.* And proceeded to forget about him. It wasn't that difficult, there'd been nothing emotional, just . . ." The blush intensified. "He was just a player. What surprised me is he'd never come *across* like one. He knew how to act romantic. Emphasis on act. Or I was just gullible."

"Did he offer you any explanation?"

"He apologized, told me I was a great girl but he needed to move on. Which I took to mean another woman."

"Did he ever mention other women?"

"Never," said Cerillos. "Some guys do that, it's moronic, but Rick never did. Are you saying he mistreated someone and they took it out on him?"

Milo said, "I wish we knew enough to theorize, Dr. Cerillos."

"But I'm not the only woman you're talking to."

"You're not. So he could come across romantic."

"Looking back, he was obviously following a routine. Pretending to be interested. The whole medical thing, he kept telling me how smart I was. Smarter than him, he hoped that wouldn't be an issue." She smiled. "I suppose it might've been had it lasted."

I said, "How'd the two of you meet?"

The smile dropped like a dry leaf. "Must I get into that? This feels invasive."

Milo said, "Sorry about that. It's just that Rick was killed pretty brutally and we haven't made much progress."

She winced. "Brutally. My God, don't even tell me."

"The point is, Doctor, anything we can learn about Rick—his habits, his approach to life—"

"His approach was obviously hooking up with gullible females."

"How'd you meet?"

Her small frame shifted forward. "At a restaurant. The Proud Rooster, it's in Brentwood, they have a cocktail lounge where you can get a light dinner. I live nearby, had been there a couple of times. That particular night, I'd had a tough day. On call for someone else's patient, fifteen-hour delivery and then the baby ended up being born with a defect that hadn't been picked up on screening. I drove straight from the hospital to the Rooster, ordered a sandwich and some wine, and tried to decompress. Not at the bar, they have tables, I don't sit at bars."

Milo said, "Why's that?"

Ellen Cerillos said, "It's been my experience that men who spend extended time at the bar can be less than . . . appropriate."

I said, "Rick was also at a table."

She nodded. "Two tables away, also by himself. I didn't see him at first, in between us a couple. But when they left Rick and I had a clear view of each other. He didn't notice me at first, then he did and smiled. Friendly, not gross. I thought he was cute. More than cute, he's—was a solidly good-looking guy, obviously took care of himself. We exchanged a few more looks and then he went to the bar and bought two drinks, one for me, one for him. I said sure, sit down."

She looked to the side. "Am I the first on his call list you're talking to?"

"Why would that be important, Doctor?"

"I wouldn't want to think that you're prioritizing me. There's absolutely no reason to do that."

"No, there've been others."

"A whole bunch, I'd imagine." Cerillos frowned and pushed the stethoscope to the side. "I need to cut this short. I'm just out of my fellowship and have a ton of student debt. Getting this job was a great deal, I can't risk having it jeopardized."

Milo said, "Our showing up jeopardizes you."

"Agnes told me everyone was looking at you."

Milo said, "We came here in person because we left messages and no one got back."

"Messages with who?"

"Your front desk."

"Oh, shit, Agnes—she can be . . . well, whatever. That's all I know about Rick."

Milo said, "Four dates then he cut it off."

Ellen Cerillos blinked. "Precisely. That's certainly nothing to kill someone over. And please don't give me that line about woman scorned, hell hath no fury. In my experience it's men who get angry and stalk."

She licked her lips.

I said, "You're speaking from experience."

Cerillos fiddled with the tubes of her stethoscope. "My second year of med school. A respiratory therapist got it in his head that we were destined for each other. We'd never even gone out, just had coffee in the cafeteria. Then he asked me out and I said no. Then a second time. And a third. That's when the problems started. He never got violent but he did get scary. Threatening demeanor, calling incessantly, showing up at my apartment with flowers. Eventually, he was arrested for stalking three other women. One he beat up. They wanted me to testify. That terrified me and I refused and the police did their best to make me feel guilty. So you can see why I'm not thrilled when you drop in and dredge up my personal life."

"What happened to your stalker?"

"He pled guilty and got a couple of years in prison. It was a tough time for me." Looking at the desk. "But you probably know that."

"Pardon?"

"You're the police. You also probably know I got a DUI."

"It came up, Doctor."

"It could've affected my licensing," she said. "But it was a stupid arrest. I was .85, instead of .80. My lawyer got it turned into a ticket and told me I didn't need to report it."

"Glad it worked out," said Milo. Out came his pad. "What's the name of the guy who stalked you?"

Rusty eyes widened in terror. "You *can't* tell him I told you!"

"We have no intention of contacting him, Doctor. We'd just like to know where he is."

"Why?"

"For your sake. What if he's in L.A. and found out you dated Rick?"

"All those months ago?"

I said, "Was he rational to begin with?"

"Oh, God," said Cerillos. "It *can't* happen again!"

Milo said, "How about this, Doctor. The moment we find out where he is, we'll let you know. Most probably he's nowhere near and you'll be reassured. Because you have wondered, right?"

Slow head shake.

"I also promise you that he'll never know we spoke to you, Doctor. Scout's honor."

"Scouts," said Cerillos. "I was a Brownie." She exhaled twice. "Tibor Halasz. With a 'z' at the end."

Milo pulled out his phone.

She said, "What are you doing?"

"Just what I said."

"Now? You can do that? On a phone?"

"Sure can."

"Scary," said Cerillos. "Orwellian." She snatched up the stethoscope.

Milo worked, I waited, Cerillos opened a drawer and applied lip balm.

He said, "Here we go. Mr. Halasz moved to Illinois and got into more trouble. Aggravated assault four years ago, nine-year sentence in a state penitentiary starting a year ago."

"He beat up another woman?"

"Doesn't say, Doctor. In any event, he's in no position to bother you."

"Or to kill Rick," said Cerillos, dropping her head, then looking up. "Thank you, Lieutenant."

"So what else can you tell us about Rick?"

"There really isn't much to tell. Simple guy."

I said, "Into his basic needs."

"*Very* basic," she said. "For him it was all about physicality. Which isn't a problem if you don't force it. And he didn't. But at some point, if you've got a brain in your head, you want more. Like substantial conversation."

"Rick didn't supply that."

"Never. Small talk and then . . . predictable, I suppose. I came to realize he did me a favor by not prolonging something that wouldn't have gone anywhere. So I don't resent him and I'd certainly have no reason to hurt him."

She hung the stethoscope around her neck. "This is going to sound mean but after I got my head straight, he didn't mean anything to me. I hadn't thought about him at all until Agnes came in and told me why you were here. Now I do have to go."

"Fair enough, Doctor. Here's my card."

Cerillos took it and scanned. "Homicide. What an ugly word."

Back in the waiting room, we passed through a visual gauntlet. Nursing women shifted their babies away from us, others stared.

In the car, I said, "Nice of you to run Halasz."

"Did it for myself. Maybe I'd actually have a suspect. But should life be easy?" He started up the car. "So what do you think about Gurnsey's choice in women?"

I said, "Cerillos and Blunt are highly educated and extremely bright. Other than that, it doesn't seem as if he went for a type."

"More like who he could pick up and put against a wall. You find Cerillos any more interesting than Blunt?"

I shook my head.

"Damn," he said. "Great minds moving in the same futile direction. How about the fact that the other women dumped Gurnsey but Gurnsey dumped Cerillos?"

"She could've told us different," I said. "Maybe some of the others did."

"Making themselves look good. Good point. Unfortunately."

He phoned Reed, told him to add the Proud Rooster to his canvass list.

Reed said, "Sure, it's right on the way, just finished at Shutters and Loew's. No one remembers Gurnsey. I also called a few animal shelters, see if anyone adopted two pit mixes. Waste of time, L.T. Pits and Chihuahuas make up a big proportion of roundups, we're talking thousands of dogs. Record keeping is sketchy and we have no idea when these two dogs were actually acquired. Plus, they could've come from another source—puppy-milled, bred for fighting, bought in a parking lot."

"A dog's life," said Milo.

"On the bright side, Sean had good luck with Roget's phone records, they're coming tomorrow."

"Fingers crossed, Moses."

"Speaking of crosses," said Reed, "be nice to crucify this bastard."

CHAPTER 18

We stopped for coffee at a diner on Moorpark near Fulton. Twenty-year-old retro refit of what had once been a chain restaurant. Two decades of paradigm shift made it an L.A. antiquity.

The place was thinly occupied and smelled of vintage grease. Pastries revolved in a slo-mo, sugar-flecked case. Milo glanced at them, contemplated, shook his head.

A middle-aged waitress in a too-tight brown dress came over smiling, took our coffee order, and straightened her lips when Milo said, "Just coffee."

"We've got nice pies, boys."

Milo glanced at the menu. "Okay, throw in a slice of your 'famous berry-merry.' "

"There you go, bone-apperteet."

"Is it really famous?"

"Sure," she said. "Isn't everything, nowadays?"

◆

A copper-colored thermal pitcher, two mugs, and a wedge of pie bleeding crimson on two sides arrived moments later.

Milo's fork descended like a hawk blitzing a nest of hatchlings. Half the pie vanished before he put it back down.

"Cerillos just put our working hypothesis into words: Gurnsey demeaned the wrong woman. Likely one who knew the Benedict house. But maybe not because she'd partied there, because she once owned it."

"Mrs. Ansar?"

"Why not, Alex? Same scenario Joan Blunt described: cheating husband, nasty divorce, time for some fun. How about calling your judge buddy and finding out when Mrs. A. left the country."

I tried Bevilacqua's chambers. His Honor was gone for the day but the paralegal who picked up was someone I knew, a veteran named Linda Montrose, long assigned to family court, long past mere cynicism and into a tortoiseshell view of the world.

"Alex. Didn't see your name on the docket."

"Nothing pending, Linda."

"So what's up?"

"I'm wondering if you could do me a favor."

"Depends on what it is."

"The Ansar case—"

She groaned. "The paper storm? More like a used-*toilet*-paper storm, totally clogging up the system. Don't tell me you're on it, now. I thought we were full-up with shrinks."

I said, "I'm not, this is a police matter. Someone was murdered on the property and I've been asked to check something out."

"Murdered," said Montrose. "*That* one, Beverly Hills? Paper made it sound like a gang thing."

"It wasn't."

"The cops think one of *them* did it? Oh my, wouldn't that be cool, finally get rid of the case so we can concentrate on someone else's misery."

"They're not suspects, Linda. And if you could keep this call to yourself, I'd appreciate it."

"High intrigue," she said. "*I'm* intrigued. What do you need to know?"

"If you could check when Mrs. A. left the country—"

"Don't need to check, I've had to read and collate so many whiny motions that I know everything by frickin' heart. She took off seven months ago, give or take a few days."

"Has she ever returned?"

"Nope. The latest jokes around here have her in the desert with the kids, turning them into mini-ISIS types."

I said, "Afghanistan is the Taliban."

"Doctor Detail," she said. "That's why Big B likes you. Anything else?"

"That's it, thanks, Linda."

"When can I tell someone?"

"I'll let you know the moment it goes public."

She laughed. "Make it a moment *before* and we'll stay friends."

I relayed the news to Milo.

He said, "Boom. That's the sound of a hypothesis blowing up. Want some pie?"

"Small piece."

"Really? You're actually indulging? That's a switch."

"Why turn my nose up at fame?"

He was driving back to the city and I was on my phone checking messages when his played something heavy and Teutonic. Maybe Brahms during one of his depressive episodes.

He scanned the screen, switched to speaker.

Basia Lopatinski said, "Hey, guys!"

A woman who cuts up corpses all day and is constitutionally cheerful. I wondered what she thought of Brahms.

Milo said, "What's up?"

"Good news and more good news. I hydrated your female vic's fingertips and got enough ridge to send to AFIS. The first AFIS database I tried was kind enough to give me a name. I emailed it to your office computer, you should have it but I wanted to tell you personally."

"You're a saint, Basia."

"Normally," she said, "I don't like it when men tell me that, it means they expect too much. But from you, I accept it."

He pulled over and checked his mail. Said, "Bingo," and handed me the phone and resumed driving.

Mary Jane Huralnik, fifty-nine years old. Much younger than I'd thought. She'd looked elderly for a decade of progressively sadder mugshots.

No felony arrests but plenty of misdemeanors up and down the state over a thirty-three-year period. Public drunkenness, public indecency, vagrancy, shoplifting, petty larceny, illegal panhandling, trespassing, failure to show on a slew of warrants for many of those offenses.

The most recent charge, an indecency bust eighteen months ago. Defecating on a sidewalk in the Sixth Street tunnel downtown.

I said, "Not that far from where Benny worked."

He said, "Like we said, someone prowling downtown for vulnerables. I'll call a Central D and ask if she knows Huralnik."

This time he phoned while in motion. I continued to read. No jail for Huralnik on the tunnel offense; with the crowding situation, the priority is those who draw copious blood.

Overall, her incarcerations had been limited to days, not weeks. With that type of abbreviated sentence, no probation or parole. Also no address, phone number, or DMV listing.

Milo hung up. "Shireen Walker has no knowledge of her. Her record say anything to you?"

"She entered the system when she was in her twenties, which would fit mental illness. No violence in her history but the indecency busts make me wonder."

"Uninhibited."

"The kind of person who *would* be vulnerable."

"To what?"

"Attention, food, dope, an offer of kindness."

"Psychopath lures her and turns her into a prop," he said. "Same probably goes for Benny. And the dogs. But why the *need* for props, Alex? If we're right about Gurnsey inspiring someone's rage why not just off him and pull out his dick and leave him in a gutter for the world to see?"

I said, "Good question."

"No, no, bad question. As in neither of us has a clue."

CHAPTER 19

We returned to Milo's office and set to work tracing Mary Jane Huralnik using separate pathways.

Beyond her minor arrests nothing further on any law enforcement database. A Social Security number issued fifty years ago yielded nothing, including disability payments. No claims on money she could've gotten. Someone low on self-care.

She didn't show in my Google search but the uncommon surname provided an edge.

Four Huralniks in the U.S. John in Omaha, Louise in Columbus, Ohio, Hampton in Dover, New Hampshire, a Honda dealer named Randall Huralnik in Stockton, California.

Milo said, "Like the trendoids say, keep it local," and started with Randall. Forty-two years old, no criminal record. An internet photo showed him corpulent and ruddy with a mop of brown hair and a pendulous nose.

Milo said, "Forty-two. I luck out and he's Mary's kid, *she* was a kid when she had him."

He phoned the dealership, asked the woman who answered to put him through to Randall Huralnik.

She said, "Randy? Hold on."

We endured several minutes of Beatles music bowdlerized to easy listening before a hearty voice boomed, "This is Randy! How can I help you today?"

"Lieutenant Sturgis, L.A. Police Department."

"L.A.?" said Huralnik. "What's going on down there?"

"Sir, are you by any chance related to Mary Jane Huralnik?"

"Aunt Mary? She finally got herself in some serious trouble?"

"The worst type of trouble, sir. I'm afraid she's deceased."

"Oh. That's real sad news, Lieutenant." Randy Huralnik's sigh sounded like a gust of static. "I guess I'm not surprised. Alcohol poisoning?"

"She was murdered, Mr. Huralnik."

"Oh. Huh. Well, that's *terrible* news. Who did it?"

"That's what we're trying to find out. What can you tell us about your aunt?"

"Tell," said Huralnik, as if practicing a foreign word. "Not much *to* tell. She's my mom's younger sister, left when she was young and only came back once in a while. To get money from my parents. Which was crazy, there were all kinds of benefits she could've gotten but she claimed the government would hunt her down and put her in a cage."

"Mental issues."

"To say the least."

"Did she have kids of her own?"

"Nope, never married, no kids." A beat. "There was a thought that she was, you know, gay. My dad used to say that but my mom disagreed. I couldn't tell you who was right."

"Any family connections beyond your parents?"

"Nope, that's it," said Randy Huralnik. "I guess you'd call her a loner."

Milo said, "How often would she visit to get money?"

"Not often. Maybe . . . two times a year, three? And not every year."

"Any idea how she supported herself?"

"Dad said she was probably prostituting, Mom said no way. Again, can't tell you. She hasn't been back in a *real* long time, sir. Since before my dad died, which was twelve years ago, so, say . . . fourteen? Couple years later, Mom passed. I would've invited Mary to the funeral, but I had no idea how to reach her."

"What's your last memory of her?"

"Last one . . . okay, I was at the house helping my dad, he was sick with the Alzheimer's. Suddenly Mary's there, didn't even hear her. Dad was on a walker but she didn't ask how he was, just went in to see Mom. She looked terrible. She had problems."

"Alcohol?"

"Sure, that," said Randy Huralnik, "but I always thought she was off even without the drink. She was just . . . you know, different. Never looking at you, walking around with her lips moving."

"Talking to herself."

"That's what it seemed to me. My dad called her the wolf the pack would've left behind. I know that sounds mean but I respect his opinion."

I mouthed, *Mom.*

Milo said, "Your mother didn't agree with him?"

"It was an issue between them, yeah," said Huralnik. "But not a big one, she wasn't around much."

"Did Mary ever talk about friends, acquaintances, people she hung out with?"

"Not that I heard, sir. She and Mom would have conversations but I stayed away from them. Life's hard enough without bringing extra problems on yourself."

"That's for sure," said Milo. "So she never asked you for money?"

"Never," said Huralnik. "She had, I'da said no. Maybe she knew that. Maybe she wasn't *that* crazy."

◆

Milo scrawled a few notes and sat back. "Schizophrenic?"

"Probably."

"Completes the picture: victims with no connections." His cell rang. A number he didn't recognize. "Sturgis. Oh, hi, Dr. Bauer."

He switched to speaker.

Andrea Bauer said, "This is probably nothing but the employee you spoke to—Justine—just called in a panic because another employee, Marcella McGann, is two days overdue and still hasn't shown up. I'd already brought someone from another facility to sub and Justine's done a few doubles, she's exhausted. So I'm bringing an additional worker and sending Justine home for an extended weekend."

Lots about her situation, very little about McGann.

Milo heard it, too, and rolled his eyes. "Marcella was due back Wednesday."

"That's right."

"She was the one on shift when Benny Alvarez didn't come home."

"She was," said Bauer. "I supposed this could be just a vacation overstay but Marcella has always been dependable. In any event, I thought you should know."

"Thanks. Why's Justine panicking?"

"Obviously because of what happened to Benny," said Bauer. "Not that I can see any connection to Marcella being late. But Justine's young and I suppose working alone could be tough. This is going to sound terribly sexist but the sub's a man and the second person will be, as well."

"You feel you need extra security?" said Milo.

"I don't, it's more a matter of reassuring Justine." A beat. "And I suppose reassuring myself. I don't feel any sense of personal responsibility for Benny but it is horrible. Any progress?"

"We're working our way."

"I see. One more thing, Lieutenant. According to Marcella's Facebook page she'd be at a Cabo hotel called Hacienda Del Sol. Obviously,

I wanted to talk to her about scheduling so I called but they told me she's not there. I asked if she actually had a reservation, thinking maybe she'd just changed her mind. They refused to tell me, even though I speak decent Spanish. I must admit, that bothers me a bit. Mexico, you know how it is, nowadays. My husband and I used to vacation in Acapulco. Now you're taking your life in your hands."

"We'll check it out," said Milo. "As long as I have you, let me shoot a name your way: Mary Jane Huralnik."

"Who's that?"

"A street person Benny might've encountered."

"A dangerous street person?"

"Another victim."

"Oh," said Bauer. "Well I'm sorry for that and it's certainly a disgrace the way we let people live wretchedly. But I don't see Benny developing a relationship with any of those people."

"Why's that?"

"Benny was trained in proper behavior. As are all our Level Ones. I've reviewed our procedures and they're totally appropriate. The residents wouldn't want me to tighten up. They wish to be treated like functional adults. Hope your luck improves, Lieutenant. And thanks for keeping things quiet."

Milo said, "Every time I talk to her I start off thinking maybe there's a heart of gold buried somewhere beneath the cashmere. Then she throws in an ulterior motive."

I said, "Can't think of one that would cause her to call about McGann."

"Hmph."

He found Marcella McGann's social network page, learned the surname of chubby boyfriend Steve: Vollmann.

At the Hacienda Del Sol Resort and Spa in Cabo San Lucas he was met with the same stonewall Andrea Bauer had described. Unlike Bauer he had police credentials and the persistence of a retrovirus.

Three transfers later, a manager named Umberto Iglesias confirmed, in unaccented English, that the reservation had been made in Stephen W. Vollmann's name and had not been "honored by the customer."

"Meaning?" said Milo.

"By no-showing, they canceled a package deal," said Iglesias. "Nonrefundable, nontransferable. We gave the room to someone else."

"Did you try to contact Mr. Vollmann?"

"*We* call *him*?" said Iglesias. As if Milo had suggested he amputate his own nose. "Package deals are the customer's responsibility."

"What was the package?"

"Discounted room rate, full breakfast, tour of a tequila factory, ride on a dolphin."

"Sounds like fun."

"People enjoy it," said Iglesias. "The police calling from L.A.? Is this guy a criminal?"

"Not to my knowledge."

"So why didn't he show up?"

Milo said, "Why, indeed," and hung up.

CHAPTER 20

Further research on Stephen Wayne Vollmann revealed a thirty-one-year-old Iraqi war vet employed as a pool maintenance man for a Granada Hills company named Agua Fresca, Ltd. No priors, wants, or warrants, good driving record. A six-year-old blue Camaro was registered at an address on Cochran Avenue in mid-city that matched Marcella McGann's.

A call to Agua Fresca, Ltd., earned him an earful from the owner, a hoarse-voiced man named Lachlan Lindley.

"Him? Totally flaked on me."

"Since when?"

"Since Wednesday when he was supposed to be here. Why are the cops after him?"

"He and his girlfriend were scheduled to go to Mexico but never showed up. We're looking at them as missing persons."

"Oh. Steve's never flaked before. It *is* kind of weird."

Milo said, "Did he talk about his trip?"

"Just that it was at some big resort, he was going to ride a dolphin," said Lindley. "He was pretty excited, first time south of the border. He never showed up? Damn. You think some cartel got him? You know what it's like. They're mowing people down and the cops there are in on it."

"Did Steve talk about his girlfriend?"

"Just that she was going with him. Shit. You think *she* did it? Shoved him off a boat or something?"

"Why would I think that?"

"'Cause it happens," said Lindley. "People are in a relationship and someone goes nuts. There was that guy in New York, goes boating, chick he thinks loves him shoves him into the river, he's drowning and she's sitting there eating a sandwich. Talk about evil."

Milo said, "Vollmann's chick isn't a suspect. You ever meet her?"

"Nope, didn't even know her name," said Lindley. "Don't socialize with the staff, period. They do their routes, I mail them their checks."

"Relaxed setup," said Milo.

"If everyone does their job it is. I used to service myself, loved anything to do with water, swam at Cal State Northridge. Then I dove the wrong way and ended up in a wheelchair."

"Sorry."

"For what?" said Lindley. "You play the hand you're dealt."

"Thanks for your time, sir."

"Got plenty of it."

I said, "The road not taken leads to Mexico."

"Hmph. Let's see what Sleepy has to say."

He punched a number he had stored in his head and connected to his contact at Homeland Security. A man I'd overheard on speaker but knew nothing about.

A slurred, somnolent voice said, "I don't need anything from you so it's not trading season."

"It's not complicated," said Milo. "Just wanna find out if two people flew to and maybe from Mexico during the last week."

"Fugitives? Ask the marshals."

"Missings. Marcella McGann and Stephen Vollmann, L.A. to Cabo."

"You know for sure they flew."

"It's what, fifteen hundred miles? Don't see them driving."

"Eleven hundred forty-four," said Sleepy. "Three days at a relaxed pace. I'm asking because it's a clusterfuck at the border, someone drives or walks into TJ, I can't always access it right away."

"I'll take my chance with flying. Stephen with a 'ph,' middle name Wayne, Vollmann, two 'l's, two 'n's, Marcella McGann, capital 'M,' small 'c'—"

"I'm an intuitive speller, got it already," said Sleepy. Long luxuriant yawn, then typing clicks. "Neither passport has been active for the past twelve months. He traveled a few years ago to Canada, nothing since, she got hers a few months ago, never used it, period. Do I really need to check the airlines?"

"Guess not—"

"Oops, already pushed the magic FAA button. No flights in or out for either of them. And now because you've already upset my circadian rhythm and I need to slow my brainwaves, I'll try those border checkpoints."

Thirty seconds passed. "No walk-throughs I can find but like I said, that's not infallible. Now you seriously owe me."

"Name it."

"When the time's right."

Yawn.

Milo put down the phone.

I said, "Maybe Justine's onto something."

"Something happened to Vollmann and McGann? Why would they be targeted?"

"McGann was Benny Alvarez's caretaker when he went missing. Suppose she got upset enough to go looking for him, learned something, and made herself a threat."

"Her and Vollmann."

"She took him along for protection."

"And he couldn't protect her . . . looking for Benny woulda meant between the home and his job."

I said, "An area where someone like Mary Huralnik would hang out."

He phoned Bogomil. "Where are you, kiddo?"

"Strip mall on La Brea and Olympic, working my way east looking for Roget's ads. Still nothing but I'm not sure that means anything. Free posting means no one at the register pays attention."

"Time to shift gears," said Milo. He told her about I.D.'ing Mary Jane Huralnik.

She said, "Homeless like we thought."

"Homeless and mentally ill and doesn't collect benefits so she wouldn't be crashing at any SROs or shelters that collect government dough."

"But maybe a nonprofit," said Bogomil. "Church-run, that kind of thing. Or she just stayed on the street."

"Exactly, Alicia. Forget the ads for the time being, head downtown and start looking for places. Now that we've got a name, maybe someone's memory will get jogged."

"On it, L.T."

"I owe you lunch. You like pastrami?"

"Not really, too fatty."

"You and Moe, both."

"Nah, I'm just a girl trying to stay healthy," she said. "Moe's another species."

He put BOLOs out on McGann's Sentra and Vollmann's Camaro. The second request elicited an immediate ping.

He said, "Excellent." Then: "Damn."

CHAPTER 21

A call to an Inglewood detective named Marcus Coolidge gave him the details: Two bodies had been found in that city the Monday after the Benedict bloodbath.

Male victim in his thirties sitting in the front passenger seat of a blue Camaro, female vic in the trunk of the car. As with the limo, the paucity of blood said the killings had taken place elsewhere. Best guess of TOD based on decomposition was Sunday. Same day the limo had been found.

The Camaro's registration plus the age and physical stats of the male victim suggested he was Stephen W. Vollmann but no formal verification.

Coolidge said, "I'm sure it's him but like I said there was decomp and we're talking a shotgun, 12-gauge, not much face or teeth left. Vollmann's got no prints on file so until the DNA comes in, I'm not allowed to make it official."

Milo said, "He's a vet, the army may have prints."

"Ah. Good. I'll get on that, thanks."

"Vollmann had a girlfriend—"

"Marcella McGann," said Coolidge. "Found her on his Facebook, the photos I saw of her match my female in general terms. But she got hit even closer-range than Vollmann and no prints from her, her hands were obliterated, probably from holding them up defensively."

"Nasty."

"Worst scene I've had in a while. One weird thing: The pathologist also found a knife wound in Vollmann, nonfatal, between the ribs, missed organs but damaged muscle. Would've caused big-time pain and made Vollmann easier to control and shoot. Vollmann's pretty good-sized so maybe cutting him first was insurance. But I've never seen that before and a shotgun's more than enough to get the job done."

"Where was the car found?"

"Hindry Avenue, industrial area. Behind a painting supply warehouse."

"Tough area?"

"This is Inglewood, man. Tough's our thing. Including citizens making wrong turns on their way to the airport, you'd be amazed at some of the directions the stupid computer kicks out. Which is what I've been thinking for these two."

"They were planning a trip to Mexico."

"There you go. We've got four major gangs operating in and around and with no wallets, I.D., or jewelry, I've been figuring it for a robbery gone *really* bad. Which is a sensitive topic, you know?"

"Bad for tourism."

"Bad for tourism," said Coolidge, "plus the racial thing. White people get killed, there's two rules from the bosses: Keep your mouth shut and be right about everything."

Milo said, "If it was a robbery, why bother shooting them elsewhere and transporting them in the car? Why not rip off the car, for that matter?"

"Interesting questions. I catch the offender, I might get answers. So far nothing from my informants and every gangster I've talked to denies having anything to do with it and I have to say they're coming across righteous. Why're you interested?"

Milo told him.

Coolidge said, "Oh, boy. So it could be totally different from what I figured."

"If it's connected to mine, it's big-time different."

"Amazing. My situation, you don't get too many surprises. We should meet, no?"

"Definitely."

"Your shop or mine?"

"Anything to learn from your crime scene?"

"Nah, it's long cleaned up and there was nothing important in the first place, just the car between a couple of dumpsters, low branches from a tree hanging over it."

Milo said, "Not hidden but not look-at-me, either."

"My thinking exactly," said Coolidge. "Weekend's coming up, I'm off shift in an hour. How about we meet today, your shop. I live in Playa, getting home after rush hour won't be as bad."

"You hungry?"

"I could eat."

"How about a deli?"

"Never met a deli I didn't like."

"Place called Maury's." Milo gave the address. "When can you be there?"

"Traffic, detours?" said Coolidge. "Give me forty. I'm late, order me a pastrami on rye. Don't trim the fat."

Milo said, "More bodies in a car," stood and stretched and rubbed chin stubble. "Gonna be a long weekend, time to change my shirt and shave. You have something to keep you occupied while I'm nice to myself?"

"Always."

"Yeah, yeah, active mind."

When he was gone, I dialed Robin's cell.

She said, "Hi, darling."

"Hi. Still working?"

"Just stopped and ran a bath. About to step in."

"The image will sustain me."

"Will it? Okay, I'm loosening my hair and *bending* and . . ."

I said, "Now you're endangering my health."

She laughed. "Would a discussion about nutrition be apropos?"

"If you're up for a late dinner, I am, too."

"How much later?"

"Hard to say."

"Something came up with the Big Guy."

I said, "Two more bodies. He's meeting with another detective."

"Over food."

"What else?"

"What kind of food?"

"Deli. I'm not hungry, can last till I get home. But if you are, don't wait."

"Two more bodies," she said. "Similar to the other one?"

"Inglewood, a smaller car. The female victim took care of Benny Alvarez."

"Oh. I can see why he'd want you there. Deli, huh? Haven't had that for a while. Bring me home a pastrami on rye and get something for yourself, we're running low on leftovers."

"With or without the fat?"

"However it comes off the slicer," she said. "Too much I can trim, not enough's a drag. Besides, I like mapping my own destiny."

As we walked to Maury's, Milo smoked a cigar and blew perfect rings up at the darkening sky. Not a word uttered.

We passed a grizzled, legless man holding a hand-lettered cardboard *Help Me* sign. Amputation mid-thigh.

Milo stopped, fished a ten out of his wallet. "Here you go, amigo."

"God bless you, sir. There's a mansion awaiting you in heaven."

"Great, I'm ready for an upgrade."

"A big mansion with a swimming pool."

"How about a pool table?"

"Of course, sir."

"Let me ask you a question, compadre. Ever hear of someone named Mary Jane Huralnik?"

The man's face screwed up. "Mary? Is she a saint?"

"Who knows?" As Milo turned to leave, I added my own ten.

The man said, "Bless everyone! We'll start a celestial suburb."

Three steps later, I said, "Good karma."

"Don't know your motivation but mine's not cosmic, it's simple gratitude."

"For what?"

He tapped both his knees. "For these."

CHAPTER 22

Maury's Deluxe Delicatessen was a generous, glass-fronted room, dill-and-salty aromatic. A clutch of people waited to be seated. I'd never been there but Milo had because we were pulled ahead of the queue and given a corner booth by a jubilant hostess who said, "Great to see you again!"

Cops tip generously; my friend kicks up the average.

Familiarity didn't stop him from studying the menu as if it were an arcane shred of papyrus.

A waiter, white-haired, paunchy, and hunched so severely he resembled an angle bracket with shoes, shuffled over. "The chief of police graces us with his presence, the world is safe." Heavy lids, phlegmy, bored voice.

"Chief's a crap job, Mel. Thought you liked me."

"I love you. Not that way, but we could be brothers." Mel gave a wheezy laugh. "If Mama had a lo-ong gestation history. Okay, I'll settle for you're my large, Gentile nephew. Who's this?" Wink wink. "The *guy*?"

"*A* guy," said Milo. "Dr. Alex Delaware."

"Isn't *the* guy a doctor?"

"He is. But he's not *this* guy."

Mel looked at me. "By any chance do you shave bunions and take Medicare?"

"He's a shrink, Mel."

"Okay. You do neuroses and take Medicare?"

"Coffee, please, Mel," said Milo. "The usual."

"Strong and black, Mr. Macho. You?"

I said, "The same."

Mel said, "So decisive, Dr. Freud. Shouldn't someone of your training be hinting, not delineating?"

I said, "If you brought coffee, it could theoretically be beneficial."

Another wheeze. "Not bad, Doc, but don't give up your day job. So we're two for dinner?"

Milo said, "Three."

"A crowd." The old man braced himself on the table and leaned in close. "So. An ISIS guy is crawling through the desert. He sees another guy off in the distance and heads for him. Turns out to be an old Jew selling neckties. 'Gimme water,' he screams. Jewish guy says, 'Got no water, just neckties. Good-looking silks, designer labels, terrific prices.' ISIS guy goes nuts, threatens to cut off the Jewish guy's head. Jewish guy says, 'My fault all I got is ties? By the way, there's a few rayons left, they look like silk and are even cheaper.' ISIS guy is going *crazy,* now. Reaches for his knife to cut off the Jewish guy's head and realizes he doesn't have it. Doesn't have nothing. Plus, he's weak and tired and thirsty. Jewish guy says, 'I also got some knits, very Ivy League, but if you want water, there's a place a mile up.' ISIS guy takes off. An hour later, he crawls back to the Jewish guy, looking even more *shtupped* up, tongue out, panting, he's a mess. Jewish guy says, 'What, you couldn't find it?' ISIS *meshugenah*—he's barely talking, now, more like croaking—he says, 'I found it all right, but they require a tie!'"

Without waiting for a reaction, he scurried off.

When I stopped laughing, Milo said, "He's ninety-two, eats everything, I find him inspiring." His eyes swung to the right. "This is probably our new buddy."

A squarely built, shaved-head six-footer with skin the color of hot chocolate stood near the crowd. Fiftyish, gray sharkskin suit, black shirt, silver tie. After appraising the room, he nodded and headed for us.

Milo shifted to his left, allowing space for Marcus Coolidge to sit between us.

Coolidge said, "Good to meet you, Milo."

"Same here, Marcus."

"Marc's fine." Coolidge unbuttoned his jacket, revealing a trace of shoulder holster. As he slid in, his eyes shifted to me.

Milo said, "Dr. Alex Delaware, our consulting psychologist."

"Doctor." Coolidge and I shook hands. When he'd settled and smoothed his tie, he said, "Psychologist. You have one full-time?"

"Nope, as needed."

"My situation, hard to say what I'd need, psychology-wise. Maybe some hypnotism, convince the predators they're lemmings and herd them off a cliff?" Coolidge arranged a napkin on his lap. "Pastrami on its way?"

"We haven't ordered yet." Milo looked at the counter and nodded. Mel baby-stepped our way, carrying two mugs of coffee. It took a while for him to reach the booth. Placing the cups down with great care, he looked at Coolidge. "Finally, we get the chief of police?"

Milo said, "This is Detective Coolidge."

"Two detectives and a shrink. Walk into a bar. Uh-oh, nope it's a restaurant. You want coffee, too—is your first name Calvin?"

"Marc. I'll take tea. Earl Grey if you have it."

"*Veddy* sophisticated," said Mel. "What'll it be food-wise, Oh Ye Three Magi?"

Milo said, "Detective Coolidge and I are having the pastrami."

"I recommend with the fat," said Mel. "Otherwise there's no taste."

"Absolutely," said Coolidge.

"Cholesterol bravery, we need that in detectives. You, Carl Jung?"

"Coffee for now, a roast beef and a pastrami to go."

"What, you eat in private? Ain't that some kind of neurosis?"

"Taking it home to my girlfriend."

"Girlfriend, not wife? Why not commit—don't answer that," said Mel. "I got one of those myself. A girlfriend. *Did* the wife thing. Twice. So I get it."

He got close enough for me to pick up his scent. Old clothes plus Old Spice. "You want to make it sound exotic, Doc, call her your *paramour.*"

He shuffled off.

Marc Coolidge said, "Entertainment and no cover charge?"

Milo said, "West L.A.'s a full-service shop."

"Mine, I'm lucky to get fast food."

A young waitress brought Coolidge's tea. "Mel's on break, I'll be taking over."

From the counter, Mel waved, then resumed talking to a woman a couple of decades his junior and a head taller.

Marc Coolidge said, "Ready to hear about your case."

Milo filled him in.

Coolidge said, "Four in a limo, I get two in a Camaro. What's next, one in a Prius? Half of one on a Harley?"

"Bite your tongue."

"Consider it bitten. So the link between my victims to yours is McGann worked at the place where this Alvarez lived?"

"That's it, so far."

"You're thinking she found something out about Alvarez and stuck her nose into it and got into trouble?"

"At this point, it's the only thing that seems to make sense."

"Unless there's just a bastard who enjoys killing people and stashing them in vehicles."

Coolidge sipped his tea, placed the bag on the saucer of his cup.

"I'm sure you feel like I do about coincidences. So yeah, it's hard to see McGann as *not* related, but there *are* differences. Your thing sounds elaborate. All that posing—like one of those Christmas things—a crèche, but evil."

"Alex calls it a production."

Coolidge thought about that. "Sure, that, too. Mine, on the other hand, seemed to be what I usually get. Strong-arm 211, get rid of witnesses and turn it into a 187. Those cases, they usually do the guy first, he's bigger, more of a threat, then the girl. Sometimes she gets raped. But so far no sign of sexual assault on McGann."

I said, "There could be another reason for that sequence. The Camaro's trunk space is eleven or so square feet and the opening's small. Tough to get someone Vollmann's size in."

"You know the dimensions by heart," said Coolidge.

"Looked them up on the way over."

Coolidge turned to Milo. "You're a lucky man—that's a good point, Doctor. As is, McGann was curled up like a fetus."

Milo said, "Not enough blood for it to happen in the car. Something else we've got in common."

Coolidge nodded. "I checked the driver's-seat position and it fit Vollmann. But he's six feet tall, which could be plenty of guys. All that moving and driving and dumping, been wondering about at least two killers. Which isn't weird for me, a gang thing and all that. I just busted a quintet doing home invasions."

Milo said, "Our vics were posed."

Coolidge said, "Yeah, nut-so. No, nothing like that and no dog blood—man, that *is* bizarre. Truth is, you hadn't called me, I'd never have assumed anything psycho. Maybe there isn't."

Milo said, "But coincidences."

Coolidge nodded. "We're atheists about coincidences."

I said, "If McGann was just a problem to be solved, there wouldn't necessarily be anything psycho."

A long sip of tea brought beads of sweat to Coolidge's forehead. He loosened his tie. "So the key might be finding out what, if anything, McGann knew about Alvarez."

Milo said, "God willing, Marc. There's something else common to both scenes: Our vic Gurnsey was stabbed in the upper torso like Vollmann."

Coolidge sat up. "Really? How many times?"

"Three cuts, all potentially fatal."

"Oh. So not the same."

I said, "The killer could've had time with Gurnsey but been under pressure with Vollmann. Unless he's a surgeon, aiming a blade that precisely would be a challenge."

"Even so, Doctor, he misses the first time, why not just keep stabbing?" He pantomimed three rapid thrusts. "Vollmann's already in shock, wouldn't take that much time to hit an artery or something."

I said, "My bet is our four were killed separately but Vollmann and McGann were taken simultaneously. And while Vollmann was being killed, McGann would have to be managed, meaning additional time pressure. Nothing quicker than a shotgun."

Coolidge tapped the table. "She's screaming, crying. Yeah, I can see that. When was their flight?"

Milo said, "Don't know yet, just that they never made it."

"Like I told you, my pathologist best-guesses it as Sunday morning."

"After ours but around the time ours were found."

"If it is the same bad guys, we're talking busy busy." Coolidge rotated his cup, spilled a few drops, mopped them with a napkin.

"Here you go, guys." The waitress served the sandwiches. Both detectives dug in stoically, as if consuming was their latest assignment.

"Still nothing for you, sir?"

"Bring him a salad," said Milo.

Her eyes darted from him to me. "What kind?"

Milo said, "Anything green and virtuous."

"All lettuce is virtuous, Lieutenant."

Coolidge laughed.

Milo said, "Dressing on the side, doesn't matter what type, he's not going to have much."

The waitress stared at me. Problem child being discussed by the adults.

I said, "Mixed green."

When she was gone, Coolidge said, "I make your rank, I also get to run the world?"

Milo said, "You bet, it's in the contract."

"Hah. So what do you figure next on this mess?"

"We both keep working."

"Yeah, what else is there," said Coolidge. "Though it used to be more fun, right? You see this year's FBI report? National close rate for murder is down to fifty-four percent. Mine's a little higher but not much."

Milo's solve rate had remained perfect for years. He said, "Too many stranger homicides."

"That and just plain crazy stuff, what a world," said Coolidge. "Reason I'm doing better than national is because my criminals are young, stupid, and have big mouths. You'd be amazed at how many we catch because they shoot off on social media. I had one genius last year, got a tattoo across his chest depicting how he shot a guy. Used an excellent artist, more detailed than our sketchers."

Milo said, "Talk about a still life."

Coolidge laughed. "More like a war scene. Brain-dead dumbo lays it out: setting, weapon, what they both were wearing. I didn't even need to ask motive, there's a big banner across the fool's nipples spelling out his gang motto and the need to avenge some dude who got wasted the month before. Idiot's lawyer shows him the photos of his torso, he's like, 'Oh.' "

"Amazing."

"I say pass a law against any education in prison. Criminals smarten up, the rates drop even lower." Coolidge looked at his remaining half sandwich. "Think I'll take it home. Got one of my kids for the weekend, he's a carnivore."

Milo said, "Got *no* kids," and dove into what was left of his dinner.

Coolidge watched him with admiration. "I don't see any obvious way to go on mine other than keep checking in with informants."

"Sounds like a plan, Marc."

"Not much of one."

"I'm not exactly blazing a pathway to victory."

"But there's a difference, my man," said Coolidge. "Your case is whack and you've got a psychologist."

Outside the deli, Milo said, "You want I can get the victim's warrant on Vollmann and McGann's place."

"No argument there." Coolidge glanced at the curb. A sleek black Audi, a few years old but beautifully maintained, was parked in front of the deli.

Milo said, "Yours? Nice."

"Be good to myself," said Coolidge. "This year's resolution. Same as every other year."

CHAPTER 23

Saturday morning I slept in until eight thirty. More rehab than recreation; trying to squeeze some brain-rest out of a night filled with bloody images.

Nearly a week had passed since the horror on Ascot Lane. People abused as children get good at compartmentalizing and I'm no exception. For most of the week, I'd intellectualized the slaughter, putting on blinders by concentrating on the details.

Now the totality was hitting me. Another pile of pictures never to be deleted.

Robin's side of the bed was empty. I found her in the kitchen, drinking coffee and reading. One hand dangled and tickled the top of Blanche's knobby head.

She put down her book and warmed me with a smile. "Morning, darling. Eggs okay?"

"Perfect."

She got up and I caught her midway to the fridge and kissed her. When I let go, I made sure to show her a smiling face and relaxed shoulders. Then I sat and took over massaging Blanche.

Neither of the females in my life was fooled.

Blanche looked up at me with a cocked head, big brown eyes full of pity. Robin took out the egg carton and said, "Tough night, huh?"

"I kept you up?"

"Only when you thrashed—don't apologize, we all go through it."

"Not you."

"Oh, yes, I'm perfect, darling. Remember two months ago? That piece of Adirondack spruce I paid a fortune for, I get it here and it splinters?"

"Don't remember you thrashing."

"I'm a jaw-grinder. Had headaches for a week." She cracked five eggs into a bowl and whisked. "You gently rubbed my temples."

"Did it help?"

"The fact that you cared helped. Plain scrambled or with stuff? There's some of that pastrami from last night."

"Stuff sounds good."

"Bring whatever you want from the fridge then call Milo."

"About what?"

"He phoned half an hour ago, we didn't get into details, you know how he shields me." She smiled. "Not wanting to upset perfection."

How much *I* tell her has been an issue for us. This time I'd given her enough basics not to feel marginalized. But no sense piling on the cruelest details.

I said, "Gallant."

"When he pushes the right button, he's got it in him."

I headed for my office.

Robin said, "When he asked where you were, I told him you were snoozing."

"And he made a crack, right? Let me guess: Prince Charming getting his beauty sleep. Babe in dreamland?"

"Nope. He said you deserved it."

◆

No answer at Milo's office phone. I tried his cell.

He said, "Risen and shiny? Cucumbers off the eyes, yet?"

"Like you said, salad's virtuous. What's up?"

"Waiting to hear from McGann and Vollmann's landlord. Meanwhile, Alicia gets a five-course dinner, place of her choosing. She found two shelters Huralnik drifted in and out of. At the second one she got tipped to an encampment where Huralnik slept when she was in the mood for not-so-fresh air and *that* led to two others."

"Any of the places near Skaggs?"

"Four miles away, warehouse district, the jungle keeps expanding east. Several homeless told her the same thing: Huralnik would disappear for days, even weeks. One guy swore to seeing her in Santa Monica. So she coulda been anywhere when she got abducted."

And yet, he sounded buoyant.

I said, "Doesn't narrow it down much."

"True but I'm taking a page from your optimism book: It doesn't *eliminate* the area around Skaggs. Main reason I'm calling is something else they said about Huralnik. She could suddenly get hypersexual. That a symptom of schizophrenia?"

"It can be. What did she do?"

"Her thing was to approach someone in an encampment—male or female—and offer to trade money for sex. If she was refused, she'd pull down her pants and say let's do it anyway. If the answer was still no, her reaction was unpredictable. Sometimes she'd walk away muttering but other times she'd turn aggressive—wheedling, insulting, even pushing and shoving. A few men called her 'the grabber.' As in reaching for what one guy called 'my manly manhood.'"

"The pose with Gurnsey," I said.

"Art imitating life, Alex. Until now, the two of them being paired seemed like a sick joke. Now we know they had something in common."

"Behavior and maybe motive: payback for coming on too strong."

"O great mystic mind reader."

"That would mean Gurnsey and Huralnik hit on the same person."

"Why not? With Gurnsey it coulda been a bona fide date, with Huralnik just some crazy thing that happened on the street."

"She groped the wrong person," I said. "So how does Benny figure in?"

"What, I'm supposed to know everything? My question to you is, would someone overreacting like that have a history of being abused?"

"It's certainly possible."

"Could you spring for 'likely'?"

"You know what I'm going to say."

"Yeah, yeah, insufficient data. But it's not *un*likely."

I laughed.

He said, "I'll choose to take that as an endorsement. You have a nice weekend planned?"

"Nothing on the calendar."

"Enjoy. No reason to watch me toss Vollmann and McGann's place. Probably won't learn a damn thing, 'cause no one writes anything down anymore. I'm lucky, one of them will have a laptop they didn't pack. I'm not, it's back to the phone companies."

"You need me, let me know."

"You're the top of my call list."

Nothing from him until Sunday at six p.m.

"Finally got into Marcella and Steve's apartment. No laptop but miracle of miracles, one of them did write down their flight info and magnet it to the refrigerator. Sunday morning, like Coolidge's pathologist guessed. Called the airline and verified. No cancellation, just a no-show. So Coolidge is probably right: waylaid on the way to LAX."

I said, "How early Sunday morning?"

"Seven forty-five."

"They'd have to leave while it was still dark and the streets were relatively deserted. Perfect for running them off the road or some other type of blitz."

He said, "The time frame also fits: Benny goes missing on Friday, McGann, by herself or with Vollmann, goes looking for him that day or Saturday, by early Sunday she's history. But what bothers me is if she learned something, she didn't report it."

"Maybe she didn't realize she'd learned anything, just had the bad luck to ask the wrong person the wrong question. Someone capable of the limo slaughter wouldn't balk at taking out insurance. The question is, Where would McGann go searching? My guess is somewhere between the facility and the art gallery. Maybe the gallery, itself."

"Benny did get to work," he said. "He just never left alive . . . Jesus . . . hold on."

A minute passed.

He said, "Called Verlang, a woman answered, so they're finally open. You have time for a little culture?"

CHAPTER 24

I picked him up in front of the station at six thirty-five p.m. Dressed as close to stylish as I'd ever seen: gray suit, black shirt, skinny brown tie. Pointy black oxfords instead of the desert boots.

I said, "New shoes?"

"Italian. Rick's."

We took the Seville at his request: "We're talking art and your wheels are a lot more aesthetic."

The drive downtown was a surprisingly smooth cruise on the 10 East slowed by construction detours and the need to navigate mostly empty one-way streets.

I found parking at a lot on Sixth and we walked to Hart Street, passing dark storefronts and several homeless people with placards, all of whom Milo ignored. No less altruistic by nature than with the legless man; preoccupied.

We stood across the street watching as a swarm of people crowded the sidewalk in front of Verlang Contemporary. A sign in the window read *Melted Visions: An Opening.*

The two neighboring galleries remained dark, as were the jeweler and the building's top two floors. The only other illumination on the block came from The Flower Drum motel's empty lobby. Clerk sitting alone in a glass-encased booth working his phone.

Milo said, "Hipster crowd. Think we can fake it?"

I pointed to the tie. "That doesn't do it, we could go arm-in-arm if you don't tell Robin and I don't tell Rick."

He laughed but not for very long. Narrowing his eyes, he watched the crowd for a few seconds. A single car passed. Then a bicyclist wearing a knit cap, pedaling a rattling one-gear with effort.

"Okay, here we go."

No security at the door, just a thin girl in a matte-black dress and matching hair offering every arrival a plastic flute of something amber-colored and bubbly followed by a nearly inaudible "Welcome." Her eyelids were smeared with something waxy and charcoal-colored. Hollow cheeks, painted-on eyebrows, the right-hand arc pierced by a little black ring.

The robotic greeting and a faraway stare said human contact was a contagious disease.

Not even a glance at Milo's tie.

The gallery was jammed with mostly thin people and a few obese exceptions drinking when they weren't moving their lips. The layout was a single long room painted flat white and floored in scarred pine. Track lights suspended from a central beam fifteen feet above showcased twenty or so large canvases.

The artist: Geoffrey Dugong.

Milo said, "Isn't that some sort of seal?"

"Sea cow."

"Now I know why I brought you."

The thickest clot of chatterers had collected in the center of the room, as if herded by a sheepdog. More eyes on one another than the art. Milo and I circulated slowly and gingerly so as not to be noticed. No need to worry, not a lot of other-directedness going around.

We finally arrived at the edge of the crowd and got a look at Geoffrey Dugong's work.

The name of the exhibit was literal: loose acrylic renderings of the same white candle in various stages of liquefaction over a black background.

We took one-page bios from a stack on a card table. Dugong's bio specified little beyond his birth in Key West, Florida, and his work on fishing boats. On the flip side, a brief note by the gallery's owner, Medina Okash, was even less informative. Written in the least comprehensive language on the planet: artspeak.

Geoffrey's assumption of the identity of an endangered benthic mammal: simultaneously idiomatic and conceptual.
Growing up near the Atlantic, the pedestrian impulse would be to morph-adopt-become a local avatar: the manatee.
With incisive contrariness abandoning all notions of entitlement, loftiness, and class, Geoffrey made the excruciating choice to lade his consciousness with the unknown, a snouted denizen of African/Pacific/non-Atlantic nobility: the dugong.
Swimming against all tides, neap, ebb, and tsunami, represents Geoffrey's approach to making art.
Be unexpected. Be woke. Be brave.
The candle is by nature transitory. So is life.
So is reality. So is meaning.
Everything changes.
Everything melts.

Milo said, "Now I understand."

We edged past a couple of the paintings. A man with a narrow goatee long enough to be constricted in two spots by gold rings said, "I did this one when I was thinking about migraines and perspiration." Midforties, long, wild curly gray hair, deeply tanned, hawk-face. When he spoke, nothing but his mouth moved.

The woman listening to him said, "Sweat purifies. Lakota or Chumash?"

Beard-ring walked away from her. She turned to a bald, scowling man behind her. "I like his attitude, maybe we should buy one."

"Are you fucking crazy? He's an asshole."

"Exactly, Dom. We could use some of that energy. A little pushback to the Warhols."

Bald walked away. The woman, alone, saw us and smiled.

Milo said, "When I hear sweat, I think Turkish bath."

"That's true," said the woman. "Are you an artist?"

"More of a craftsman."

"What's your medium?"

"Rare."

We walked away. The woman looked at the painting, then into her purse.

We made our way to a corner with another card table, this one used for empty glasses. Our bubbly, untouched, found a home. Milo worked his phone and pulled up an image.

Pie-faced woman in her thirties. Blue-gray eyes, pageboy dyed the purplish gray of an old bruise, complexion pale enough to suggest Kabuki makeup.

Medina Okash was more into biography than her featured artist. Born thirty-six years ago in Seattle, B.A. in fine arts from the University of Oregon, certificate in curatorial science from the Gurnitz Institute in Bern, Switzerland, employment at a minor New York auction house followed by stints at Lower Manhattan art dealers.

She'd opened her own gallery six months ago.

Her mission statement: Be fearless.

Armed with the image, finding her was simple. Same everything except for the hair, now electric blue. She held glasses in both hands, drank from each in turn as she nodded at whatever a pair of men in matching black suits and red T-shirts was telling her. Identical twins down to the anorexia. They traded off speaking, one sentence at a time.

Medina Okash's head moved from side to side, following the duet. A couple of times she threw back her head and laughed loud enough to be heard over the crowd.

Milo said, "Friendly, maybe that'll extend to us."

The merriment seemed staged to me. I said nothing as we waited. When the twins drifted away, we walked up to her.

Appraising smile. "Hi, you two."

Milo said, "Good show."

"Geoffrey's a force to be reckoned with." Okash looked at her drinks, then at our empty hands. "Don't like Prosecco? It's muy tasty."

Milo patted his gut. "Moderation."

"Is for people who doubt themselves," said Medina Okash, placing a fingertip on his gut and rotating slowly. "Feels luscious and gorgeous to me."

Milo managed a smile. The things we do in the call of duty.

She switched to me, fingertipping my turtleneck precisely over my navel. "A little more L.A.-toned for you . . . ooh, an innie. So where do I know you guys—the Harrison thing last month? Or was it Art Basel Miami?"

Milo flipped his lapel just wide enough to show her his badge.

Generally that evokes shock. Medina Okash's affect didn't change. "Police. Let me guess: Benny."

Milo nodded. "We came by earlier but you were closed."

Okash took in the crowd behind us. "Obviously, this isn't really a good time so if you could come back tomorrow—ya know, scratch that. Time is nothing more than the longest distance between two places."

I said, "Tennessee Williams."

A painted eyebrow arched. She knuckled my arm lightly. "A cop who appreciates literature. Let us chit and chat."

We followed her to a door at the back of the gallery. She opened it and waited as we stepped through. Brushing Milo's arm as he passed. Doing the same to me and adding an instant of hip-to-hip pressure.

Expressionless throughout the contact; the who-me? demeanor of a kid trying something naughty.

The back room was a storage area set up with floor-to-ceiling vertical racks. Every gallery rear I've seen is crammed with canvases. Verlang Contemporary housed less than a dozen paintings, all wrapped in brown paper.

Medina Okash said, "I'm assuming you're here because Marcella told you Benny worked here."

Flat voice, matching eyes.

Milo nodded. "You know Marcella McGann."

"Not well enough to know that's her surname," said Okash. "To me she's Marcella the woman who takes care of Benny. She got Benny hired."

"Did she."

"Oh, yes. She showed up one day, told me about the place she worked, and asked if I could help out by giving one of her residents something to do, he liked to draw. My first thought was, *Who needs the complication?* Then I thought, *You've always appreciated outsider art, Medina. Why not help an actual outsider?*"

"What did Benny do here?"

"Swept up, straightened, accepted deliveries. If I was here cataloging he'd let me know someone was at the door. I'd send him to get food if a yummy truck was nearby. Mostly he just hung around. No problem, very sweet. And actually very diligent. At first Marcella or someone else from the home would walk him and pick him up. Then, maybe a week in, he began making the trip himself."

I said, "Did he ever report any problems during the walk?"

"Never," said Medina Okash. "So he still hasn't come home? That's not good."

Sympathetic words. But no affect to match.

Milo said, "When did Marcella drop by?"

"Saturday morning."

"Do you remember what time?"

"Maybe . . . ten? I came in through there." Pointing to a second back door. "I wasn't open for business, caught up prepping for the show. I heard pounding on the front door, figured some homeless person is going bonkers, went out to see. If it looked sketchy I was ready to call 911."

"Have you done that before?"

"Not yet but one needs to keep one's eyes open, right?"

"Right. So Marcella was the one knocking."

"She and some guy. He's just standing there but she's waving her hands and looking agitated. I let them in and she goes on about Benny not coming home the day before. You're here so I guess he still hasn't."

Milo said, "He'll never come home, Ms. Okash."

"What do you mean?"

Out came the card.

Okash read it, eyes scanning slowly. "Really? Oh, fuck, that's disgusting. That is truly dis*gust*ing. What the fuck happened?"

Not shocked; annoyed.

"That's what we're trying to find out," said Milo. "Did Benny show up for work on Friday?"

"Sure, the usual, around elevenish. Normally, he leaves between two and four, I'm flexible. That day I had to be out for the afternoon, got back at four thirty and assumed he'd left."

"Benny was here by himself."

Okash folded her arms across her chest. "He wasn't a child and the deal wasn't I had to babysit him."

"He could just let himself out."

"The door self-locks."

"So Marcella showed up Saturday. You'd heard nothing from her the day Benny didn't come home?"

Okash's eyes turned icy. "All these questions. I have to say I'm starting to feel uncomfortable."

"About?"

"Being questioned like a suspect. I did someone a favor, that's all—and yes, turns out Marcella did call me on Friday. I was busy, didn't check for messages."

"Don't mean to upset you," said Milo. "It's just in cases like these we need to talk to everyone."

"There's talk and there's inquisition."

The door to the front room swung open hard enough to bang against the wall. Letting in crowd noise and Geoffrey Dugong. The painter's body canted forward.

Unlike Okash, an animated face: eyes blazing, cheeks flushed, mouth working.

"You leave me the fuck alone out there! I'm supposed to talk to these fuck-brains by myself?"

Okash regarded him the way a pedestrian looks at dogshit. "I'll be out in a second, Geoffrey."

"You better—who the fuck are *you*?"

Milo said, "Maybe potential clients."

Dugong's head snapped back. "Yeah. Fine. Doesn't give you the right to fuck up my opening."

He stomped out.

Medina Okash said, "Artists." As if she couldn't care less.

CHAPTER 25

As we made our way out of the gallery, I searched for Dugong in the crowd. In a corner, blocking one of his paintings as he sulked and gulped Prosecco. Not even pretending to listen to a shaved-head, six-foot woman's arm-waving description of something.

Angry eyes. No red dots on any of the paintings indicating a sale. Reacting to that or was his emotional thermostat set permanently on high?

We stepped outside into soothing silence and headed up Hart. The same homeless people plus a few more. The stench of self-neglect assaulted the cool spring air in noxious bursts. This time Milo handed out money. A few blessings, a lot of stupor.

He said, "The mayor lets it get this way and also thinks he can be president—problem is maybe he can."

I said, "Geoffrey's got a temper problem."

"He does, indeed. What'd you think of Medina?"

"Never had my belly button appraised before."

"Touchy-feely but cold," he said. "The way she stood in the doorway and did this." Caressing his sleeve. "Like being prodded during a physical."

"I got that plus a love-bump, here." Patting my flank.

"Now I'm jealous—fine, you're cuter."

"She's also got a protégé who comes unglued easily and the gallery was Benny's last destination before being killed. I find all that interesting."

"Fascinating," he said. "I mean it."

As I drove, he ran Okash through the databases. "Well, well, well, our girl's got a record, all in New York. Three DUIs and one cocaine but also an assault conviction . . . looks like she cut up another woman outside a Lower East Side bar, served seven months of a two-year sentence at the Bedford Hills women's prison. One bust but it's still serious violence. Maybe she just got craftier."

I said, "One thing for sure, she learned to suppress her emotions. Or never had a problem in the first place. Dugong's a loose cannon but she wasn't thrown an inch by his tantrum."

"Yeah, I saw that, patronizing. You're an idiot child, Geoffy."

"She didn't mention Dugong being with her on Saturday when she was setting up his show but artists often participate. And the prep could've begun earlier. As in Friday, when Benny was there."

His shoulders bunched as he pushed his palms against the glove compartment door. "Okash coulda lied about leaving Benny alone in the gallery. If Dugong could get that pissed about Okash ducking out for a minute, a slow guy like Benny making some kind of mistake could've really set him off. He drags Benny to the back, shoots him in the head. Poor guy went in but never came out."

I said, "Small-caliber bullet, the mess would've been manageable. But the show was coming up so the body needed to be moved. Friday, Benny doesn't return, McGann gets worried about Benny and phones the gallery. Okash ignores her, so the following morning, before she's due to leave for Mexico, McGann and Vollmann show up and ask the wrong questions. Like Coolidge said, Vollmann was a big guy, so he was subdued first with a knife then obliterated by a shotgun in order to delay identification. Okash and Dugong find the airline tickets, wait until after dark, and dump the bodies near the airport, where it'll look like what Coolidge assumed: a wrong-way gang thing. They use Vollmann's Camaro for transport and another vehicle to get away."

He stayed silent. I maneuvered the downtown interchange, got on the 10 West, and passed three exits.

I said, "The only problem is Benny's murder being an impulsive lashing out by Dugong doesn't fit with three other victims and the choreography we saw in the limo. So what if by the time Benny showed up on Friday he'd been long groomed for victimhood. Because he fit a role in a script. The worst kind of casting call."

"Back to the production thing." He slapped the glove compartment door. "I've got something fits better, Alex. What planet do Okash and Dugong inhabit? Maybe we need to start thinking about performance art."

My gut tightened. Good sign. "I like it."

"I'm developing a major *crush* on it—okay, time to check out this *artiste's* history."

He returned to his phone, clicked awhile, and sat back. "Just petty stuff in Florida, some under Dugong, most under his real name, Jeffrey Mitchell Dowd." He scrolled. "Weed, weed, DUI, weed, DUI, cocaine, weed. All personal use, total of . . . five days' jail time over twelve years. Why the hell couldn't he be cooperatively violent?"

"What if meeting Okash changed that?"

"Femme fatale?"

I said, "She could be his patron in more ways than one. From what I saw, if they do have a relationship, she's the dominant one. Meaning she could be free to explore sexually, like with Ricky Gurnsey. And it's not a stretch to see Gurnsey being attracted to all that sexual energy."

"Medina and Ricky against a hedge. Hmh."

I said, "Geoffrey goes along with it until he doesn't."

"The two of them work through their relationship issues by killing four people?"

"More like taking it to the next step."

As I cruised the 10 West at the ambient thirty per, Milo conference-called Reed and Binchy, caught them up, told them to begin a two-man surveillance on the gallery and Okash's address on Fountain Avenue, in Hollywood.

Reed said, "What about sea-mammal guy?"

Binchy began humming "I Am the Walrus."

Milo said, "Glad I caught you kids during happy time. No local address on Dugong, so far. He home-bases in Key West. You get lucky, he's staying with Okash and one watch handles everything."

"Got it," said Reed, sounding a bit chastened. "How should we divide it up?"

"As you see fit. And *stay* happy."

Next step: educating Alicia Bogomil and assigning her to return to the homeless camps where Mary Jane Huralnik had slept rough.

She said, "Still working Roget's ads with nothing to show, so thanks for letting me shift gears. These people sound bizarre, L.T. Who picks an ugly animal for a name?"

"And here I was considering Willy Warthog for my new avatar. Yeah, they're different."

"Hart Street," she said. "Not a huge hike from some of the home-less camps."

"Just saw a bunch of homeless on the same block, for all we know Mary Jane got lured inside right there. So, yeah, ask if anyone's ever seen her near there."

"On it, boss. And here I was thinking arty types were delicate."

◆

I was nearing the Western Avenue exit when Milo's phone abused Beethoven's Fifth by repeating the first four notes at a frantic pace and chipmunk frequency.

"Sturgis—oh, hi, Doctor. No, sorry, I wish there was . . . when? Of course. I can meet you at your father's place or you're welcome to come to the station . . . sure, see you then."

I said, "Roget's son?"

"He's here along with his sister. Coroner okayed releasing the body, they're taking care of business, want to meet tomorrow."

"What time?"

"Nothing to tell them so don't bother."

"Can't hurt to know as much as possible about the victim. When?"

"Three p.m."

I handed him my phone. "Use the TrackSmart app and check my schedule."

"Look at you, all computer-courant . . . says here you're booked until one thirty."

"What's the address?"

"Two can play cyber-efficient," he said, typing. "I'm entering the data directly."

CHAPTER 26

Dr. Hillaire Roget was five-six in shoes, compactly built, with a closely cropped head of dense white hair and a mustache to match. He wore a beautifully tailored olive-green suit, a white dress shirt, and perforated shoes the color of peanut butter.

His sister, Dr. Madeleine Roget-Cohen, was at least five-nine in shoes, slim and broad-shouldered with an artfully styled head of straightened, hennaed hair.

I'd seen their father's corpse and knew him to be tall. My guess was short mother, one of those random shuffles of the genetic deck.

They sat close to each other on one of two spotless, matching blue sofas in what had once been Solomon Roget's living room. The apartment was what I'd expected from Milo's account of his search. Sparely but adequately furnished, impeccably kept when you considered no one had tended it for the week-plus since the murders. Photos of a young Solomon with a pretty wife shared space with shots of the children from toddlerhood to med school graduation, then the grandkids. Where lineage didn't rule the walls, Roget had hung prints of Haiti portrayed as a tropical Eden.

Before Milo knocked on the door, he'd asked if I should be identified as a psychologist.

I said, "Why not? How people react is always interesting."

The Roget sibs had reacted by nodding, shaking my hand briefly, then looking away. After Milo and I sat, Madeleine said, "Does that mean there's a psychiatric component to the crime?"

Milo said, "When I spoke to your brother, Doctor, I told him I couldn't get into details. That's still true but what I can tell you is your father wasn't the only victim. There were three others, in the back of his limousine."

Hillaire said, "We know that, Lieutenant. Googled and came up with a crime that fit."

Madeleine said, "All the accounts list the location as Beverly Hills but when we ran map searches, it's in Los Angeles."

"True," said Milo.

"So there may be other inaccuracies?"

"There usually are."

Silence.

Milo said, "Everything points to your dad being an innocent bystander. He drove the wrong client."

Hillaire said, "Does that mean one of the three in the back was the killer?"

"No chance of that, sir. Best guess is they were already dead by the time your father picked up the killer."

"He was used for his car," said Madeleine.

"That's the working assumption, ma'am."

"And you have no idea who this devil is."

"The problem is your father didn't have an online presence, he didn't leave behind any written logs, and the only number on his phone list that conceivably matches the time frame belongs to a non-traceable pay-as-you-go phone."

"The kind criminals use," said Madeleine.

"Yes, ma'am."

Hillaire said, "So you've searched here in the apartment?"

"Soon after," said Milo.

The siblings looked at each other.

Milo said, "You thought I hadn't?"

Madeleine said, "It's so tidy, doesn't look as if anything's been disturbed."

"I try to conduct my searches with respect."

Hillaire sighed. "Please excuse us for thinking you were dilatory." His voice choked. "Thank you for honoring our father's home."

"Of course. Have you done any looking around?"

"This morning," said Madeleine. Small smile. "We weren't as neat as you. We also found nothing that seemed—would the word be 'probative'?"

"Evidentiary," said her brother.

"In any event, we learned nothing, Lieutenant. Though we did come up with some photos of our parents back when Mother was alive."

Milo said, "Small leather album in the top right-hand dresser drawer."

Madeleine smiled.

Hillaire said, "Father was always on us to be tidy."

Madeleine said, "We weren't always compliant." Her turn to choke up.

Both of them began to cry.

Milo tapped his supply of tissues and gave one to each of them.

Madeleine was the first to break the silence, letting out a raspy laugh. "You certainly come prepared."

Milo smiled.

"What a job you have, Lieutenant. Maybe it's good you're here, Dr. Delaware. Maybe we could use some therapy."

◆

We listened as son and daughter reminisced about Solomon Roget's virtues as a single parent, his pride at their accomplishments, their wish that he'd moved to Florida and lived closer to them.

Madeleine said, "We're not going to get caught up in if he had, he'd still be alive." A brief turn-down of her lips said she'd been there and hadn't quite moved on. "What would be the point? Father was a proud, independent man. We needed to respect that."

"As if we had a choice," said Hillaire.

His sister touched his wrist briefly. "Exactly, as if."

"We have our own kids," said Hillaire. "We have expectations but in the end everyone has to live their own life."

Madeleine said, "Father lived a good one."

"Exemplary." Flash of anger in Hillaire's eyes. "Lieutenant, whoever did this needs to be held accountable. From my understanding, you have the death penalty in California but it's a joke, you never actually use it."

Milo said, "Unfortunately, that's true."

Madeleine said, "Years of stupid appeals, the devils get to live out their lives with TV and gyms and three meals a day."

"In Florida," said Hillaire, "we execute devils. Too bad Father *didn't* move back."

She put her arm around him. "Don't, Hill."

"You're right—I suppose this will continue for a while. The process."

She said, "Fluctuating emotionally."

Both of them looked at me.

I said, "It will."

Profound, scholarly contribution. But the Roget sibs seemed to appreciate it, loosening their shoulders and facial muscles.

"Well," said Hillaire, "it's good to know we're not notably maladjusted. Thanks for meeting with us, Lieutenant. You, too, Doctor. I know we have nothing to offer but this has been helpful."

"Another step," said Madeleine.

Milo looked at Hillaire. "Dr. Roget, when we spoke last week I asked if you had any idea where your father posted his ads. Any new thoughts on that?"

"What ads?" said Madeleine.

Hillaire said, "You know, those little tear-offs he used because he refused to modernize?"

She turned to us. "Why would you want to know about that?"

Milo said, "Some locales that provide space for free ads—markets, convenience stores—have closed-circuit cameras. If we could get a look at who tore off your dad's ads during the weeks before his death, it could conceivably help. We've searched within several miles of here and haven't come up with anything."

"Conceivably?" said Hillaire.

"Often the cameras don't work or they provide poor images or they're not aimed where we want them to be. It's also possible the killer found him another way—say, word of mouth."

Madeleine said, "The tear-offs. I can think of a place."

Her brother's head whipped sideways.

"Maybe it's nothing," she said, "but there's a market Father liked to go to. Not close to here, so you wouldn't find it. He'd make the trip because he claimed he could get the best Caribbean groceries."

Hillaire said, "J&M! My God, I'm so stupid!" Slapping his own cheek.

His sister lowered his arm. "You're human not a computer."

He shook his head.

She said, "Really, Hill. It may not even be relevant."

Hillaire stared straight ahead.

Milo said, "Doctor, your sister's right, we grasp at lots of straws. But I'll check it out." Out came his pad. "J&M—"

"J&M Caribbean Market," said Madeleine. "Western Avenue, near the university."

"Rotten neighborhood," said Hillaire. "I told Father he could get plantains somewhere else but he insisted." Head shake. "Why didn't I *think* of it? Okay, let's be logical. What kind of paying client would Father hope to find there? To rent the limo, no less. Ghetto thugs with money—drugs, maybe one of those so-called aspiring rappers?"

"You know how Father felt about *those* people, Hill. He'd never have worked for them."

"He worked with *someone* evil."

No answer to that.

We offered a bit more sympathy and left them to the process.

The Seville was parked half a block from the Impala. Milo walked me over, waited as I unlocked, settled in the passenger seat, and began clicking.

"J&M Caribbean Market, still in business, Western and Thirty-Fifth."

I said, "Definitely gang territory."

"Same as Inglewood." He shut his eyes. "All I need, a whole new direction."

He phoned Sean Binchy.

"Loot, what's up?"

"Are you on Okash's place or is Reed?"

"I am, cut out at eleven but Moe came over from the gallery and watched all last night, so he's catching Z's."

"Nice of him to double up."

Binchy chuckled. "I'm the one with kids, Loot. Unfortunately, no action. Okash was home by eight, never came out until this morning at nine when she went to a Whole Foods, bought two bags of whatever, took them back to her apartment—it's a four-story multi-unit with a sub-lot, mailboxes inside the lobby so we don't know her unit. At ten twenty-three, she drove to the gallery, turned into an alley on the south of the building. I followed on foot and saw there's a cruddy-looking parking lot where she put her BMW. It also occurred to me that the building is pretty deep, so there's probably more space behind that storage area you diagrammed. Not much to the lot, not even painted slots, but it is card-key entry. That early, no one else there except her."

"Good work, Sean, stay on her."

"What do we do about Dugong? So far he hasn't showed up."

"He does, Moe loses sleep. Or if it's near the gallery, we pull Alicia in from skid row."

"Roger Wilco, Loot."

Milo suppressed a smile. "Over and out."

CHAPTER 27

Milo said, "Let's check out that market. You mind driving? I need to think."

I took Olympic east to San Vicente, continued past La Brea where the street turned to Venice Boulevard, hooked a right on Western, and drove a block south of Jefferson.

Tough neighborhood since the fifties, ravaged four decades later by the self-destruction sparked by the Rodney King riots. During the ensuing decades, no shortage of talk about renewal from politicians. But L.A.'s not a movie town for nothing; people get paid well to act.

Some of the storefronts had been rehabbed. More were boarded or empty and the overall feel was drab and sad.

J&M Caribbean Market was one of the bright spots, a single story of cement block painted lemon yellow and lime green, with hot-pink, bubbly-font signage asserting itself under a spotless red awning. A rolling iron accordion fence was pushed to the right side of the building.

Caribbean Food *** Natural Herbs *** Spiritual Oils.

A parking lot to the left was secured by a sliding metal-picket gate, now wide open. Two cars in the lot, a wine-colored Cadillac DeVille and a gold Buick Century. I parked between them. Three American sedans grouped like that evoked Detroit in its prime.

We walked around to the market's entrance. Dead-bolted glass door. Milo rang the bell, someone moved behind the glass, and ten seconds later we were beeped in.

The market's interior was immaculate, well lit, and fragrant—florals, citrus, a heavy layer of allspice. Fresh maple laminate covered the floor. High white walls were banded at the top by a belt of Z-Brick.

White display cases showcased bags of red beans and rice, pre-cooked meat meals, packages of "fruta" and "gandules." Conventional produce was stacked alongside plantains, okra labeled as "gumbo," and tubers I couldn't name. The beverage case cooled American beer along with Prestige from Port-au-Prince, Red Stripe and Gong 71st fruit beer from Jamaica. Cans of Coke and Pepsi and Mountain Dew shared space with golden Cola Couronne and Pineapple Ginger soda.

Behind the register, candles and the heralded herbs and oils.

One customer, a woman in her seventies, pushing a cart. A young Hispanic man swept the floor, careful to get into the corners. A dread-locked woman in her thirties worked the register.

She smiled. Warmly, instinctually. Took a closer look and said, "Police?" but held on to a sunny face.

Milo said, "Want a job as a detective?"

The woman giggled, then turned serious. "Please don't tell me something bad happened on the block. Usually I hear about it before you get here."

"Nothing, ma'am, sorry if we alarmed you. We're looking for a message board but I see you don't have one."

"Oh, we do," she said. "Juan removed it to clear and clean a few days ago—we soap and water it regularly, all those hands? When it dries out, it goes back there." Pointing to four feet of wall space at the right of the door.

"Did you by any chance hold on to any of the postings?"

"No, they're tossed. Out with the old, in with the new, that way more people get to post. Why're you interested in the board?"

"A man who we're told shopped here was murdered last week and we're trying to find a connection between anyone he did business with."

"Murdered?" Both hands took hold of her chin. "So something *did* happen."

"Not here, ma'am, on the Westside."

"The Westside—that's a switch. Who's this person?"

Milo showed her Roget's picture.

"Mr. Solomon? Oh, no."

"You know him by name."

"He wasn't a regular but he did come in enough for us to chat. And yes, he did post his ads. A chauffeur, right—poor Mr. Solomon. You think someone who hired him killed him?"

"We're looking into everything."

"It couldn't be my customers," she said. "I don't get gangsters, and the Rastas who buy from me are serious about their faith. I even get white folk. Students and faculty from USC and Mount Saint Mary's. I used to work in administration at Mount Saint Mary's, my husband's an electrician there. Last week he sent me a dean of nursing and she bought up all of my sausage. We're getting a reputation, some of those downtown hipster types are starting to come in, it's a well-behaved clientele, I wouldn't tolerate otherwise."

"Got it, Ms. . . ."

"Frieda Graham. Why would anyone hurt Mr. Solomon? He was such a gentleman . . . I know, it's a foolish question."

Milo said, "We ask ourselves the same thing pretty often."

"Some job you have. Anyway, sorry I couldn't be of more help."

"Could we show you some photos?"

"Of who?"

"People who might be involved—not suspects, just involved. We'd like to know if they've ever been here."

"I can't remember everyone, but I'll give it a try, why not."

Visual pop quiz, Frieda Graham's focus intense, her responses immediate.

Rick Gurnsey: "Nice looking . . . no."

Benny Alvarez: "*He* looks kind of frail . . . no."

Mary Ann Huralnik: "*She* looks totally out of it . . . no."

Geoffrey Dugong: "That beard, we do get some like that, like I said hipsters . . . no, not him. I'm pretty sure."

Milo said, "Pretty sure but not certain?"

"Ninety percent," said Frieda Graham. "Because if I'd seen him clean-shaven, he'd look different. But like this—those beard-rings—he reminds me of that wrestler . . . Captain Lou Albano? My dad used to watch him."

She used her hand to block the bottom half of Dugong's face, studied the eyes. "Ninety-*five* percent no, I'd remember those eyes, they're kind of crazy—have you seen Van Gogh's self-portrait?"

Milo let her stay with the photo. She handed it back, shaking her head. "I'm gonna say no. Those eyes, though—is he like a semi-suspect?"

Milo smiled and showed her Medina Okash's DMV photo.

She said, "Yes."

CHAPTER 28

"She's a customer," said Milo.

"Definitely," said Frieda Graham. "That hair—I think last time it was purple. But definitely yes, that face. I remember her because she was touchy."

"About what?"

"Not touchy-sensitive, touchy-feely. Like this."

She leaned over the counter and dabbed his shoulder lightly with a green-nailed fingertip. "Like a pecking bird. Kind of annoying but you know, the customer's always right. Hold on. Juan? Come over."

The sweeper joined us. "She's been here, right?"

He nodded.

"I told them she liked to do this." Repeating the dabbing on Juan's arm.

He laughed. "Mosquito."

Milo said, "She ever give you problems, Juan?"

"No. Just mosquito." Jabbing air. More laughter.

"Thanks."

Juan returned to his broom.

Milo turned back to Graham. "Can you remember the last time she was here?"

"Hmm," said Graham. "Not recently—maybe a month? Five, six weeks? Could even be longer. What I *can* tell you is she always bought the same thing: prepared jerk chicken dinner and Red Stripe—that's a Jamaican beer. Also veggies—yellow and purple yams. That hair, I figured her for an artist. Am I right?"

"Art dealer."

"Oh. That also makes sense. I assumed artist because one time she had a painting tucked under her arm—or maybe it was a drawing, I never actually saw it. Big, thin square wrapped in brown paper. She saw me looking at it and said she didn't want to leave it in her car. Did she pull off one of Mr. Solomon's tabs? Sorry, no idea. It's a courtesy we extend to the neighborhood, we just make sure to keep the board squeaky clean."

I said, "Don't see any security cameras."

"Oh, I've got some," said Graham. "Two in the parking lot and another outside the rear door leading to the delivery area. But for the store, I rely on my rolling gate, my dead bolt, and my alarm. So far, we've been okay. Three false alarms during the fourteen months we've been here. Old wiring."

"Do you have tape from the parking lot?"

"No, it self-cleans every forty-eight hours."

"Thanks for your time, ma'am."

"Of course. I hope you get whoever hurt Mr. Solomon."

Milo crossed his fingers and we started for the door.

Frieda Graham said, "Can I give you guys something for the road? Just got some sandwiches made by a guy who runs the best Caribbean food truck in the city."

Milo said, "Sounds great, but no thanks."

"You're sure?"

His voice and face said he was far from certain.

"Oh, c'mon." Chuckling, Frieda Graham produced four sandwiches from under the counter and handed them to him. "It's in my best interest. You'll taste and want to come back. Two chickens, one crab, one ham and pineapple. All on hard-dough bread Robert bakes himself."

Milo said, "You're too kind."

"So I've been told."

I waited for a traffic lull and turned north onto Western. "Mosquito."

Milo said, "Well equipped for drawing blood." He punched a pre-set on his phone.

The call to Deputy D.A. John Nguyen produced no surprises:

"Your intuitive suspicions of Okash might even be right but they're worthless from a legal standpoint."

"So I'm stuck, John?"

"But for my creativity you would be," said Nguyen. "Her violent assault conviction combined with the store owner's confirmation of her presence where Roget hung his ads is, in my opinion, just enough to justify a two-month phone subpoena. As in skin-of-the-teeth enough."

"What about Dugong?"

"Don't push it." Nguyen laughed. "What a fucking stupid name."

CHAPTER 29

Two hours later, Milo had commandeered the same interview room and set up a whiteboard. The only other equipment: a box of muffins from a bakery in West Hollywood.

No writing on the board, no complex mesh of directional arrows. That's for the movies where plot elements need to be explained to the audience.

This was four knowledgeable detectives and me looking at a three-by-two array of victim photos to the left and enlarged DMV shots of Medina Okash and Geoffrey Dugong to the right.

Milo summarized what we'd learned at the Caribbean market.

Bogomil said, "So we know Okash had access to Roget's little tabs but we can't prove she actually took any."

"Small steps, Alicia. Speaking of which, we get to subpoena her phone. That burner Gurnsey and Roget both talked to can't be documented but maybe she carried a cell with an account and we can GPS her locations. Anything from the homeless folk?"

"I wish, L.T. No one remembers Huralnik at all, let alone any sexual bad habits."

Reed said, "They're transient, someone who did know her could be anywhere by now."

Bogomil said, "Transient and brain-damaged. I saw one woman with these festering sores on her legs. I offered to call the EMTs. She told me to fuck myself in the ass."

Milo said, "No good deed, it's my version of Newton's law."

"Which one?" said Binchy.

"All of them, Sean. Moses, anything more from New York on Okash's assault?"

Reed said, "One of the D's who worked it is deceased, I reached the other, he's in corporate security. He said he remembered the case 'cause it was different, one yuppie white girl pulling out a blade and slashing another across the face. Other than that, he was fuzzy, couldn't recall motive. If he ever knew it. I finally got the victim's name from the Seventh Precinct. Contessa Welles. No social network presence, no employment or death records, so maybe they got the name wrong."

Bogomil said, "Or she avoids the limelight. Someone slashed my face, I might." Touching her own smooth cheek.

Milo said, "Knife attack. That's no catfight."

He turned back to the board and jabbed Dugong's beard. "Despite his dope busts, this prince isn't currently known to Key West PD, under his marine-mammal moniker or his real one, Jeffrey Dowd. Sergeant I spoke to said they've got twenty-five thousand residents and a couple million tourists each year, it's a constant balancing act between keeping bad behavior low and not pissing off the chamber of commerce. When I told her Dugong was an artist she suggested I try some of the galleries. So far I'm zero for eight. Until six years ago, the guy's got no employment history, which fits day labor on a boat, like his bio said. Alex did find a website for his art."

I said, "Six years ago, he began doing macramé, then switched to photographic collages. Painting started three years ago but he hasn't produced much so he still may be working under the table—deckhand, fisherman, landscaping, maintenance."

Bogomil said, "Tying knots and pasting up magazine photos. Any actual talent going on there?"

I said, "Put it this way: He's got a loose brush."

Laughter.

Milo said, "From what we saw his salesmanship skills are lacking."

"A failure with a bad temper," said Reed. "That's combustible."

"Exactly, Moses. He came across stupid angry, like a kid who habitually tantrums. We don't see him as controlled enough to plan the limo."

"Okash is the boss?"

Milo looked at me.

I said, "If the two of them are involved, she's running the show."

Bogomil said, "She aims Dugong, he shoots."

"Makes sense," said Reed. "We've been thinking more than one offender. So what's the overall theory of how it went down, Doc?"

I said, "Best guess at this point is Okash and Rick Gurnsey had repeated sexual contact. She could be the woman seen with him at the fundraiser back in January. At some point, whatever they had went bad. We've heard two things about Gurnsey that could've led to that: He's been known to cut off relationships without warning or explanation and he could get pushy about sex, including pressuring women to do anal. The women we spoke to dealt with it and moved on. Maybe Okash didn't."

"Agg assault with a blade," said Reed. "Wrong woman to pressure."

Reed said, "So she thinks up a way to get back at Gurnsey with Dugong's help. Why the others? Why the limo?"

I said, "I'd been thinking about it as a theatrical production but Milo pointed out it could be performance art. Okash may even think of herself as an artist, so it's possible she constructed a tableau."

Up to that point, Binchy had remained uncharacteristically mute. Now he spoke in a low voice. "Human collage. Dugong was once into cut and paste."

"Good point, Sean."

"Once in a while I come up with one." Still subdued. At odds with his usual cheer. Milo and Reed and Bogomil looked at him. He shrugged.

I said, "Whatever the exact motivation, Gurnsey was placed in a humiliating pose. Along with Mary Jane Huralnik, who we also know acted out sexually and who may have accosted Okash downtown. Solomon Roget I'm still seeing as collateral damage—murdered for his limo. Benny Alvarez is more of a question mark. He worked for Okash, he may have seen something he shouldn't have. But as to why she'd want him in the picture? No idea."

Milo walked to the board, pointed to McGann and Vollmann. "Seeing something is our working theory on these poor folk. They show up at the gallery on Saturday because McGann cares about Alvarez. Vollmann's there because they're heading to Mexico in a few hours. The two of them are shotgunned and dumped in Inglewood."

Bogomil said, "If it's true, these people are monsters."

Binchy said, "Crazy art." Looking down at the table, tight-jawed. "'Scuse me, need a pit stop." He hurried out of the room.

Last year he'd encountered a murderous power freak and nearly died in the process. I'd saved his life. Since then, he'd feigned being okay and we'd never really talked about it.

Everyone knew. No one spoke because this was the job, not group therapy.

Milo said, "Have some muffins, kids. They're fresh."

Binchy returned looking as if he'd been sick.

Milo ignored that and sketched out the new plan: The four of them would divide the watch on Okash into six-hour shifts beginning with Binchy at six tonight, Milo taking over at midnight, Reed handling six a.m. to noon, and Bogomil working the afternoon.

If Dugong's L.A. residence could be determined, there'd be improvisation: a looser watch on him with Milo handling most of the extra hours. Milo would also pursue and analyze Okash's phone records.

Bogomil said, "Full plate, L.T."

"That's why I get the big bucks." He looked at the uneaten muffins. "Plenty of nutrition to go around— Don't grimace, Moses. Once upon a time you ate for pleasure."

With the interview room emptied, Milo began folding up the whiteboard.

I said, "What do you need from me?"

"Stay smart."

"Seriously."

"I'm being serious. Go home, I need you, I'll ask. One thing I've never been accused of is reticence."

I took Sepulveda to Sunset and drove east. My return trip would normally end at the Glen, well west of Benedict Canyon. But I said *Why not?* and continued past the Glen into Beverly Hills.

Three thirty p.m. was theoretically early enough to beat the northern commute to the Valley. But early home-goers had already queued up north of Sunset, turning the ride into a stop-and-go.

That was beneficial, enabling my peripheral vision. A mile short of Ascot Lane, during a stop phase, something caught my eye.

Blue hair, electrified by sunlight, far brighter than the surrounding vegetation.

Medina Okash's dress helped, as well. Red, short, tight as sausage casing, a shiny fabric that bounced solar rays like a prism as she toted a four-by-four brown-paper square to the front door of a house just off the main road.

During the meeting, she'd left the gallery, eluding notice.

The square was the same size and wrapping as the canvases we'd seen in the back of her gallery.

The dress was a good sign: You didn't attire yourself that way if you knew you were being watched.

I took advantage of the next traffic lull by making eye contact with the motorist facing south and eliciting a weary go-ahead nod. Hooking into a driveway on the west side of Benedict, I pulled off as quick a three-pointer as the Seville would allow and drove back to where I'd seen Okash.

The street was named Clearwater Lane, a steep slash of blacktop not unlike the one leading to the old bridal path that terminates at my house. I got there just in time to see the front door of a house close. Kept climbing until the road flattened, reversed, and descended.

No street parking on the north side of Clearwater, permit-only after six p.m. on the south. That hadn't stopped a vehicle from stationing itself where Okash had gotten out.

Not Okash's BMW; a brown Toyota RAV4. A man sat at the wheel. Not Geoffrey Dugong. Older, heavier, swarthy, working his phone.

Another male friend? Another potential weapon? Then I saw the black-and-white Uber windshield sticker.

The driver kept his head down and his fingers manic, caught up in cellular narcosis. Betting that would hold, I backed up, swung around, and repeated my climb up Clearwater. This time I settled with a clear view of the SUV and waited.

The house Okash had entered was a pale-blue fifties ranch with a flat gray roof and decorative wooden slats over the front windows.

Unassuming and at odds with the white Rolls-Royce parked in front. Better fit with the white Volvo station wagon positioned next to it. I copied down the address.

During the sixteen minutes Okash remained inside, her hired driver never looked up. When she reappeared, her hands were free and she high-stepped with a bounce that flexed her calves and quivered her rump.

Victory prance.

She got into the RAV's rear seat. The driver started up and turned right on Benedict Canyon.

North, toward Ascot Lane. But the driver continued for less than a minute before stopping well short of the B.H.–L.A. line and performing his own three-pointer—this one rash and rude and met with horn-blares.

Bumping the curb, he slued wildly across both lanes, raised more protest, headed back toward Sunset.

The direction you'd take to either Okash's place on Fountain or the gallery downtown.

In one of those eternal traffic mysteries, the drive had sped up to a smooth cruise that kept me moving at eighteen mph with no chance to turn off. As I continued north, I barely caught a glimpse of Ascot Lane, now blocked by a chain-link rent-a-fence.

I phoned Milo and told him about Okash.

He said, "I'll tell Sean to position himself near her crib. She doesn't show up in reasonable time, he'll go to the gallery. What's the vehicle?"

"Brown RAV4." I gave him the house address.

"Got it, thanks, Alex. What were you hoping to see in the first place?"

"I thought I'd check out the crime scene but obviously it's off limits now."

"Cart, horse, ain't that the way it usually is? Any particular reason the scene interested you?"

"Hoping for inspiration."

"Aren't we all? I've been up there myself a couple of times, nada. So Okash looked pleased with herself."

"Profit will do that to you."

"Vamping," he said. "She loves herself, our Medina. What do you always say—self-esteem is good for good people, bad for bad people? Okay, gracias again for keeping an eye out. Now go home per prior executive order. Kiss Gorgeous for me. And canine Gorgeous. Be sure to give me the credit."

When I stepped into the house, Robin was curled on the sofa nearest the door reading, Blanche's bratwurst body molded to her and ruffling with slow, sleepy breaths.

One canine eye opened. Serene dog. I thought about the luck of the draw.

It was earlier than Robin's usual quitting time but she was out of her work clothes and into a black cashmere hoodie, black tights, black platforms that boosted her to five-five.

I said, "We're going out?"

"Italian or Thai, take your pick."

I said, "The comfort of a limited choice. What's the common factor, noodles?"

"Such deductive powers." She got up and kissed me. Blanche bounded off the chair, stood on her hind legs panting, rubbed her knobby bulldog head against my leg, then hugged it with both her forepaws.

Robin said, "She's making me look bad."

I said, "So nice to be in demand. I'll go change."

Blanche's compensation for being left at home was an oversized bone-shaped, tooth-cleaning treat the color of a new lawn and the consistency of marble.

Twenty minutes later, Robin and I were sharing a corner table at a small family-run place on Westwood Boulevard south of Olympic. Gregarious family, homemade pasta, early enough to get in without a reservation.

Over bread and Sangiovese, I asked Robin about her day. When she finished telling me, she said, "Your turn."

I told her about the new suspicions of Okash and Dugong.

"The art world," she said. "Yeah, it can get really vicious, one of the many reasons I left school. I think it's because artists get a pass—talent confused with being a good person, they don't think the rules apply to them."

I said, "Caravaggio?"

One of the greatest painters who'd ever lived had been a rage-prone murderer.

"Of course, Caravaggio. But Degas and Mapplethorpe were bigots, Gauguin was a syphilitic pedophile, we won't even get into how Picasso treated women and stocked his studio with stolen artifacts. If we move on to musicians, we'll be here until morning—ah, here's our food."

Over fruit and coffee, she said, "Violence as performance art . . . like Chris Burden having someone shoot him in the arm. Or one of those classic grotesques—Bosch, that kind of thing."

I said, "Maybe Geoffrey Dugong in his pre-candle days."

"He was into gore?"

"No idea because no images from his early days have turned up. Maybe because they're not fit for public consumption."

"He could've used another nom de paintbrush." She shook her head. "Dugong. What was the guy thinking? Did he figure on growing flippers? That could sure limit your brush control."

When I stopped laughing, she said, "*Now* you're relaxed. When we get home, we'll have a *leisurely* dessert."

CHAPTER 30

Strenuous dessert. Followed by a long bath and a couple of hours watching *Foyle's War.*

I'd intended to stay up after Robin fell asleep as I often do. Wanting to wring info from the computer on Dugong/Dowd and if that didn't produce anything, search real estate sites for ownership of the house where Medina Okash had delivered the painting.

The next thing I saw was a blade of golden light riding the top of the bedroom curtains. Seven forty-eight a.m. Still in bed. No memory of the intervening hours.

Robin's side of the mattress was empty. Slow, steady snuffling from my side led me to look down.

Blanche snoring joyfully, one paw resting in one of my slippers.

She waited, smiling, as I brushed my teeth and put on a robe, then padded after me into the kitchen. Coffee in the pot, two slices of rye toast on the table.

I said, "Where's Mom?"

Trotting to the service-porch door, she sat.

I filled a cup and grabbed a piece of toast and the two of us went out to the garden. Pausing at the pond, I scooped a handful of pellets from the old porcelain Japanese urn I keep near the water's edge and tossed them in. A few fell to the ground and Blanche was rewarded for her vigilance. The koi splashed her as they gobbled. She shook herself off and smiled some more. Not at me, at life, in general.

The right way to start the day.

Nothing on knife-attack victim Contessa Welles but the computer was more than happy to tell me who owned the house on Clearwater.

Privately held company named Heigur, LLC. Nothing anywhere about what it peddled.

I called Milo. He said, "Saw that, looked up the business license. Real estate, no details, no transactions for a while. Caught a picture of the house, doesn't look like much."

"But they do have a Rolls."

"White, right?"

"How'd you know?"

"Your basic B.H. retiree drive."

"There was a Volvo, too."

"Probably the maid's," he said. "We could be talking venerable types who went for one of ol' Geoff's masterpieces. In terms of Okash, Sean was there when she Ubered home and I had a fascinating night watching her stay there. Reed got all the action: At eight she drove her own car to a breakfast place on Eighth Street near Vermont. Still there. Meanwhile, no word where Dugong's crashing."

I said, "He could've gone back to Florida."

"If he flew, there's no record of it."

"Just thought of something: Roget's kids live in Florida."

"Don't wanna brag but that also occurred to me so I called them. Neither has heard of Dugong and Ocala's not close to Key West, nearly five hundred miles north. I also emailed Okash's photo to Rick Gurnsey's roommate, Briggs. He's never seen her, doubts Ricky dated her, too much of a fat-face, quote unquote. Briggs ain't the most observant fellow and we know Gurnsey didn't bring every conquest home so no doors are closed. I sent the same photo to civic-minded Ms. Kierstead. She had nothing to add."

I said, "I couldn't find anything on Okash's victim."

"Me, neither, but I haven't dug deep. You're thinking people disappear for all sorts of reasons. Let me see if I can find a death certificate somewhere—hold on, incoming call—Marc Coolidge, I'll call you right back."

He didn't.

But at three thirteen p.m. he rang my doorbell.

I said, "Coolidge found something?"

"What—no, he was just letting me know he got another D to work with him, the two of them want to check out every CC camera they can find between McGann and Vollmann's crime scene and the two nearest freeway exits. We're talking enough video-viewing to earn a degree in film history."

I said, "Conscientious."

"The fact that his case could be tied in to something bigger has gotten to him." He stepped into the living room, sat. "The reason I took the liberty to grace your doorstep is guess who just called? Todd Leventhal the precocious party meister. Sounding scared out of his gourd."

"Of what?"

"He wouldn't say but asked to meet soon. More like demanded. Don't enjoy indulging brats but at this point, anyone wants to talk to me, I'm a cheap date."

Leventhal had asked to meet on Spalding Drive south of Olympic, a short drive from his high school. The black Challenger was in place when we arrived, parked in front of a red-brick condo complex that took up half the block.

Plenty of spaces across the street but the boy had chosen to sit squarely in a red zone, blocking a fire hydrant.

Milo said, "Entitled little prince."

I said, "Or he thinks you can protect him from the parking nazis."

"Delusions abound." He U-turned at the next corner, glided to the curb across the street from the Challenger, and rolled down his window. "Todd."

Leventhal, hands fixed rigidly on his steering wheel, turned jerkily and nodded. None of the bravado he'd shown the first time.

He said, "Um, where?"

"Here." Milo hooked a thumb toward the Impala's rear seat.

"We're taking a ride?"

"No, we're taking a meeting. C'mere."

The boy looked around and got out. Gray hoodie, bright-blue board shorts, orange sneakers. The thunderbolts etched into his hair had been highlighted yellow. He crossed the street, got into the backseat behind Milo, and immediately began fidgeting. "Smells weird back here."

Milo said, "New cologne, Todd. Eau de Felony. So what's on your mind?"

"This." Reaching into his jean pocket, Leventhal produced a single sheet of paper.

Screenshots of several Twitter posts.

The same poster: V-I-M Numero Uno.

Similar messages, one day after the other, all within the last week:

TL and SA socialize suckalize screwalize.

TL and SA and their ilk are like elk. hunted.

TL and SA have low genetic life expectancy. dna do not allow.

TL and SA party partially perish permanently.

TL SA MD MD MD MD MD MD MD MD MD MD MD.

Milo said, "Someone doesn't like you and Shirin."

"No! It's more!" The boy's new voice was shrill, constricted. "Look at the bottom one—look!"

"Lotta MD's. Something to do with a doctor?"

"No! It means 'must die'!"

"You figured that out because—"

"I didn't figure, I know! Motherfucker comes up and whispers it to me, online he doesn't want to get kicked off so he hides it with code. Look at his handle! It's obvious!"

"V-I-M . . ."

"Vengeance is mine! He says that, too!"

"This person has threatened you to your face."

"He always looked at me weird," said Leventhal. "Now he's saying it. Whispering. Like he's telling me a fucking secret."

"Who are we talking about?"

"Piece of shit autistic spazz-whack named Moman."

"First name?"

"Crispin." Snickering at the sound of the name.

"Crispin also goes to Beverly."

"Not like a normal person," said Leventhal. "He was like home-schooled 'cause he's fucked up, started this year so he could like go to Harvard or something. He misses a lot 'cause he's fucked up. Allergies, flus, whatever. But when he's there he's being psycho with me and Shirin."

"Why you?"

" 'Cause he's an asshole!"

"When did he begin seriously harassing you?"

"Like a month ago. When he found out."

"About what?"

"The party! The one where it happened. He comes up to me Friday, says 'I want to go,' I'm like 'Fuck off, loser.' "

"You and Shirin both told him that."

Silence.

Milo said, "Just you."

Leventhal nodded. "She likes me to be in charge."

"But now she's being targeted along with you."

"Zactly. You gotta do something. It's your job."

"Have you talked to campus security?"

"Useless fucks," said Leventhal. "They're gonna bring his parents in, my parents will have to come in and hers, there'll be shitloads of useless bullshit. *You* need to check it out. Not just for me, for you."

"For me, how?"

"Your case. He *lives* there."

"Where?"

Leventhal's eye roll said he was dealing with a garden slug. "*There.* Where it happened—like a block or two, whatever."

"Crispin lives near the party house."

"That's what I'm trying to tell you! I tell him fuck off but he shows up anyway dressed like a geek—suit, tie, shiny-shine shoes. Tries to go in, the footballers block him. He starts crying. Monday, *this* starts." Pointing at the paper. "Okay? Now you need to handle it. He's a fucking loon, eats his own boogers, tortures animals."

"Really," said Milo. "You've seen that?"

Shrug. "People talk. He's *nuts*! *Okay?* I'm doing what you said. Calling you with clues. I'm giving you *awesome* clues!"

"Thanks for the information, Todd. Anything else?"

Leventhal folded his arms across his chest. "Like what?"

"Anything you think would help."

"What would *help* is you do what I *tell* you."

Flinging open the door, the boy stomped to his car, revved the engine, roared off.

"Well," said Milo, "looks like we've been given our marching orders."

He examined the posts, handed them to me. "Diagnosis?"

I said, "Twitter allows you two hundred eighty characters. All of these are a fraction of that."

"Meaning?"

"Maybe a boy of few words because verbalizing is a challenge. Then there is the matter of the animals."

He exhaled. "So there is."

Working his phone he searched *crispin moman.* "No address, no surprise, he's a minor . . . here we go: An Adrian Moman lives on the 1200 block of Benedict, could be Mommy or Daddy. The Beverly Hills side but yeah, not far."

He googled. "Daddy." Showing me a thumbnail of a small, bespectacled, blow-dried man in his fifties with the smile of a carnival barker.

"Agent at CAA . . . it's worth a look-see. School won't be out for a while but if Todd's right and the kid misses a lot, he could be home. Want to take a chance and stop by? Meet another child of privilege?"

CHAPTER 31

The house was a two-story white Georgian Revival with a black door and matching shutters. Ungated succulent garden in front, double-width driveway, a silver Mercedes taking up half.

At the front door, Milo let a bronze, lion-shaped knocker fall on solid wood.

A maid in a black-and-white lace uniform opened. "Yes?"

Milo's badge made her step back. "Is Crispin home?"

"One min."

The door shut for two and a half minutes before opening on a pretty blond woman in her forties wearing pink velour sweats and black-and-white checked sneakers. The pale end of blond, a smidge past gray, thick mop of it, pushed back from an unlined forehead by a rhinestone band. A scrunchy circled one wrist, a fitness watch the other.

She said, "I'm about to head for the gym. Police? Why in the world?"

Milo said, "Are you Crispin's mom?"

"I am." Quick glance toward the house. Trembling lips.

"Sorry to bother you but we've had a complaint about Crispin."

"I see." Unsurprised. "What'd he do? Say something inappropriate to an overly sensitive teacher or student?"

"A little more than that."

Pink velour shoulders rose. "Meaning?"

"Our report is he threatened some other students. Is he home?"

She slid a silver nail under the rim of her watchband. Flicked leather a couple of times. "It's complicated. You can't just approach him like everyone."

"Could we talk to him in front of you?"

"Who'd he supposedly threaten?"

"Could we talk inside, ma'am?"

"Don't you need a warrant?"

"We could come back with one, ma'am. But if it turns out to be nothing, why make a big deal and have it recorded as an incident on Crispin's record?"

"Hmm." Freeing the nail and inspecting her cuticle, she began stepping in place. "Okay, here's what's going to happen: You'll talk to me first and if I approve of your approach—*and* if Crispin's receptive—we can reach out to him. With sensitivity."

"More than reasonable, Ms.—"

"Haley Moman." Eyelash flutter. "I used to be Haley Hartford."

As if we were expected to know that.

Both of us faked it and said, "Sure," at the same time.

That made her smile.

She said, "C'mon in, guys."

The house was a precisely calibrated mix of taupe and aqua. A taxidermy shark took up one high wall, a wooden frame filled with stuffed teddy bears, another. Wall three hosted a scatter of family photos: Haley Moman née Hartford, blow-dried, shorter than her by half a head, and a boy, always caught with his head down, features obscured by long, lank, tan hair.

Wall four was a life-sized painting of Haley Moman née Hartford in a strapless silver gown with an abdominal cutout that honored her navel.

"Taken from a red-carpet shot at the Emmys," she said. "Back in the back-then. Wait here."

She crossed the living room and an adjoining dining room, passed through what was likely a kitchen door, and returned moments later holding a bottle of Vitaminwater.

Milo muttered, "No graham crackers, shucks."

Haley Moman said, "Pardon?"

"Nice house."

"We try." Sitting down with the poise of a yoga master, she dangled one leg over the other and swung it from the ankle down, uncapped the bottle, and took a long swallow.

"Okay, go. What's the *alleged* claim?"

Milo showed her the tweets.

She said, "This reads like teenage garbage—and this part about the doctors is absolutely nothing dangerous. Crispin is reflecting his reality. He's always being trucked around to appointments. Allergist, pediatrician, ENT, orthodontist, behavioral optometrist." A beat. She bit her lip. "His psychotherapist. So you see we are aware that he's got issues. But this? It's a joke."

She handed the paper back to Milo. "Really, guys, I can't believe you're wasting your time on something so childish."

Milo said, "According to the complainant, 'MD' doesn't refer to medical doctors. It's Crispin's code for 'Must Die.' "

"His code? Nonsense," said Haley Moman. But her voice lacked conviction.

I said, "Does Crispin have strong computer skills?"

"Isn't he entitled to a plus? Yes, he's great with computers."

"So he's used to codes and coding."

"Oh, *please.* That's advanced math and whatever, this is a stupid letter thing. To me 'MD' means 'medical doctor' and until you can prove different, that's the way it's going to stay."

Milo looked at me.

I said, "We're really sorry if this is upsetting you but as a parent you can see that we need to follow up."

"On the basis of this?"

"The complainant said Crispin also made verbal threats."

"Where?"

"At school."

"Hah. As if he's there often enough to even talk to anyone—you need to understand, Crispin's different but not in a bad way, he's just different. Until his senior year, he was homeschooled. His therapist felt he needed a social experience before college, even with the adjustment challenges that were likely to occur. We go by what she says. She's brilliant, a professor at the U., a doctorate from Yale. So please excuse me for trusting *her* and not *this.*"

"Could we talk to her?"

"Absolutely not—oh, hell, why not, she's only going to back up what I'm saying. Dr. Marlene Sontag. Go for it."

Lucky break. Someone I knew and liked.

I said, "Could you please call Dr. Sontag and give your consent?"

"You bet, sir. You *bet.* Now can we end this and let me get to the gym?"

"We were also told Crispin had issues with animals."

Haley Moman's eyes zipped to the right. Lowered. Aimed at her lap and stayed that way. "Oh, Jesus—I thought that was resolved."

I said nothing.

"I can't believe this—it was a *squirrel* for God's sake. They're disgusting rodents, they carry diseases. It might as well have been a rat. They're basically rats with fluffy tails."

"What happened?"

"Nothing," said Haley Moman. "This was months ago. Right after Crispin began at Beverly. During lunchtime, that's all, nothing disruptive in class. Out on the *lawn.* Do you think anyone would take the time to reach out since the time he got there? As if. So he was all by himself, eating, and a stupid squirrel ran up to him and bared its teeth. Blatant. Aggressive. I mean that's not normal, right? Normally they're afraid of people, right? So this one had to be sick. Maybe even rabies. Or some other horrible disease."

I said, "Crispin felt threatened."

"Wouldn't you? I mean, let's face it, everyone's into animals nowadays. I don't mind, I gave up my furs. But animals aren't perfect, there are mean ones just like there are mean people, and this one was obviously vicious. Baring its teeth unprovoked at a child? What was Crispin supposed to do, sit there and get mauled?"

"What did he do?"

She tented her fingers then ran them down the sides of a perfectly styled nose. "What did he do? He protected himself."

"How?"

Her eyes dropped down again. "Look. I had no idea he had it with him. It was a gift from his grandpa. My dad, he ranches cattle in Montana, to him, a knife's a tool. This was a stupid little two-inch blade for whittling. Dad gave it to Crispin when Crispin turned six. We took it away because we're fiercely anti any sort of weapon. Crispin must've found it."

Milo said, "So no firearms in the house."

"Of course not!" said Haley Moman. Appalled, as if he'd suggested she was old. "No instruments of destruction, period."

Her chest heaved. "From the beginning, we knew Crispin deserved special consideration. That means zero tolerance."

"Crispin got hold of the knife."

She threw up her hands. "I kept it 'cause of my dad, hid it in my bathing suit drawer, somehow he found it. He said it was just for that day, he was planning to pick up a tree branch and whittle—he tries to be artistic. So he had it with him and he ended up using it."

"On the squirrel."

Haley Moman faced me, cheeks flushed, brown eyes narrowed. "The stupid thing was baring its *teeth* at him, he felt *threatened.* For all we know he was in danger of being exposed to the plague or something. So he used it. So big *deal.*"

I said, "You're making a good point about disease. Did Animal Control ever analyze the body to see if it was infected?"

No reaction from Haley Moman. Then she tugged at her hair, picked up her water bottle, uncapped, recapped. Put it down hard on a taupe travertine table.

"No," she said. "There wasn't much left to analyze."

She ran out. This time she was gone for a while, returning with her eyes raw, her hair loose, clutching a fresh water bottle.

During her absence, Milo had done some research. Twenty years ago, Haley Hartford had worn a blood-red bathing suit for two seasons of a show called *Tideline.* First marriage to an actor who'd O.D.'d. A couple of boyfriends in between the marriage to Adrian Moman. Crispin's age said Moman was likely his stepdad.

"All right," she said, tossing the hair. "Crispin has agreed to meet with you."

Secretary clearing the boss's calendar.

Milo said, "Great," and we stood.

"But," said Haley Moman, "you must stick to only relevant topics and avoid nonsense."

"Such as?"

"I'll direct you." She racewalked toward the rear of the house, speeding past three bedrooms on both sides of a skylit corridor. At the back, a space the width of the entire structure was set up with aqua leather theater seats and a hundred-inch screen on one side, a wet bar and a pool table backed by a floor-to-ceiling aquarium filled with marine fish on the other. Taupe drapes covered every window. Light courtesy dimmed LEDs in the ceiling.

All those toys still allowed for plenty of square footage in the center of the room. A queen-sized bed shared the space with a black leather Eames chair and six feet of Lucite bent into an upside-down U. Atop the Lucite: two laptops, three twenty-inch screens, half a dozen Rubik's cubes, and a large, yellow softcover book.

MIRE PANDEMIC: A GUIDE TO MINDCRAFT VOID-SATIATION

On the bed, his scrawny butt barely taking up a corner of mattress, perched a pitiably thin, undersized boy with long, straight hair colored a curiously waxy tan. Spidery soft-looking fingers rested on bony knees. Skin so pallid and blue-veined it verged on translucent.

Crispin Moman was seventeen and a half but could've passed for fourteen.

This time he revealed his face, expressionless but for the merest sense of expectancy in narrow-set gray eyes. His features were well set but skimpy, as if a sculptor had roughed in then run out of clay. The exception, his eyes, purplish blue, luminous, and huge, fringed by long curling lashes.

The oddly colored hair was cut in a pageboy with straight-edge bangs that bisected a high, white brow. Already sporting brow lines his mother had avoided through lucky genetics or botulin toxin. He wore a dark-green polyester jumpsuit that evoked an old guy loafing in Palm Springs decades ago. *Ralph* embroidered across the right breast. Black wingtips, no socks. Four red strings banded a flimsy-looking wrist.

He looked at us but didn't seem to see us.

Haley Moman said, "They're here, honey."

Crispin didn't react.

She looked at us and wagged a warning finger. *Don't push it.*

Milo walked over and faced the boy. "Crispin, I'm Milo."

Without looking up, Crispin said, "What's your title?"

"Pardon?"

"Your real identity has a title." Nasal voice, tremolo modulation, the volume dialed a smidge too high.

"Lieutenant."

Crispin Moman said, "Lieutenant Milo . . . ?"

"Sturgis."

"Lieutenant. Milo. Sturgis." One of the hands extended.

Milo took it and shook gently. The boy's fingers held on until Milo unpeeled them, then flopped back to their knee-perch.

"My identity is Crispin Bernard Moman."

Milo grinned. "How 'bout that. Mine is actually Milo Bernard Sturgis."

Haley Moman shot him a doubtful look. *Lying to manipulate my child?*

Crispin said, "You didn't include that initially."

"Don't use the middle name much, Crispin."

"Incomplete data," said the boy. "Can lead to errors."

"Ah."

Without acknowledging me, Crispin said, "What's your full identity?"

"Alexander Dumas Delaware. I go by Alex."

Milo gaped. He'd never known about the flight of literary fancy cooked up by my mother before the postpartum depression set in and never left. Leaving me to be disparaged throughout my childhood as "sissy-boy Froggy" by my violent sot of a father.

The initials didn't help, either: A.D.D. I'd tired of the ridicule at school, abandoned the offending "D" on my Missouri driver's license and every document since.

Haley said, "Bernard is my dad. Crispin likes going to Montana to visit him."

Crispin picked up the book and began reading.

Milo said, "Do you know why we're here?"

"I threatened Todd and Shirin."

Haley said, "He means you think that."

Crispin said, "I mean I know that."

Milo said, "So you did it."

"Of course I did it."

"Todd and Shirin got pretty upset."

"That was the goal."

"To make them upset."

"Yes."

"Because . . ."

"I hate them," said Crispin. "They hate me. Expecting pleasantries in a situation like that is unrealistic."

"Would you ever act out on the threats?"

Haley said, "Of course not!"

Her son regarded her as if she was beyond reasoning with.

Milo said, "Crispin, would you ever—"

"No. It's an inefficient and stupid strategy."

"How so?"

The boy's withering glance shifted to us. "Why would I endanger my freedom for the short-term pleasure of harming them? At least not under current circumstances."

Haley said, "Oh, Crispin, stop screwing around and just tell them the truth."

"I'm being truthful. Mother. In the current situation, all of us being adolescents, there's zero probability I'd act out."

I said, "But?"

"Three of us on a deserted island together, enough food for only one? Or two? I'd do my best to survive."

Haley said, "That's a fantasy, Crispin. Give them reality. *Please.*"

"Then excluding fantasy, there's no probability of harm. I attempted to arouse them because they—he, actually, not she—was acting out against me verbally."

I said, "Shirin was okay."

"Neutral," said Crispin. "No hostility, no expression of support. I included her because she's meaningful to him and I wanted to strike at his core."

Sudden, lopsided smile. "Apparently, I've succeeded."

Haley said, "You have, Crispin, but you need to stop."

Long silence. She wrung her hands.

Crispin said, "Okay."

Milo said, "Okay what?"

"I'll stop."

"Completely."

"That's what stop means, Milo Bernard Sturgis comma Lieutenant. There's no rheostat, it's either or."

"Good."

"Not good or bad," said Crispin. "Reality. There'll be no need for you to return and worry Haley. I won't be going back there."

"To Beverly Hills High School?"

"Honey, I thought we agreed you'd try to—"

"Circumstances have changed, Haley. It hasn't been positive and is unlikely to become positive. I can learn more by myself."

"But the counselor said Harvard and Yale—"

"The counselor went to Pitzer," said Crispin, sneering. "I'll follow my own judgment."

He looked at Milo. "No need to come back and cause her stress, M.B.S. comma L."

Milo said, "If you don't give us reason to come back we won't."

The boy held up a hand. "Promise-pledge-swear. If it makes you feel better, bring me a holy book and I'll place my hand on it."

"Are you religious?"

"I believe in belief."

"So no more threats?"

"Nary a one." The boy smiled at his own phrasing. "Nary." As if tasting the word. "Nary more scary."

Milo said, "Fair enough," and extended his hand.

Crispin said, "We already did that but all right." This time he was the first to let go.

"Thanks, Crispin."

"For what?"

"Talking to us."

"I talk to people. I'm not a robot." Leveling the purplish eyes at his mother.

She said, "Of course, honey."

Another condescending smile aimed her way.

We turned to leave.

Crispin said, "They pretend to be adults but they're not."

"Who?"

"He and she, the party people. They pretended the party was all theirs but they were lying, it wasn't."

I said, "How do you know?"

"After they barred my entry I planned to conduct a commemoration of the confrontations. I walked over there and saw parents so I knew I didn't have to bother."

Haley Moman said, "You went over there? Ohmigod."

Crispin said, "Don't waste anxiety on events that didn't occur."

Milo said, "What were you planning to do?"

The boy's lopsided smile reappeared and grew, filling the entire span of his lips. Gradually, as if joy were a gas that could inflate tissue.

Haley said, "Do I want to know this?"

"No, but they do," said Crispin. "The plan was to deposit a large bowel movement on the property. At the entrance where stepping in it was most likely."

His mother gasped.

Crispin flashed a V-sign. "I brought toilet paper and was going to also leave the used portions. Then I saw the parents and realized the plan should be aborted because they were liars and barring me had been a false gesture of dominance. So why bother donating my body chemistry to insignificant ants?"

"Oh, Jesus." Haley hung her head.

I said, "How many parents did you see?"

"A mother and a father."

"You knew they were parents because . . ."

"They weren't adolescents. Their shape was adult, they walked with adult confidence and drove off."

"Did you see their car?"

"It was dark," said Crispin. "I heard it so it was there. Then it wasn't because they left."

"Did you hear these people say anything?"

"No."

"Which way did they go?"

"North."

"When did this happen, Crispin?"

"Exactly Saturday, exactly two fifty-eight a.m."

Haley said, "You left the house at three in the morning?"

"I do it when I can't sleep."

"Oh, Crispin—"

"You take your Lunesta and he takes his Ambien. You know what I think about medication, Haley."

"Being out there at night is more dangerous than medication."

"I challenge that idea, Haley. Vehicle traffic is infrequent and I stay away from the road."

"But in the dark, by yourself—"

"The dark is neutral. There are no people. One time I saw a raccoon. We looked at each other and went our separate ways. I've also seen deer. They're afraid of me. Even the large ones."

"I can't believe this—where do you go in the middle of the night?"

"Early morning. Typically I walk around our backyard. Atypically when I remain wide awake, I go outside in front and walk a few paces south or a few paces north. This was the first time I had a goal and a destination."

I said, "Wanting to make a statement."

"A gastrointestinal statement. At dinner, I ate a lot of fiber." To his mother: "Remember? The chili and the salad and then cereal? You approved of my having a good appetite."

"Oh, Crispin!"

"When I saw the parents and felt better about how pathetic he and she are, I knew it was time to change the plan. The fiber was working and I made it back here just in time and used my toilet. Then I sprayed that organic orange spray you like, Haley, and took a shower and went to bed."

His mother rocked and placed a hand on her temple. "I feel a migraine coming on, we need to end this."

Milo said, "Just a coupla more questions. These parents, Crispin, what did they look like?"

Blank stare.

"Son—"

Haley said, "He has no idea."

Milo said, "Tall, short, fat, skinny—"

Blank stare.

"Hair color?"

Silence.

"Clothing?"

No response.

"Is there anything you can recall?"

Emotionless head shake.

From voluble to mute. As if the boy's brain waves had changed.

Haley Moman got between Milo and her son. "This is *over.* You have to leave *now.*"

Crispin returned to his book.

"Out," she said, pointing to the door and staying close behind us as we retraced toward the front of the house.

Back in the living room, she said, "You need to understand: He has *zero* facial recognition. By now, he's forgotten what *you* look like so *don't* waste your time and mine."

She flung her front door open. "You're not going to make troubles for him, right? He's obviously no danger to anyone."

Milo said, "So far so good."

"What does *that* mean?"

"Now that you're aware, I'm sure you'll be paying close attention—"

"Like I don't *already*? Like I haven't been paying attention every single *day* since he started to show his *differences*? You people are *unbelievable.*"

She glared from her doorway. Held the pose as we drove away.

Milo said, "Making new friends every day. So the kid sees a man and a woman early Saturday morning right before three. The timing's right."

I said, "A two-person job like we thought. One of them drove the limo, the other brought a second vehicle for getaway."

"And I've got an eyewitness who can't recognize faces." He laughed. "Some kid. What do you think about his dangerousness? I don't see grounds for any kind of charge and now that he's going back to home-schooling, I can't see involving BHPD."

"A few coded messages and no weapons in the house? No action would be taken. Like you said, all she can do is keep an eye on him."

A mile later, he said, "There *was* that squirrel. Then again, he and the raccoon parted ways amicably. Poor thing. Her. From a beach hottie to that. But enough compassion, time to redouble on Okash and Weird Beard."

CHAPTER 32

We were back at my house by five forty. Twenty minutes to go for Moe Reed's watch on Okash. As the unmarked idled, Milo phoned him.

Reed said, "No movement, L.T., her lights are still off and her car's still here."

He recapped the talk with Crispin. "Let Alicia and Sean know."

"Kid probably saw the murderers," said Reed, "but no facial recognition—that psychiatrist—Oliver Sacks—Liz gave me one of his books, he had the same thing."

"The way my luck's going, he'll be my next potential witness."

"He passed away, L.T."

"Proves my point."

Silent house, Robin working, Blanche assisting. I made coffee, drank it on my battered leather couch, and wondered if there was anything else I could do. The databases had yielded little about the woman Medina Okash had slashed but the D's had been too busy to dig deeper, so why not give it a try?

I keyworded *contessa welles*. Nothing. Maybe a nickname. Or as Reed had suggested, an NYPD clerical error.

I began pairing *welles* with *connie, constance, consuela* and ran into the opposite problem: too many hits. The two most interesting were a character in a Robert B. Parker novel and a wounded Andean condor in a Peruvian bird sanctuary. Avian Connie had learned to nibble treats daintily from her keeper's hand.

The flood of names drained quickly as I filtered by age and geography, assuming Okash's victim was around her age, give or take five years on either side, and had lived in or near New York. I repeated the process with *wells* with no greater success. Returned to *contessa* paired with surnames that a tired desk officer might confuse with Welles.

Welch, Welsh, Walsh, Walls.

Ping.

Two bottom-of-the-page paragraphs in the *Newark Star-Ledger*'s online archive reported the death, two years ago, of Contessa Walls, age thirty-six.

The decedent had been found hanging in an isolation cell at the Edna Mahan Correctional Facility for Women in Clinton, New Jersey. Six years into a ten-year sentence for attempted murder; she'd spent most of that time in the prison's mental health facility. At the time of her demise, she'd been in isolation due to disruptive behavior but not on suicide watch.

Note was made of a scandal the previous year involving male guards sexually abusing female inmates.

I searched for *contessa walls medina okash* and got a single hit. With Okash's name crossed out, so much for that. But the content gave me a lead.

Online sympathy message posted to the O'Reilly Funeral Home in Newark a week after Walls's death.

****Contessa Jane Walls. Your life was a challenging one.****
But there was purity in your soul.

I pray that your next life brings you
salvation and the joy you deserve.
**** Emeline Beaumont ****

One woman by that name, living locally.

Sister Emeline Beaumont
Assistant Director
Servants of St. Theresa
Los Angeles, CA 90049

A convent in Bel Air? I looked up the address. Sure enough: the foothills north of Sunset and west of the U.

I went out to Robin's studio. She had on her full-face safety helmet and overalls. The exhaust fan whirred. A rosewood guitar back was held steady on her bench. Pretty wood but toxic dust. A routing jig Robin had designed and built was clamped perpendicular to the tabletop.

She was busy channeling hair-like layers of multicolored wood binding into place. Delicate work. I held back so as not to distract her. She saw me anyway, flipped up the helmet's plastic shield, shut off the fan with a foot pedal. "Hi, babe. What time is it?"

"Six forty."

"I got caught up. Some of this binding is satinwood and it loves to snap. I want to do it in one swoop, avoid irregularities."

"No prob, I'm going out for a short ride."

"Where?"

"A convent."

She smiled. "I won't ask but at least it's not a monastery."

"Want me to pick up dinner?"

"How about fish and loaves? No, I'm fine with leftovers if you are. Big Guy coming over?"

"No plans."

"Then we'll definitely have enough. C'mere and give me a kiss."

CHAPTER 33

The drive was ten minutes on Sunset under a black sky, then a right turn east of Mount Saint Mary's college. I was figuring the convent would be part of that campus but it wasn't and I had to travel another 3.3 miles, well past the point where the views turned panoramic.

The address led me to a two-story, white stucco Spanish Colonial mansion, the kind you glimpse in the more venerable areas of Santa Barbara and Montecito, mostly hidden behind walls and gates. This property was open to the street. I wasn't expecting to see much in the dark, but generous outdoor lighting said I'd been needlessly pessimistic.

The house was perched atop a high mound of lawn dotted with old palms and orange trees and a three-trunk sycamore whose branches stretched over an Italianate cement bench. A fountain of similar style burbled in the center of the property. To the right was flat asphalt parking hosting two blue vans and two blue Kias.

No signage, no crucifix, no steeple; nothing to suggest the place was a religious institution. That same anonymity extended to the clothing of the woman leaving the building and walking toward the lot, something green and shiny tucked under her right arm.

Long-sleeved blouse, knee-length skirt, uncovered dark bob. She was on the short side with a solid build and a jaunty walk. When she reached one of the compacts, she unfolded the green thing.

Several plastic shopping bags rolled up like a jelly pastry. She dropped one, bent and retrieved it, saw me get out of the Seville, smiled and waved.

I waved back and began climbing. The woman descended and we met halfway.

Thirty-five to forty, smooth complexion, strong nose, cleft chin, twinkly pale eyes.

"Dr. McCarthy? Glad you caught me. Thanks so much for the generous donation." Softly contoured southern accent. Her hand extended.

I gave it a brief shake. "Sorry, I'm not Dr. McCarthy."

She pulled away. "A donor I've never met said he might be dropping off a check. I figured a nice vintage Caddy—my apologies."

"I'm Dr. Delaware. I'm a psychologist who—"

"So is he! Dr. Jerry McCarthy. Do you know him?"

"Actually, I do." One of the most respected neuropsychologists in town. I said so.

"Feel free to join him in psychological generosity, Doctor. Are you coming to visit? It's after hours and I was about to leave but if what we do inspires you, I'm happy to show you around."

I showed her my LAPD consultant's badge. Out of date and essentially useless, except for making a first impression.

"Police? Oh, dear. We haven't made any complaints."

"I'm looking for Sister Emeline Beaumont."

All traces of good cheer withered. "Why would the police be interested in me?"

"They're not, Sister. It's about Medina Okash and Contessa Walls."

"How did you connect them to me?"

"Your funeral message to Ms. Walls."

"Poor Connie—well, that was a while ago."

"Do you have a sec?"

"Is it going to take long? I was about to go shopping for our residents. We've only got three, currently. Teenage girls about to be moms. We offer them support throughout the process. Voluntarily. I emphasize that because with all that's going on, the church has gotten a pretty bad reputation. A lot of it unfortunately justified. So how much time do you think you'll need?"

"Just a few minutes."

"Then let's have ourselves a nice sit outside under Gargantua—that big old monster. A botanist from the U. came and did dendrochronology. Gargantua was planted over three hundred years ago and has healthy roots."

"Happy to make his acquaintance."

Sister Emeline Beaumont laughed but the sound faded fast.

Once we'd settled beneath the sycamore, she placed her hands at her sides and her feet on the grass.

"So," she said, "seeing as Connie's departed, I'm assuming this is about Medina Okash."

"As a matter of fact, it is. How did you—"

"We were all friends, once. What has Medina done?"

"That's unclear."

"It's clear enough for the police to send a psychologist to track me down. Does it have to do with some sort of mental situation?"

"I'd answer that with a question but I don't want to be a walking cliché."

This time her laughter was durable. "You're a high-spirited man, Dr. Delaware. For a psychologist—sorry, couldn't resist. So is that it? Medina's done something off?"

"Sister—"

"Emmy's fine."

"Emmy, I apologize but I can't go into any details."

"Fine, I get it, the secular confession booth," she said. "But obviously something serious is going on. I mean, they're not going to send a psychologist out on a jaywalker."

"Medina committing a serious crime wouldn't surprise you."

"Wish it would," said Emmy Beaumont. "You know what she did to Connie, right?"

"Knife attack."

"Cut her open right here." She drew a slashing diagonal line from the right-hand top of her face to her collarbone and beyond. "Just sliced open her face and kept cutting down her chest. Muscle and bone, so many stitches. Horrible. But . . . what I'm going to say might sound uncharitable—Connie had issues, as well. She'd hurt Medina. Not as seriously, punches and kicks, but several times when they got into it."

"They had a volatile relationship."

"To put it mildly. And I have to say mostly Connie was the instigator. Her mood swings could be terrifying." Sighing. "Looking back she was probably bipolar. Drugs and alcohol couldn't have helped. Not that I'm telling someone of your training anything."

"How far back did the three of you go?"

"All the way back to our freshman year in high school," said Emmy Beaumont. "Holy Cross Preparatory in Annapolis. *Their* nuns looked the part!"

Sudden smile but again, just as sudden decay.

I said, "Are you from Louisiana?"

"You can tell, huh? My dad was an admiral, I was born in New Orleans and lived there for a while when he was at the naval air base, then we moved when he began teaching at the academy. Medina came from up Seattle way, her mom was a hippie but her dad switched to born-again religious. Connie was a local girl, her folks put her in boarding school to squash her rebellious tendencies. We ended up as roommates and then we parted ways for college, then we met up again in New York after college and that's where it happened."

"You were there."

Her eyes shut and opened. "Unfortunately I was. It took a long time to stop the nightmares."

"Are you able to tell me about it?"

The fingers of both hands drummed the concrete bench. "They were rooming together downtown. I was going to Columbia and lived in Harlem so I wasn't with them as often. The night it happened we had dinner in Chinatown. I wanted to go home but they insisted I come with them to a club, a place they'd been before. When I got there I knew it was a mistake. It was a lesbian bar."

She turned and faced me. "I'm celibate now, but I wasn't always. And I definitely wasn't gay."

"Medina and Connie were."

"More like bi-curious. I guess I should've known. They were always together, sometimes they'd sleep in the same bed and giggle. But I never actually *saw* anything. Tell the truth I was pretty naive, assumed they had one of those girlie things. Later they roomed together but so what, they both worked downtown at art galleries. They'd studied art history in college and spent time overseas. In Switzerland."

"Both of them were in Switzerland?"

"Briefly. They always had a tight bond. At Holy Cross, there'd been times I felt the odd woman out. Sometimes it bothered me. Later, when I began living by myself during grad school, it felt liberating. When the three of us were together they could get a little . . . in-jokey."

"So the three of you went clubbing . . ."

Sad smile. "You really want me to turn back those pages . . . yes, we did, and yes we stayed far longer than we should have and drank far, far more than we should have and at some point something happened on the dance floor, I can't really say what. But I can guess."

I waited.

She said, "Someone probably flirted too much with Connie, that was always happening, she was the gorgeous one. Tall and slim like a model, long legs, a gorgeous mop of blond hair. I suppose Medina always had to cope with her jealousy. I wasn't aware because I never really knew that they were . . . in any way together. They also went after guys. Aggressively . . . anyway, something happened on the dance floor, the two of them began arguing, then tussling—pushing and shoving. Then Connie slapped Medina across the face. Hard. Medina tried to do the same but Connie got hold of her wrist and twisted hard. I'm watching this, appalled. Shocked to begin with about being in a place like that, plus I've got a test later in the morning and my head's swimming from Zombies—that's what we were drinking, they insisted and I, being a total wimp, went along with it."

She flicked the edge of her shopping bag roll. "So now Connie's hurting Medina's wrist and Medina's trying to scratch at Connie's eyes and Connie's just laughing at her and calling her terrible names and the bouncers come and throw them out. I follow behind the bouncer and he tells them to behave, he's going to call them a taxi. And they obey. Just like that, the two of them stop fighting and stand there like little kids called to the principal's office. I'm standing a few feet away, can't wait to get out of there, in fact I've called my own taxi. Then Medina tries to kiss Connie and Connie laughs at her again—a really demeaning laugh, you know—and calls her more names and Medina reaches into her purse and then she does what looks like taking a slap at Connie's face and chest. Like you'd swipe a credit card. Which looked odd to me. Then I saw the look on Connie's face. She's clutching her chest and blood's coming out of her cheek and her chest. She was wearing a thin, gauzy top. No bra. You could see the wound spreading. Growing darker. And she falls down and Medina stands over her and she laughs. Then she starts crying and bends over Connie and tells her not to die. Meanwhile, I've called 911. And that's it."

"Were you subpoenaed to testify at Medina's trial?"

"I feared I would be," said Sister Emeline Beaumont. "But there was no trial, Medina made some kind of plea and went to prison for a long time."

"How did Connie react to that?"

"I couldn't tell you. I went to see her several times in the hospital and she was pretty much out of it. One day I showed up and she'd been discharged. I phoned her a few times but never got an answer. At that point I figured I should wait for her to call me. She didn't. I never saw her or spoke to her again. The same goes for Medina, though she did reach out from time to time. Not personally, once in a while a sort of art thing invitation. To tell the truth, I didn't want to rekindle anything with Medina. The way she'd stood over Connie, smiling. Even though she cried right after. I got the feeling she was crying for herself—for her own loss."

"No genuine empathy."

"Maybe I'm judging her uncharitably. It was a bizarre night. We were all drunk." She shook her head. "Now you're going to think that's why I joined an order but it wasn't like that. I got my MSW, worked with disadvantaged kids in Bed-Stuy—Brooklyn. Another Saint Theresa place. One of the good ones, there was absolutely *nothing* untoward going on."

She said, "Delaware. Is that French? Are you Catholic or Huguenot?"

"More like a mongrel."

"Mixes are the strongest, right? Anyway I was impressed by the work the sisters were doing and I'd found relationships with men not to be satisfying, so I applied as a novitiate, liked it, and stayed. It's a peaceful life."

She eyed the convent. "We get to do our work without controversy. We have a nickname. The California sisters do. Among ourselves we're the Saint Terri Girls. Anyway, that's the story with Connie and Medina."

"Connie ended up in prison herself."

"I know. Attempted murder. My parents called to tell me. They said she'd died in prison, was serving time for attempted murder. Some conflict over a woman but I don't know the details. Do you?"

"We're just starting out."

"With what?"

"Looking into Medina's past," I said. "Some sort of romantic conflict. Same story."

"I suppose so. My father put it down to homosexuality. He was big on stories having morals, Dad was. Very religious behaviorally, never missed Mass or confession when he was ashore. One of his sisters was a nun so you'd think he'd approve of my choice. But I was an only child and that meant no grandkids so he convinced himself there was something irregular about my sexuality."

She winked. "I couldn't exactly tell him about my youth. Though it was pretty tame compared with Medina and Connie."

"Could I run a few names by you? People Medina may have known?"

"If it's a short list, I really would like to get my shopping done."

No reaction to any of the victims. When I said, "Geoffrey Dugong," she said, "That's a real name."

"He's an artist Medina represents. Born Jeffrey Dowd."

Silence.

"Emmy?"

"That's Medina's brother. Half brother. Like I said, her dad was a hippie, had a child with another woman when he was married to Medina's mom. Jeff's involved in whatever this is about? I guess that shouldn't surprise me. He was always kind of tightly wound."

"How so?"

"Irritable, easily distracted, jumpy. He's in Medina's life now?"

"That's surprising?"

"They never really seemed to have much of a relationship, Doctor. At least the few times I saw them together."

She leaned forward. "She used to refer to him as 'Daddy's little bastard.'"

"She resented him."

"Maybe the affair was a factor in her parents' divorce. I can't say for sure, the one time I brought it up she got angry."

I said, "Anger's always been an issue for Medina."

She stared at me. "Why do I feel I'm in therapy? Yes, she could go zero to sixty like this." Snapping her fingers. "So she's done something. What a shame, I was hoping the experience would change her. You must think I'm odd. Two friends who ended up incarcerated. But I had other friends, my academic cohorts."

She laughed. "That sure came across defensive, didn't it?" She stood. "I really have to get those groceries. Pregnant women work up a hunger."

I walked her to the car. She tried to step ahead, failed, settled for ignoring me. Reluctant to offend. Maybe it had saved her life.

When we got to the top of the hill, I said, "Thanks for talking to me."

"I'm not sure what you really got out of it. And truth is, I don't want to know the details. What's the point?"

CHAPTER 34

As she drove away, I called Milo.

Straight to voicemail at work and home.

I said, "Learned some interesting things about Okash," and got out of there.

Robin was in the kitchen, hair toweled, wearing her Japanese robe and reading *Cook's* magazine. Blanche stretched a few feet away, attending to a jerky stick. Both of them looked up and smiled. Robin got up, fetched a couple of plates and two bottles of Grolsch from the fridge, set them on the table.

Turkey sandwiches, potato salad, Greek olives, apple slices.

I said, "Impressive leftovers."

"Easy when you start with good stuff. So how were the nuns?"

"One nun, nice person."

I summed up what Emeline Beaumont had told me.

She said, "Two lose their freedom and the one who's left chooses self-restriction."

"Interesting way to look at it." I popped the bottles.

Robin said, "So now you know this woman's capable of calculated violence and has a brother with anger problems. That must've been some family."

We were clearing the table when Milo called.

He said, "You'll never believe who I've got sitting in an interview room."

"Okash."

"Her brother."

"Dugong."

A beat. "There goes my punch line. How the hell did you find that out?"

"I left you a message explaining."

"Saw it but didn't read it, yet. Too busy with Geoffrey. You have time to bop over?"

I looked at Robin.

She said, "He's coming over? Sure, I'll make more sandwiches."

"He wants me at the station. The angry brother showed up."

"Then I guess you'll have to go. Civic duty and all that."

"I can tell him no."

She stroked my cheek. "Naysaying's not your strong point, darling."

Milo had placed Geoffrey Dugong in a room he rarely used because it flanked a small observation area with a one-way mirror and he didn't like being observed. Dugong was on his feet, pacing. A gray wheelie bag and a green duffel sat in a corner.

Medina Okash's half brother wore a black leather jacket, red T-shirt, black jeans, orange sneakers. Tattoos wriggled from under his cuffs and ivied the sides of his neck. The rings sausaging his beard were gone, leaving a coarse fan of dark hair that reached his pectorals.

His circuits were slow, a bent-over trudge that traced the walls of the room. Dispirited, none of the anger we'd seen at the gallery. Younger than Medina Okash but he looked older.

I said, "Different Geoffrey."

Milo said, "He's been hitting the sauce hard, fear of flying. His story is he had a flight three hours ago back to Florida, Ubered to the gallery where Okash was supposed to meet him and drive him but she didn't show up."

"Why not go straight to the airport?"

"Money. She was gonna pay him for the two paintings he sold, said she needed to get a business check. He shows up, the place is dark, he hangs around, walks to the back, finds her car there and knocks on the back door, nada. He tries to call her, no connection, returns to the front, waits some more, gets antsy, tries the back again. At that point Binchy, who's been observing all this, follows him, ready for a confrontation. Instead, he finds a scared drunk guy who asks for help."

"What's so scary about a no-show?"

"Maybe it's the booze talking or whatever personality issues he's got. But what he claims is Okash is big on punctuality, it just didn't feel right." He eyed the mirror. "You wanna watch him go 'round in circles a few more times?"

"No, enough entertainment."

The moment we cracked the door, Dugong stopped, stared, and tottered toward a table in the center of the room.

I shook his hand.

"Yeah, I saw you the first time." Sharp gust of grain alcohol. He burped. "Sorry, I fill the tank before I fly. Scares the shit out of me, I like boats." Slurred voice, red eyes, cracked lips. In a few years he could hang with the likes of Mary Jane Huralnik.

We sat down across from him.

Milo said, "So you were saying Medina's never late."

"I mean, she didn't used to be."

I said, "Back when you were kids."

"Yuh."

"You guys grew up together?"

"No, no, my dad—our dad—he moved around." Head shake. "He was a dog and a total asshole. Our mothers hated each other." A beat. "So we also did."

I said, "Fighting your mothers' battles."

Dugong chewed his lip. His eyes narrowed in concentration; weighing a novel concept. "Guess so."

"So when did you and Medina start talking again?"

"Last year. I . . . okay, I'll be straight, I had a meth problem, got out of rehab but couldn't find a job on a boat, you know? So I started painting again. I always done it. Drawing, painting, doing collage, anything art. In rehab they said I was good. So I went to Art Basel, it's this big winter thing in Miami."

I said, "Showing your stuff there is huge, Geoff."

Dugong looked at the table. "I wasn't showing, I got hired to move stuff around."

"Like a grip?"

"What's that?"

"Guys who move stuff on movie sets."

"Yeah, like that. It was shit work for thirteen an hour with faggots ordering you around. But I figured get close to the art, see what's selling. That's when Medina saw me. I'm pushing a hand truck, she's with these rich assholes, dressed in white like a cruise ship, speaking European. We knew each other right away, had saw each other ten years before. *His* funeral. I wouldn'ta said anything but she did this."

He held up a wait-a-second finger.

I said, "Wanting you to stick around."

"Yeah. She finished with the Europeans, it was almost my break so we had coffee. I was like, what do you want, we never got along. But turned out to be a good deal, she's mellow, we talk, she finds out I paint, she just got her own gallery in L.A., if I come up with something she can use, she'll look at it. So I walked out on that shit job, got back to the Keys, and went crazy painting. Did a couple of water scenes and sent her a photo and she said great but she needed something more conceptual. I'm like what? She's like an idea—a concept. Then she tells me about the candles, I say sure, that's easier than water. I do a candle, send her a photo, she says great, now we're in business, do a bunch more. She pays to have everything sent here, pays to fly me out. Round-trip."

"She handled everything."

"She's good at that. Organized, you know? So when she's not there, it feels wrong. 'Cause yeah, she is big on time. Doing things organized. Then your redhead dude shows up—what was he doing there, anyway? Cool guy, though. For one a your—he was okay to me."

I said, "What's behind the back door?"

"Huh?"

"The door that leads to the parking lot."

"The back room."

"We saw a small storage room but there's something behind that."

"Another back room, empty," said Dugong.

Milo said, "So you got worried."

"Fuck, yeah, you *think*?" Sharp glints livened Dugong's eyes, jagged, like fissures in overheated glass. The spade of beard quivered, large, inked hands rolled naturally into fists. His knuckles were glossy, heaped with keloid scarring.

Souvenirs of the red zone. Which was where he was edging now, without warning.

Milo sat taller and stared him down.

Dugong forced his hands open, rubbed the side of his neck, tried, without success, to smile. "Sorry, sometimes I get inpatient."

"No prob, Geoff. You're under stress."

"Zactly. Makes no sense, like at the show, she gave me shit for being ten minutes late and it wasn't even my fault, driver was some Armenian asshole, got messed up by one-way streets. Ten minutes and she reams me. Like really *reams* me. It put me in a shit mood. That's why you saw me being in a shit mood."

He cracked his knuckles. "I'm working on it. Keeping it even . . . maybe I'm making a big fucking deal but it feels off, that's all I can say. I don't want problems with you guys so when Redhead Dude says he's calling the boss, I say sure, flight's already gone, what the fuck."

Milo said, "Where've you been staying in L.A., Geoff?"

"Caribbean Motel in Hollywood. I been in worse."

"You never stayed at Medina's place."

"No way, we both like our space. We *never* lived together, *he* just went back and forth depending on who he wanted to fu— He was a dog and an asshole and now we agree on that."

I said, "You and your sister are used to living separately."

"I never thought of her as my sister," said Dugong. "Even now, with the show, it wasn't a family thing, more like . . . we had something we could both do. She hung my stuff, threw the party, we sold a couple, we both made out. So are you gonna look for her?"

Milo said, "Definitely, Geoff. Have you checked to see if she went back home? Maybe left her car at the gallery and took her own Uber?"

Dugong thought. Slow-breathed with effort that creased his forehead. A man fated to battle emotion. Maybe neural pathways disrupted by meth. Maybe he'd gone for speed because something had always been wrong.

Milo said, "I'm not trying to stress you, Geoff."

"I know, I know." Dugong took hold of his beard, squeezed, let go. "Sorry, it's just the questions, it's like a storm in my head . . . I told you her phone doesn't answer, how can I check?"

"Good point, Geoff. Sorry, I'm just used to asking questions."

"She had my money and she promised to take me—I'm not making this up in my head."

Convincing himself.

Milo said, "Of course not, Geoff."

Yank of the beard. "Good, good—sometimes I need to know I'm making sense." Dugong licked his lips.

Milo said, "Want some water or coffee?"

"Nah, I'm good."

"Change your mind, let me know, Geoff. Now I'd like to show you some pictures and you tell me if you've ever seen any of these people with Medina."

"What kind of people?" said Dugong.

"Possible social contacts. Maybe folks who were at the show."

"Why?"

"If we're gonna do a good search, Geoff, we need to know as much as we can about her social life."

Flimsy premise. Dugong said, "Sure, go for it."

No reactions to any of the victims until he saw Benny Alvarez's photo.

"That's the retarded dude, worked at the gallery." Red eyes slitted. "Why you showing me that? He got killed."

"Medina told you?"

"She said that's why you were there. She was pretty freaked out."

"That he was killed or that we were there?"

"Both. I guess. This was later, after the show. She was pissed off and not talking to me. I say okay, here goes, own your shit, asshole, like they tell you in rehab. So I say *sor-ree.* She shines me on, I say it again. She says I couldn'ta picked a worse time, she's trying to run a show and sell my stuff and I'm acting like a big baby and on top of it you guys just showed up and told her the retarded dude got killed."

I said, "His name's Benny."

"She said that, too."

"What was Benny like?"

"Like? He was retarded, didn't talk much. Little dude, didn't seem like he'd get in anyone's face. So who killed him?"

Milo said, "We're trying to find out."

Dugong's eyes bugged. "Oh, shit. Oh, holy fucking shit." He buried his face in his hands.

"Geoff?"

Red eyes rose. "I see what you're getting at. Oh, fuck."

"What, Geoff?"

"He works there, she works there, you think the same could happen to her as him. Something about that place? Bad karma, whatever? Oh, shit. I didn't think about that."

"Let's not get ahead of ourselves, Geoff."

Dugong pouted. Curiously vulnerable moue, out of place on a grizzled face. "What do you mean?"

"There's no reason to connect Medina to Benny."

"Really? You're not shitting me?"

"Absolutely not, Geoff. First thing we'll do is head over to Medina's place, for all we know she came down with something and decided to go to bed."

"We? You and me?"

Milo smiled. "No, just us, Geoff."

"She's sick why wouldn't she call me? She knew when my flight was leaving because she'd boughten the ticket—oh, fuck, I need to buy another—you think maybe they'd give it to me free 'cause it's not my fault? Oh, fuck, I need to find out when there are other flights."

He held the sides of his head. Murmured, "All this shit to do."

Milo said, "No guarantees, Geoff, but we'll talk to the airlines, tell them it was an emergency. Why don't you find out first if there is another flight."

"Yeah . . ." Dugong reached into a pocket and pulled out an older Android with a cracked screen.

Milo glanced at me. Not a burner.

He clicked for a while, made errors, cursed, finally connected. "Okay . . . there's another in . . . like five hours. I got to get over there. So you'll write me a note or something?"

"We'll do better, Geoff. We'll drive you over and talk to the airline personally. What's your cell number?"

Dugong told him. His fingers waved wildly. "I need to get my cats from the dude I left them with."

I said, "You're a cat person, huh?"

"Got three strays, they love me."

"No dogs?"

"Cats are better, do their own thing."

"Medina into dogs?"

"Not that she said. Can we go? I need to go?"

"Anything else you want to tell us, Geoff?"

Dugong tapped a foot, blinked, played with his beard. "I hope she's okay. I want to sell more art."

CHAPTER 35

We left him in the room and called Sean up from the big D-room.

Milo told him his new assignment.

"Am I looking for something specific, Loot?"

"Nope, don't ask questions and for sure don't challenge the guy, he was a meth freak, still acts like one, and is tanked up on booze. Stay mellow and maybe he'll drop some nugget of info. He does, don't react, just remember."

"Sounds kind of like being a therapist," said Binchy. "You come up with the plan, Doc?"

Milo said, "Give me credit, kid. Conceived it all on my lonesome."

Sean flushed. "Sorry, Loot."

Milo clapped his back. "Relax. You're the man for the job."

"I am?"

"You bet, he thinks you're a good guy."

"Really," said Binchy.

Far more cheered by Dugong's evaluation than he should be.

Appreciating every brick in the crumbling walls of his identity. One day we'd talk.

He went to get Dugong out of the interview room, came out carrying the duffel followed by Dugong wheeling the bag.

They walked down the corridor, side by side, Binchy talking about something, Dugong listening. Probably music. Sean loves to talk about music.

Milo and I headed the opposite direction, to his office.

He said, "Here's my take on Rembrandt: not too bright in the first place, additional brain cells popped by substance abuse. And tragically, he was being totally straight with us."

I said, "Tragic because of the way he described Okash's reaction to our drop-in."

He leaned against the doorpost. "Freaked out by Benny's death? Not a good fit for her being our bad girl."

"Unless," I said, "Okash suspected or knew she was being watched and decided to use Dugong *because* he's a dull-witted addict and a starving artist who's come to depend on her. She insists on driving him to the airport, incentivizes by promising to pay him, then stands him up knowing he's likely to react emotionally rather than just get his own ride. He's observed by Sean, gets taken here, tells us exactly what she wants us to hear."

"That's pretty elaborate."

"So was the crime scene."

He exhaled in several bursts and took the single stride that led to his desk. Plopping into his chair, he made it whinny in protest. "So where the hell is she?"

I said, "If the key was setting Dugong up as an unwitting character reference, she's anywhere but where she was supposed to be. That could mean she never left the building but is out of view—like that back-of-the-back room. Or she got away without being spotted—walked a few miles west and was picked up, maybe by her co-conspirator."

He rubbed his face. "Who isn't Dugong. All right, let's go for horses, not zebras, and try her damn apartment."

I drove and Milo called Sleepy, asking him to get Dugong a free ticket on the next flight to Key West.

"You like being in debt?"

"We'll find a way to even up."

"This guy's a C.I.?"

"Something like that."

A beat. "If there's a cheap seat, I'll do it," said Sleepy, "but man, you're compounding interest."

Seconds later: texted verification of the flight number.

Milo called Binchy. Binchy whispered, "Great, he'll be happy."

"Why the hush-hush?"

"He fell asleep, Loot. Maybe emotional overload?"

Milo clicked off. "My designated bleeding-heart. Think he could use some therapy for the balcony stuff?"

"Yup."

"Should I order it?"

"Give him more time," I said. "I'm keeping an eye out."

He smiled. "Such a nurturing environment we've created. Okay, let's get a look at Medina's natural habitat."

Not to be.

Okash's building was well maintained, full security, with an in-house manager, a woman named Ada Mansour who responded to Milo's buzzer-push with a snappish "Police?" and took her time appearing.

Fifties, stocky, bleached blonde in a brown shirt with faint military overtones over tan stretch pants and a scowl that looked sewn-on.

She sidled through one of a pair of glass doors, folded her arms across her chest as she listened to Milo's request.

Responding before his final word faded. "Nope, can't let you in."

Milo said, "It's a welfare check, ma'am."

"Based on what?"

"Ms. Okash is missing."

"For how long?"

"She didn't show up for an appointment a few hours ago."

Mansour smirked. "That's missing? No way, Jose, it's not going to work again."

"Again?"

"My son used to play in a band, bunch of them were sharing a dive in the Valley. Cops claimed it was a welfare check so they could bust the door. Ali got arrested for drugs and he doesn't even use them. Cost me a fortune."

"There's nothing like that going on now, ma'am."

"So you say. My lawyer got everything dismissed because you guys shouldn't have entered in the first place. Cost me an arm and a leg and a lot of time and energy so forget it."

"How about this?" said Milo. "You go into her apartment and check."

"Check for what?"

"Is she there, is she okay."

"She's out," said Mansour. "I saw her leave and she didn't come back. She looked fine."

"How can you be sure she didn't return?"

"My unit's near hers. If she was there, I'd know it."

"She a good neighbor?"

"Now the questions start?" said Mansour. "She's quiet and pays her rent. That means good. You suspect her of something? The owners don't want no problems, you guys hide something and something happens there'll be lawyers, believe me."

"It's a welfare check, ma'am."

It didn't fail because it was a lie. Mansour was primed to refuse. "Ma'am, huh? That's what all of yous called me when I had to bail out Ali. Ma'am this, ma'am that. Meanwhile they're putting me through the wringer."

She turned to leave.

Milo got in front of her and tried to give her his card.

She kept her hands by her side. "Ugh. What do I want with this?"

"I'm available in case of problems. Ms. Mansour."

"Like you care," she said. "Like I believe anyone about anything anytime anyplace."

Back in the Seville, he laughed. "Checked the weather this morning, didn't see any storm warnings."

I said, "Nowadays, everything's personal."

"Ain't that the truth. So what's next . . . maybe whoever owns the gallery building will have a friendlier attitude. Let's see who that might be."

I started the car. "West to the station or east to downtown?"

"You always say optimism's healthy. Let's aim for Hart Street."

The ride was quiet but for grunts and clicks as he worked his phone.

Disgruntled bear harassed by crickets.

He sat back frowning. "Plug in the address and an outfit called AOC, Limited, comes up. But a search for business licenses and DBAs pulls up nothing. The only link I can find is an outfit in Macao: Asian-Occidental Concepts. I go on *their* website and everything dissolves. One more try."

His thumbs worked. "Now it's frozen."

He switched the phone off and on. "Know anything about Macao?"

"Part of China, I think they like casinos."

"Hmph—okay, it's the—get this—Special Administrative Region of the People's Republic of China. I'm visualizing a mail-drop in a dim sum joint."

I said, "Sounds like a trade center with tax benefits. Is there a chamber of commerce?"

"Hold on . . . there is, indeed . . . but it's gobbledygook . . . okay, here's something: The place has cultural agreements in Europe. Company calls itself Asian-Occidental, maybe that'll lead somewhere."

He muttered as he worked.

"Lisbon, Portugal . . . nada . . . Coimbra, Portugal, nada . . . one more place in Portugal . . . Porto—that where the wine's from? I could use some . . . also zilch . . . next stop . . . *c'mon* Linköping, Sweden . . . thanks for nothing, Blondie . . . okay, *here* we go, Brussels, Belgium."

He gave the thumbs-up and returned to the screen. "The Belgium-Macao Friendship Society lists a whole bunch of companies and top of the list is AOC. Along with . . . three subsidiaries. First one is . . . hold on, this is a mouthful . . . Nieder . . . schön . . . hausen Fine Arts . . . then Western Import-Export, then Heigur, Limited. Why's that third one familiar?"

I said, "Owner of the house where Okash delivered the painting."

"Okash sells two paintings and one goes to her landlord?"

"Maybe some kind of swap for rent. The building isn't exactly booming."

"Okay, forget downtown, go west, young man."

No cars in the driveway of the blue house on Clearwater Lane. Mail overflowed a tarnished brass box to the left of the front door. Bulk junk addressed to *Occupant.* Milo put it back, rang the bell, got the expected silence.

"Not exactly Xanadu. They have a Rolls, huh?"

"And a Volvo."

"Automotive yin-yang . . . the place is obviously *not* a mail-drop."

I said, "Maybe it's a layover for Macao execs when they're here on business. Or some sort of tax dodge—keeping the ownership overseas where the rates are lower and depreciating the real estate here."

"How does that work?"

"Above my pay grade," I said. "I did have a custody case last year, couple was worth six hundred million, most of it in property. They bought, sold, traded up, kept depreciating, and paid no income tax. The wife threatened to expose it but it turned out to be legit."

"She owned half and wanted to blow everything up?"

"You bet," I said. "She hated her husband that much."

"Nose, spite, face—doesn't that level of ugly get to you?"

"This from you?"

"I live in one nasty world, you occupy two."

"I've got a fulfilling outside life."

"Feeding the fish?"

I smiled. "That's part of it."

He tried a gate on the east side of the house. Bolted. "When Okash brought the painting someone was here to let her in."

"Definitely. She stayed inside for sixteen minutes."

"You timed it?"

"Nothing else to do while I watched."

"So if we keep popping by there's a chance of catching someone. Let's get out of here."

He slouched toward the Seville.

I got behind the wheel. "Back to the gallery again?"

"You've got energy for that?"

"Sure."

"Titanium man. Nah, I'm bushed. Drop me at the station then go feed your finny friends."

CHAPTER 36

He dozed as I drove, rasping through his nose. A mile from the station he was roused by a text beep, sat up sharp and speed-dialed.

Marcus Coolidge said, "Hey. A couple of us have been reviewing any closed-circuit footage we can find within a mile of my crime scene. Mostly phony cameras, malfunctions, lousy quality when we get anything. But an hour ago, Albert—my guy, a loaner from Auto-Theft—spotted something a little less than half a mile away. The same car drives toward the dump site at the right time and is spotted going the other way sixteen minutes later. It's the only vehicle we've seen doing that. It's an industrial area, that hour no traffic to speak of. Disk is too blurry to make out the tags but the make's clear. Volvo sedan, you know how boxy they are. Leon's a motorhead, says mid- to late nineties 850."

I said, "White."

Coolidge said, "Who's that?"

Milo said, "Dr. Delaware. Is it white?"

A beat. "You already know this?"

"We didn't until you called, Marc." He told Coolidge about the cars at the Clearwater house.

Coolidge said, "That and a Rolls, one for show, one for the dirty work? So who are these people?"

"That, my friend, is unclear. All we've got so far is a business," Milo summed up.

Coolidge said, "Macao. Where's that, the Caribbean?"

"China. Low taxes and casinos."

"So we could be dealing with Asian mafia types?"

"Who knows, Marc? The company seems to do art and real estate and Okash does business with them. She was seen coming and going with what looked like a painting."

"Business and nasty," said Coolidge, "if that Volvo is theirs."

"We just stopped by, neither car was there and at least a couple days' mail was in the box—all junk, no addressee names. Given what you found, you up for a meeting tomorrow morning, my shop? Bring Albert, you'll meet my team."

"Team? How many you got?"

"Three D's, all on loan."

"Same as here. My boss calls the Auto boss, cashes in a favor, and gets me Albert. Guy knows cars like I know my right hand. Not sure he can make it but I'll be there. When were you thinking?"

"Ten work for you?"

"No prob." Coolidge yawned. " 'Scuse, looking at that video is like a slow drip of vodka, I need to crash."

CHAPTER 37

Next morning, same room. I was starting to feel at home.

Clean whiteboard, six chairs assembled in two rows like a classroom. Milo had amped up the catering: two boxes of pastries, another of assorted bagels, lox, cream cheese, paper napkins, a coffee urn, hot water, tea bags, Styrofoam cups. All on his dime.

Enthusiastic consumption all around. Even Reed, succumbing to a whole-wheat bagel.

He sat in the back row with Binchy and me. In front of us were Marc Coolidge, his Inglewood colleague, a six-foot-five Kobe Bryant look-alike named Albert Freeman, and Alicia Bogomil.

Up at the board, his jacket freckled by crumbs, Milo wielded a wooden pointer.

He'd been over the basics: no additional data on any of the four victims, no sightings of Medina Okash. Even with her car behind the gallery, the inactive look of the entire building suggested she'd slipped out and had been picked up by someone.

That combined with the mail pile-up at the blue house caused the room to go quiet.

Milo tapped Geoffrey Dugong's face. "He's gone, too, but to my mind, he's a low-probability suspect. Unless he's a consummate actor, and I don't think he's bright enough. Either way, we had nothing to hold him on so he's back in Key West, courtesy a flight paid for by Homeland Security."

Albert Freeman said, "How'd you pull that off?"

"Personal charm. Meanwhile, I've kept watch on the gallery and Alicia's been surveilling Okash's apartment. A warrant's out of the question and I still can't convince the D.A. a welfare check isn't going to get us in evidentiary trouble. But one thing I did get from Dugong was Okash's cell number and I've issued a subpoena for her records."

Coolidge said, "So despite what the whack-a-walrus said, she's high-probability."

"She's got a history of violence, the last place Benny Alvarez was seen alive is her gallery, she patronized the market where Solomon Roget posted his ads. And now we've got your Volvo lead and her connection to Clearwater. We've been figuring this for at least two people."

"Her and some dude with a Rolls."

"The reaction we saw to the murders was a one-eighty from what she showed Dugong."

Milo turned to me.

I said, "Calm to the point of being flat and extremely flirtatious. So she may have been one of Rick Gurnsey's flock of sexual partners, possibly the woman seen with Gurnsey at the house last January."

Coolidge said, "So what's the motive?"

Milo said, "Given Okash's business, we might have some sort of sick performance art."

More silence.

I said, "I just thought of something. The burner Gurnsey was talking to before he got killed has a Baltimore number and Okash went to high school in Annapolis."

"It's a burner, Doc," said Binchy. "Random numbers."

Alicia cleared her throat. "Not exactly. In the early days you could pay for an area code. And sometimes codes actually matched where they were sold. Least I saw that in Alburquerque."

Milo said, "That so? Okay, maybe another brick in the wall."

He pointed to a photo of the blue house on Clearwater. "Onward to this place. Still haven't found any names associated with the property, just a company, AOC—Asian-Occidental Concepts."

The pointer shifted to the right. Enlargements of a white Volvo and a long, sleek Rolls-Royce the same color. "These aren't actual cars and in fact none are registered to AOC. But these exact models *are* registered to one of their subsidiaries, an outfit called Heigur, Limited. Making it even more interesting, another subsidiary, Western Import-Export, owns the building that houses Okash's place as well as the two other galleries on the ground floor. Neither of which we've ever seen actually doing business."

Coolidge said, "Some sort of front."

"That's what it smells like," said Milo. Tap of the Volvo. "This one's a '96 850, just like you figured, Detective Freeman. Wanna I.D. the Rolls?"

Freeman walked to the board, put on glasses, returned to his seat. "Lower radiator, extended wheel base, got to be a Mark Three Silver Dawn. In terms of the year, about the same vintage as the Volvo: '93 to '96."

"Impressive," said Milo. "DMV says Heigur's Rolls is a '95."

Reed said, "Rolls-Royce, a house in B.H., mega-money."

Freeman said, "The house maybe, but not necessarily the car. Market's soft as a baby's butt, you could get one of these for twenty-five, thirty K."

Binchy said, "You're kidding."

Alicia said, "Thinking of upgrading, Sean? Putting a surfboard on the roof?"

Binchy smiled. "Maybe, if there's enough belts for the car seats."

Coolidge said, "Both cars are from the nineties so maybe that's when these Asian folk came to town. Meaning they *could've* bought the Rolls new and we are dealing with a big-bucks thing."

Milo said, "So far, we've found no other vehicles registered to Heigur, so maybe. In terms of what that means for the case?" He shrugged.

Reed said, "What I was getting at is that with corporate types or Chinese gangsters, there could be lots of flying in and out. For all we know Vollmann and McGann got dumped near the airport *because* it was on the way to a fly-out."

Al Freeman said, "Maybe they are jet-setters but here's the thing: Cars can't just sit there, they get garage rot, the engine freezes. So if both vehicles are operable, someone's driving them on a semi-regular basis. And servicing them. There are plenty of places to handle the Volvo but the Roller's more specialized. Besides a couple of dealers, there are like four guys in L.A. County you'd go to. It might narrow things down."

Coolidge turned to regard his colleague. "You going on *Jeopardy!*? See why I brought him?"

Milo said, "Could you call the four, Al?"

"Sure, get me the VIN and I might be able to nail it, specifically."

Milo grinned. "I didn't know better, I'd think you owned one."

Freeman shrugged.

Coolidge nudged him. "C'mon, give it up, man."

Alicia whistled.

Freeman said, "Got a '76 Shadow couple of years ago."

Hoots all around followed by brief applause.

Freeman got up, bowed, sat down. "No big deal, picked it up for thirteen K."

Coolidge said, "Bet you don't tell the ladies that."

Milo said, "Which of the four mechanics services your car? You could start there."

"I do it myself."

Coolidge stared at his friend. "That *and* college basketball? Where's your cape, Ironman?"

Alicia looked at Freeman intently.

He said, "It's not rocket science. Spent some time with a guy in Van Nuys, yeah I'll start with him."

"I'll email the VIN," said Milo. "Thanks."

Alicia had loaded a photo of a '76 Silver Shadow on her phone. "*Nice.* What color's yours?"

Freeman said, "Shell gray, red interior."

"Sounds gorgeous."

"I take care of it."

She smiled at him. He smiled back.

Milo said, "In terms of where to go from here, we just keep watching Okash's places. Same rotation if that works for the three of you."

Reed, Binchy, and Bogomil nodded.

I said, "Another canvass of Benedict Canyon might be a good idea. Neighbors who weren't there the first time, people who remember something new."

Milo said, "If we can fit it in, maybe."

Alicia said, "What about that autistic kid? He claims he was actually out there when the killers left. Are you sure he told you everything?"

Milo said, "He's a minor and his mother was pretty protective so I don't see getting access."

Alicia said, "We've got a psychologist."

Everyone looked at me.

I said, "I'll give it a try."

CHAPTER 38

I drove home thinking about how to approach Crispin Moman. Then I backed up and remembered the job I'd been trained for and looked at the big picture: Ethically, *should* I approach him?

This was a boy who'd been dealt an unusual hand. I couldn't see any benefit he'd get from getting more involved. And if his name found its way into the murder book, he could conceivably find himself on a witness list.

If he was my kid, I'd say no.

As someone licensed to take care of people, *I* said no.

At the next red light, I texted Milo, told him I'd changed my mind and why.

My phoned pinged immediately.

Yeah, thought about it, figured you might say that. No worries. M.

I continued to drive west on Sunset, veered north on Benedict, came to Clearwater Lane, and hooked a right.

Still no cars at the blue house. More mail, spillover from the now full box, piled haphazardly in front of the door. I sifted through it.

Occupant. Resident. Homeowner.

Maybe Reed was right and whoever lived here was on the other side of the planet. With or without Medina Okash.

I returned to the Seville. Just as I turned the key, another text came through.

When are you coming home?

Five, ten minutes. Everything ok?

I'm fine. Just come home.

Robin met me at the door, still in her work overalls, hands drumming her hips, bouncing on her feet.

Not like her, and Blanche was also keyed up, snorting and rotating her head.

I said, "What's going on, girls?"

Robin took my hand, led me to my office, pointed at my computer. "Sent it to you from my laptop because your screen's wide."

Faded color and curvaceous form filled the monitor.

A painting, blurred, busy.

From a distance, the interior of what looked to be a Renaissance drawing room. Voluptuous folds of satin and velvet and embroidered cloth, intricate brocade, tides of sable and ermine fur. All that excess punctuated by gem-like dots of metallic trim.

Luxuriant heaps of far-too-much in a confined space suggested imminent collapse.

I sat down, took a closer look, and amended my first impression: not a room; a horse-drawn coach crowded with people.

Up front a driver gripped the reins in a white-gloved hand as he craned back toward his passengers. Beyond him a star-flecked night sky, in front of him a hint of dappled equine haunches.

Black man. Literally. His skin rendered in inky tones limned blue and lilac.

Scarlet lips, milky teeth, the sclera of eyes tinted butterscotch as he leered at his passengers. No subtlety to racist intention.

He wore the type of Moorish garb that had filled the fantasies of Europeans travelers centuries ago as they indulged in "Orientalist" art: three gold hoops in one pendulous ear, grape-purple livery edged in silver, a creamy white turban.

The leer cartoonish.

I shifted to the objects of the driver's attention.

The passenger sitting farthest from the viewer—next to the coach's window—was a sallow, child-sized man of uncertain age with a tiny, scrunched, capuchin-monkey face. His slight frame was covered by a grass-green, high-buttoned tunic hemmed at the bottom by yellow triangles ending in bells.

Hooding his tiny head was more green cloth adorned by floppy donkey ears.

Bucktoothed smile.

Professional fool, on the job.

Closest to the eye, bathed in a ray of what had probably been bright-golden light centuries ago but was now ecru, sat a handsome, young, rosy-cheeked man, resplendent in blue silk and white lace. Glossy ringlets of dark hair trailed below his shoulders. Gold epaulets on his shoulders suggested military rank. So did a royal-blue cavalier's hat balanced on his right knee.

The smirking expression of a spoiled adolescent. A waxed mustache and a wispy triangle of hair on his chin failed to add maturity. Nor did slumping posture, drunken eyes, and an agape mouth molded into a besotted grin. In the center of the mouth, a tongue tinted and shaped like a Japanese eggplant curled backward, a fleshy nautilus probing the innards beyond.

Sitting between the men, pressed close to the cavalier's right flank, was a hook-nosed crone in a fraying, dust-colored dress, the garment baggy but unable to conceal a barrel of girth.

A black beret roosted lopsided atop strands of white hair so wild they appeared electrified. Drool beaded on her chin. The dress was cut low and square, exposing puckered cleavage that dipped to the withered roseate of the woman's right nipple.

Like the three men, smiling. Crafty smile, as if a spell had been cast. Two brown teeth on top, a single incisor below.

The hag's right hand, gnarled and liver-spotted, circled the young man's penis. Small organ, but erect.

On the floor of the coach, two snub-nosed dogs, tongues drooping, observing the merriment. Resting on a bed of scarlet taffeta.

I turned away, heart racing. Robin's hands alit on my shoulders and stayed there.

I put my hand on hers. "How did you find this?"

"The more I thought about what you described, your suspect running a gallery, the more I wondered if someone had tried to re-create an actual work of art. My first thought was Hieronymus Bosch or someone like him but I came up empty. So I keyed *erotic art* along with the basic victim descriptions. *Black man young man old woman.* I wasn't sure how to characterize the mentally challenged guy but finally I said to heck with political correctness and put in *fool.* Because that's how I saw a cruel murderer viewing him. To my amazement, this came up right away on a website called youdidntinventsexstupid.com. There's all sorts of racy stuff on it. Apparently, Rembrandt went for outdoor sex, did a bunch of etchings, the most famous is *The Monk in the Cornfield.* Then there's Picasso, Egon Schiele, Japanese woodcuts. But also this."

"Who runs the site?"

"A woman named Suzanne Hirto. Art history professor at Swarthmore, she directed it to 'the smug, entitled brats who invade my classroom.'"

I said, "Not a great career move."

"You've got that right, she was fired. Not for erotica, for hurting the poor dears' feelings. But she keeps the site up, message of defiance and all that. Anyway, here it is: *The Museum of Desire,* painted sometime around 1510, probably in Venice by one Antonio Domenico Carascelli. He was rumored to be a student of Titian but that can't be proved. This is the only known work attributed to him and even that's up for grabs. But putting aside taste issues, he was good, don't you think? So maybe."

I stared at the image. "How long did you work on this?"

"You know," she said. "You get caught up."

"Where's the painting now?"

"No one knows. I emailed Hirto—she's retired, sculpts and paints. She answered right away, said she got the image from a catalog put out by a Holocaust survivor group back in the seventies."

"Nazi art?"

"Yes, but not what you'd think. This wasn't stolen from Jewish collectors, it was part of Hermann Göring's personal collection. Most of which *was* plunder. Great stuff—Velázquez, Renoir, Monet, all stolen. Like a good Nazi, he left handwritten lists that finally got cataloged a few years ago. But the bastard also bought and hoarded erotica that he didn't record. This may have been an exception because of the Titian link, but no one knows for sure. The survivors tried to get compensation for reparations but they were poorly funded, relinquished control to a larger group who's *still* struggling to get the stolen stuff back. So no interest in a dirty picture by an unknown artist."

"Unbelievable," I said. "That you found it."

"It turned out not to be that complicated, hon."

"That's like saying all a drag racer needs to do is drive straight." I got up, took her face in my hands, and kissed her hard. "Brilliant. Absolutely brilliant."

"Aw," she said. "Now I need a bigger hat."

◆

She and Blanche returned to the studio and I studied the painting, feeling queasy rather than triumphant.

I began to send the image to Milo. Decided phone-miniaturization would lessen the impact and texted instead.

How close are you?

Still at the office. Everything okay?

Fine. Come over.

Paraphrasing Robin. Why mess with brilliance?

CHAPTER 39

I filled the time waiting for him trying to find other references to *The Museum of Desire,* Göring's porn stash, Antonio Carascelli.

Nothing.

I checked out Suzanne Hirto's site. Two headshots of her on the homepage: a photo that showed her blond, midfifties, with an open smiling face, and a self-portrait in oils that distorted her countenance to the shape of a dog bone and tinted it bilious green under a thatch of plaid hair.

The bell rang. I put the painting back on the screen and went to open the door.

Milo charged in. "What's up?"

"A whole lot."

He said, "How the hell did you find this?"

"Robin found it."

"Jesus. What *is* it?"

I told him.

He said, "Obscure? So whoever knows about it coulda seen it on this site?"

"Could be."

A third look at the painting. "Unbelievable. What's her email?"

I logged back onto Suzanne Hirto's site. He pointed to the grotesque self-portrait. "What's that about?"

I said, "Maybe a confident woman."

"Don't see a visitor count. Push *Contact,* I'll do the begging."

Dear Professor Hirto,

This is Lieutenant Milo Sturgis of the Los Angeles Police Department. You were contacted recently by Robin Castagna, an artist who resides here in L.A., about a painting titled The Museum of Desire. I believe the painting may be related to a case I'm investigating. I know this is a difficult request because of privacy issues but would there be any way for you to be comfortable releasing the email addresses of people who've logged onto your site? It's possible one of them is involved in this crime. I assure you no one innocent will be contacted or otherwise hassled.

Thanks and best, Milo

He exhaled. "She'll probably ignore me."

Seconds later:

Hey, Milo. Really? That's crazy and creepy. What type of crime?

Suze.

Thanks for getting back, Suze. Unfortunately, murder.

Holy shit! I have no problems giving you the info, no one should get away with killing someone. Problem is I don't pay attention to the site anymore, never kept a user file in the first place and I delete my emails every week or so cause I don't want shit piling up.

Understood, Suze. Would you be willing to have one of our tech people take a look and see what they can come up with?

Hmm. Don't know about that. A little too black helicopter, you know? Not being paranoid, just prefer to live a quiet life. Speaking of which, major oops: How do I know you're who you say you are? Are you going to ask me to send cash to Nigeria?

Hahaha. Promise I'm legit. Here's my office number at LAPD, West Los Angeles Division. You can also google me. I've solved a few cases.

A minute passed. Two, three, four.

Milo said, "So much for that. I'm amazed a professorial type even answered."

"Ex-prof," I said. "She got fired for speaking her mind."

"Ah, a woman of taste and discretion." Fourth look at the painting followed by a headshake. He paced, returned. "Okay, let's think about which way to go on this."

Ping.

A few cases? You're downright Sherlockian, sir. I phoned the #, got transferred to someone named Reid, he assured me you're his boss. So okay, let me think about it. I don't like assholes getting away with spilling blood. My brother's a lawyer, I check everything with him except clay, tools, paint, and brushes. He oks it, maybe but no promises.

More than I could hope for, Suze. Muchas gracias.

Bilingual, huh? Hasta la vista. S.

I rotated my index finger.

He said, “What?”

“Picking up a nuance of romance in the air.”

“If she only knew.” He grinned. “Hey, she comes through for me, maybe I can be flexible. Scroll back to the masterpiece.”

A few squinting seconds later. “Talk about un-fine art. So what, Okash always wanted to be a painter but has no talent, decides to work with human flesh?”

“I still think it began with Gurnsey and expanded. Look.” I tapped the screen. “The young guy’s the center of the composition. The light hits his face.”

“Okash and Ricky at that party,” he said. “Something happens that pisses Okash off—maybe being caught by Candace Kierstead, she blames Gurnsey for roping her in.”

I said, “We know she’s got a violent temper. Rage kicks in, she decides on payback, knows about the painting and goes about assembling the rest of the cast. Probably beginning with poor Benny Alvarez. Small-stature, challenged guy sweeping up her place.”

I tapped the jester. “She could’ve seen it as an omen.”

“Huh. Talk about a gift from the Devil.”

“After that, finding a hag would be easy with all those street people downtown. So all she needs to find is a black coachman and poor Roget has the bad luck to fit. She snags his number from the Caribbean bulletin board, calls him, hears his accent, asks where he’s from. He says Haiti, the casting phase is over and the execution begins.”

He grimaced. “Okash and someone who lives at the Clearwater house. That package you saw her bringing there, could it be this?”

I scrolled beneath the image, enlarged the legend below. Title, possible attribution to Carascelli, dimensions. Thirty inches wide, twenty-four high.

I said, "No, too small."

"So Mr. Rolls could have more of this garbage . . . Göring. Now a Nazi angle, wonderful . . . Robin here?"

"In the studio."

"Let me say it in person."

CHAPTER 40

Hugs, kisses, a proclamation of "Genius!"

Robin said, "Aw shucks, just doing my job."

Milo: "As what?"

"Loyal girlfriend."

"More like Supergirl. What you did is incredible." He eyed her bench. "What's that?"

"Renaissance lute," she said. "Something that pretty boy in blue might've strummed."

Milo left, nearly running to the door.

Alone in my office, I wondered how to sink an informational hook into Asian-Occidental Concepts. The parent company had covered its tracks. Maybe one of its subsidiaries had opened a cyber-door.

I struck out with *heigur* and *Western Import Export.* Not expecting much, I tried *niederschonhausen.*

Fourteen-million-plus hits.

A district north of Berlin, in a borough of the German capital called Pankow.

Pairing *niederschonhausen* with *art* filled the screen with narrative.

Schloss Niederschönhausen, a Baroque castle in Pankow, had been the site of a gallery established in 1938. Furnished with over twenty thousand works of art stripped from the walls of German museums after being labeled "degenerate" by leaders of the Nationalist Socialist Party.

Germans during the thirties were a conforming bunch and sales fared poorly due to der Führer's bad review. Many of the paintings and sculptures ended up in Switzerland, long a bastion of amorality pled down to neutrality. In Basel, Zurich, and Bern, museums, collectors, and dealers attracted by bargain prices pounced energetically, with the pieces soon dispersed around the globe.

The man in charge of what had essentially been a large-scale fencing operation was one Heinz Friederich Gurschoebel.

That made me sit up.

Hei-gur.

I typed.

Well educated, and respected as an art historian until he'd turned war profiteer, Heinz Gurschoebel had been a favorite of the Nazi high command and had also been implicated in selling the treasures of Jewish and gay art patrons sent to death camps. Captured by the Allies in 1945, he'd avoided prosecution by falsely claiming status as an undercover resistance agent and, some said, bribing Russian officers with icons and jewelry.

Gurschoebel had also lied about losing his personal art collection in the Dresden bombing, having sent it in installments to Damascus, where his wife and children had fled in 1942. The family had subsequently moved from Syria to Algeria to Sweden, then Argentina, then Belgium, where Gurschoebel and his wife had settled and died of natural causes.

Nothing more on the family.

Asian-Oriental Concepts had named one of its corporate offshoots after a Nazi agent and another after the site of his plunder-fest, so not a huge leap imagining a link to *The Museum of Desire.*

As a favorite of the Nazi high command, Gurschoebel might well have had access to Göring's stash. Had he taken some or all of the collection after Göring's cyanide suicide?

Passed choice pieces to his descendants?

Did *The Museum of Desire* hang in some clandestine chamber, to be appreciated in solitude?

Had randy oil paintings been only part of the inheritance? Had Gurschoebel also passed on a cold, callous nature?

The kind of malignant narcissism that segues easily to sadism.

Owning a masterpiece you could never exhibit. Pity.

Oh, well, reinterpret it in human flesh.

I spent hours grouping *heinz friederich gurschoebel* with *museum of desire macao asia, asian occidental concepts aoc asian art, medina okash,* and the addresses of the two galleries bordering Okash's. Came up empty and tossed in Geoffrey Dugong's given and assumed names, then those of the four victims in the limo.

A harvest of dead branches.

I left a long message on Milo's office phone and went for a run. Ended up pushing myself harder than usual, reaching the top of the Glen and continuing half a mile east. I got back home drenched and sore, swigged a quart of water, showered, dressed, began heading back to the office, and stopped.

My body was thrumming but my brain felt like a chunk of cement.

Time to follow the advice I give to patients when they talk about feeling stuck: back off, regroup, rest the gray cells.

CHAPTER 41

I was playing guitar when Milo phoned just after nine p.m.

"More Nazi stuff, like it wasn't weird enough? I put in a call to the Holocaust center, maybe they can tell us something. Still watching Okash's locales, still nada. Meanwhile, I need your help. Got a call from Haley Moman—Crispin's mom. While she's talking to me, the kid's screaming at her in the background. Apparently he decided he needs to convene with us again, won't say why. Mom told him no, he had a fit. She has no idea about what, just that he's freaking out. I told her I could send a psychologist—that she already met you. She said why didn't you tell me that in the first place, what, you assumed my son's mentally ill? I said given Todd and Shirin's complaint, it seemed the cautious way to go. That shut her up for a second then she says I don't need *your* shrink, Crispin already *has* one. Meanwhile, the kid's ranting in the background. I said maybe the two doctors could collaborate. That didn't go over well with the lad, he's screaming at the top of his lungs, wants 'the Dumas guy.' Even after Haley told him you were a shrink. Kid says, 'Even better.'"

"Rigid and repetitious. That's consistent."

"Don't sell yourself short. Anyway, Haley called the kid's therapist and she said nice things about you so everything's set up. Sooner would be better than later, though I'm not convinced the kid really has anything to say. Probably just craves attention."

I checked my calendar. Custody interview in the morning. Third-time meeting with a cranky, resistant father. I'd warmed him up a bit but more needed to be done.

"I'm free around one."

"Great, I'll tell her," he said. "The kid's at home all day, don't imagine you'll need an appointment."

At twelve fifty-five, I pulled up to the white Georgian. On the way, I'd slowed and glanced at Clearwater Lane—a quick scan. No cars in front of the blue house.

Haley Moman opened the door, hair combed out, her face coated with full makeup. Cosmetics couldn't mask weary eyes and worry lines.

"So you're a therapist. You couldn't tell me that?"

"It didn't seem necessary."

"Honesty's always necessary . . . lucky for you, Dr. Sontag says you're solid. A professor."

"I do some teaching."

"Yeah, yeah, at the med school crosstown," she said. "I looked you up. You worked with kids with cancer. That had to be depressing."

"For the most part, it was rewarding."

"Was it? Anyway, you've been vetted and approved so I'll allow you to talk to my baby, let's get this over with."

"Any idea what Crispin wants to tell me?"

"As if."

Crispin sat cross-legged on the floor, facing the massive aquarium. Gaudy fish glided through a coral forest, pecking and browsing and nose-jabbing one another. Bubbles carbonated and broke the surface of the water, setting off glints of light.

Haley Moman cleared her throat.

Crispin waved his hand dismissively. "Go."

She flinched. Took her shame out on me with a kill-the-messenger glare.

"Go, Haley!"

Fighting back tears, mother fled son.

I walked toward Crispin, evoking no reaction. He wore the same green, old-guy poly jumpsuit and the out-of-place black wingtips. His pageboy was a mess, beige hairs spiking in odd directions. His skin had broken out, what looked like a crop of miniature pomegranate seeds on the cramped pallid face.

"Hello again, Crispin."

"Sit or stand."

I got down beside him.

"Just as I thought."

"Pardon?"

"You want to establish rapport so you sat. I knew you would. I gave you a fictitious choice." He continued to stare at the aquarium. But not at the fish; no eye movement. "Alexander Dumas Delaware. Writers are professional liars. Apparently so are psychologists. You're named after a professional liar. Was your mother dishonest?"

I laughed.

He said, "Do you think I'm funny or are you still trying to establish rapport?"

"That was pretty funny."

"That your mother was a liar?"

"That you see the world in an interesting way."

"*That* sounds like rapport-building. I have a supposed therapist. She's always pretending to be nice."

I knew his therapist. Genuinely nice.

A few seconds passed. He said, "Don't bother with what I think of you. I could think you were dog excrement and I'd tell you what I brought you here for."

"Okay."

"Aren't you going to ask what that is?"

"You'll tell me when you're ready."

He half turned toward me. Regarding me with purplish eyes, narrowed and impermeable. Returning to the aquarium, he set about picking a zit. Drew blood and transferred the activity to a ring finger cuticle and raised a crimson thread that traced the bottom of his nail.

"I lied," he said.

"About . . ."

"Complete the sentence. Add an object. About . . . ?"

"You lied about what?"

"Good," he said. "You're being cooperative. People don't like to cooperate with me. People don't like me."

I said nothing.

"Good," he repeated. "You didn't argue." He uncrossed his legs, extended his feet straight out, wiggled the tips of the black shoes. "When you were here with Milo Bernard, I lied about what I saw. Ask me why."

"Why did you lie?"

"I don't know. That applies to much of what I do and think. I have trouble coming up with easy explanations. It makes me more interesting to me."

I said, "You prefer questions that can't be answered."

"Are you ridiculing me?"

"Nope."

He got to work on an index finger cuticle. Thicker blood trail. He licked it. "I sometimes drink myself. Recycling."

I said, "Was your lie false information or incomplete information?"

Pick, pick, lick. He rubbed his eyes for a long time. "Tell me what I told you the first time."

"You went over to the party house Saturday morning close to three a.m., heard two adults talking, heard them drive away."

"I went over intending . . ."

"To shit on the property."

"Ha. Hahaha. Haha. Ha." Nasal, barking laughter continued to burst from his skimpy mouth. Impersonal, like rounds from an automatic weapon. "Hahaha. Haha. Hahahah. Did I tell you I shit?"

"You said you didn't."

"Ha. I did. Not on the property. On the road. I found leaves for wiping."

His smile was unsettling. Dealt a tough hand but he'd chosen to be mean.

I stayed silent.

He said, "You're disgusted with me."

"I didn't see it or smell it, Crispin, so not really."

His head whipped toward me. "*Are* you ridiculing me?"

"Same answer as the first time you asked."

He pouted. "Alexander Dumas paid other writers to write for him."

"Is that so?"

"You're his namesake and you didn't bother to learn about him?"

"Nope."

"That is inappropriate," he said. "When you have a name, you need to learn about it. 'Crispin' means 'curly-haired.' Haley didn't know that, she just liked the sound of it, like you, she's not curious. Saint Crispin is the patron of shoemakers. Saint Bernard is the patron of mountaineers. 'Bernard' means 'bear-like.' Haley didn't know that. She named me after her grandfather. Milo Bernard is bear-like. Bernard fits him but not me. That makes me feel inauthentic. I'm more fox-like. I should be named Reynard. I looked up the origin of Milo. There are two opinions. It could be derived from a German word meaning 'to pulverize' or it could be Slavonic for 'merciful.' Milo Bernard looks more like a pulverizer than a merciful person. I didn't know anything about Slavonic. I looked it up. It's an Orthodox Christian church language. That's esoteric. I felt better about not knowing, I can't know everything though I try. At this moment, I'm satisfied with myself that I had the authority to summon you and you arrived. Are you intensely interested in what I'm going to tell you?"

"I'm here."

"That is inferential not a direct answer."

"I'm extremely interested."

He stared at the aquarium and bloodied another cuticle. Suddenly he sprang up and tapped the glass hard. The fish scattered.

He sat back down. "The clown trigger was about to bite the dorsal fin of the heniochus. I can tell from the look in the clown trigger's eyes and the way his body orients when he's preparing to attack. When I see that, I scare him. That's why I'm here watching. I plan to be here until the behavior is eliminated."

I said, "Deconditioning."

"Re-education," he said. "Like Mao Tse-tung told the Chinese to do. He never bathed, just swam. He took young girls to an island called Hammer Island and raped them."

I said, "Nice guy."

"I read his red book, it's inane but inane people still follow him."

He hiked his knees to his chin. "The minor lie I told you was about not shitting, the major lie I told you is I didn't see details. I did. They both wore dark clothes. He was tall with light hair. She was medium-sized with dark hair. I also lied when I said I didn't see their car. I did. It was a white Rolls-Royce. He drove, she was on the passenger side. I thought they were spoiled-brat parents, driving a car like that, spoiled imbeciles breeding other spoiled imbeciles. I'm rich but I've developed independently because people don't like me so I do what I want and think comprehensively."

"What else do you want to tell me about the people in the Rolls?"

He pouted, unhappy at the topic shifting away from him. "Who says anything?"

"It's up to you to say."

"And I will," he said. "Why wouldn't I? Initially, they drove north then a few minutes later they came back down. I was on the side of the road wiping with leaves. That's when I got a better look at them. They kept going south until I couldn't see their taillights anymore. South is toward Beverly Hills, that confirmed my hypothesis."

"Makes sense. This is extremely helpful, Crispin."

"Because it adds to your data bank or because it confirms a prior hypothesis of yours?"

"Sorry, I can't get into details."

Surprisingly, no reaction to the refusal. Just the opposite; he created a near-smile. "It's extremely helpful."

"It is."

"Love that love it love that. So I will be called to testify if you apprehend them based on my information and they're taken to trial rather than settle with a plea."

"We're a long way from that, Crispin."

"I understand that," he said. "But given those contingencies, will I be called?"

"You want to testify?"

"Very much so. So I will be invited?"

"It's complicated," I said. "You're a minor, your parents would need to—"

"By that time I likely will have reached majority and Haley and him will have nothing to say about it. Will I be allowed?"

"It won't be up to me, Crispin. Why the desire to testify?"

"It would be interesting and recreational."

I said, "A lot of people would be worried about testifying."

"A lot of people are low-functioning automatons who care what other low-functioning automatons think of them. I want to get up in the witness box and be asked to swear on a Bible and refuse in a loud voice because I'm an atheist. Given the quality of my information, after a protracted debate among the lawyers and the judge, I'll be allowed to affirm my truthfulness the way I see fit. Once that's settled, I'll inform everyone in the courtroom what I saw but I will fix my eyes on the two of them. I'm certain to be a star witness. What do you say about that?"

"I'm sure you'll be convincing."

"I will be," he said. "I can make people think things."

CHAPTER 42

He sprang up again and gave the aquarium another poke, setting off piscine panic. Then he walked to his glass desk, shoved the collection of Rubik's cubes to the floor, and began working one of his laptops.

Screenful of geometric designs. As he manipulated, he hummed atonally.

"Is there anything else you want to tell me, Crispin?"

"On your way out inform Haley I'm ready for breakfast. I want anchovies."

No sign of his mother. The maid was in the kitchen, wiping counters with something that smelled of vinegar.

I said, "Crispin's hungry."

She said, "He's always hungry," and kept washing.

I saw myself out, sat in the Seville, and phoned Milo.

He said, "One of a kind. Mentioning the Rolls says he's probably being straight."

I said, "The woman's description fits, too."

"Midsized and dark-haired, yeah, that sums up Okash. The light-haired guy's probably our Herr Whatever. Okay, thanks, this goes in the book. Not that the kid would ever want to testify."

"Quite the contrary," I said. "He's pawing the dirt and waiting for the starter gun. It might even be the reason he called me back."

"Why would he put himself through that?"

"For the attention."

"Huh. From what you saw, could he handle it?"

"He probably wouldn't spook on the stand but I'm not sure the case would survive." I told him about the boy's yen for confrontation over his oath.

He said, "Can't you see Nguyen dealing with that? All right, hopefully we won't need him. I did get Okash's friendly manager to go up and take a look at Okash's apartment. She refused to do anything but a once-over, says no purse, phone, or keys in plain sight, no Okash, that stench of escape is growing. Maybe I was wrong about Dugong and he tipped her off. I got Key West PD to do a drive-by at his home, guy lives in a shack-type place, is in front painting away. Sleepy can't find any flights Okash has taken but she could be with The Herr driving somewhere. Still waiting for Okash's phone records and that's it. Thanks for practicing your craft. Or is it an art?"

I said, "I'm steering clear of art."

CHAPTER 43

Custody paperwork filled the rest of the day, followed by dinner with Robin that I cooked and catching up with psych journals. I went to sleep at eleven p.m., woke up at midnight, one a.m., two thirty.

As four a.m. approached, I remained wide awake, eyes open, muscles tight, synapses jangling. I tried to deep-breathe myself back to sleep. *Doctor-soothe-thyself* failed and at four forty-five a.m., I got out of bed, made my way to the closet, and got dressed in jeans, a sweatshirt, and running shoes.

Robin stirred. I kissed her forehead and went to the kitchen. Blanche stirred from her service-porch crate.

I opened the unlocked grate, received a somnolent lick.

After writing a note to Robin, I left.

When you're compulsive, even new habits die hard.

No doubt where I was going.

Rolling down the private road topped by my house, I had to brake hard to avoid a buck with a full-on rack of antlers. He stared at me, flexed chest muscles, and bounded off into the brush. Moments later an enormous owl soared out of a pine tree and was swallowed by a lavender-black sky.

The Seville's windows were open. Cool May air and scurry-noise blew through. I got cold and shut the window. Didn't like the ensuing quiet and put the radio on.

KJazz. Stan Getz playing "Desafinado." Nice and mellow but it didn't matter.

The Glen was free of vehicles. I sped to Sunset, made an easy left turn, and drove toward Beverly Hills. Thinking about Crispin Moman making his way up Benedict Canyon, intent on fecal revenge.

Driven by forces he'd never understand.

Lucky him.

Easy to take my time on a deserted Benedict Canyon. I spotted it well in advance.

White car backed into the driveway of the blue house.

I checked the rearview, backed up illegally, turned east, and, as I had the first time I'd been here, drove to the top of the street, just out of view. Exiting the car, I walked downhill, blanketed by darkness, hoping my footsteps didn't set off someone's guard dog.

I descended just enough to see lights on in the blue house. A faint driveway bulb clarified the car: the Volvo. I took a few more steps.

No mail piled up in front of the door.

As I stood there, the door cracked.

I backed up and watched as a tall, silver-haired man stepped out and locked the door. Three brown-paper rectangles under his arm.

I raced back to the Seville, had rolled a few yards downhill, headlights off by the time the Volvo sped out of the driveway and turned left on Benedict.

Southward, the same direction the Rolls had taken as Crispin watched.

I kept my distance as the boxy white car rolled through the red light at Sunset and turned right.

West. The same route I'd take to go home. A strange thought flashed: What if this was a neighbor?

But at Beverly Glen, where I'd normally head north, the Volvo drove south, then west.

The car hooked south on a side street and continued halfway down the block before swinging a wide arc in the center of the road and backing up into the driveway of a house. Idling as a black-iron gate twenty feet up slid open. Behind it another car facing the street; the unmistakable imperial verticality of a Rolls-Royce grille.

The Volvo took its place in front of its glitzier sib. The gate closed.

I got out of there, caught a red light at Beverly Glen, and used the time to text Milo.

Five a.m. Something to greet him when he woke.

No reply until seven thirty-four: his knock on my front door.

CHAPTER 44

Red-faced, red-eyed, back rounded, rolling his shoulders restlessly, my friend sat down in the living room, opened his attaché case, and yanked out his pad.

He dropped it in his lap, unopened. "Candace Kierstead's place. Unreal."

I said, "The guy looks like the picture of her husband."

"She was playing me."

"Probing the investigation."

"And putting herself in the middle of it? That's beyond high-risk, Alex."

"Part of the thrill," I said. "Like telling us that baby possum story. 'I love animals.' "

"Jesus. Before I came here, I checked my notes. Don't think I told her anything that matters."

"You didn't. And you can use her overconfidence—their overconfidence—against them."

"Supportive therapy. I feel better already."

He got a text, read, replied.

"Al Freeman, he found the Rolls's owner. Sig Kierstead. I shot him a thanks with five exclamation points. Didn't have the heart."

He opened the pad. "Unlike the Clearwater house, there's no corporate fog obscuring the Conrock deed. A little over two years ago it was bought by the marital trust of Stefan Sigmund Kierstead and Candace *Walls* Kierstead."

I said, "Candace is related to Okash's victim."

"Gotta be. She's the right age for an older sister. With a big grudge against Okash. Except why, then, would she become Okash's landlady?"

"Playing with her the way a cat worries a mouse. And how better to keep tabs on her while she plans her revenge? How long have the Kiersteads owned the gallery building?"

He flipped pages. "Twenty months."

"And Okash opened her place eight months ago. Someone able to sit with us the way Candace did has a suppressed nervous system. My bet is she enjoys the stalking as much as the kill. It's possible meeting up with Okash was accidental but Candace saw it as confirmation. When Dugong ran into Okash at Art Basel she was chatting up potential clients. Maybe it was the Kiersteads. Maybe Okash doesn't know who Candace is but Candace realizes what she's been gifted with. She owns gallery space, Okash wants to have her own place, talk about karma."

"Revenge eaten way cold," he said. "Yeah, she's an icy one, goddamn graham crackers, playing good citizen. But why wouldn't Okash know who she was?"

"Sister Emeline said the Walls family had issues. It's possible Connie never brought friends home. Candace, on the other hand, could've recognized Okash's name from court documents or similar."

"Connie gets cut, ends up sliding down hard, hangs herself in prison," he said. "Yeah, that's plenty to seethe about."

"Let's see if I can confirm the sisterly connection."

I put my phone on speaker, punched buttons.

A melodious voice trilled, "Good morning, Saint Theresa's!"

"Sister Emeline, this is Alex Delaware, the psychologist who came by a few days ago."

"The police psychologist." Wariness drained the music from her voice.

"I have a question about Contessa Walls's family. Did she have siblings?"

"Connie, again? Yes, she had two older brothers and an older sister."

"You met them."

"No but she talked about them when her mood got low."

"Not a happy family."

"Distant, icy, rejecting. That's why I never met them. They never visited the dorm, not even the parents, and Connie rarely went home during vacations. Sometimes she'd be alone, sometimes she'd tag along with us. She was physically beautiful but such a sad girl, Dr. Delaware."

"Do you happen to know the siblings' names?"

"I do know because when Connie griped, she'd *use* their names. Cormac orders me around like I'm a servant, Cormac used to hit me and pinch me, Charlie—no, *Chuck* laughs at me and makes me feel stupid. The big complaint about the sister was she shut Connie out, never included her . . . what was *her* name . . . something else beginning with 'C,' I guess the parents had a thing for 'C' names . . . Candy, I think. Yes, definitely. I remember thinking, *That girl doesn't sound very sweet.*"

"Thanks for the information, Sister."

"If your thanks are *sincere,* donate *generously* to our food drive. Every single can, jar, box, and bottle goes to those in serious need."

"Will money do?"

She laughed. "Money always does." The lilt, restored.

◆

Milo said, "Sisterly revenge. Now I'm thinking Okash didn't rabbit, she's probably history. So what does that have to do with wiping out six other people?"

My head filled with white noise. I went to the kitchen, filled two coffee cups, took my time returning. Sorting, contextualizing. Imagining.

I handed him a cup. "Let's start with the simplest motive: McGann and Vollmann were eliminated because they asked too many questions about Benny."

"They asked Okash, not the Kiersteads."

"Maybe not. The Kiersteads own the building and two dummy galleries. What if Okash wasn't around when McGann and Vollmann came by but the Kiersteads were? They put on compassionate faces, invite McGann and Vollmann in."

"And boom." He rubbed his face. "Fine. What about the limo?"

"What I said yesterday. Gurnsey and Okash humiliated her. That sped up Okash's execution date and earned Gurnsey spillover hatred. Once he was targeted, *The Museum of Desire* came to mind. The level of planning and cruelty we saw in the limo stinks of long-standing sadistic fantasies. It's possible the slaughter would've occurred without Gurnsey but he provided an aha moment."

"They're evil, the painting fills in the blanks?"

"These are people who choose Nazi references when they name their companies. It's all about game-playing."

His turn in the kitchen. He came back chomping an apple viciously and working his phone.

Downloading Candace Kierstead's DMV photo, he called the Caribbean market.

"Ms. Graham? Lieutenant Sturgis."

"Oh, hi. What's up?"

"You were really helpful when we were in and I wondered if I could send you another photo."

"Of course. You're making progress on Solomon?"

"Slowly but surely." He sent the headshot. Seconds later, Graham called back. "Sure, that's Candy. She's a great customer, likes our beers and our fresh vegetables. She and her husband come in all the time. He told me he developed a taste for spice when they lived in Asia and then in the Grand Caymans."

"Did they ever come in with the other woman I showed you?"

"No, they're more recent—the last few months. Very nice, always pay cash."

"Thanks."

"That helped you?" said Graham.

"Inch at a time."

"Just like starting a business."

Milo demolished the apple as if it were a threat, dangling what was left from the stem. I said, "The Kiersteads probably heard about the market from Okash, discovered Roget on the bulletin board."

"They do their thing with the limo, save Okash for last, do her on the sly."

"No reason to display her," I said. "She didn't fit the painting, they could toss her like garbage."

He put in a call to John Nguyen, got voicemail, tried a judge with the same results and went silent. Tossing the apple, he returned eating a nectarine, getting juice on his chin and dabbing. "Candace worked me like a goddamn piece of clay." He laughed. "The art metaphors just keep coming."

He demolished the nectarine. "What were you doing driving around at five in the morning?"

"Information overload. You were also up early, had time to research the Kiersteads."

"Got your text at five forty, it threw me, all of sudden Candace is in a new light. Once I steadied my neurons with a shot of WhistlePig, I woke up the kids. Bogomil's assigned to the gallery building, the lads are taking turns driving up and down Benedict and every third time, cruising Conrock. Can't do a sustained watch on Conrock. Too quiet, no street parking, everything's conspicuous."

"Get the lads a Bentley from the impound lot and have them wear ascots."

He exploded into laughter. Wrapped the nectarine in the napkin and said, "I saw eggs. Can you spare some?"

CHAPTER 45

Two thirty p.m., that day: new whiteboard.

The stars of the display: enlarged DMV shots of Stefan Sigmund Kierstead, fifty-four, and Candace Walls Kierstead, forty-one.

Sleepy had confirmed the couple's numerous trips to and from Hong Kong, Macao, Bern, Basel, Zurich, and Stockholm but still no information on where they'd lived before moving to L.A.

Further digging on the Walls family revealed that Candace's parents, Charleston and Cinthia, were both deceased, as was brother Cormac. All three deaths had been registered at Johns Hopkins Hospital in Baltimore. Hepatitis, liver cancer, liver failure.

Brother Charleston Jr. was alive and a resident of the Federal Correctional Institution in Cumberland, Maryland, six years into a twenty-two-year sentence for manslaughter and drug possession with intent to sell. A chat with an assistant warden revealed the specifics: running over a meth-dealing competitor with his car. Twice.

According to prison records, Walls was a no-problems inmate, hampered by diabetes, heart disease, and liver disease, loosely connected to the Aryan Brotherhood but not a member. A mugshot revealed a shaved-head, facially tattooed, sunken-eyed con with a goatish white chin beard bottoming a pale, collapsed face. Forty-eight but looking closer to seventy.

Marc Coolidge said, “Bunch of alkies, quality family.”

Al Freeman sitting next to Alicia Bogomil, their legs occasionally bumping, said, “Same old story.”

Alicia said, “Ain’t that the truth,” and smiled at him. Bump.

Milo said, “There’s no record of any domestic calls to the family and outwardly they look respectable. Dad was an IRS lawyer and they lived in a nice neighborhood.”

Moe Reed said, “Putting up a façade.” His voice emerging from Milo’s laptop.

He and Binchy were linked in to the meeting on FaceTime, Binchy now back on the Hart Street watch, Reed soloing Benedict Canyon and Conrock. So far, no movement at either location and neither the Volvo nor the Rolls had emerged from behind the black gate.

“The good news,” said Milo, “is I just got arrest warrants for both of them along with paper to enter both houses and the entire gallery building. We can also confiscate Okash’s car, which is still parked out back. I don’t wanna confront the Kiersteads or make a show of entering the gallery. Too many unknowns so we’re in a holding pattern, hoping to spot them on the road and take them.”

Coolidge said, “Avoid a hostage situation.”

“That and giving them time to destroy evidence. These are people responsible for at least six murders, likely seven. Once they’re in custody, we’ll separate them and take our time. Any questions?”

Al Freeman said, “They’re Nazis and her brother’s linked to the Brotherhood. Any connection?”

“Not so far and prison records say Candace never visited him. In fact, he’s gotten no visitors, period. The nun told Alex they weren’t exactly close-knit.”

“Bastards,” said Alicia. “Those poor dogs.”

Freeman said, “Hating’s an overall thing.”

"Ain't that the truth."

Bump.

I checked my watch and stood and headed for the door.

No surprise on Milo's face. Freeman and Coolidge and Bogomil stared.

He said, "Dr. D.'s got a woman to talk to."

CHAPTER 46

Identifying Jane Leavitt had been easy: On the Daylighters' website, her face was displayed prominently above the motto *Vanquish Breast Cancer!*

Executive chairperson of the group. For the past five years, also head of the steering committee for the group's annual Newer Than New Year's Fling.

No listing for Candace Walls Kierstead, despite her claim. I'd also failed to find verification of dancing ballet in San Francisco.

Reaching Jane Leavitt had proved a challenge. She hadn't responded to Milo's calls of a few days ago; his emails remained unanswered as did voicemails left on the group's business number.

I gave it a shot, texting an oncologist I'd worked with at Western Pediatric Medical Center and asking her to call Warren Giacomo, M.D., professor of clinical medicine at the U. and the Daylighters' medical advisor.

Giacomo phoned me at one forty-five p.m. He proved to be a genial sort who'd heard about the Benedict murders and termed them "unbelievable, way too close for comfort." He had no idea who Candace Kierstead was but assured me, "Jane's a sweetheart, let me see what I can do."

I said, "So it's a good group?"

"Sterling. Older demographic, mostly survivors and relatives. They've been extremely generous and once they give money they're not pushy about how to spend it. So the police think something happened at their party?"

"They do."

"Wow, I was there," said Giacomo. "Now that you mention it, Jane did seem upset toward the end of the evening. I didn't push it. Golden goose and all that. Let me try her personal email."

"I really appreciate it."

"No prob, I live on the 500 block of Roxbury. Not a hop-skip but close enough to give my wife and daughters serious creeps."

Three minutes later, a 310 number flashed on my phone screen.

A throaty voice said, "Dr. Alex Delaware, this is Mrs. Jane Leavitt. Dr. Giacomo informs me you wish to talk about our last fundraiser."

"That and Candace Kierstead."

"You bet, sir. Four p.m. You darn well *bet*."

The house was a half-timbered, fieldstone-faced, slate-roofed Tudor on the 800 block of North Camden Drive in the Beverly Hills flats. The English gentry thing was thrown awry by a dense palm forest out front. L.A. improvisation, part of what makes the city great.

A pearl-gray Lexus LX was parked in an impeccably clean driveway. A bumper sticker read *Kill Cancer!*

Before I got to the front door a woman opened it. Seventy or so and tiny—five feet tall, ninety pounds after gorging. A narrow, powdered face was topped by a stiff, black bouffant that swelled like a turban. She wore a pale-blue sweater set, pink quilted Chanel flats, and silver lorgnette opera glasses suspended from a seed-pearl chain.

"Dr. Delaware, Jane." Quick once-over. Sly smile. "You're so young. And handsome!" A bird-hand grasped mine and shook with astonishing vigor. Maintaining her grip, she swung me toward the entrance.

As I stepped in, Jane Leavitt's arm slipped through mine. Chanel perfume. Lots of it.

She half pulled, half pushed me through a foyer with niches holding urns, then down three steps to a sunken living room that looked out to a walled garden crammed with more palms.

Expensive interior decades ago, now charmingly dated: hand-scored, peg-and-groove pecan floors, walls covered in linenfold pickled oak, a coffered ceiling of the same wood. Chairs and sofas were upholstered in velvet, paisley, and bright florals. A Chagall fiddler painting looked real, as did a Warhol soup can, a Lichtenstein comic strip send-up, and a massive Frank Stella chevron.

Candace Kierstead had set out graham crackers and coffee. Jane Leavitt had turbocharged the concept of hospitality.

A silver-and-glass coffee table was laden with bone china plates of croissants, raisin bread, sesame flatbread, and brioche rolls. A tub of soft butter sat next to a tub of strawberry preserves. Gigantic purple grapes were presented in triads dangling from stems, haloing slices of cheese arranged like the folds of a geisha's fan. In addition to all that, bowls of nuts and dried fruits and pink meat sliced tissue-thin.

"Parma ham, Doctor, if you're a protein person."

All that food but nothing to drink. Then a hefty, middle-aged blond maid in a black, white-lace-trimmed uniform appeared carrying a flute-edged gilt tray.

"The Blue, ma'am."

Jane Leavitt said, "Thank you, Sophie. Cream and sugar, Doctor?"

"Black's fine, thanks."

"A man of discretion and taste," said Jane Leavitt, advertising first-rate bridgework. "With the finest coffee there's no need for dilution. This is the highest grade of Blue Mountain. My husband, rest his soul, was in the coffee and tea business. I can still obtain anything."

I smiled. The maid poured. Jane Leavitt raised her cup and I did the same.

We sipped. She purred. Put her cup down. "Try the grapes, Doctor. They're from a sustainable farm in Chile and they're fabulous."

No sense bucking authority. I plucked and tasted. "Delicious."

"Stan also wholesaled fruit. And nuts. All kinds of high-end comestibles. I sold the companies but I've maintained my connections and I employ them. As in our fundraiser. Our appetizer buffet is legendary."

I smiled again.

She said, "You really *are* handsome." Sharp, brown eyes lowered to my hands. "I don't see a ring."

"I'm in a relationship."

"Alas." Theatrical sigh. "No surprise there, the good ones are always taken. Please don't find me cheeky, I have a terrible habit of inquiring for my daughter."

She pointed to a large silver-framed photo displayed conspicuously behind the food. Marilyn Monroe look-alike in a strapless black dress.

Gorgeous woman but haunted eyes.

"That's my Karen. It was taken professionally back when she thought she'd be an actress. Now she's studying to be a therapist. Not like you, a Ph.D. She's finishing her B.A. in communications and plans to work with drug rehab patients."

A wave of anxiety washed across chalky skin. "Based on her own experiences. You understand."

"I do."

"Oh, well, I suppose it might work out," said Jane Leavitt. "Provide her a certain level of experience that could help others. But I do wonder about her being exposed to the wrong people. What do you think, Doctor?"

"I don't want to be evasive, Ms. Leavitt, but I don't know enough about your daughter to pontificate."

She laughed. "Pontificate. I like that. Spoken like a true cautious scientist—Warren's like that. Dr. Giacomo. Can't be pinned down.

Very *scientific,* everything must be verified and reverified and what's the word—replicated. I respect him for that and I see you're cut from the same cloth—have some cheese. It's from a Basque village where the goats are pampered."

Again, I obeyed.

Jane Leavitt said, "So. You want to know about *her.* What exactly has she done?"

"I'm afraid I'm going to have to be evasive again."

"Fair enough," she said. "But obviously if the police send a psychologist, it's got to be something nasty and bizarre. *Good.* I want the full weight of the law brought down upon her. I want her to reap the fruits of her rotten character."

Angry words but a serene tone.

I said, "Something happened at the fundraiser."

"The fundraiser is important to our cause—more than that, it's *vital.* The moneys we raise go straight into research. We underwrite every bit of overhead, not a penny goes toward administration. Last January we welcomed a small but promising crop of potential donors. The fundraiser was our opportunity to put on our best face and *she* nearly ruined it and for that I can *never* forgive her."

"What did she do?"

"She allowed some of her low-life friends to crash and they . . . oh, why beat around the bush, they had an *orgy.*"

"Really."

"Well," she said, "perhaps that's an exaggeration, but not much of one."

She took a deep breath, placed a hand on her chest. "Everything was going along swimmingly. I run a tight ship, brief speeches, no dead time, a wonderful band versed in the American Song Book. Ample drink as well but everyone tipples in moderation. We're a *mature* group, Doctor. That's our hallmark. Maturity. I shouldn't have listened to her in the first place."

"About what?"

"About allowing her to get involved. She was pushy, that alone should've been the tip-off, I don't do pushy. But she caught me at a bad time. Karen was just out—no matter, she convinced me. The first thing she screwed up was the venue. In the past, we've used members' homes, so many of our members have *lovely* homes. *She* convinced me to try something new. That hideous pseudo-castle, she knew the owners because they'd bought art from her and that tight-sphinctered husband of hers so we could get it at deep discount. When she told me the figure, I said, why not, be adventurous. Because with members' homes we have to take out serious insurance."

"How did Candace come to the group?"

"She emailed me, said breast cancer research was their passion, a first wife of his had died of it. So when I met him at the fundraiser I offered my sympathy and empathy but he gave me a blank look. As if he had no idea what I was talking about. Then, as if he was trying to cover for himself, he said oh, yes, that was terrible, Gertrude would be so pleased. *That* should've tipped me off. Gertrude? When's the last time you heard of a woman under eighty named Gertrude? But as I said, I was distracted. Plus I give people the benefit."

Her jaws clenched. "Until they prove otherwise. After that?" She rubbed her palms together then let each hand fly. "Good riddance to bad rubbish."

I said, "The party crashers—"

"Two of them. A lounge lizard and a floozy with blue hair and a Pillsbury Doughboy face. Clearly neither of them was one of *us*. *She* let them in, the layout of that hideous dump, it was impossible to monitor. All the cars jamming up on Benedict—have you seen the place?"

"I have."

"Vulgar. The interior was gloomy and the outside lighting skimpy. Lesson learned, next year we'll be using one of our members' manses in the Palisades designed by Wallace Neff. Wesley and Denise have their own personal vineyard and we'll be tasting their private reserves—try the bleu, Doctor. It really is yum."

She watched with satisfaction as I obliged. After swallowing the dry morsel, I said, "This orgy—"

Jane Leavitt's eyes danced with merriment. "I suppose I must get into details."

She took her time selecting a macadamia nut from a bowl, bit it in half, and chewed one fragment thoughtfully. The other she placed on her plate.

"I discovered it by mere chance. Looking for *her.* She'd promised me more than enough Chardonnay and we were falling short and I wondered if it was stashed somewhere in that vault of a place."

A tongue-tip moistened her lips. "I looked all over that dreadful property, finally spotted something going on at the back. Correction, I heard something. Such poor lighting, one couldn't see until one got up close."

Deep sigh. "Now you'll want to know what I heard. All right, here goes. Grunts, gutturals, vulgar heavy breathing." Another sigh, longer, louder. "I suppose I *must* get into further details."

"Not if it makes you uncomfortable—"

"I volunteer with cancer patients, Doctor. Nothing makes me uncomfortable."

Another tongue flick.

"What I saw was a disgusting scene. Lounge lizard and floozy were . . ." She gave a limp wave. "No sense shilly-shallying, Karen's always telling me to be direct, it's the modern way." Wink wink. "What I *saw* was the two of them standing up and fucking like bunny rabbits."

Moving her index finger back and forward. "They were panting like heart attack victims. His family jewels were jiggling. Then I saw it wasn't just the two of them. *She* was kneeling behind him with her head up there like a badger nosing for bugs."

"Candace Kierstead."

"That's who we're talking about, right?" said Jane Leavitt, inching back and luxuriating in the memory. Another half a macadamia nut entered her mouth to be slowly pulverized.

"Yum. From the Big Island . . . where was I . . . oh, yes, the badger. I was at loss for words and trust me, Doctor, that doesn't happen often. What did I do? I just stood there. Appalled. Then I told myself, *Jane, leadership comes with responsibility,* so I cleared my throat."

Sitting up straighter, she demonstrated, producing the growl of a semi with a busted ignition.

"You can bet *that* got their attention, Doctor. The three of them jumped up, began zipping and buttoning and straightening and what-not. *That* was something to see."

Soprano laughter ended in an operatic trill.

"It could've been a terrible blot on my fundraiser but thank goodness no one else realized what had happened. Even, I suppose, her husband, because he was nowhere to be found. Looking back, I suppose there's some comedy to the whole thing. But that's memories for you. Like fine wine, they taste so much better with age."

"Absolutely. So they all left."

"I allowed Iguana and Pie-Face to scoot their derrieres away, but when *she* tried to leave, I blocked her and gave her my blue-ribbon stare-down, Karen calls it the death ray."

Cashmere sleeves clamped over a pigeon-chest. Her face took on the steely frown of a dyspeptic drill sergeant.

"I just stood there and dressed her down visually. She knew her goose was cooked. Finally, when she was starting to wilt, I said, 'Go and never come back.' And that was it."

I thought: *You have no idea.*

CHAPTER 47

As four thirty p.m. rolled around, I was itching to go but Jane Leavitt said, "I've so enjoyed chatting with you—please enjoy more high tea."

I conceded another slice of cheese, two additional grapes, a water biscuit, and a slice of raisin bread. Thinking: *Big Guy, you blew it.*

Managing to withstand her urging to "try the butter, just a smidge, it's from Denmark—okay, cholesterol, I get it. Then at least the jam, it's a mixture of Alpine and conventional strawberries, a family in Milan—wait here one sec."

She strutted out of the room and returned toting a leather-bound folio with both hands. Karen Amilyn Leavitt's brief acting career was preserved between sheets of plastic. Semi-literate puff-piece reviews in a Beverly Hills throwaway paper, some dating back to high school days, had been preserved with additional photos from the Marilyn-clone shoot. Emphasis on come-hither headshots, lingerie glams, and air-brushed bikini poses.

Jane watched as I flipped pages. When I closed the book, I said, "Terrific."

"She had so much potential." She turned away, dabbed at her eyes.

I checked my phone and stood. "Oops, so sorry, I really need to go."

"Police business? Something to do with *her*?"

"Yes."

"Then be off," she said. "Just as well. I've got a party to plan. The garden club, they love my palms."

She directed my exit the same way she'd guided my entry: arm in arm, followed by a firm propulsion outdoors.

"When will you be able to clue me in, Doctor?"

"Soon as I can."

"Grand," she said, clapping her hands. "I want all the gory details, each and every one."

Be careful what you hope for.

I drove south to Lomitas Avenue, hooked a right at Walden Drive, pulled over, and phoned Judge Martin Bevilacqua.

His clerk said, "I think he's free," and rang him in chambers.

A second later, Marty came on. "What's up, Alex?"

"One more question about the Ansar divorce."

"No new facts."

"You mentioned art was part of the dispute."

"Why does that matter to you?"

"It may connect to the murder."

"One of *them* is involved? Oh, shit."

"No direct involvement," I said, "but our suspects claim to have sold to the Ansars. Any idea what?"

"Oh, man," he said. "No, not a clue, Mister absconded with all of it according to Missus and she has no record other than it's supposedly gazillions."

"You have your doubts?"

"You know what it's like. Everyone lies or at least exaggerates."

"What kind of art does she claim he took?"

"Priceless Old Masters but she's up the creek because there's zero evidence. Are you telling me he hung out with really bad people?"

"He could've just been a customer."

"Is there something weird about the art?"

Good nose. I said, "No details yet."

"Alex, is this going to hit the papers?"

I said, "Not in the near future."

"But maybe at some point."

"It's possible."

"All right, thanks for letting me know. And if you do get any evidence that relates to the damn divorce, let me know and I'll make sure you get paid for your time. By who, I don't know, but by someone."

Milo picked up his desk phone after one ring. "Nothing to report."

"Get me into the staff lot. I'll be there in twenty."

Milo said, "What's going on?"

"Twenty."

A uniform was waiting by the barrier arm to the lot. He checked my I.D. and, still looking dubious, slipped a card into a slot. By the time I walked out and crossed Butler Avenue, he was gone.

I hustled upstairs and found Milo hunched at his desk, typing away. Long paragraph. Reply to a departmental questionnaire. Dated a month ago.

He logged off. "Seventeen minutes. Take a load off."

Between Jane Leavitt's high tea and driving, I'd sat enough and remained on my feet as I told her story.

He listened the way a good detective does. Silent, focused. Took a moment to consider before responding.

"January. So Candace was manipulating Okash for a while. The party thing threw me, sure, but I was kind of figuring the Kiersteads had taken premeditation to a new level. Okash named her gallery Verlang. I wondered why and looked it up and found out *verlangen* is German for 'desire.' Wanna lay odds who suggested it? So how do you see Gurnsey getting sucked in?"

I said, "Candace could've been one of his bar pickups. She suggested a threesome with a friend. From what we know about Ricky, he'd have jumped and asked how high. Unfortunately, they got nailed. Momentary embarrassment for Gurnsey and Okash but a lot worse for Candace. It cost her the social status the Daylighters affiliation was supposed to bring her. Killing Okash had been on the back burner, one way or another she was history. But she probably would've just dropped Gurnsey the way Joan Blunt did. Then the rage kicked in."

"She screws up but she's angry?"

"Psychopaths never take responsibility. It didn't take long to convince herself Okash and Gurnsey were to blame. Grunting too loud, who knows what. The idea of replicating *The Museum* had also been percolating for a while but after the debacle she began planning in detail. Taking her time casting."

"Five months," he said. "Taking dogs out of a shelter to sacrifice them. And we ate her crackers and drank her goddamn coffee."

He got up, took the one long stride that gets him out of the office, marched to the end of the corridor and back three times.

"This is so premeditated and twisted even John can't stay constipated."

He called Nguyen and pled his case.

The DDA said, "Yeah, it's sick . . . but borderline at best—"

"John—"

"Hold on, I'm thinking it through . . . you do have eyewitness confirmation of Kierstead with Gurnsey . . . fine, give it a try, long as you understand the risk. You've got nothing on the husband and if you bust the wife and come up with nothing, she knows you're after her and she'll be free as a bird. People like that can lam internationally the way a ghetto thug slinks around the block."

"I want to bust both of them."

"What do you have on him?"

"At this point guilt by association and probable Nazi but you know as well as I do he's involved. I get into that gallery building and his houses, I'm gonna find something."

"Hmm," said Nguyen. "Hell, why not?"

"Thanks, John. Any judge in particular?"

"I'll make the call," said Nguyen. "If they really are fucking fascist psycho lunatics, they need to go. Sit tight."

For the next six minutes, Milo alternated among reading long-neglected email, muttering under his breath, playing with an unlit cigar, rubbing his face, and taking another trip up and down the corridor.

He was at the far end when his desk phone rang.

I said, "Hi, John."

"Alex. You stirred something nicely. Long as I have you, it would help if you memorialize your conversation with that rich lady eyewitness sooner rather than later. Either dictate it to him or write it down yourself and he can stick it in the book."

"No prob."

"Nothing's ever a prob with you. They teach you that in psychology school?"

"More like acting school."

"You did that, too?"

"Nope."

He laughed. "Where is he, in the john?"

"Pacing."

"Ah, that. When he comes back tell him the arrest warrants came through courtesy Judge Cohen, I'm emailing them over. Ciao. As in breezy Italian, not Chinese food."

I went out to the hallway and waved Milo back.

He said, "Please say good news."

"The best. Check your email."

CHAPTER

48

At five fifteen p.m., Milo printed two copies of the arrest warrants, held on to one, and filed the other in the murder book.

He scanned the wording. "Lots of latitude, perfect. Time to contact the troops."

Marc Coolidge was in Inglewood, working a pistol-whipping/armed robbery at a liquor store.

"It's not homicide, Milo, but we are talking blood and teeth all over the place. I'll be stuck here for a while, let you know when I'm free."

"What about Al?"

"Sure, give him a try," said Coolidge. "Stolen wheels don't usually feature teeth."

Freeman was in East L.A. in the crime lab's parking lot checking out a ten-wheel transport van hijacked on the way to the cargo section of the airport. No injury to the drivers beyond being yanked out of the cab by four suspects who'd fled when the sirens sounded.

Milo said, "So you're wrapping up."

"As if. Now I've got to go through a huge load of washing machines, dishwashers, and fridges bound for Dubai, record serial numbers, then escort it to the plane."

Milo said, "I'm here to rescue you."

Freeman said, "Man, I'd love to be rescued but my captain's here." He lowered his voice. "Involved."

Milo said, "One jacked truck brings out the brass?"

"The flight supervisor is my captain's sister."

"Ah."

"Ah, indeed," said Freeman. "I get free, you'll be the first to know."

Next step, conferencing with the regulars. He told Binchy to replace Alicia Bogomil downtown, ordered her to alternate with Reed on the Westside drive-bys. It seemed a needless bit of shuffling. Then I got it.

Everyone said, "Yes, sir."

When he hung up, I said, "Despite what John said, a Westside bust is more likely and you want to keep Sean out of it."

He shot a long look my way. "All of a sudden you analyze human behavior? Oh, yeah, that's your gig. Am I wrong? Sean hasn't been himself since the balcony."

"You're not but once this is over I'll talk to him."

"Thanks—it's pushing six, let's get some grub."

We walked north on Butler into the din and haze of Santa Monica Boulevard at rush hour.

I said, "Here's more analysis. You haven't told me to go home because you think it'll get psychological."

"It already is," he said. "The whole thing is out there. I can't tell you how much three a.m. time I've spent thinking about the limo and trying to get it." Big grin. "Now you're gonna tell me there's no explanation."

"Congratulations. You have now added oracle to your résumé. Where are we eating?"

"Indian okay?"

"Always."

Given Milo's appetite and, more important, his Diamond Jim tipping, he gets warm welcomes at every tavern and restaurant we enter. The Indian storefront around the corner from the station kicks it up to adulation.

Over the years, he's handled a few disruptive customers and street people, convincing the bespectacled, sari-draped woman who owns the place that he's invincible.

This evening, the place was humming, mostly with uniforms and plainclothes cops. She grants Milo credit for that, as well. There's some truth to it; he's left brochures in the big detective room and has been known to talk the place up.

The table he likes—at the rear, facing the street—was unoccupied and topped by a *Reserved* place marker though he'd made no reservation. The woman beamed like someone spotting a long-lost relative at an airport arrival gate.

Heads turned as she hugged us—me, briefly, Milo, longer.

Heads rotated back to nutrition when Milo shot the room a George Patton scowl.

Before our butts hit the chairs, the woman was pouring us spiced iced tea and leaving the pitcher on the table. A jog to the kitchen and back produced naan bread, crisp chili-laced wheat crackers and dip bowls of chutney, hot pepper sauce, and cilantro with garlic.

As Milo tucked a napkin under his chin, she said, "There's lobster and lamb, both are extremely fresh."

"Can't refuse that—you?"

I said, "The same."

"Excellent! I bring a platter."

She brought creamed spinach with homemade paneer cheese first. And butter chicken. *And* three varieties of kebab.

Four types of lentil.

As the table filled, Milo's eyebrows climbed.

"Appetizers, Captain."

"Lieutenant."

"You will be captain one day. Then general."

When she left, he said, "She doesn't realize she just hexed me."

We began eating.

Six minutes later, with lobster and lamb yet to arrive, Moe Reed phoned.

"They're on the move, L.T.! Left the house in the Rolls, drove to Sunset, and are heading east. I'm two lengths behind."

Milo ripped off the napkin. "Damn, both Alicia and Sean are in transit. Any idea how close they are?"

"I called them first, they're both in traffic. Alicia's at Beverly and Western, Sean's on Santa Monica near La Brea. Waze says at least twenty for both of them. I figured they should both hold till we know if the Kiersteads are going downtown or stopping somewhere else."

"Good thinking, Moses. For the time being, have them pull over and stay ready. Tailing the Rolls any problem? Not the tac band, I don't trust it, let's keep it cellular, everyone on conference."

"Got it, L.T. Finally something happens."

We stood and put cash on the table. Milo scooped up my contribution and stashed it in the breast pocket of my jacket. His payment was three times the cost of a lavish feast.

The woman emerged with a family-sized bowl of salad. "No! Lobster is almost ready!"

"Emergency, sorry."

"I will pack it up for you."

"Thanks, but no time." He eyed one of the plainclothes cops. "Bill, just got a Code Two, would you mind taking whatever she gives you and putting it in the big fridge?"

Bill said, "Sure, but I might kype some."

The woman said, "No need, sir, I'll put in extra for you. For assisting *him.*" She scurried off.

Bill said, "You some sort of god? Maybe the one with the elephant head?"

"Blasphemy," said Milo as we rushed out. He paused at the door. "The name is Ganesha."

CHAPTER 49

We took Milo's Impala. Just as he turned east on Santa Monica, Reed phoned in again.

"I was wondering if they'd go north on Benedict but they just passed the Beverly Hills Hotel. She's driving, he's kicking back and smoking what looks like a doobie—okay, they're turning south onto Beverly Drive . . . now we're at that insane intersection where all those streets come together . . ."

Honks in the background.

"That was close," said Reed. "Texting idiot in a Maserati just ran the stop sign, nearly T-boned a tourist bus . . . everyone at the intersection trying to figure when to go, who designed this . . . okay, the prey's turning left onto Canon Drive . . . staying on Canon going south . . . full stop at Elevado . . . have to make a full-fledged full stop, hopefully they haven't made me, no reason they should . . . I'll pull over and keep visual contact."

Thirty seconds later. "Still south on Canon, got two cars between us again, the Rolls is easy to keep tabs on . . . another stop at Carmelita . . . they roll through . . . he's a litterbug, flicked his butt out the window . . . she's driving slowly, doesn't look like they're talking so they definitely haven't made me . . . okay, now there's a line of cars stopped at the red at Canon and Santa Monica, they're not in the turn lane so they're continuing south."

I said, "Canon's the new Restaurant Row in B.H., so maybe dinner."

Milo said, "If we're lucky. Be fun to ruin their appetite—Alicia and Sean, you still hearing this? Head over here. Code Two, no sound effects."

"Roger, Loot," said Binchy.

"Same here," said Bogomil.

Reed said, "The light's green but no one's moving, more fools texting . . . all right, now we're crossing Santa Monica . . . you're right, Doc, tables on the sidewalk, people stuffing their faces everywhere. A whole bunch of pedestrian traffic . . . the Rolls just pulled over to a valet stand, looks like it handles . . . a bunch of restaurants. I'm pulling over in a loading zone thirty, forty feet up, watching through my rearview . . . they're out of the Rolls . . . both are wearing white, not exactly virgins, huh? Sunglasses . . . she just handed the keys to a valet then . . . here we go, a place called . . . La Pasta. They just walked around to the side and went in . . . nothing yet, maybe they're staying inside . . . nope, here they are, being shown to a sidewalk table right in front . . . maître d' or whatever you call him is smiling at them . . . now he's gone . . . they're settling in . . . taking off their sunglasses . . . I'll find legit parking—okay, there's a city lot across the street, I'll circle back on foot."

Milo said, "We'll be there in ten, Moses. Observe from where you won't be seen. That goes for everyone."

He phoned the Beverly Hills Police Department, used his rank until he reached the lieutenant in charge, a man named Fosburgh.

"We need to arrest two homicide suspects on your turf. I thought you should know."

"Homicide," said Fosburgh. "Shit. We talking gang guys coming to our turf to party? We should probably get involved."

Milo said, "Nothing like that. Outwardly respectable folk from Little Holmby."

"You're kidding. What'd they do?"

"The Benedict Canyon limo thing."

"That? I was wondering how it was going. Rich psychos or ghetto trash renting in Holmby?"

"Respectable," said Milo.

"Wow," said Fosburgh. "Guess I should thank you 'cause a few yards south it would've been ours. What do you need?"

"Nothing at this point, I'm figuring to keep it extremely low-key, just wanted to do right by you."

"You did. They in a house or an office building?"

"About to dine at La Pasta."

"That place," said Fosburgh. "Overblown reputation but always busy, Eurotrash and rich tourists. They carrying? Maybe you should wait until they're finished and get 'em where there're fewer people."

"They valet-parked, no jackets, all-white clothes, can't see anywhere to put a weapon except maybe her purse. But I don't think they have a clue and you don't want an auto pursuit."

"No-o, that would be uncool. Canon's the new Restaurant Row, except for the occasional drunks, it's mellow. A few years ago we did bust some Mafia-wannabes from the Valley doing a loan-shark thing in a patio right across the street. You don't think you'll need any backup?"

"There's four of us. I'm aiming for a nice quiet walk-up."

"That's how I'd do it," said Fosburgh. "All right, appreciate you giving me the one-up. Here's my direct number. You need *anything,* use it. And let me know once the situation's over."

"Will do. Thanks, L.T."

"You too, L.T. You can call me Eric."

CHAPTER 50

Milo parked the Impala in a one-hour zone on the 500 North block of Canon Drive, residential, just north of Santa Monica Boulevard. We continued on foot.

Restaurant Row was concentrated on the east side of the street. The west had some eateries but also boutiques and other retail businesses, all closed. Plenty of pedestrians window-shopping. Milo said, "Let's join them."

La Pasta was one of the largest establishments, outfitted with a double-wide outdoor area girded by waist-high iron. A gate in the center was slightly ajar. We looked for Moe Reed and spotted him across the street half a block away.

I said, "The gate's a good thing. You can get them out without going through the interior."

"I'll interpret that as God loves me."

We took our time, blending in with the foot traffic but keeping our eyes on the two people in white. As the crowd thinned and thickened, Reed flickered in and out of view. Leaning against the front of a store and pretending to study his phone.

He wore a gray sport coat in the slightly too-short Italian style, a black T-shirt, and jeans. Every seam working hard to contain his muscles.

Milo said, "He looks like a personal trainer. For other personal trainers."

A couple of wiggly young brunettes in halter tops, black tights, and impossible heels clickety-clacked past us and toward Reed. When they saw him, they smiled, and one woman finger-waved near her hip.

Reed pretended not to notice. The women stared at each other as they walked on. When they were five yards up, Reed made eye contact with us and cocked his head toward La Pasta.

The Kiersteads had scored a choice curbside table just south of the gate. Glasses of white wine in both their hands, the bottle between them.

Stefan "Sig" Kierstead sipped and studied the menu. Sitting high; a tall, broad man with a long torso. His hair was pewter-colored, brushed back and worn full at the sides. Too far to make out his features but his skin tone was blatant: intense tan.

Candace Kierstead, brown hair streaming down her back, glints of gold at her earlobes and wrists, was positioned to her husband's left. She fanned herself with the menu, put it down, fanned again, looked around at her fellow diners as if searching for something.

But not some*one*. Smallish table for two, there'd be no guests tonight. Another bit of luck. I said so. "God definitely loves you."

"Compassionate deity that He is."

We watched. Sig read; Candace drank. No interplay. She said something; he nodded.

Putting her glass down, she checked out her surroundings again.

I said, "She's jumpy and she's met both of us. Maybe the kids should do the frontal and you come up from behind."

"No, if there's gonna be a problem, the front's where it's gonna be and I need to be responsible."

"At the least, you might want to approach from his side."

"That I can work with." His hands flexed and shut and opened. He dropped them to his side. Looked at the Timex and lengthened his stride. We were three storefronts from Reed when a break in the retail array appeared: open passageway leading to an outdoor area.

Milo said, "What's good for the Mafia is okay by me," and ducked in. I followed, and the two of us positioned ourselves just out of eyeshot from other pedestrians.

Behind us was a small patio filled with potted plants not in their prime. The surrounding shops—watch repair, jewelry, chocolatier, hairdresser—were dark.

Milo took a quick look at the Kiersteads. "We're in the alcove, c'mon over, Moses. Sean and Alicia, what're your ETAs?"

Sean Binchy, his voice strained, said, "I'm stuck. Some kind of emergency drain deal on Santa Monica just past San Vicente. Water's flowing, manholes are off, hard hats with *Slow* and *Stop* signs are running the show. I'd go past 'em but every lane's closed off and there are sawhorses all over the place. Sorry, Loot."

"Don't worry about it. Alicia?"

"It's monster traffic all over this damn city," said Bogomil. "I hit an incredible clog near the Beverly Center but fortunately nothing like what he's going through. I'm making the turn at Palm Drive, should be there in five."

"Good for you," said Binchy, sounding anything but pleased.

Milo said, "Alicia, park as close as you can, even a red zone. Sean, text me when you're five away."

Reed entered the patio, swinging his arms. The movement caused the front of his jacket to flap against his massive chest. The bulge of his shoulder holster was visible for an instant; then he rolled his neck and stood up straight and it was gone.

"Anything to be aware of, kid?"

"They got seated right away and served wine without asking for it so I'm figuring regulars."

"The good life," said Milo. "As soon as Alicia gets here, we go. Candace knows me so I'll approach from the north. Alicia will be with me and you'll come from the back. Go to the bar, order a soda, look cool, and come out behind them. Try to get closer to her because she's edgy. Sean makes it in time, he'll be with you."

"What about Doc?"

"Observing from a safe distance. On the way over, he worked up ideas about how to approach them. Everyone take a listen."

I said, "With so many people around, the key is to avoid disruption and any sort of collateral damage. Cuff them as soon as possible and once they're restrained, try to ease them up and out through that little gate in front. Obviously, they'll be put in separate cars. Read them their rights and switch your phones to *Record*."

Milo said, "Book 'em immediately but don't get 'em into interview rooms as soon as possible. Alex?"

"Once they're in the rooms, no pressure, go the soft route, try to give them the illusion of control. But the truth is, none of this may matter. These are sophisticated people. They're bound to lawyer up."

Milo said, "The key will be finding evidence at their houses and the gallery. They lawyer up, they're locked up."

His phone beeped and a second later so did Reed's. A brief little electronic duet.

Alicia said, "Driving south on Canon. Can't see you."

Milo stuck his head out.

"Okay, now I can—got a nice little red zone right . . . here."

Moments later she'd joined us, hair in a tight bun, wearing a black leather jacket, black crewneck, gray skinny jeans, black running shoes. As if she and Reed had color-coordinated. Or the assignment had inspired somber tones in both of them.

Milo said, "You hear everything?"

She said, "I did."

Another beep. "What's up, Sean?"

"Moving finally, Loot, but like a snail. I'm stuck behind ten cars at Doheny, every time the light changes it gridlocks."

"Just stay with it, kid. We're gonna move in a few."

"You don't need me?" said Binchy.

"I always need you. There'll be plenty to do. This is just the beginning."

Just as we were about to cross Canon, a waiter emerged from the restaurant and placed food before the Kiersteads. Refills of wine, the empty bottle removed.

Sig dug right in, sawing at something and eating with gusto. Candace picked at her plate.

Milo gave Binchy one more try.

"Still haven't crossed Doheny." Mournful.

"We're going, Sean. I'll use you to drive one of them."

"Sure, Loot." Not consoled.

Milo shut down his cell, the rest of us did the same. "Let's do this."

CHAPTER 51

Milo, Alicia, and I walked back to Little Santa Monica, taking the brief detour in order to remain out of view. Crossing Canon, we made our way back toward La Pasta. Reed had headed in the opposite direction, crossing at Brighton Way and continuing toward the restaurant's entrance.

As we reached the edge of the iron railing, Milo unsnapped his holster but kept his gun in place. Stepping in front of Alicia, he led the way. I stayed back. But close enough to see.

I watched as Milo stepped up to Sig Kierstead, who paid no notice. Busy cutting a petite steak topped with some sort of green sauce.

Candace paid plenty of notice. She squinted, tensed. Said, "Lieutenant?" and put down the fork she'd been using to halfheartedly spool fettuccine.

Her husband looked up. Confused. Then amused. "Lyu-tenant? This is your police friend, Candy?" Smooth Middle European voice.

"It is. And you are?"

Alicia said, "Alicia."

"Your girlfriend, Mr. Lyu-tenant?" said Sig. "You're eating here? Excellent choice."

Milo said, "Actually we came to see you."

Candace gripped her fork. Fixed on us and not noticing Reed appearing behind her. He sidled between the neighboring table and the nape of her neck. That she noticed. She whipped her head back toward him.

Reed kept walking and she relaxed.

"Us? Why in the world?" said Sig, putting his knife and fork down and daintily dabbing at clean lips. Unperturbed. Cold gray eyes. Why not? The world was his plaything. At that moment I knew he'd been more than a sidekick.

He smiled. The tan was spray-on, yellow borders visible where it met pink flesh.

Candace said, "Something new has come up?"

Milo said, "Best to talk somewhere else."

Sig said, "Out of the question. We're recreating."

"Still, sir. Please come with us."

Gray eyes turned to pond pebbles. "I don't think so, Mr. Lyu-tenant. Call and make an appointment."

Candace said, "What is this about? Just tell us."

Milo produced handcuffs.

Sig smiled. "Really? Fine, suit yourself." Producing a small navy-blue tin from his pant pocket. Navy enamel, printed with white Chinese characters. "I'm a polite man, conversation calls for fresh breath." Picking out a white, pillow-shaped lozenge, he rested it on his tongue, closed his mouth, swallowed. "Delicious."

Candace gaped. "Coward!"

"That's not nice, Candy." Swooping up his steak knife, he plunged it into the center of her throat, thrust then slashed viciously to the left.

One volcanic spasm before her head dropped to her chest.

No longer all in white.

Sig smiled at his handiwork. Winked.

Someone shouted, "He stabbed her!"

People began screaming, shooting to their feet, tripping over themselves and their companions, upending chairs in the haste to escape.

Someone yelled, "Decapitation—ISIS!"

Milo lunged at Sig Kierstead and Reed did the same from the back.

Kierstead sat there, offered no resistance as they cuffed him.

Not a glance at his wife, spurting and leaking and dribbling blood over clothing, her food, the tablecloth, the sidewalk.

She deflated, sliding low. Hair dipping into blood, a head hanging from sinews collided on the table with a wet hollow sound. Her plate was knocked to the sidewalk.

Blood landed in her wineglass.

Swirling, as if before a tasting.

White to rosé to red.

Milo and Reed yanked Sig to his feet. He went limp.

Doing the Gandhi?

Then his eyes dilated. Rolled back, exposing the whites.

As the detectives struggled to hold on to him, froth started streaming from between now slack lips. His mouth dropped open. Filled with a bubble bath of foam. He convulsed. Spewed internal suds.

Projectile vomit followed by violent convulsions.

People continued to stumble and scream. Someone cried. The sounds of shock and torment continued until every table was empty.

Then a strange, unsettling quiet. The sidewalk clear because Alicia had been smart enough to keep it that way.

Sig Kierstead shuddered once, then again. His body sagged with a different type of flaccidity.

Gray began seeping from beneath the spray tan.

Whatever cheap imitation of a soul he'd possessed was gone.

CHAPTER 52

Milo and Reed let the body drop to the ground. Milo stood guard, Reed did the same for what remained of Candace, and Alicia kept control of the sidewalk.

No challenge for her. The street had emptied as far as was visible. Instant ghost town. The last time I'd seen it like this was after the Northridge quake.

Then the quiet gave way to din as sirens began wailing. Loud louder deafening; an avant-garde composer gone berserk.

A figure ran toward us from the south.

Sean Binchy, pumping his arms, ginger hair blowing. Dressed like the ska-punk bassist he'd once been in an untucked floral shirt, blue cargo pants, and Doc Martins.

Alicia stepped aside to let him pass. He looked around panting, eyes hyperactive. "It's over?"

I said, "We need to talk."

"About what?"

"C'mon."

◆

As I guided him away from the carnage, talking softly, steadily, hypnotically, five Beverly Hills police SUVs zoomed up, screeched to a stop, and formed a motor queue in the middle of Canon Drive. Seconds later two hook-and-ladders turned off onto the brief block between Santa Monica Boulevard and its smaller southern neighbor, South Santa Monica Boulevard.

The firefighters remained in place. Ten uniformed Beverly Hills officers got out and stood in front of their vehicles. Six males, four females, all young, all working at stoic but mostly failing.

Seconds later an unmarked green sedan roared in and discharged a gray-haired, potato-faced man. He took a moment to look around, walked straight up to Milo.

"Eric Fosburgh."

Brief handshake. Milo's hand was steady. Mine weren't.

Fosburgh said, "What the fuck, our 911's going psycho." He looked at the bodies. "Oh, my God, what the hell happened?"

Milo said, "It turned psycho."

Fosburgh's eyes settled on Candace. "That's her? What the *hell*?"

"And that's him." Milo pointed to the sidewalk. "He cut her throat without warning after taking some sort of poison pill."

"Right here? Fucking *insane,*" said Fosburgh. Sweat beaded his face, collecting in a deep-cleft chin tinted by five o'clock shadow. "Unfuckingbelievable—all right, at least it's not terrorists or an active shooter, which is what a whole bunch of callers claimed."

"Fake news," said Milo.

Fosburgh took another look at the bodies. "Sitting right there . . . shit, they could be anyone."

"They're anything but."

"He just hauled off and cut her?"

"Straight in then around to her right carotid. Two seconds."

"Fuck," said Fosburgh. "Someone also called in about a guy getting punched out and croaking of a heart attack. I guess nothing like that. What kind of poison?"

Milo took a deep breath. "He pulled that little blue box on the table out of his pocket, swallowed a little white dealie, and said it was a breath mint."

"Like those Nazi suicide deals in the movies?"

"That would fit."

"He's a Nazi, also?"

"It's complicated, Eric."

"Yeah, yeah, yeah, yeah. Sorry it went to shit, I know what it's like when things go to shit . . . you know, your color isn't looking so good. Maybe you should sit down."

"Thanks, but I'm fine."

Fosburgh studied him, shook his head. "Your call." He looked back at his officers. "This is crazy but I'm not going to lie, I'm relieved it's not an active shooter. When's the crypt van coming?"

"They've been notified. Traffic, who knows?"

Fosburgh took a step closer to the remains of Candace Kierstead, flinched, and retreated. "God, that's awful, doing her right here, in front of all those people . . . all right, I'm going to leave as many of my troops here as I can afford. Some may get called away."

"Whatever you think is best, Eric."

"Not that you'll need us if it stays this quiet—totally dead. No pun intended. Or maybe yes, pun intended . . . a good thing, I guess. The quiet. No civilian pains in the ass, easier to preserve the scene. Not that the scene's a big deal, no whodunit, you saw it . . . all those fake news calls . . . not going to lie, my friend, I'm glad it's you and not us."

"It's definitely us, Eric."

"It is. Definitely." Fosburgh patted his shoulder the way Milo sometimes does when he's feeling avuncular. Milo didn't react.

Fosburgh, one eye twitching, resumed prating. "That's the job, eh, Milo? Nothing happens then it does. Between us, when it happens to the bad guys, I say great, save on a trial, move on. In the end this might work out for you. Not being personally involved, I can say all that with some . . . perspective. Never did homicide, never wanted to . . . did some burglary and fraud, last few years it's been traffic, that's a big deal, here, traffic . . . guess it's relevant right now, keep the street clear, what's done is done."

Milo nodded.

Fosburgh said, "Doesn't get more done than this—all right, so I'll leave all ten until someone gets called. Want me to also tell the fire studs you don't need them?"

"Good to have them here, Eric. If you can ask them to move one truck and block Brighton."

"Sure. Good idea. Box it in, keep it mellow. All right, I'm off, got to call my chief, she's at a conference in Arizona. Tell her everything's under control. Anything else I can do for you?"

Milo shook his head.

Fosburgh said, "Know what you mean. You've got yourself a situation. Good luck."

Translation: *You're on your own, pal.*

CHAPTER 53

By the time the coroner's vans arrived, darkness had fallen. The fire trucks remained in place but three of the police cruisers had been called away.

The remaining four cops had resorted to working their phones. Looking up briefly as the bodies were loaded.

Sean had hung on the periphery, looking miserable. Milo handed him the search warrant on Medina Okash's apartment. "Take your time, do every single inch. Landlady's a peach, she may give you attitude."

"I can handle that, Loot."

"Exactly."

Milo's next call was to the LAPD Safe Detail, requesting locksmiths for entry to the Clearwater and Conrock houses and the gallery building on Hart. The last would take time, Central Division smiths tied up at a pair of ultra-high-tech-secured toy district warehouses suspected to be the storage facility for a violent home-invasion gang.

He assigned Alicia the houses.

When she was gone, Reed gave an expectant look.

"You and me, downtown, Moses. It's a big space. If I can get Coolidge and Freeman, I'll use them, too."

Next communication: his captain. Who referred him to a deputy chief. Who told him to contact the Public Affairs office. Which was closed.

He texted a message, got a call two minutes later.

Dr. Basia Lopatinski said, "Just got your message." I didn't know he'd left one.

He said, "No mystery on cause and manner but any guesses about the poison pill?"

"What did it look like?"

"Little white square thing, came in a blue tin with Chinese lettering."

"What were his symptoms and how long did he take to die?"

"He got weak, started foaming at the mouth, vomited, seized, and that was it. Maybe half a minute start to finish."

She said, "Except for the half minute I'd say potassium cyanide, which usually takes a couple of minutes. It's similar to what the Nazis used. Also Tamil, for bombers in Sri Lanka and various other fanatics. I suppose it *could* be KCN kicked up by a chemical accelerator. An antidepressant would do."

"Could we be talking literal Nazi stuff saved from back then?"

"With Chinese lettering? Doubtful. Their factories make all kinds of illegal products. Including most of our fentanyl."

"Any legit uses?"

"Here, only industrial purposes. Photography, mining, fertilizer manufacture. And for those you'd use liquid, not pills. In the Wild East, who knows? Hold on . . . *here* we go. I'm going to send you a picture from an alleged assisted suicide website and you'll say, hey, that's the one."

Seconds later, an image.

He saved. "Hey, that's the one. Why alleged?"

"It's obviously a commercial site aimed at exploiting depressed people. They also sell a clone of Nembutal to ensure that death is as quick and painless as possible."

"You get this on the dark web?"

"No, it's out in the open. Was the decedent chronically depressed?"

"No idea. Met him for the first time today."

"I see . . . well, in China anything goes, they put garbage in baby formula. It could be a rat poison cocktail turbocharged by ephedra or meth or cloned Ritalin. Get him here and I'll try to find out. How are you doing, otherwise? I heard about what happened—the decapitation."

"Word spreads."

"Oh, yes," she said. "No secrets, the world spins faster and faster."

A couple of techs began doing their thing and a sixtyish, crew-cut crime scene investigator named Donald Hartfield who had to be retired law enforcement showed up moments later. "Obviously don't need me for an I.D., sir, but I still have to make notes for the file. Anything you want to tell me?"

Milo said, "Whatever you need."

Hartfield said, "This is related to that limo thing, right? George Arredondo worked that, said it was horrific."

"George spoke the truth."

"Guess like breeds like. He says he still dreams about it."

Milo, Reed, and I left the scene and walked to the Impala. Milo said, "Come with me, Moses, keep it simple."

He got behind the wheel, I sat up front, and Reed took the back. Like a suspect. He didn't seem to mind. Impressively calm, overall. If you didn't notice his hands crabbed above the tight denim sheathing his knees.

Traffic had eased up a bit and twenty minutes later we were halfway to the gallery when Marc Coolidge called in.

"Man, you are all over the news."

"Really. Didn't see any reporters."

"Who needs reporters?" said Coolidge. "Joe Blow has a cellphone with a camera, the media's got their feed. Sounds like a mess."

"Understatement. We're on our way to the gallery. You free?"

"Just got free. What can I do?"

"Join me for art appreciation."

CHAPTER 54

A *Going Out of Business Sale* banner striped the front window of New World Elegant Jewelers. The Flower Drum motel was doing some sort of business; four women in minimal clothing dispersed as we arrived. So did three vagrants nearby.

I thought of Mary Jane Huralnik being plucked off the street.

No sign of the locksmith. Milo parked in a red zone in front of the gallery building, scanned night-blackened windows, and pulled out a panatela that he actually smoked.

The smoke bothered Reed. He moved a few feet away, stretched and flexed, did a quick ten push-ups on the sidewalk, racewalked back and forth.

I used the time to phone Robin.

She said, "It's in the news. Sounds horrible. My first thought was are you okay?"

"I was never in danger. Not even close."

"I figured that out when they said one female victim. Her?"

"At the hands of her husband. Who poisoned himself and died on the scene."

"So two victims, not one," she said. "They can't even get the basics right. You saw it?"

"Unfortunately."

"Oh, baby, sorry. Are you all right?"

"Fine."

"Okay." Doubtful but too loving to say it. "What's next?"

"When a locksmith shows up, we check out the gallery building."

"Big place?"

"Three stories."

"So you'll be late."

"They can do without me, I'll Uber home."

"Your brain, your eyes? No, I'll sacrifice for the common good. But soon as you can swing it—when your mind's really free of this—let's go somewhere, okay? Maybe a beach—no high culture."

I laughed.

She said, "That's a lovely sound."

Marc Coolidge showed up just before nine p.m. The locksmith's ETA was twenty minutes minimum.

As we waited, Alicia called in from Clearwater. "No one lives here, L.T., it's basically a storage facility. Alarm went off, phone started ringing, I convinced the security company I was the real deal."

Milo said, "Art storage?"

"Nothing but, L.T. Every room's piled high. There seem to be two kinds that I can make out: The bulk is posters and prints and a few junky-looking paintings including that candle deal by Manatee Man. There is one bedroom at the back with extra bars on the windows that has maybe thirty paintings that look like good stuff, bubble-wrapped, those carved gold frames. I'm assuming you don't want me to unwrap, better to wait for some kind of expert."

"You assume right," said Milo. "Anything else?"

"Like blood or signs of a struggle? Nope, it's basically a high-priced storage locker. On to Conrock, maybe there'll be juicier stuff there."

"Do it."

A beat. "That was some scene, L.T."

"It was."

"Beyond the pale," said Alicia. "Not even sure exactly what that means but it sounds right."

Six minutes later, Sean phoned from Okash's flat.

"It's a pretty small place, Loot. One bedroom, one bath, not much in the way of furniture. Or art—no art, as a matter of fact. I found her purse in a nightstand drawer along with her phone. All her calls and texts were deleted but I'm sure the subpoena can tell us who she called."

Milo smiled. Still waiting for records, everything academic now.

I said, "With her purse there, she was taken and brought to the gallery."

Sean said, "That you, Doc? Yeah, I guess. Only there's no sign of struggle, everything's neat as a pin."

"Someone she knew."

"Makes sense. Like I said, it's small, I'll go over every inch."

Milo said, "Go for it."

"When I'm finished," said Binchy, "just tell me what else to do."

The locksmith was a rotund, apple-cheeked, toolbox-toting extrovert named Guillermo Tischler wearing LAPD overalls and a big grin.

"At your service." He looked at the three doors. "Which one?"

Milo said, "All three and once we're in, probably some interior doors."

Tischler said, "Looks like it was a bank. Maybe there's a safe I can play with?" He gloved up and inspected each of the three dead bolts. "Nothing special. Any reason to play nice?"

"Nope, everything belonged to my suspects and they're both dead."

"Yeah, heard about that." Humming, Tischler produced a power drill from the box. Grind grind grind. Three doors swung open.

He cupped an ear. "No alarm, the sound of silence. Good song. Here you go."

AB-Original Gallery was smaller than Medina Okash's place: a single slit of a room, no storage area.

Nothing to store. Blank dusty space, not a stick of furniture. Milo tried the light switch. Dead. He took out his Maglite and strode to the back. An unmarked door sprung by a turn-latch opened to an unlit parking lot.

Guillermo Tischler said, "Business this bad, I can see why they killed themselves."

No one laughed but he was one of those people who don't care about being appreciated and resumed humming.

I said, "The name of the place. Maybe AB-O? A thing for blood?"

Milo, Reed, Coolidge, and Tischler stared at me.

Coolidge said, "That makes creepy sense, given what we know."

Tischler said, "They did themselves bloody?"

Milo said, "Next."

He led the procession back outside and into The Hoard Collection.

Same size and layout as Okash's place. These lights worked but most of the bulbs on the overhead tracks were out and the stingy light available told a story of disuse. As did the bare shelves of the rear storage area.

Unlike its neighbors, no door to the lot.

I said, "At one time, this place and AB-O were probably connected."

Guillermo Tischler said, "That makes total sense."

Moe Reed examined the wall bordering AB-Original. Tapped with gloved hands. At a spot just west of center, he said, "Hollow, yeah, there was a door here."

Guillermo Tischler said, "This empty stuff keeps up, you're going to have an easy night."

Milo said, "Next."

◆

Verlang Contemporary was just as we'd seen it, minus people, wine, and Geoffrey Dugong's paintings. Desk, phone, lights.

Tischler opened his mouth. Milo said, "Yeah, it's hustling and bustling."

He hurried to the storage area, now empty, tried to open the door leading to the mystery area. Locked.

"Go," he told Tischler.

Tischler rapped the door once. "Hollow crap, I could kick it in." Out came the drill.

The door shuddered as the bolt came loose but when Tischler tried to turn the knob, it resisted.

"That's a surprise—oh, okay, just stuck." He kneed the door ajar. We walked past him.

More empty space, closet-sized, lit by a single bare bulb.

Limited geography but *two* doors.

One, dispatched easily by Tischler, led to the parking area. The other, on the left wall, reacted with a thud to Tischler's poke and made him frown.

"This is solid. And oversized."

White slab, an L-shaped handle painted the same color. Below, three bolts.

Tischler tapped twice. "Yup, this is metal. From the resonance, probably some pretty serious steel."

Milo said, "Maybe the vault you want to play with."

Tischler ran his hand over the middle of the slab. "Doubt it. A vault door would have a central wheel in the middle, don't look like anything's been patched or painted over. But it could be a security door leading to the vault . . . serious security hinges. This much steel, probably weighs a ton and a half minimum."

Milo said, "You have what you need to pop it?"

"What do you think?" said Tischler. "These locks are newer, look like . . . twenty years ago and nothing special."

He got down on a knee. "Two Yales, one Schlage, here comes Poppa!"

The drill did its job. Tischler reached for the handle but Milo got there first, turned hard, and stepped into darkness.

Reed and I filed past Tischler.

He muttered, "Someone's in a hurry," and brought up the rear.

Milo's Maglite located the light switch. One flick and everything turned bright.

We'd entered ten square feet of windowless space with walls covered by intricately patterned green, white, and red tiles. The floors were white subway tiles feeding to an ornate steel staircase.

Flight and a half, the steps granite, the railing adorned by vines and flowers and newel posts shaped like snarling lion's heads.

A curious, yeasty smell.

Milo held us back and began climbing.

Twenty footfalls later: "Clear."

At the top of the stairs was brick-walled loft space, sixty or seventy feet long and half as wide, backed by a partition on the north end that failed to reach the ceiling and gapped six feet on either side.

Towering ceiling, at least thirty feet, stripped to raw boards, the ducts naked. Double-stacked windows had provided the illusion of a three-story.

Lighting, harsh, ashy, pervasive, suffused with dust, came from four tracks that paralleled the ceiling's center beam. The floors were wide-plank pine, pitted and scarred and burnished by decades of foot traffic.

The yeast stronger, here.

Paper.

Half the loft was filled with ten-foot stacks of posters grouped by the hundred or so, piles of mailing tubes bound together by metal strips, and heaps of flat brown cardboard, the makings of shipping cartons.

The top poster, a low-res copy of *Irises.* A label on the back was printed in Chinese characters. One bit of translation:

Van Goe

A second stack featured a soup can.

Warhol

Tischler said, "Their spelling improved. So what, these were junk art dealers?"

Reed said, "Something like that."

"Hate that, ruining art. I paint. Used to make a living at it in Chile. Commercial. You respect art, you don't tacky it up."

Milo said, "Hold that thought." He walked through the opening on the left side of the partition.

No *Clear* call for what seemed like a long time.

Guillermo Tischler said, "You okay?"

Milo reappeared. "You can go now, my friend. Thanks."

"I don't get to hear the punch line?"

"Thanks for your time. A man of your skills, I'm sure you can find your way out."

"Really?" said Tischler. Sighing, he picked up his toolbox and left.

When the sounds of his footsteps died, Milo turned to Reed, Coolidge, and me. "I won't say ready because you can't be."

CHAPTER

55

Equally cavernous space on the other side of the partition.

This lighting different, miserly, courtesy of a single track running down the center.

Warmer bulbs, though. Calculated focus.

The objects of illumination: two easels. Heavy-duty, solid oak professional artist models, both positioned along the room's central spine, separated by twenty feet of open flooring.

The word "curation" has become a well-abused cliché. But it applied here.

An exhibit.

Perched on the nearer easel was a painting cased in glimmering gold leaf.

Hand-carved frame festooned with miniature gargoyle heads.

I knew the dimensions. But still, *The Museum of Desire* was surprisingly small.

Vivid colors unsuggested by Suzanne Hirto's muddy file photo spoke to recent restoration.

Beautifully, horribly done.

The painting the product of a gifted hand but failing to rise above cartoon.

Because the intention had been nothing but shock value.

The four of us stared, stunned into silence. I was still staring as Milo and Reed and Coolidge moved on to the second easel.

Coolidge gasped. Reed's hand shot to his mouth.

Milo stood there. I caught up.

An even smaller painting, maybe ten inches square.

Similar hues, similar style.

A tag affixed to the easel. Loopy handwriting in fountain pen.

Fate of a Harlot

Antonio Domenico Carascelli

c. 1512

Cherry-sized lumps began coursing up and down Milo's jawline. The muscular tic that afflicts him when he fights internal combustion.

I braced myself and looked at the painting.

Black background, chiaroscuro lighting directing the eyes toward a triad of images.

Three gleaming silver salvers on a table draped in whiskey-colored velvet.

In the left-hand tray, a severed hand. On the right, a foot.

Filling the center tray was a woman's head, dark ringlets streaming over a fluted edge. Eyes wide open but vacant. Mouth formed in a final oval. The skin, chalky gray accented in mauve and sea green and in strategic spots, red.

Marc Coolidge said, "Oh, God." His eyes trailed to the far end of the room.

Something in a corner the track lighting neglected. Barely visible in the sooty gloom.

The four of us got closer. Details materialized.

Six-foot white rectangle.

A deep freeze.

Again, Milo held us back and walked toward it. Lifting the lid, he peered inside and stumbled back involuntarily.

Reed, unused to seeing his boss off balance, managed a single croaked word. “Her.”

Milo said, “Blue hair,” and began lowering the lid.

His hand slipped.

It slammed.

CHAPTER 56

There'd be no trial in the matter of what the bloggers, the rumormongers, the conspiracy theorists, and the media, playing catch-up, had labeled The Stretch-Limo Massacre.

No quick resolution out of the public eye, the department doing its best to control leaks.

Impossible task. Gratifying the bloggers, the rumormongers . . .

Luminol tests of the gallery building revealed oceans of blood from several human sources, most of it upstairs throughout the loft. But evidence of mop-up was also found in the rear anteroom leading to the staircase, and those samples traced to Marcella McGann and Stephen Vollmann.

The charnel house would take time to sort out, and the DOJ lab could've been convinced to prioritize. But Milo's bosses had decided on a go-slow strategy, hoping the internet noise would die down and they could stop fielding annoying questions.

As Alicia had said, the Clearwater house revealed nothing but art storage. The same combination of cheap poster art and centuries-old paintings yet to be cataloged.

The paintings were transferred to a temperature-controlled vault at the crime lab. Milo suggested Suzanne Hirto be brought in. His bosses felt otherwise and hired an art history professor from the U. who arrived with a squadron of eager graduate students. When their expertise was found lacking, the prof brought in Suzanne Hirto.

It took a while but the team managed to divide the trove into two categories. Nearly three hundred paintings ranging from Renaissance to impressionist were believed to have been looted by the Nazis, fifty-nine of them labeled with the business card of Heinz Gurschoebel.

That leaked out quickly, eliciting a hailstorm of demand letters from the legal departments of museums around the world, organizations claiming virtue, and lawyers representing Holocaust survivors.

A smaller grouping—thirty-four oils on panel—had been set aside in the smallest Conrock bedroom. A collection of grotesque, pornographic, often sadistic genre scenes, not dissimilar to the two paintings displayed in the loft.

Those, Hirto was willing to certify, likely came from Hermann Göring's collection of grotesquerie, a claim later supported by twenty-year-old correspondence unearthed in the Conrock house indicating that Stefan Sigmund Kierstead was a grand-nephew of Gurschoebel's wife and she'd willed him the lot.

The Conrock house also gave up two exquisitely fashioned Fabbri shotguns from Italy, a more utilitarian Mossberg, an AK-47, eight handguns, and a collection of Japanese kitchen knives. Blood blowback on the Mossberg matched to Marcella McGann and Stephen Vollmann. Microscopic specks of blood on a cleaver, a boning knife, and a butcher knife matched to the four limo victims and Medina Okash. Okash's blood was also found on a band saw in the Conrock garage.

Along with the saw and other tools, Milo found a box containing forty-four burner phones, most still in their wrappers but a few used sparingly.

One of those was the cell Candace Kierstead had employed to communicate with Richard Gurnsey. Their correspondence consisted of texts that grew increasingly explicit over the five months Candace and Gurnsey had cohabited. Some of their sessions had taken place in hotels and parks, others in Candace's marital bed with Sig watching and masturbating appreciatively.

In a Conrock desk drawer, Alicia found papers documenting the transfer of ownership, a week prior to the murders, of two dogs from the high-kill animal shelter in Riverside. The recipient: *S. Smith.* The handwriting was a match to Candace's.

A pair of pit bull mixes, one male, one female, estimated to be three and five years old, respectively.

Picked up as strays, they'd never been named.

No communication was found between Richard Gurnsey and Medina Okash, and Sean had found little of interest in the five-hundred-square-foot apartment. The exception was a dozen explicit videos downloaded from the internet and saved on a laptop Okash kept on a kitchen counter.

Erotica of a single theme: threesomes featuring two women and one man.

Sean told me about it in my office. Blushing, his freckles receding as the surrounding skin reddened. For all the things he's seen, there's always been an innocence about him.

He turned to religion years ago. That and the comfort he finds in family and clarity of values generally help him maintain a cheerful outlook. But even structure and support can fall short when you've come inches from dying terribly.

I waited awhile before suggesting he come by to talk. Prepared with an explanation but he said, "Sure, Doc," and didn't ask for clarification.

He arrived dressed for work, in a blue suit, white shirt, tie, and the usual Doc Martens. The tie, patterned with Fender Precision Basses.

He doesn't drink coffee so I'd set out a bottle of water.

He said, "Thanks, Doc," and drank. "So what's up?"

I said, "You'd know better than me."

He looked around the office. "I'm always impressed when I come here how quiet it is. Must be nice."

"It is."

"So," he said.

"So," I said.

"First can I tell you what I found in Okash's place? The only thing really."

You're not a child. Then again, maybe part of you is, given what you've been through.

I said, "Of course."

He finished the bottle. The blushing began. "It's not going to be in the book, Loot says the brass don't want it there, there's enough going on without feeding the wolves."

"Makes sense."

"I guess . . . okay, let me tell you about her laptop."

When he finished, I said, "Consistent theme."

"Exactly, Doc. Maybe it isn't evidence, but I'm thinking it's still psychologically meaningful. Like once they found out about her . . . about what she liked, they could set her up. For what happened. At the party."

"That makes sense, Sean."

"Does it? Great." He ran his fingers through the ginger thatch atop his head. "I always like when I get it right."

I said, "You don't need me to tell you."

"I don't?"

"You're a skillful detective, Sean."

"Am I?"

"Definitely."

"Definitely . . . well, definitely is better than not."

He looked away. A young man caught between the blessings of instinctual sincerity and positivity and the job he'd chosen.

"Sometimes I wonder, Doc. Is this what I should be doing forever. Then I think, *What else is there,* and I can't come up with anything—Doc, tell me straight, am I having PTSD?"

"Are you experiencing flashbacks?"

"Nope."

"Panic attacks?"

"Nope. But sometimes I just kind of . . . I find myself thinking about what happened. Not reliving it. More like . . . just remembering it. And then I feel kind of flu-ish for a few minutes—maybe even an hour. Then I'm basically okay."

"What you went through," I said, "isn't something that can be just filed away and forgotten."

"It's normal?"

"It's a normal reaction to an extreme situation."

"That's what my wife says."

"She's right."

"She also said I need to talk to someone until I'm feeling myself again. The thing is, I don't want any disability situation. The department thinking I'm defective."

He sat forward. "I don't want to be off the job for one second."

"I've got a good referral for you. Someone with flexible hours."

His face fell. "You couldn't do it?"

"We work together, Sean."

"Yeah . . . Becky said that, too."

He looked at the floor. Forced his eyes upward. "Also, you saved my life."

Tears filled his eyes. "I never really thanked you. And sometimes—I'm ashamed to say this, Doc, sometimes when I see you it makes me think of what happened and I don't feel that great."

"That's to be expected."

"But I don't want us to—I don't want it to be different. I know how Loot feels about you, you'll always be on the tough ones. That's what I want. To be on the tough ones. To work with you and not remember."

"No reason that can't happen."

"You're sure?"

"I am, Sean. The best thing you can do is take care of yourself and stop worrying. Things have a way of working themselves out."

"With the Lord's help." Sheepish smile. "At least that's how I see it."

We need all the help we can get.

I said, "Use all your resources. You'll be fine."

He let out a long gust of air. "Doc, this is going to sound weird but can I get up and shake your hand?"

"Of course."

We stood at the same time. Before his fingers reached mine, he pitched forward, threw his arms around me and squeezed.

Then he pulled away, as if stung.

"Sorry, Doc."

I said, "Nothing to be sorry for."

"I owe you my life, Doc."

"Yours is a life worth saving, Sean."

"It is?—no, scratch that. It *is.* I actually could use more water."

Dr. Larry Daschoff called later that day, thanking me for the referral, saying he liked Sean, was feeling good about the situation.

The following morning, Robin and I flew to Hawaii.

Don't miss the gripping new thriller featuring Alex Delaware and Milo Sturgis

Out in February 2021

ALSO AVAILABLE

An uninvited guest. A missing identity. A trail of deadly secrets.

When a horrified bridesmaid finds the body of a young woman at a wedding reception, it makes the bride and groom's choice of a Saints and Sinners theme all the more macabre.

There are no means of identification and nobody knows the victim.

It's up to brilliant psychologist Alex Delaware and LAPD Lieutenant Milo Sturgis to uncover the truth. They have a hundred guests to question, and a strong suspicion that the motive for murder is personal . . .

The party's over – and the hunt for the killer is on.

arrow books